PRAISE FOR
*Manchester Christmas*

"Sweet, romantic, and suspenseful,
*Manchester Christmas* is an unexpected gift."
—**Richard Paul Evans,**
#1 *New York Times* best-selling author of *The Christmas Box*

"Stuffed to the seams with wholesome holiday cheer,
*Manchester Christmas* is an adorable Christian romance set in a
snow globe-worthy small town in Vermont."
—**Foreword Reviews**

"Gray has authored three children's books and has released his debut
novel, a heart-filled book about a young writer who is drawn to a small
New England town in search of meaning for her life. She encounters
kindness, romance, and is pulled into a mystery. It has the sort of happy-
ending story that everyone could use right now."
—**Berkshire Magazine,** Massachusetts

"*Manchester Christmas* is a fun story,
perfect for those times when you like a happy ending
that brings a tear to your eye and a smile to your face."
—**CatholicMom.com**

"The author brought to life the spirit of rural Vermont on every page.
The characters are engaging. The story twists and turns in ways
that make it difficult to close the book."
—**The White River Valley Herald,** Randolph, Vermont

"*Manchester Christmas* also might be coming to a screen near you.
The movie and television rights are being optioned by Brian Herzlinger,
who is known for directing 'Christmas Angel,' 'My Date with Drew,'
and 'Finding Normal' among others."
—**The Daily Gazette,** Schenectady, New York

FOR MOM AND DAD.
*Your love made my dreams possible.*

# Chasing Manhattan

## A Novel

# John Gray

author of *Manchester Christmas*

## PARACLETE PRESS
Brewster, Massachusetts

2021 First Printing

*Chasing Manhattan: A Novel*

Copyright © 2021 by John Gray

ISBN 978-1-64060-671-5

The Paraclete Press name and logo (dove on cross) are trademarks of Paraclete Press

Library of Congress Cataloging-in-Publication Data
Names: Gray, John, 1962- author.
Title: Chasing Manhattan : a novel / John Gray.
Description: Brewster, Massachusetts : Paraclete Press, [2021] | Summary:
  "Chase lands in the center of a new mystery when silent messages begin
  to appear, urging her to help those closest to her who are in peril"--
  Provided by publisher.
Identifiers: LCCN 2021014088 (print) | LCCN 2021014089 (ebook) | ISBN
  9781640606715 (hardcover) | ISBN 9781640606722 (epub) | ISBN
  9781640606739 (pdf)
Subjects: BISAC: FICTION / Christian / Contemporary | FICTION / Women |
  GSAFD: Mystery fiction.
Classification: LCC PS3607.R3948 C48 2021  (print) | LCC PS3607.R3948
  (ebook) | DDC 813/.6--dc23
LC record available at https://lccn.loc.gov/2021014088
LC ebook record available at https://lccn.loc.gov/2021014089

10 9 8 7 6 5 4 3 2 1

Published by Paraclete Press
Brewster, Massachusetts
www.paracletepress.com

Printed in the United States of America

# Chasing Manhattan

## CHAPTER 1

# 59th or 50th?

For the first time in her life Chase Harrington was hiding. A self-imposed witness protection plan, made necessary because she wrote a book that inspired strangers to pack up their lives, drive cross-country, and seek her help fixing what was broken. In most cases, their lives. But a person cannot give what they no longer possess, and whatever magic Chase had conjured in the past, if it ever existed at all, was gone.

The true account of what happened to Chase in an abandoned church in Manchester, Vermont, and how she healed a hurting town was the stuff of legend, but it was over. The visions, or whatever they were, had vanished like a morning fog on a warm autumn day.

Chase was deeply in love, and it was the object of that love that held her hand tight and told her she needed to get away, at least for a while. Chase was smart, so she figured if the best place to hide a grain of sand was on the beach, then the perfect place for her to disappear was a big city, like Manhattan. And that's where, for the last twelve months, Chase opened her eyes each morning with her faithful dog, Scooter, at her feet. This is where our story begins.

It was a beautiful fall day in the city that never sleeps. Maple trees with leaves the color of molten lava lined the sidewalks, their branches slowly swaying back and forth in the breeze as if dancing to music only they could hear. Chase needed to get outside and breathe it all in, knowing because she was anonymous here, she was safe.

As sunlight peeked over the tall buildings to her east, Chase could see it was a perfect morning for a jog. Her Australian Shepherd always tagged along for her runs in the country, but here, with so much traffic, it was too dangerous. Scooter didn't mind hanging back, though, because of the fun he would find in the coffee shop that sat directly below the apartment Chase was renting.

After Chase did a quick stretch on the wide, rust-colored steps of her Manhattan brownstone, her pink and white Nike sneaks bounced lightly along the dirty and cracked streets of Gotham. Her thick auburn hair was tied back in a ponytail, as the matching blue lululemon pants and top hugged her size-four frame, causing more than a few heads to turn. Her pace was slow enough for her to stop on a dime, watching out for all manner of mayhem in such a busy place. Those bike messengers were the worst, flying by silently with some top-secret package to deliver.

Step by step she made her way from her overpriced apartment in the Lenox Hill neighborhood on the Upper East Side, toward Central Park for her daily three-mile run. The smell of sausage and peppers from the corner carts filled the air, awakening her empty tummy. Whitney Houston was singing about wanting to *dance with somebody* in the tiny white pro-beats that clung precariously to her ears, a birthday gift from her loving boyfriend, Gavin.

It was exactly seven blocks from her apartment on York Avenue to the entrance to the park on Fifth, but these were Big Apple blocks, so it took nearly a mile to cover it. Once in the park, she'd turn left and make her way toward the famous Plaza Hotel. There, horse-drawn carriages carried tourists on a half-hour loop through the park, as drivers with top hats and exotic accents pointed out where they filmed *Ghostbusters* or the rock where Macaulay Culkin met the pigeon lady in *Home Alone 2*. Chase smiled, thinking how she'd better watch out for those "sticky bandits" who chased little Kevin around.

Halfway into her run the singing was stopped by the sound of her phone ringing. It was tucked away in the small blue knapsack strapped to her back, next to a bottle of Fiji water. She assumed it was her driver, Matthew, wanting to know where to pick her up after her run, so she touched her left ear and said, "Hello?"

A warm male voice, one that still made her knees buckle, responded, "Hey, babe. You sound out of breath. You okay?"

"Yes," Chase replied, "Just out for my run. Where are you, hon?"

Gavin Bennett, decked out in torn jeans and a red sweatshirt with the word GAP across the front, peered out of his silver and black Dodge pick-up trying to find a road sign. His dirty blonde hair was still like an untamed forest, framing that GQ-model face and ocean-blue eyes. Eyes scanning the landscape while trying to stay in his lane, he said, "Oh, there it is. I'm passing some place called Ram Map Oh."

Chase laughed and said, "I think they pronounce it Ram-Uh-Poe. Like Edgar Allan Poe but with a ram at the front."

Gavin smiled, picturing her with her hair back in a ponytail, wearing some perfectly matched outfit, weaving among and around pedestrians.

He finally responded, "Well whatever they call it, the GPS says I'll be to you in forty-five minutes."

Chase, not breaking her stride, replied, "Sounds good, cowboy. That should time out perfect. All I'll need is a quick shower and we'll grab dinner someplace nice."

Gavin sipped the blue bottle of Gatorade that was resting in the cup holder and said, "Anything but sushi; we had that the last two times, my sweet."

Chase loved the Japanese restaurant kitty-corner to her building, but knew Gavin was more a steak and potatoes guy. Still, you couldn't blame a girl for trying to expand a farm boy's palate. Plus, watching his face turn red when he put too much wasabi on a salmon roll was priceless.

"Don't worry, Gav, I have a surprise for you. I'm taking you to Spark's Steakhouse in Midtown. It has a perfect score on Zagat, serves up juicy steaks, and—you'll love this part—it was home to a famous mob hit back in the eighties," she said.

Gavin laughed, "So I'm going to eat where Tony Soprano got whacked? That sounds appetizing."

Chase giggled as she ran. "It's actually supposed to have great food."

Before Gavin could reply, Chase's ear bud made a beeping sound, letting her know someone else was calling. "Hey, babe, that's my other line. Let me grab that and I'll see you in less than an hour."

Gavin was good about getting off the phone when Chase said she had to go, especially since the book came out and Chase's life—heck, all of their lives—got turned upside down. So, he said, "No worries, hon, see ya soon."

Chase tapped her left ear once again and gave another slightly breathless, "Hello?"

A familiar older man's voice said, "Are we doing 59th or 50th for the pickup?"

It was Chase's driver, Matthew Rodriguez, a retired New York City detective who came highly recommended by Sheriff Erastus Harlan back in Vermont. A friend of a friend in law enforcement is how Harlan found the guy, and Chase was so glad he did. Smart and honest, Matthew didn't look at Chase like so many lesser men did, as some conquest. He had become almost a father-figure to her in these past twelve months, and even though he didn't know all her secrets, he could tell Chase needed protecting, and he was more than up to the task.

"Hello, earth to Chase—can you hear me?" Matthew repeated to the silence on the other end.

"Yes, sorry, bud, my mind was wandering. Um, it feels like an East 50th kind of day."

Matthew, sitting comfortably in the leather seats of his black 7-series BMW sedan, nodded, then said, "You got it. Oh, and by the way, Chase?"

Still running, but now with Fifth Avenue and the old FAO Schwarz building in her sights, Chase replied, "Yes?"

Matthew put the car in drive and said, "Someday you going to tell me why you keep going there? For real. And don't tell me you're praying, 'cause nobody prays that much or that fast."

Chase waved him away in her mind with a quick, "Yeah, yeah, yeah, someday, Matthew, but for now . . ."

He checked his mirrors to make sure the coast was clear before pulling into traffic, responding, "But for now just drive the car. Keep it up and I'm gonna start calling you Miss Daisy."

Chase stopped running for a moment to grab a quick drink out of her pack. "Miss Daisy?" she asked, confused.

Matthew laughing, "Oh, I keep forgetting, you were like two when that movie came out. Never mind, I'll see you at East 50th and 5th in two shakes of a lamb's tail."

Chase was the one smiling now. "You and those lambs. You would have fit in great back where I lived in Vermont. Lambs, cows, horses as far as the eye could see. I'll catch you in a bit."

A push of the button and Matthew was gone, replaced by Beyoncé singing about *all the single ladies.* The morning run finished, Chase was walking up Fifth Avenue now toward a big stone building she visited at least once a week. She was thinking, *I'm a single lady, well sort of. But, probably not for long.* She could tell Gavin was getting itchy to take things to the next level, and while Chase loved him, she needed time right now to get her life in order and figure out what came next, besides a wedding cake and place settings.

She walked by the famed Tiffany's store and stopped in her tracks as a memory flooded her. Chase had taken a trip to New York City the summer before she started college, a graduation present from her grandmother. A handful of her high school friends were planning the trip, all the way from Seattle, but there was no way Chase's mom could swing the plane ticket, hotel, and money for spending.

Grandma Margaret, "Marge" to her friends, overheard Chase telling her best friend, Cadence, on the telephone that she couldn't go because she was broke. That's when Marge took her husband's old coin collection, collecting dust on the shelf, down to a dealer in Tacoma and got a thousand dollars for it. Those silver dollars, Buffalo nickels, and Liberty dimes certainly added up.

That was such a generous gift for a teenage girl who had never been more than fifty miles from where she was born. They stayed at the Hilton on West 54th Street, bought half-price tickets to the Broadway show *Rent* at something called the "TKTS Booth," and ran around Times Square until 3 a.m. pretending they were Angel and Mimi from the show. *Today for you, tomorrow for me,* was the call of that crazy night.

Before they flew back home, the four girls walked up ritzy Fifth Avenue to see where the rich people shopped, and Chase went into Tiffany's with her last fifty bucks, hoping to buy a souvenir. She didn't care what it was, as long as it came in that famous light blue Tiffany box. An older employee, a well-dressed woman with blonde hair, saw how much money Chase had to spend and gently pulled her away from the other customers so no one could hear their conversation.

She whispered in Chase's ear, "I'm sorry, sweetie. The cheapest thing we have in the store is a key chain, and those are seventy-five dollars."

All of a sudden, after playing bigshot for the past forty-eight hours, the girl from the Pacific Northwest felt small and poor again. It stung.

The woman then did something incredibly kind, grabbing an empty Tiffany's ring box from behind the counter and placing it in Chase's hand. "Here, take a box and use it to hold something special. Someday, you'll come back, and, on that day, it won't be empty."

Chase stood, lost in that memory, in front of Tiffany's, making people in a hurry walk around her. She gazed through the windows at the fancy store, knowing she could purchase pretty much anything she wanted now, due to the success of her book. Funny thing was, she had no desire to go in. Every time she walked by though, she hoped she'd catch a glimpse of that older woman who had been kind to her that hot summer day seventeen years earlier.

She'd say, "You don't remember me, but you were very nice to me when I was young and poor and pretending to be rich."

It's funny how moments like that don't just leave a mark, but sometimes come back to take another bite. You can't make friends with some memories, no matter how hard you try. The first time Gavin visited her in Manhattan they walked by Tiffany's and he asked if she wanted to go in. Instead, they sat and had coffee at the Carnegie Deli, and she told him the story about the kind woman giving her the empty blue Tiffany's box. She could see his heart breaking for her as she told it. It was another reason Chase knew she loved Gavin, sharing something so personal and knowing he was truly listening.

The thought of Gavin in the deli that day holding her hand made her smile when, "EXCUSE ME MISS," someone said in a loud rude tone, reminding Chase that standing still in the middle of the sidewalk on busy Fifth Avenue was an invitation for a collision.

"Sorry, sorry," she replied sheepishly, getting her feet moving again. As she passed a group of teenagers taking selfies outside the Versace store to her left, the all too familiar stone spires of her destination were beginning to come into sight. Parked outside the historic building was the black BMW with her charming driver, Matthew, behind the wheel.

He looked up from his *New York Post* and locked eyes with Chase, shaking his head with a tiny smirk that said, *You're nuts, young lady, but go ahead. I know you can't help yourself. Go on in.*

Chase threw him a quick wave and then went up the steps where a security guard recognized her from her frequent visits and gave her a friendly nod.

No vehicle, big or small, is allowed to linger long on Fifth Avenue, especially at the corner of East 50th near Rockefeller Center, but Matthew had no intention of circling the block or even shutting off the car's engine. He knew that ninety seconds after Chase disappeared behind those big wooden doors, she'd pop back out and come directly to the car, hop in the front seat, and say, "Drive, please."

Sure enough, as if he were timing a soft-boiled egg, Chase did exactly that, exiting the building as quickly as she'd gone in.

The security guard wished Chase a good day as she skipped down the steps, passing a large group of tourists who had just gotten off a Greyhound bus. They were young and wearing matching yellow t-shirts so they wouldn't lose each other, cameras at the ready, heading toward the large stone structure. This particular building was a *must stop* for anyone visiting New York City for the first time.

As Chase placed her hand on the door of the BMW to get herself home for a romantic dinner with her sweet Gavin, she heard the guard announce to the noisy tourists, "Welcome to St. Patrick's Cathedral."

CHAPTER 2

*A Quarter to Spare*

It was a short drive from Rockefeller Center to the Lenox Hill area of Manhattan, and Chase refused to sit in the back seat, even though she was paying Matthew to drive her. It felt as if she'd be saying to the world, *Look at me, the fancy girl with the fancy driver.* She preferred instead to sit up front and chat, although today she was uncharacteristically quiet, her tongue still, her mind wandering, and her gaze out the car windows fixing on nothing at all.

Chase adjusted herself in the seat and felt a jab in her right hip, revealing something in her pocket, poking her. She wiggled around a bit to gain leverage, pushed her small fingers inside the tiny pocket and fished out a single shiny quarter. Chase rubbed the coin between her thumb and fingers, and it worked like a time machine, transporting her to a memory and place far away.

As the car eased its way through the Upper East Side, Chase looked down at the coin and said quietly, "Some kids don't have a quarter, so I'd leave them one."

Matthew, not taking his dark brown eyes off the road said, "I'm sorry, what about quarters?"

Chase liked and trusted Matthew, but in the year he'd been her driver she had never let him into her real life. She couldn't tell you why. After all, he came across as one of the most stand-up men she'd ever met, as solid and trustworthy as he was handsome for his age. Yet today, there was something about the way he asked her that last question, a kindness in his voice, that caused Chase to let her guard down.

"Back where I used to live in Manchester, Vermont," she began, "They had a store called Orvis; it was an L.L. Bean-type place."

Matthew nodded, "Okay."

"Outside this store was a big pond filled with trout of all shapes and sizes. I mean these things were HUGE."

She saw he was listening, so she continued, "By the back of the store, near the door that led to the pond, they had a gumball machine with fish food inside, and you could fill up a little paper cup with the food if you put a quarter in. You know what I mean?"

Matthew, following along, said, "So instead of getting candy like a regular gumball machine, you got fish food."

"That's right," Chase replied, "and when you threw the food into the water the fish went crazy trying to gobble it up."

Matthew could imagine the feeding frenzy in his own mind right now.

She continued as she looked down at the coin, "I was just thinking about that place and saying to myself that some kids didn't have a quarter for the fish food. Some kids are broke, ya know?"

Matthew smiled, "I do. I used to be one of them."

"Me too," Chase said, smiling back. "Anyway, once a month I'd stop at Bennington Bank and buy a roll of quarters for ten bucks, then I'd leave it with Liana Bonavita, the nice lady who ran the Orvis store."

Chase hadn't thought of Liana since she left Vermont, prompting her to smile again and say, "Isn't that a great name, Liana Bonavita. It's almost lyrical."

Matthew chuckled and said, "It is. It sounds like an exotic place you'd go on vacation. 'Sorry, can't talk, I'm catching a flight for Bonavita.'"

They were both smiling now at Matthew's silliness.

"Anyway," Chase continued, "I'd leave the quarters with Liana, and she'd keep them separate from the register, and when some kid was looking for fish food and didn't have any money, she'd say, 'Hold up, I have a quarter to spare,' and hand them out, making a child happy."

Matthew considered the kind gesture and in a thoughtful voice said, "Well, that was nice of you, Chase."

She smiled and said, "I didn't have a lot growing up, so things like that, not even having a quarter sometimes—I don't know, I guess when I see a kid like that I want to help."

Chase looked out of the car's windshield at the busy traffic, but then her grin fell away as she remembered standing on a small wooden bridge that crossed the pond full of fish in Vermont. She and Gavin stood there more than once, talking, but the last time was an unhappy memory. It involved a very difficult conversation with Gavin, one where, in the end, she knew she had to leave Vermont, a place she adored.

Telling the man, you love, "I can't stay here," causes an ache that never quite leaves you.

Matthew saw the sadness in her face and said, "I know you are a private person, Chase, but I also know you are hiding from something here in Manhattan, and the thing is, I can't protect you properly if I don't know what it is."

There was a long silent pause, then Mathew added, "Why are you here, Chase?"

Chase liked Matthew. He looked like a fluffy Antonio Banderas, the silver in his hair growing whiter by the day and the creases around his eyes telling you this was a man who had seen some things in his years as a cop. Even though he had retired from the force he still dressed like a police detective, with a neatly pressed dress shirt, slacks, and shoes. Appearance was important to Matthew.

Chase had ducked his polite inquiries for months, but seeing those kind eyes searching for a way to help her, perhaps it was time, she thought, to take the trust he had earned and put it to use.

She decided to just say it. "I'm a writer, Matthew, and a couple of years ago when I went to visit a small town in Vermont something happened to me that led me to write a book."

Matthew considered her words and replied, "Something happened. Was it something good or bad?"

Chase put both feet on the front seat and pulled her knees up to her chest, wrapping them with her arms the way a child would who was about to tell a secret.

She went on: "No, not bad. Just strange. I lived in an old church building and started seeing things in the windows that ended up coming true."

Matthew then, "You mean—literally seeing?"

"Yes, I mean I'd see something in the stained glass that wasn't there before, and it turned out to be a clue to help someone in town," she replied.

Matthew sat in silence as she added, "And before you ask, no, I'm not psychic. It hasn't happened before or since."

Matthew immediately thought about all the times she had finished her daily jog by taking a quick walk through St. Patrick's Cathedral, and then his mind shifted back to what she just said about the church in Vermont. "Hang on, let me park first."

After pulling the car into an empty spot in front of the dry cleaners Chase used often, Matthew turned facing her now and said patiently, "Go on."

Chase locked eyes with his and said, "When I looked at the church windows, I saw people in town who were in trouble, and so I helped them. That's all. I'm a writer, so I wrote a book about the experience, and when word got out, things got weird for me."

Matthew was thinking hard now, trying to make sense of it, then asked, "What do you mean when word got out? You mean when people read the book?"

Chase nodded, "Sort of. Here's what happened. I write and publish the book and it does all right, in sales, ya know."

Matthew just nodded as he followed along.

"Then a TV station in Boston hears about it and sends a reporter from four hours away to Manchester to interview me. I do it, thinking I'm just talking to people in Boston."

Matthew was confused now. "You weren't?"

"No," Chase began, "they do the story and put it up on the satellite and give it to CNN. Next thing I know my story and book have gone viral."

"Well, that must have been good for sales, right?" Matthew said.

"Right, it was. I was on the bestsellers list two weeks later. But then people from all over who had troubles in their lives started making this pilgrimage to Manchester, asking me to look at the church windows and tell them if their mom was in heaven or where their lost cat was."

Matthew thought for a moment then said, "And you had no clue."

"No, I didn't, and most of them just stared at me with these lost, sad eyes like . . ." Chase let out a deep sigh and didn't finish the thought.

"Hey, hey, It's okay. I get it now. So, you needed to get out of there for a while?"

Chase reigned in her emotions and said, "Yes, that's why I'm here in a big city where nobody knows me."

The two sat in silence another moment when Matthew finally asked, "Is that why you keep going to St. Patrick's? Are you looking up at all those windows for something?"

Chase felt relief rush over her. It was good that someone understood and knew she wasn't crazy.

"Yes," she answered, "I literally do a quick loop inside, looking up at all that stained glass, and it always looks exactly the same. Whatever happened in Vermont, stayed in Vermont, and is apparently finished with me."

Matthew touched her hand like a father trying to comfort a child, "Is that a good thing or a bad thing?"

Chase threw her hands in the air, shrugged her shoulders, "Beats me. I have a book everyone read, a bank account full of money, and here I am running around churches like some fool."

Matthew didn't say a word, just listening now.

Chase added, "And you wanna hear the funny part?"

Matthew nodded silently.

"Before Vermont, I'm not sure I even believed in God. I rarely went to church, so I keep asking myself the same question . . ." Her voice trailed off.

"Why you?" Matthew said firmly.

"Exactly!" Chase replied, "Why me?"

After another slight pause Matthew asked, "So how many more times am I picking you up at East Fiftieth?"

Chase responded, "You mean how many more times am I running through the church there?"

She pushed away a tear from her left eye, embarrassed she was getting this emotional about it. "Oh, I think we're done. I think today was the last time."

She looked at her watch, signaling that she really had to go.

Picking up on the signal, Matthew said, "Hey, before you duck out, did I ever tell you why my name is Matthew?"

Chase liked the fact that he was changing the subject. "Nope, I don't think you did."

Her thoughtful driver continued, "My mom was super-religious, and of all the stories in the Bible she loved the fact that Jesus chose Matthew as one of his special twelve."

Chase wasn't following. "I don't read the Bible, so I don't get the significance."

He continued, "Matthew was a tax collector and only cared about money. He's the last person you'd think Jesus would want for an apostle. He even told Jesus when they met, listen dude, I'm NOT the guy you want."

Chase giggled. "He called Jesus 'dude'?"

Matthew laughed. "Probably not, but you get my point."

Chase thought a moment and said, "Maybe my mind is foggy today. What's your point?"

He finished saying, "My mom always said even if you don't believe in God, he believes in you, and he sometimes uses the least likely among us to do good things."

Chase was on the verge of tears again, thinking about what Matthew said, replying in a slightly cracked voice, "And you think that's me, huh?"

Matthew was the one shrugging his shoulders now. "Beats me, but why not? You're a good person, Chase. I saw that the first day I met you. And I appreciate you trusting me enough to tell me about Winchester, Vermont, and the church windows."

Chase laughed, "Manchester, it was Manchester, but . . . thank you, Matthew."

Chase felt like a twenty-pound weight had been lifted from her shoulders as she smiled at her driver and said, "Gotta go. Thank you for listening."

Matthew Rodriguez watched his one and only client exit the vehicle and make her way toward the front door of her well-appointed building.

He noticed she left the quarter that was in her hand, the one that triggered all those memories, behind on the dashboard. Matthew scooped up the emotional landmine, tossing it into a dish with the rest of his loose change.

As he watched Chase pull the rubber band tie out of her hair, causing it to fall softly on her shoulders, catching the late morning light, Matthew had one powerful thought cross his mind.

He said it out loud, as if doing so made it more real, "I'm not going to let anything happen to you, Chase. I promise."

What Matthew didn't know was that he had the situation exactly backwards. It was Chase who would someday save his life.

## CHAPTER 3

# Fur-Ever Java

The Brownstone where Chase lived alone with her pup was four stories high. She rented the second floor, with tenants above and a one-of-a-kind coffee shop taking up a very lively residence down below. Chase smiled every time she approached the front door and looked up to see the large red and white sign that said *Fur-Ever Java*. The casual observer would assume it was just a play on words, but within thirty seconds of entering the coffee house, you'd understand what the *Fur* was about.

Chase was about to reach for the doorknob to let herself in when she heard her best friend call out to her. Scooter, an Australian Shepherd she'd saved from a shelter outside Seattle, was already in the window announcing her return. Scooter was smart and knew exactly how long his mommy's morning jog took. One hour after she left, his piercing, light blue eyes would scan the block waiting for the black car to arrive that carried everything that mattered to him in the world.

Chase pulled the door open and braced herself for the two front paws that would hit her legs hard, just above the knee, Scooter's way of saying *I missed you*.

"EASY, buddy," she said, scratching the top of his furry head.

"Did he behave?" Chase asked the busy café, tossing the question to whoever wanted to catch it.

Raylan, the owner, said, "Are you kidding? He's smitten with that Pug who just came in, Penelope. The two were thick as thieves while you were gone."

Chase's eyes scanned the café, and waddling over was a small dog with a light brown body and a jet-black face. Around the Pug's neck was a handmade white cloth collar with the name PENELOPE sewn right in. The animal shelter on Bleeker Street in Greenwich Village had a volunteer sew those collars so any dog that was up for adoption would be easy to identify.

Chase leaned down to give her a pat on the head when Scooter suddenly pushed himself between them as if to say, *Um, mom, she's mine.*

Chase looked at Raylan and said, "You're not kidding, he likes her. It's gonna break his heart when she goes."

Raylan, a man in his forties, with a face that told a hard story and a crisp white apron tied around his waist, continued wiping down a table and replied, "Oh yeah, he'll be heartbroken until the next girl comes in to visit."

A well-dressed woman in her sixties holding an expensive Hermes bag was looking at pottery, specifically a clay bowl made by a local artist. Raylan was kind enough to offer a free shelf in his café to any of the local artisans so they could sell their wares. He wouldn't even take a cut, letting them keep all the profits. In Raylan's mind everyone needed a hand up sometimes, especially a struggling artist.

The woman holding the bowl asked in a rude tone, "Can I ask you why you have so many dogs in here?"

"GOUT, It's definitely gout, Raylan." The words came from a different woman with short red hair who worked part-time at the café and was busy *not* ringing up customers. Instead, she was staring at a laptop computer that didn't belong on the front counter. She shouted to Raylan something about gout with a look of horror on her face.

Raylan turned from the customer who asked the question about the dogs toward the woman with the laptop and said, "Hang on, Deb. You can tell me about your horrible disease in a minute. I'm talking to a customer."

Deb slammed the computer shut and walked in a circle talking to herself, "Gout, I knew it. And everyone said I just banged my leg on the stairs. It's probably creeping toward my brain as we speak."

Raylan, no stranger to Deb's hypochondria, heard that last comment about it *creeping* and started laughing out loud.

The wealthy woman holding the pottery looking annoyed, asking, "Did I say something funny?"

Raylan straightened up, "No, ma'am. I was laughing at my worker. Every day she comes in here with some ailment and instead of RINGING UP CUSTOMERS," Raylan said loudly in Deb's direction, "She gets on the internet and puts in her symptoms and about twenty seconds later she's convinced she has some horrible disease."

Raylan could see the woman wasn't amused or interested, "I'm sorry. What was your question again—why so many dogs in here?"

The woman folded her arms in front of her in a defiant stance and said, "Seems like a health hazard in a place you sell food."

Raylan had gotten the question before and was growing tired of answering it. Chase, holding Scooter by his collar, was eavesdropping, so she decided to help him out.

"Mrs.?" Chase began with inquiry in her voice.

The woman turned a cold eye toward Chase and said, "Wainwright. Delores Wainwright. And you are?"

"Chase," she replied with a smile.

The woman crinkled her nose, "Chase? Aren't you a girl?"

Chase let go of Scooter's collar now so he could go rub noses with his new girlfriend, Penelope, saying, "Yes, last I checked. Anyway, Mrs. Wainwright, can I ask you a question? I saw you looking at the pottery there . . . it's pretty, isn't it?"

The older woman paused, then said in a calmer tone, "It is."

Chase continued, "Were you thinking of maybe buying some?"

The woman cleared her throat, "I suppose I was, but . . ."

Before she could continue, Chase said, "Not to interrupt, but I'll bet you when you walked into this coffee shop you planned on getting coffee, not pottery, but because it's here you happened to see it and like it and now you might get it."

The woman was curious where this was going and said only, "Right."

Chase continued, "This Fur-Ever Java café is spelled like *Fur*, F-U-R, for a reason."

Now it seemed everyone in the café had stopped what they were doing and was listening to Chase. She went on, "At any given moment there are hundreds of cats and dogs sitting in animal shelters in the five boroughs of New York City. People don't adopt them because they don't see them."

"Raylan here," Chase continued, now pointing over to her landlord and the coffee shop owner, "Raylan has agreed to bring two dogs in at a time from the shelter and let them kinda wander around the shop and meet the customers. And before you ask or look where you stepped, they have to be housebroken and friendly or Raylan doesn't take them in."

The woman was looking down at Scooter when Chase added, "Oh no, not this one. This pup is mine, but Penelope here and that white dog who is sleeping over in that corner are from the shelter."

Delores noticed the other puppy, mostly white with dark swirl markings, all curled up and leaning against a wall with her eyes closed.

Raylan jumped in at this point adding, "I take in two dogs at a time and let them live here, and my regular customers get to know them. Nine out of ten times they get adopted by someone who has been around them a few times and likes them."

The woman considered what she was hearing and asked, "And the health department allows it?"

Raylan scratched his chin, just below a large scar on the right side of his face, and said, "Let's just say it hasn't been a problem because nobody ever complained. The dogs and I have an arrangement. They agree to behave, and I save their lives. It's a pretty fair deal."

Penelope the Pug walked over, almost if on cue, and wagged her cropped tail, looking up at the older woman with loving eyes.

Delores couldn't help but smile and said, "Well, they won't hear any complaints from me. The health department, I mean."

With that she took a small blue handmade pottery bowl and moved toward the register, causing Raylan to raise his hand and stop her.

"You must have missed the sign out front ma'am. Every customer who Penelope wags her tail at, gets a free bowl today. So, it's on her. You have a wonderful day."

The older woman, feeling almost ashamed of her ill-temper, smiled and said, "Very kind of you."

She then surprised everyone when she reached down and patted the puppy on the head, "Thank you for the bowl, Penelope."

Delores Wainwright took her new pottery and the coffee she'd already paid for and headed for the door.

Chase smiled and said to Raylan, "You're going to go broke if you keep doing that, bud."

Raylan laughed and brought his hand up to cover the scars on his face, an automatic reflex born of embarrassment. With Chase, and a few others he trusted, Raylan forgot the scars were even there. And the truth was, living above the coffee shop for a year now, Chase no longer even noticed what Raylan unceremoniously called his *present from the war.*

"GOUT, ravaging my body as you give away pottery." Deb said out loud so the whole café could hear. She shouted louder, "CREEPING TOWARD MY BRAIN AS WE SPEAK."

Raylan turned with a wicked grin and shouted back, "When it gets there it will find a vacancy sign." Chase shook her head, laughing, and took up Scooter's leash to take him upstairs to her apartment and get ready for Gavin and dinner.

Raylan couldn't resist asking Chase, "Is stud muffin farmer boy coming into town again? More sushi? Is he thinking about moving in? I mean, in fairness, it is supposed to be an apartment for *one.*"

Chase shot him a look and said, "And that's how it will stay. I told you Raylan, I'm an old-fashioned girl. There will be plenty of time for that stuff later."

Raylan replied, "You mean after you're married."

Chase answered, "Of course, but there's no rush."

Curious now, Raylan asked, "So where does he stay when he drives down to visit?"

"His buddy from college lives just outside the city and has an extra room where Gavin can crash anytime he likes," she replied.

Raylan smiled, "Well, I admire the traditional values."

Chase started toward the door, with Scooter in tow, when Raylan called after her, "Hey, can you do me a favor? Take the box on the end of the counter, the one covered in tin foil, and leave it on the side steps as you head up to your apartment?"

Chase looked confused, so Raylan added, "It's food, day-old stuff. I was gonna throw it away. Just leave it on the stairs. Please."

Chase did as she was asked, and a half hour later the box of goodies was gone. She'd find out soon enough who took it and why.

## CHAPTER 4

# Carrie Bradshaw Lied

C hase's jaw fell to the floor when, one year ago, she opened an email from a man with a strange first name and saw what he wanted for a one-bedroom apartment in Manhattan. Chase's first place after college in Seattle was $850 a month and that included utilities. When she rented an old church in Vermont, they wanted $1,200 a month, which was a big step up for her pricewise. But this was a whole new universe, paying $3,700 dollars for a 900-square-foot flat with a leaky showerhead and a bedroom that offered a spectacular view of a brick wall.

Still, Chase checked around and saw that in the higher-end neighborhoods where she wanted to live, not far from Central Park, what Raylan was asking was more than fair, especially when you consider that the place came with two parking spaces at a nearby garage. Perfect for a woman with a vintage ragtop Mustang and a boyfriend with a big truck.

It wasn't as if she didn't have the money. Chase's first novel, *Manchester Christmas,* sold 600,000 copies when word got out that it was based on a true story. People ate up stuff like that, especially if there was a paranormal element to it. She even got a call from a Hollywood director, Brian something or other, looking to buy the rights to her story. He kept going on about the movies he'd made and his date with actress Drew Barrymore, when Chase politely cut him off and said, "Sorry pal, not interested, but tell Drew I said hi!"

Still, every time she turned the key and went into the tiny apartment, Chase couldn't help rolling her eyes at how little all that money had bought her.

Most women Chase's age grew up binge watching *Sex and the City* and following the amazing life of Carrie Bradshaw. They all bought in to the belief that you could write a weekly column for a newspaper no one ever heard of and make enough money to afford a large three-bedroom apartment in Greenwich Village.

"Carrie Bradshaw lied," Chase said out loud to her tiny apartment the very day she moved in.

Still, she couldn't complain. Most adults in their thirties who worked jobs in Manhattan were forced to live like sardines, three to an apartment, if they wanted the Upper East Side. Most found themselves taking trains to and from work, from one of the outer boroughs. Chase was lucky, because the book had sold so well it afforded her this option. The money also allowed her to hire a driver and avoid flagging down cabs in the rain or riding the subways at night. A young 135-pound woman walking alone in the dark in any big city was never a good idea, so her driver and friend, Matthew, was an extravagance she could justify.

Her apartment door opened into a small living space with hardwood floors that needed refinishing, which made her happy because it also meant Scooter's nails couldn't make them any worse. Mounted to the right of the door was a small coat rack where she hung her black leather jacket, Scooter's leash, and Gavin's cowboy hat if he chose to wear it. When she first moved in and he began visiting, Gavin wore the tan Stetson all the time, but he soon learned that kind of headgear earns you lots of stares and comments. More often than not lately, Gavin just left the hat on the passenger seat of his truck.

The walls of her apartment were exposed brick, making it difficult to hang photos properly, and her couch was a small two-seater, just enough room for the two of them to watch TV.

Gavin, having grown up on a farm and being used to miles of space and blue sky above, felt confined in the big city, but if this was where his sweetheart needed to be right now, he was willing to make the long drive to see her. Most men wouldn't have been so patient, a year of this back and forth, but Gavin knew a keeper when he met one, and that was certainly his Chase. Still the *give and take* was feeling a bit too much like *take* as of late, and Gavin was growing restless in this cramped, noisy city.

The kitchen was also small with a four-top gas stove and one dangerous problem. The back burners wouldn't light on their own, so you had to turn the gas on and then ignite them with a match. If you didn't get it on the first try the smell of gas quickly filled the kitchen, making your second effort with the match crucial. Raylan told her, "If you can't get it on the first or second try, shut off the gas, crack open a window and leave it be until the smell is gone." Who knew making a cup of tea could be so rife with peril?

Chase signed a one-year lease, which was about to expire, and Raylan, the landlord, hadn't mentioned her renewing it yet. He was so busy giving away pottery to people downstairs and trying to adopt out all these unwanted puppies, Chase assumed it had just skipped his mind. Chase didn't love the apartment—it was a bit claustrophobic— but she adored the neighborhood, especially the café below. Most days it felt like an island of misfit toys due to the collection of odd ducks who frequently found their way in. Raylan was damaged from the war; the scars on the outside were easy to spot, but the others, which ran deeper, remained hidden away.

Deb on the cash register was a *hoot*, a phrase Chase's grandmother Marge was fond of saying, and the locals who came in for scones and cappuccinos were fun to watch. Chase could sit for an hour at a corner table downstairs and just drink it all in.

"Characters for a future book," she'd tell herself, as she sat in silence and observed them. And now today this new mystery, Raylan having her leave trays of food on the stairs for some invisible guest, intrigued her too.

Chase hopped in the shower, trying to wash away the morning run, as Scooter lay on the thick beige towel she left folded on the floor just outside the shower door. Chase would step onto it to catch the dripping water and Scooter would lick the tiny drops off her feet, tickling them.

"Stop it, silly," she'd say to him, taking his drying technique as an expression of love.

Once dried off, she threw on a pretty pink blouse and designer jeans and was about to sit down to start her makeup when she heard Gavin's footsteps on the stairs. There was something about the way he walked that told her it was him.

She looked at Scooter and said, "It's funny how you can tell it's someone you love just by the stomping of their feet.

Gavin used the spare key Chase had given him to engage the lock.

"Babe?" he called, as he swung open the door, sending Scooter running in his direction for a hug.

"Hey buddy, where's mommy—making herself beautiful?" he asked the happy pup.

Scooter slammed his backside against Gavin's leg and then turned on a dime and returned to Chase. There was no doubt whose dog he was. Gavin saw her cell phone charging on the counter and noticed there was a missed call and a voicemail.

"You got a message, hon," he yelled toward the sound of the blow dryer hard at work on her thick wet hair. Chase's beautiful face peeked around the corner from the bathroom and said, "See who it is."

Gavin liked the fact that they held no secrets and could pick up each other's phones without worrying that they'd be upset by something they saw. He unplugged the silver iPhone and looked at the screen and read the name aloud, "It says 'Jennifer from college.'"

Chase shut off the blow dryer and moved on to brushing her teeth, catching a glimpse of herself in the mirror above the sink, wishing she was half as pretty as Gavin always made her feel. The way he looked at her was paralyzing at times. No man had ever given her that sense of adoration before.

She finished quickly and came out of the tiny bathroom to give him a peck on the lips with her minty fresh breath. "Thank you for making the drive. How's dad?"

Gavin took a seat at the kitchen table and said, "Good. Busy. Stubborn. The usual menu, I'd say."

Chase's mind just caught up with what Gavin said about the missed call and asked, "Did you say 'Jennifer from college'?"

Gavin, still holding her phone in his hand, raised it up so she could read the screen. "Yep. That's what it says. You've never mentioned her before."

Chase looked perplexed now. "No, I haven't. Gosh, I haven't heard from Jen in like five years. She's a writer like me but more a journalist."

Gavin, following along, asked, "What newspaper does she write for?"

Chase thought a moment, trying to remember, "I think she actually worked for a magazine in Chicago last I knew. Honestly, I'm not sure, it's been so long since I heard from her."

She then pushed play on the voicemail button and put it on speaker so they could listen together.

"Hey Chase, it's Jen. First up, congrats on the book. Bestsellers list! Wow. Good for you. Anyway, I'm assuming you are still up in Vermont, but if you are taking a break from writing novels, I need a really big favor. I'm at the *New Yorker* now, the magazine, and our subscriptions and web hits are a bit down right now. I told my boss we were friends in college, and she asked if I could get you to do a special guest assignment for us. At first I thought no, I'm not even going to ask, I don't like trading on friendship that way. But then something fell in my lap that I thought you'd be perfect for. Geez, I'm rambling on and this thing is probably gonna cut me off. Call me back when you get this message and I'll tell you about it. Again, congrats on the book."

With that the phone let out a beep and Jennifer from college was gone.

Gavin looked at Chase, trying to gauge her reaction, but he couldn't get a clear read on her face, asking instead, "You want to call her back? You know, to take the job?"

There was an awkward moment of silence, so Gavin stepped deeper into the murky water, now adding, "You haven't worked in a year, Chase, I mean, written. Might be good for you."

Another pause, and then he finished the thought: "To work, I mean."

Still thinking about the message and whether or not she was ready to dive back into writing, Chase finally said, "You excited for steak tonight? This place is supposed to be great." She started toward the door to grab her jacket but realized Gavin wasn't following after. As much as Gavin adored her, he hated when Chase did this, side-stepping a question she didn't want to answer, so he just kept staring at her without saying a word.

She knew that look in those pushy blue eyes, so she said, "Yes, of course I'll call her back. As far as working or not working . . . we can talk about it over dinner. Actually, there's a few things we should talk about."

Gavin could tell now was not the time to push her, but asked, "Are you going to call Matthew to come get us and drive us to dinner?"

Chase avoided eye contact as she picked up the keys to Gavin's truck off the counter and said, "I thought we could give him the night off and you drive."

Gavin knew what that meant. Whatever they needed to talk about might go sideways fast, and if they were about to have their first big fight, Chase would rather not have an audience in the front seat.

As in most things in life, Gavin was right on the money.

## CHAPTER 5

# Sparks at Spark's

G avin Bennett wasn't a magician, but growing up in the country he learned a trick that had served him well. Because the Green Mountains of Vermont surrounded the family farm in Manchester, storms and rain could easily sneak up and catch you off guard. Not Gavin, though. Gavin had learned there was a smell the air took on and a way birds behaved long before the first thundercloud peeked over the trees. When light rain was coming, he'd catch the faint scent of morning dew, and the birds would be busy gathering food, building nests, singing in the trees. But when a real storm was brewing, the air took on a heavy, syrupy quality, and birds could be seen darting about with great haste, acting like they needed to get home fast.

As Gavin and Chase slid into his truck and made their way to Spark's Steakhouse for an early dinner, he could feel those storm clouds gathering even though nothing had been really said since *Jennifer from college* made her pitch to Chase over voicemail. It felt like a chess match where they both knew what was coming but neither one wanted to make the first move, so the drive was quiet.

Even though Chase was sitting on a pile of money from the book, Gavin always insisted on paying for dinner, and Chase reluctantly let him. She knew Gavin was old-school, stubborn, and a true gentleman, so she'd find other ways to put money back in his pocket without him noticing: a full tank of gas in his truck when he wasn't watching or paying the take-out man in advance, so when food arrived and Gavin reached for his wallet the guy would say, "You're all set."

Spark's restaurant looked like something out of a Scorsese movie, with oak walls, a huge bar with thousands of bottles of liquor on display, and shadows and patches of light everywhere. It felt like a place where ten things might be happening all at once, each table and booth offering absolute privacy for the occupants. You sensed a business deal might be happening to your left while a couple was getting engaged to your right.

Chase had called a week in advance to secure the reservation, and they were given a table just a few feet from a beautiful piano that sat silent at the moment. Clean white linens adorned the tables, with heavy silverware placed neatly on top, each knife, fork and spoon precisely two inches apart. It reminded Chase of the kind of flatware your grandmother only broke out at Christmas and Easter.

A handsome waiter in a bright white shirt with a black vest introduced himself as Howard and was about to place a large leather wine list down on the spacious table. Gavin stopped him, "I can save us some time. The lady will have a glass of Merlot, and I'll take any IPA you have on tap."

Howard pulled back the wine list and tucked it neatly under his arm, saying, "We have several fine Merlots and I believe four different IPAs. If you'd like I can . . ."

Gavin cut him off politely and said, "Tell ya what, just bring us the most expensive of both."

The waiter nodded with a smile, knowing his tip just went up significantly. "Very good, sir." As he turned to go Chase shot Gavin a look that said, *You may regret that, pal.*

Gavin knew Chase's every emotion and could read her face, responding, "Don't worry, the worst they'll ding me on the beer is ten bucks. And the Merlot?" He shrugged his shoulders.

Chase smiled and said, "Yeah, you may have just bought me a thirty-dollar glass of wine, cowboy."

Gavin smiled back, "It's okay, we're celebrating, aren't we?" Chase looked confused.

Gavin tried to begin, "Your lease, it's up. You said you'd be one year away, living here in the city, and we are now at that year."

Chase fell silent and took a breath. Gavin could see she wasn't ready to think or talk about it, so he poked her a bit more, "Or did I completely misunderstand what we talked about and agreed to on that bridge outside the Orvis store?"

The waiter brought the drinks but, having been in this job for the better part of twenty years, he also could read a table with the best of them. Howard could tell immediately that either the air conditioning in the restaurant was on too high or the "chill factor" between this attractive couple had gone up since he left. He placed the drinks down and didn't bother to tell them the day's specials, retreating silently as quickly as he had come.

Chase waited until the waiter was gone, took Gavin's hand and said, "No you didn't misunderstand, and I know what I said. It's just, I'm not sure if now is the time to go back there."

Gavin's face looked a bit flush now. He brought his palms up to his head, rubbing his scalp hard without saying a word. It was a habit Chase noticed he did when he was frustrated. Had she known him all his life, she'd know it was the same thing he used to do when he was twelve years old and struck out at Little League.

Finally, after an awkward pause, Gavin began, "Home, you mean. When you say can't go back *there*. You mean home?"

Chase hated that he was upset and looked him in the eyes, took hold of both his hands, squeezing them tight. "Yes, home. Your home and what could be my home, someday."

Gavin pulled his right hand back, took a drink of the beer and was looking off in the restaurant at nothing in particular. With his frustration tamped down a bit, he said without looking at her, "So, not now?"

Chase sat up straight, then leaned in so he couldn't miss her next words and in a defensive tone asked, "You tell me and be honest. Are things back to normal there in Manchester or are people still showing up looking for me, driving everyone I mentioned in the book crazy with questions?"

Gavin put the beer down and looked back at her. "Honestly, it's still pretty bad. The tourists, the nonsense."

There was silence now, so Howard took the cue to approach. Chase, however, raised her hand up to stop, and gave him a *not now* look. He bowed his head in apology and said, "You call me over whenever you're ready."

Chase hadn't touched the wine but found herself staring at the beautiful crystal glass, taking deep breaths.

Gavin, feeling calmer, said, "So what do you want to do, stay here? Because this going back and forth is tough on me and before you say it, I know I could get a job here in the city, but Chase . . ." He didn't finish the thought.

She looked up from the glass, and Gavin looked like a lost little boy. "But it's not for you. I know that, sweetie," Chase said in a loving tone.

Then she added, "I notice you didn't have any suits with you in the truck. I'm guessing that means you're not here to go on any interviews?"

Gavin bit his bottom lip. "I tried, I really did," he said. "I went on those websites you sent me and found a couple of farming conglomerates with corporate offices in Manhattan, but it's not for me. I'd lose my mind wearing a tie all day, staring out a fortieth-floor window into nothing. I need space to breathe."

Chase touched his face gently with her soft hands, "It's okay. I know it's not you. I'm sorry I ever asked."

There was silence now, and for a moment it felt like everyone else in the packed restaurant had left and it was just the two of them trapped in this awkward moment.

Finally, Chase said, "Maybe it is time to move out of here; I'm just not sure where to go. But I do know, whatever the move is, you have to be right there with me or it won't feel like home."

Gavin smiled for the first time since they'd left the apartment and said, "Thank you for saying that, and I feel the same way. So, we can't do Manchester, at least not now, and I don't fit in here. Maybe if we put our heads together something great will come to us."

Chase liked where the conversation was going now. "I'm sure we will," she said. "And who knows, maybe something will just present itself unexpectedly. I was only supposed to be in Manchester for a couple of weeks and look what happened there."

Gavin nodded in agreement, "Yeah, I guess we can thank Owen the Realtor for showing you that old church."

Chase was lost in thought when Gavin said something that risked starting up another argument.

"Hey, speaking of church—your driver, the one who looks like Antonio Banderas . . ."

Chase tilted her head. "Matthew. What about him?"

"I called you twice the other day and it went to voicemail and I got nervous, so I called him on his cell," Gavin said.

Chase was curious about where this was going. "And?"

Gavin continued, "And he told me he was parked outside a church, St. Patrick's Cathedral, the big one."

Chase looked away now, slightly annoyed, knowing what was coming next.

Gavin's tone turned kinder. He reached for her shoulder, touching it gently, "He said you go there sometimes and then come right back out. He didn't understand why. Obviously, I do, or at least I think I do. Chase, what are you doing?"

Chase took her first sip of the wine, a generous one, then said, "I don't know. I guess I'm nuts. After what happened in Manchester stopped, I wondered why and if it would happen again."

Gavin looked understanding. "Right, makes sense. So, you went to the church here . . . and . . . what?"

She put the wine glass down hard on the table, almost causing it to slosh out onto the pretty white linen, and said, "NOTHING." She said it so loudly that people at a nearby table looked over and Gavin gave them a glance that said, *Go back to your meal, we're fine.*

Gavin paused, then whispered, "Don't get mad at Matthew, but he says you go there a lot."

Chase was the one looking off at the other diners at their tables now. She said, "He's right. I have. I did. But the truth is, I'm done. Whatever that was in Manchester, showing me things that would happen, be it

God, Taylor, the ghost of Christmas future, whatever that was, it's done with me."

She picked up the glass and took another healthy sip, adding, "But hey, I got a heck of a book out of it."

Gavin was rubbing her shoulder now. "You did more than that, and you know it. You really helped heal that town. You should be proud of that, book or no book."

They stared at each other and both let out a sigh, at exactly the same moment, causing them both to laugh.

With that, Gavin motioned Howard over and they ordered dinner, filet for him and grilled salmon for her. The food was everything the reputation promised, so they asked for a slice of the double chocolate cake to go, something they'd split back at Chase's apartment.

As they walked out holding hands, it felt as if a weight had been lifted. The future was anything but certain, but both knew whatever came next, they'd face it together.

Gavin said, "So just to recap, you're *not* staying here in Manhattan, but you're *not* going back to Manchester?"

Chase smiled. "Correct. Maybe there's some place in between where you can find fresh air and I can find a fresh start."

Gavin gave her a soft kiss on the lips, smiled warmly, and said, "Well I'm all for those, as long as this old dog is part of whatever chapter you write next."

Chase hugged him and spoke quietly. "Chapter? You're the whole book, babe."

As they waited for the valet to bring Gavin's truck, he filled what felt like an awkward silence by imitating a gangster with a Jersey accent: "Ya see this spot right here, Muggzy, this is where Castallano got it. Boom!"

Chase giggled with surprise and said, "Costa who?"

Gavin stopped goofing, returning to his normal voice, "Castallano, the mobster. Remember you told me this place had a mob hit, like, forty years ago? I Googled it."

Chase remembered. Then, in a voice full of relief she said, "You know, for a minute there I thought *we* were going to have a nasty fight."

Gavin tilted his head to the side, that dirty blonde hair and those deep blue eyes drinking in his beautiful girlfriend, and said confidently, "Us? No way. Just a few sparks at Spark's. I loves ya too much, Muggzy."

As Gavin drove them back to the Lenox Hill neighborhood to share dessert and a kiss goodnight, both were secretly nervous about where life would take them next. Both assumed the mystery and magic of Manchester and Chase's visions were well behind them. Both would be wrong.

## CHAPTER 6

# Book in Hand

G ERD!" Deb shouted, as she stared at the bright screen of the laptop placed conspicuously on the front counter at the Fur-Ever Java café. She was gripping the device so tightly you could see the whites of her knuckles. Gavin and Chase were in their usual table near the window, away from the foot traffic but not far from the "fixins station" where people added cream and sugar to their hot and cold drinks. A perfect spot for privacy, but with a full view of both the street and inside the café, depending on which way you turned.

"What did she just say?" Gavin asked out loud.

"Pay her no mind," a voice said. It was Raylan coming out of the kitchen with a small tray filled with muffins and scones. "Yesterday it was gout and today it's . . . what did you just say you have now, Deb?"

She spun the computer around so Raylan could read it for himself.

"GERD. It stands for Gastroesophageal Reflux Disease. It's why I've been coughing like this the last few days."

Raylan tried not to smile and said, "I haven't noticed you . . ." And at that precise moment Deb let out a dry cough.

Raylan nodded like he understood now, "Can I ask you a question then?"

Deb, excited he was finally interested in her daily dire diagnosis, her eyes going big and wide, exclaimed, "Of course, ask me anything!"

Raylan set the tray of breakfast treats on the counter behind the register, and began, "Are the side effects of GOOP—"

"GERD," Deb quickly corrected him. "Not GOOP. GERD."

"Oh, my mistake, sorry," Raylan continued. "Are the side effects of GERD, one of them anyway, an inability to place pastries into a case while simultaneously ringing up customers?"

Deb could sense the sarcasm and made a face as if she had swallowed a lemon. "No."

Raylan smiled. "Alrighty then, get these muffins and scones out and continue your medical prognosis later, please."

Deb closed the laptop and turned to get the muffins when Gavin spoke up. "What was your name again, Deb?"

She looked over and said, "Yes, I'm Deb."

Chase knew her boyfriend and could tell when he had mischief on his mind, so she kicked him gently under the table.

Gavin, ignoring her minor assault, continued. "My name is Gavin, and while I'm not a doctor, I did grow up on a big farm full of animals, so I've seen all sorts of medical conditions."

Deb stopped working for the moment and was enthralled with what this curious gentleman might say next. "Go on, please," she said.

Gavin stood up now, giving her and everyone else in the café a good look at his handsome physique, his tight black t-shirt tucked into acid washed jeans that were slightly frayed at the bottom, just above his brown Tony Lama boots.

He continued, "That cough doesn't sound like GERD to me. It sounds like kennel cough."

Chase looked down at her coffee cup and mumbled to herself, "Sweet Jesus, here we go."

"Kennel cough? Isn't that something dogs get?" Deb asked.

Gavin began to pace the floor, like a television marketer on late night TV selling a product. "They do, yes, they do. But humans can get it too. Can I ask you Deb, have you been around any strange dogs lately?"

Deb looked down and realized Penelope, the rescue dog from the shelter, was standing right near her, so she jumped back, clutching her chest with both hands as if afraid.

"Yes, I've been around several," she replied, staring suspiciously at poor little Penelope.

Gavin could tell he had her believing him now. "Well, that might explain it. It's not fatal or anything, but you should watch out for the warning signs in case it gets worse."

Deb walked around the counter to get closer to Gavin for this next part. "The WARNING signs?" she asked, with trepidation in her voice.

Chase looked up, trying not to laugh, saying, "Gav. Please don't."

Gavin ignored her; he was too far into this now. "Oh yeah. If you find yourself suddenly wanting to chase cars or worse, and I sincerely hope this one doesn't happen to you."

"WHAT?" Deb asked, nearly terrified now.

"If you see a new customer in the store and you suddenly want to sniff them. Or if for no logical reason you ask them to throw you a ball. That would be a sign that you should probably see a doctor."

Deb's mouth was agape, her eyes darting back and forth. She looked out the front window and saw a red car roll by and said, "Oh geez. I just saw a car and I think I wanted to chase it." With that the dozen or so people in the café burst out laughing.

Chase stood up at this point and said, "Oh, for God's sake, Deb, he's joking with you. Only dogs can get kennel cough. You're fine. He's kidding." She looked toward Gavin, adding, "Tell her you're kidding!"

Deb suddenly realized how silly Gavin sounded and saw him smirking, so she said, "Seriously? You scared me."

Gavin smiled. "I'm sorry Miss Deb," he said. "I was just teasing. It sounds like a regular old cough to me. Although if you feel the urge to drink out of the toilet . . ."

With that Deb took the dish towel that hung from her belt and threw it in Gavin's direction, "HA, HA, HA."

She was a good sport about the teasing, and just as the laughter died down, the door to the café swung open and two young women in their late teens came in with a stack of books in their hands. They looked like students from one of the many colleges or universities that called New York City home. No one paid them much mind as they made their way toward the counter to order drinks, but that's when Raylan noticed one of the books in the blonde girl's hand.

He swallowed hard and his mood changed in a flash, and he suddenly pointed at Gavin and said, "Hey you, funny man. I need to see your girlfriend in the kitchen for a moment."

His girlfriend? Everyone knew that Raylan knew Chase's name, so the request was strange. Before anyone could reply, Raylan snapped his fingers impatiently and said, "You, yes, YOU," pointing directly at Chase. "I need you in the kitchen right now, please."

Chase shot Gavin a look of confusion, but she'd known Raylan long enough to know something was up. Then, without saying a word, she got up from the small table and crossed the café, went behind the counter, and pushed open a swinging door that led into the kitchen. In a matter of seconds Chase was gone from sight behind the brown greasy door.

The young ladies, now at the front counter, both grabbed bottles of Evian water and waited to pay, as Raylan said to Deb, "Take care of them," before darting into the kitchen himself.

Once behind the door he immediately started peeking out the small window to see the front counter and the rest of the café. Chase said, "What the heck?"

Raylan brought the index finger of his right hand up to his lips and said, "Shhh . . ."

Chase was really confused now, so she approached Raylan and whispered, "What's the matter with you?"

He took a beat, waiting for the women to pay for their bottled water, and as they turned to leave the café he said, "They're going. Good."

Chase craned her neck to get her own look out the window in the kitchen door and said, "Who is going? Why are you acting so strange?"

Chase saw the two young women leaving, and as her gaze dropped down to the book in the blonde woman's hand, suddenly it all made sense. She was carrying a hardcover copy of *Manchester Christmas* with Chase's photo on the back cover. Chase saw her own face under the woman's palm as she carried the book out, and then turned to Raylan and said very matter-of-factly, "You know who I am."

Raylan let out a deep breath like they'd pulled off a successful bank heist and had just shaken the cops, when he turned to her and said, "Of course I do. I did a background check on you."

Chase looked back at Raylan and replied, "You did? Why?"

Raylan chucked now, responding, "Are you kidding? A woman who will only talk to me over email or phone wants to rent an apartment in my building. She pays me a year's rent in advance with a certified bank check, and every time I ask her a personal question she changes the subject. You'd better believe I looked into who you were. I didn't need a drug lord or something moving into my place."

Chase gave him a sarcastic look and said, "Yeah, I'm Pablo Escobar."

Raylan said, "Put yourself in my shoes."

Chase thought a moment. "I guess I can see your point," she said. "But you never said anything to me about who I am or the book?"

Raylan paused and then pointed to the scar that covered the right side of his face, "Did you ever ask me how I got this?"

Chase replied, "You told me at war but . . ."

Raylan brought his hand down from the scar that stretched from his ear lobe all the way down to his neckline adding, "But you never pressed me for details, did you?"

Chase looked away a moment, then back at Raylan, "No. I thought that was private."

Raylan nodded in agreement. "Exactly. And I figured if you went to all that trouble to hide who you were from me, I'd respect it."

Chase thought another second and said, "And those girls, the one with my book?"

Raylan nodded, "Yeah, I figured you wanted your privacy, so I didn't want them recognizing you and blowing your cover. That's why I didn't shout your name across the cafe. *Chase* is a pretty unique name, especially for a girl, don't ya think?"

Chase felt the urge to hug Raylan at that moment for protecting her, but instead said, "Thank you for that."

Gavin appeared at the kitchen door and said playfully, "Does someone want to tell me what all the cloak and dagger is about?"

Chase immediately went over and rubbed Gavin's back, saying, "Raylan was protecting me, that's all."

Gavin didn't understand what they were talking about, but he looked at Raylan and said, "Thanks, man."

As the three went to leave the kitchen and go back into the café, Chase noticed another small box with tin foil covering it, much like the one she'd left on the stairs the day before.

"Hey," she said to Raylan, pointing at the box, "Is that like the other one? Do you need it to be left on the stairs?"

Raylan looked back at the box on the counter and said, "It is."

Gavin put his arm around Chase as she asked Raylan, "Who picks it up? What's this about?"

Raylan smiled in a way that made you forget he had that nasty scar. "Just helping a guy out, that's all. Hey, if you want to meet him . . ."

With that he looked down at his wristwatch, before adding, "Bring it out in exactly eleven minutes. That's when he comes by to get it. His name is Oscar. You know, like the guy in the Muppets."

Chase loved a mystery, so she picked up the box of treats and said, "You got it."

Gavin looked at her and asked, "Does this mean we're not going for a walk in the park?"

Chase hugged him back and said, "No, we're going. I just need to meet someone first."

As they swung open the kitchen door and returned to the café, Deb could be heard back on the laptop computer, which was propped up near the cash register, "I still think it's GERD."

They all laughed as Chase's phone, which was in her front pocket, began to buzz.

Gavin looked at her inquisitively as she pulled it out and held it up so he could read who was calling: *Jennifer from college.* Again.

"She must have something good for you to be this persistent," Gavin said.

Chase paused a moment, looking at the phone, then hit the button to answer and raised it to her ear.

"Hey Jen, really quick. No, I'm not still in Vermont. Yes, I may be interested in whatever you want to pitch me, and at the risk of being rude I'll have to call you back in a bit."

Chase looked down at the tray of day-old muffins and said, "Right now I'm on the way to meet a Muppet."

## CHAPTER 7

# *Oscar*

Chase and Gavin left the café and walked around to the back of the brownstone. A set of narrow wooden stairs led to the back of Chase's apartment, and Gavin made quick use of them, dashing up and calling back to her, "I'll throw my sneaks on and get ready for our walk. It's such a nice day for it."

With that, Gavin looked up at the bright blue sky doing its best to peek through the tall Manhattan skyline, and then disappeared behind the brown door above.

Chase was holding the small tray of treats and was about to sit on the steps and wait for this Oscar fella to show up, when she noticed movement to her left. Behind the café was a dumpster, a small red picnic table, and a long black wrought iron fence with peeling paint. Attached to the fence was a long white rope that stretched a good twenty feet, and on the other end was a small white dog with a thick, fluffy tail. Even from this distance, Chase recognized the pup as one of the shelter dogs Raylan had taken in with the hope of adopting it out.

The dog looked very happy, bouncing around and wagging that tail like a well-oiled helicopter blade. The source of his joy was a man in his early forties, with dark hair and a light complexion, of average build and wearing some kind of green jumpsuit. It was the kind of outfit you saw auto mechanics wear as they worked in the garage all day, minus the grease. This green jumpsuit was pristine and fit the man like a glove.

Chase watched as the man raised his right hand and touched the tip of his nose with his index finger. Chase's eyes went back to the dog, and she could see the puppy was locked in on the man's every movement. It looked like he was training the dog without uttering a single command. He dropped his hand for a moment, then after he touched his nose again the dog sat. Then he took the same finger and made a circular motion and the pup spun itself in a circle. Chase giggled loud enough for the man to hear, she was so amused by the trick. He then held up his hand in a fist and the dog stopped and stood there. Then he touched his nose a third time and the dog sat again, prompting the man to give her a small treat he had kept hidden away in his right front pocket. After the dog took the treat, the man in the solid green jumpsuit smiled and gave the puppy a big thumbs up, prompting the dog to leap up and give him a kiss. All of this dog training happened in absolute silence.

Chase, sensing the dog's lesson might be over, approached the man with the tray of treats Raylan had set aside. She said, "Hi, is your name Oscar?"

The man smiled warmly and said, "That's what they call me."

Chase handed him the tray and said, "Hi, I'm Chase. I think this is for you."

Oscar smiled and did an exaggerated bow at the waist, saying in a fake English accent, "Thank you, milady."

"That was amazing, what you just did with that dog," Chase blurted out.

Oscar smiled like a proud papa and said in his normal voice, "Yeah, not bad, and this is only our . . ." Then he paused, scrunching his face a bit as if he were thinking, then continued, ". . . fourth time, I think. Training her. She caught on much quicker than the others."

Chase bent down to pet the puppy and noticed that her white cloth collar read *Ella*. "Hi, Ella," she said, rubbing the small dog's head. "What breed is she, do you know?" she asked.

"Beats me," he said. "She looks like she has some chow or terrier in her, but I'm pretty sure she's a mutt. And I mean that in the nicest way."

Chase was down on one knee now, continuing to rub Ella's head and chest with her finely manicured nails.

"My pup likes it when I do this. You like that, sweetie?" she said to the dog.

Oscar, stealing a glance at what was hiding under the tin foil on the tray, returned his eyes to Chase and said, "Yeah, that's right. I've seen you with your dog walking in the neighborhood."

Chase stood up and thought a moment before saying, "I don't think I've seen you, until today."

Oscar then ran over to the dumpster. "I'll bet you have. Does this look familiar?" he said, and hoisted his body up over the edge of the large garbage container and reached in, leaving only his backside and legs dangling in the air.

Chase didn't respond, uncertain of what to say. Oscar popped back out and said, "I'm a dumpster diver. Searching for empty bottles and cans for the deposits."

Chase nodded. "Ah, gotcha. I'm surprised I didn't recognize the bottom of your feet, then," she said with a smile.

Oscar rubbed his hands against his legs to dust them off before picking up the tray of slightly stale muffins and scones.

Chase noticed at that moment that he was in good shape for his age and said, "Hey, there's no way you eat that stuff every day. You'd be 300 pounds."

Oscar scratched his chin, pretending to ponder something, and said, "Maybe I have a super high metabolism." Then he gave Chase a curious look.

She tipped her head to the side, trying to figure out if this man was serious, when he said, "I'm teasing you. No, I don't eat them. I bring them to Mercy House, the homeless shelter around the corner. Have you seen it? It has a big cross above the front door. Half the light bulbs are out though, so when they light it up at night it looks more like an exclamation point than a cross."

Chase shook her head, then said, "Well, that's nice of you to come get these treats and donate them."

Oscar pointed to a large plastic bag filled with empty bottles and cans and added, "That's where the nickel deposits go, too—Mercy House."

Chase assumed in that instant that Oscar must be a man down on his luck who was doing his best to help himself and others.

Then she got an idea, asking, "Hey, are you good with all dogs? I mean not just this one here." Chase was pointing down to Ella, who was sitting attentively looking up at them.

She continued, "I ask because, well, I had a thought. If the boss in there is cool with it, would you want a job walking the shelter dogs he lets into the cafe? I'm sure he'd pay you."

Oscar bit down on his bottom lip like he was pondering some great life mystery and took a long pause to consider what she was saying.

Finally, he spoke, "Um, can I give you two answers to that question? YES, I'd love to help walk the dogs, but NO, I don't want to be paid. I'd be doing it just because."

Chase looked him dead in the eye trying to understand why a man who rummaged through garbage for nickel deposits would say no to easy cash, asking, "Just because? Don't ya like money, Oscar?"

The man in green bent down again to pat Ella on the head and said, "Oh sure, who doesn't? But for this job, helping with the dogs, I'd like to do it for fun, ya know?"

Chase could see he was sincere, so she replied, "Okay, whatever you want. But I should go in and clear it with Raylan, the boss. You wanna meet him?"

Oscar looked shy, now, turning his face away from her. "Nah, I met him once or twice before when he saw me taking empty bottles out of the trash. When I told him what the money was for, Mercy House, he offered me the day-old baked goods to take over too. He leaves them on the back stairs every day at noon. He's a nice guy and all, but since this dog walking stuff was *your* idea . . ."

Chase understood, and she finished Oscar's sentence: "You'd rather I spoke to him about it. I get it. No worries."

As Chase started toward the stairs to join Gavin for their walk in the park, Oscar said, "You're a nice lady. Thank you for bringing this tray of treats to me and for the dog walking job."

Chase stopped on the third step when the writer in her head kicked in, wondering aloud, "Hey, Oscar. When I asked you if that was your name, *Oscar*, you said, 'That's what they call me.' Is that a nickname?"

He smiled, looking up at Chase, who was standing on the stairs, and said, "Good catch. No, the truth is they call me Oscar because before I go dumpster diving, I put on this green outfit they gave me at Mercy House, to keep my regular clothes from getting dirty."

Chase was not following but said, "Okay."

Oscar continued, "And since I'm always in green and in a garbage can, someone said I reminded them of Oscar from *Sesame Street*."

Chase hadn't watched the children's show in thirty years, so she searched her confused brain, and then finally asked, "Isn't the guy in the garbage can blue?"

Oscar let out a loud belly laugh now. "Oh my, NO, that's the cookie monster. How do you not know that?"

Oscar then imitated the cookie monster's voice saying, "ME WANT COOKIES!!!!"

Chase laughed and could imagine it now. "Geez, you're right. And wait, the green one was a grouch. Oscar the Grouch."

Oscar gave her a thumbs up like the one he'd given the puppy earlier, and then said, "Now you got it."

Chase caught herself laughing and then finally said, "But wait, you don't seem very grouchy."

Oscar shook his head side to side and smiled widely saying, "God, no. I love life and people. Every day is a gift."

Chase let out a deep breath. "Well, this has been fun. I have plans with my boyfriend right now, but I'll talk to Raylan later today about the dog walking job that pays nothing."

Oscar gave the dog Ella one last hug and said, "Sounds good, Chase."

With that, Chase bounced up the stairs to tell Gavin about her new friend, as the man named after a Muppet made his way through the alley to take the occupants of Mercy House a perfect midday snack.

## CHAPTER 8

## *Raylan*

An unseasonably warm breeze was blowing through Manhattan, so Raylan took a large white stone he had found years earlier walking alongside Cape Cod Bay and used it to prop open the café's front door. Of all the t-shirts and souvenirs he'd purchased over the years on vacations, it was that silly rock he picked up for free that got the most use. His rock from Rock Harbor, he called it.

After finishing her walk with Gavin, Chase went downstairs to buy a bottle of cold water and talk to Raylan about Oscar and the dogs. She opened the door, and then stopped and stared, taking a moment to drink in the charm of the place. The building was built at the turn of the twentieth century, so the floorboards were wide and creaky, adding to the allure of the café. The scent of rich coffee filled the air as light music played over hidden speakers. The music was never too loud—Raylan made sure of that. He hated being in a place where the music was so distracting that you couldn't hear yourself think or carry on a decent conversation.

New York City is a melting pot of faces and cultures, and this was always evident in the customers that filled the chairs and tables of Raylan's place. Chase glanced around the room, taking in the patchwork of customers. Two couples, both in their twenties, were laughing out loud at something one of them was showing the others on their phone. A man with shaggy long hair and a guitar case in hand was pinning a yellow flier to the bulletin board to the left of the main counter, a singer no doubt advertising an upcoming gig or looking for work.

Then, Chase smiled as she saw a familiar face. It was the older woman from the day before, the one who was barking about a dog being loose in an establishment that served food and drinks. Chase struggled to remember her name.

"Delores something, I think," Chase said to herself.

Chase was smiling because the well-dressed older woman was reaching under her small table to pet Penelope, the rescue mutt she had just met not twenty-four hours earlier.

Chase watched a moment and then giggled as Delores took a piece of the blueberry scone from a tiny brown bag and lowered it down to feed the already chubby Pug. The dog wiggled her back end in a dance of joy, as the woman looked up and realized Chase was watching her. Chase waved hello and gave a look that said, *It's okay, you can feed her if you like, no judgments here.*

"Where's the handsome farmer?" a voice asked from behind. It was Raylan wiping down a table and clearing out some trash a customer left behind.

Chase turned and said, "He's upstairs chilling out. I came down to see you. I have a proposition for you."

Raylan kept wiping, then adjusted the empty chair, making the seat look more inviting. "Wouldn't that be a preposition?" he replied. "You're a writer, right? Don't you guys talk like that?"

Chase laughed, "Preposition, proposition, Preparation H for all I care. Do you want to hear some good news or not?"

Raylan took a seat in the chair he had just pushed under the table, placed his cleaning cloth down, and said, "Hit me with it."

Chase grabbed the chair on the opposite side of the table and began, "So, Oscar, the guy who collects bottles and you give the leftover food to: turns out he's awesome with dogs. I saw him teaching tricks to the little white one you have. I asked him . . ." Chase paused now, second-guessing her boldness in this moment.

Raylan put his elbows on the table in front of him, resting his face in both his hands like a cradle. "You asked him what?"

Chase swallowed a bit, then said, "I know it wasn't really my place, but I asked him if he wanted to walk the dogs for you, as a kind of job. And before you freak out, it won't cost you a penny."

Raylan considered what she said. "Why won't it cost me?" he replied.

Chase lit up. "'Cause he said he'd do it for free. Not my idea. I told him you'd pay him, but he said, nope, free. See what a good negotiator I am for you!"

Raylan smiled, "Oh yeah, I can see it."

Raylan liked Chase, but not because of her obvious beauty or charm. There was a kindness to her that made him feel good being around her. She made him forget how he looked.

In that instant he could tell Chase was fixated on the scars on the right side of his face, and he touched them, saying, "Oh this. Yeah. How about that. You never do ask about it. I appreciate that. You're a real friend."

Chase looked down, embarrassed that he had caught her staring, then raised her eyes to his and said, "Well you know what, because we are friends, I'm asking now. What did happen to cause that? I know you were in the military but . . ."

Before she could finish the thought, Raylan got up abruptly and started walking toward the front counter without saying a word.

Chase's heart sank, thinking she'd pushed him too hard. She called out, "I'm sorry. I didn't mean. It's none of my . . . I'm sorry."

Raylan stopped and turned back, motioning gently with his hand, then said, "Wait. Just wait a moment." He poured himself a hot coffee and, without putting cream or sugar in, returned to the table and sat across from her.

"When you're in the military and out in the field or in some desert, you can't always get stuff to put in your coffee to make it sweet. So you learn to drink it black," he said, taking a deep sip.

Raylan then placed the ceramic white mug down on the small round table between them and continued. "You didn't upset me by asking, Chase. I just knew if we were going to have this conversation, I'd want a cup of joe. So."

He reached up, touching the scar on his cheek, and continued. "How did this happen? You're right, we are friends now, so, fair enough, I'll tell you about the worst day of my life."

Chase took a drink from her water bottle and leaned back in the chair waiting for the story.

"It was early April 2003, a couple weeks after we invaded Iraq. I'm a Marine. Notice I didn't say *was* a Marine, because once you put that uniform on it never really comes off. Like a lot of young men, I joined up after Nine-Eleven and what happened here in the city. I grew up in Jersey City, just across the river, so I had a front row seat for the tragedy at the towers."

Chase was silent, taking in every word.

Raylan continued, "So, April 2003 we are in Iraq—where exactly doesn't matter—and my unit is taking on some heavy fire. Up ahead of us we see some Army boys driving right into the teeth of it and BAM, there's an explosion, about a football field's length in front of me."

Chase interrupted, "And that's how your face got hurt."

Raylan shook his head, "No ma'am. I was safe from that blast, but then the mortars came, and everyone grabbed cover."

"And a mortar hit you?"

"You know, this would go quicker if you let me . . ."

Chase smiled. ". . . finish. Yes. I'm sorry, Shutting up now."

Raylan continued. "Everyone is grabbing cover and I see an Army truck flipped upside down and the fuel line is severed and spewing out diesel. You know, fuel."

Chase leaned in closer as Raylan said, "I think I can see some movement from the truck, and I know once that fuel hits a spark, they're gone, so without thinking I drop my pack and weapon and just sprint toward the vehicle. I get there and the driver and passenger are both buckled in upside down, one is groaning and the other unconscious. I got to the passenger first, the one groaning, so I unbuckle him and drag him, face down in the dirt, out and away from the truck. I run back for the driver and check but there's no pulse. I could smell the fuel now, heavy in my nose, ya know, so I realize there's nothing I can do but get out of there."

Chase finally spoke, "And that's when . . ."

Raylan, "Yes, that's when the fuel ignited and hit me with a blast that knocked me back ten feet."

Raylan stood up then to better explain the next part. "The flaming diesel doused my whole right side, but my helmet, boots, and uniform protected most of me. It was just here . . ." And then Raylan touched his face, adding, ". . .where the fire got me. Unfortunately."

Chase didn't say a word. All she could do was imagine the pain he must have been in.

Raylan took his seat again. "I woke up three days later in a hospital in Germany and wondered why nobody would bring me a mirror. My face actually looked a lot worse. I had five different surgeries where they take skin from your leg or back and graft it here. It got to a point where the improvements were so incremental, I told them I'd just have to live with it, you know," he said, sighing.

Then he looked away, toward the street, not saying another word for a good minute.

Finally, he turned back to Chase, and said, "I know what you're probably thinking, and no, I don't regret going into the military or running toward the danger that way. I may have been young and impetuous, but I'm proud of my service."

Chase squeezed his left hand. "You should be. And Raylan, I don't think your face looks as bad as you think others see it. I'll be honest: I've known you a year and I don't even notice it anymore."

Raylan nodded his head in agreement and said, "I know. That's why I'm sitting with you now, talking about it."

After another pause Chase said in a cheerful voice, "And you're a HERO, Raylan. Oh my God, you saved that man's life. He owes you, forever!"

Raylan chuckled at that thought and said, "Yeah, that's not how I see it."

Chase gave him a confused look. "You don't. Why not? If you hadn't pulled him out . . ."

"Yeah, I understand that, but . . ." Raylan stopped himself before continuing: ". . . there's an old Chinese proverb that says, when you save a life, you are now responsible for it. I kinda feel that way. Whatever happens with that guy I yanked out of the fire, that's kind of on me now."

Raylan got up from the table and took his half-empty cup behind the counter to top off his coffee. Chase followed after him, thinking about what he'd just said, and then asked, "So if you really feel that way, why not track him down? He'd probably love to thank you."

Just then Deb came from around the other side of the counter with her laptop open and said, "I have the worst headache."

Raylan walked over and shut the computer before she could start typing and said, "Can we not today? Please. If you're ever really dying, I promise to tell you."

Deb smiled and said, "Probably just allergies anyway," as she pretended to punch Raylan in the arm and started her chores.

Raylan turned his attention back to Chase and surprised her when he said, "I did. I mean, track him down."

Chase was behind the counter now, and she pulled Raylan by the elbow away from customers who might hear. Quietly, she asked, "You did? How? When? What did he say?"

Raylan explained, "When I got out of the war and the service, the US government handed me some medals for bravery and then gave me a choice. I could take permanent disability and get a nice little check once a month for the rest of my life, or I could take one lump sum check and start my life over. I took the bigger check and bought this building, fixing up the apartment upstairs where you live and turning this space down here into a coffee shop."

Chase nodded, "Okay, but what about the guy you saved?"

Raylan continued, "After I got my life settled here, that's when I started looking for him. All I knew was he was a *Screaming Eagle.*"

Chase was confused. "A screaming what?"

"Eagle. They're from the 101st Airborne in the Army. Their nickname is the Screaming Eagles. I knew he was one because of the tattoo on the back of his neck." Raylan could see Chase wasn't following along, so he reached his hand up.

"Right here," he said, touching the back of his neck below the hairline. "He had a tattoo of a screaming eagle, so I knew he was with that unit."

Once he could see she understood, he continued. "A general who I met in Germany at the hospital told me to get in touch with him if I ever needed a favor, so I called him up and told him I wanted to find the guy I saved. It was against the rules because of privacy issues, but he got me a name and address anyway."

Chase's eyes went wide, wondering what would come next. "And?"

"His name is Peter Philmont, and it turns out he lives here in Manhattan."

Chase pushed Raylan with both hands in a friendly way. "Shut the front door!"

Raylan laughed. "I can't. There's a big rock holding it open."

After a quick giggle from Chase, he continued. "His address was over on Park Avenue, Upper East Side."

Chase considered this new information and replied, "Wait. What? He's rich?"

Raylan nodded. "Yep. You ever hear of Philmont Petroleum?"

Chase shrugged and said, "I guess. They're like Exxon or something, right?"

Raylan replied, "Not as big, but yeah, big enough. The guy I saved is a Philmont. What he was doing in the Army and in the middle of that war is a mystery."

Chase thought a moment and shot back, "Why a mystery? Didn't you ask him when you met him?"

Raylan grabbed up a dust rag and a bottle of cleaner to start wiping things down when Chase yanked them both out of his hands. "Will you stop cleaning for a second and talk to me?"

Raylan smiled. "I never met him," he said. "I went over and talked to the doorman downstairs in their building—*really* nice building by the way. Anyway, he told me several of the Philmont family lived on the upper floors, and he told me Peter was the best of the bunch. Always happy, friendly, a great tipper."

Chase was listening but her face told Raylan she still didn't understand why he didn't say hello to the man.

Finally, he touched Chase's arm. "Listen. The guy I saved is doing great. And I swear, I was going to go up just to say hello but then I caught a glimpse of my reflection in this big mirror in the building's lobby. I saw the scar and thought, I don't want to put this guilt on him. It wasn't his fault his truck got blown up and it wasn't his fault this happened to me. It's just . . . life."

Chase thought a moment and said, "I get it. I do. You didn't want him feeling guilty and you didn't want him thinking you're some charity case."

Raylan nodded firmly. "Exactly. Plus, the whole point of finding him was to make sure he was doing okay, and obviously he is."

Neither spoke for a moment, and Chase found her eyes wandering around the café and back to the older woman who was still petting the rescue dog Penelope, saying, "You see what's going on over there between those two? I don't think she'll be complaining about your dogs anymore."

The war hero with the brave heart and scarred face smiled and said, "I think you're right."

Both could sense their private talk was over, so Raylan said, "Thank you for asking and for listening."

Chase paused, then said, "I have one more question. It's about your name."

Raylan just looked back, folding his arms, waiting for some snarky comment.

"I grew up with an odd name for a girl so I'm always curious when I meet people with odd names," Chase said. "The only other *Raylan* I ever heard of was a character from an Elmore Leonard novel. Is it a family name?"

Raylan smiled. "If I told you, you won't believe me."

Chase was the one standing silent now, folding her arms exactly as he had done, waiting.

"When my mother had me at the hospital," he explained, "she needed a C-section."

Chase nodded. "Okay, so?"

He continued, "She was still a little woozy from the drugs when she filled out the form for my name, so her handwriting was off. The next day the nurse came in and asked her how little Raylan was doing?"

Chase stayed silent, still confused.

He was smiling broadly now. "She meant to write Raymond, but her scribble was mistaken for Raylan. Since she was going to call me Ray anyway, she said she kind of liked that it was different, so she never changed it."

Chase laughed. "That's wild. I love it! Thanks for telling me."

As Chase turned to go back upstairs to be with Gavin, Raylan shouted after her, "Oh, and tell Oscar that's fine with me! He can walk the dogs anytime he wants."

Chase smiled and nodded without saying a word. As she approached the stairs her phone gave off a loud "ding" and a text message popped on the screen. It was *Jennifer from college* and revealed two words in all caps, *STILL WAITING*. What Chase didn't know, what she couldn't know, was that returning that phone call would change her life forever.

CHAPTER 9

# Stonewall Jackson

The only time a cell phone wasn't in Jennifer Donnelly's hand was the five hours a night she slept, so when Chase's name appeared on the screen, she picked up on the very first ring. "Hey Rockstar, thanks for calling back. How are you? Where are you?"

Chase was sitting on the couch in her apartment gently petting her dog, Scooter, with Gavin next to her, working on his laptop. "Hey Jen," she began, "actually I'm in New York City, Manhattan. East side, a few blocks from the park."

Jennifer, seated at a desk at the *New Yorker* magazine at 1 World Trade Center, blurted out, "You're kidding me, *here* New York? Girl, I'm like a fifteen-minute cab ride from you. Why don't we meet up?"

Chase looked at Gavin and said, "Sure, we can do that, but first, tell me what this writing job is."

Jennifer opened a drawer and pulled out a light tan folder, tossed it on the desk in front of her, revealing a black and white photograph of a distinguished-looking older man. "Have you ever heard of Sebastian Winthrop?" she asked, while staring at the older man's face.

Chase now pushed the speaker button on the phone so Gavin could hear the conversation too. And looking over at her boyfriend, she responded, "Sebastian Winthrop? It sounds familiar, but I'm not . . ."

Gavin quickly tapped Chase on the knee and said so only she could hear, "Real estate guy, very rich."

Then he shouted toward the phone, "HE'S A RICH GUY, RIGHT?"

Jennifer, surprised to hear a man's voice on the call, said, "That's right, and this is?"

Chase interjected, "That's my boyfriend, Gavin."

Jennifer smiled and remembered Gavin from Chase's novel and said, "Holy moley, the handsome farmer from Manchester? Who did the picnic by the stream and had that first kiss after the firefly show? Oh yeah, I know who Gavin is. HI, GAVIN."

Chase playfully replied, "Okay, down, girl. So, what about Sebastian the rich guy?"

Jennifer got back on point, saying, "So my magazine wants a profile on Sebastian Winthrop, and since you are now a household name in literature, with a bestseller, we thought . . ."

Chase wasn't sold on the idea immediately, asking bluntly, "Okay, so he's rich. What's the angle to the story?"

Jennifer started turning pages in her folder. She continued, "Well, the story, my dear, is he starts from nothing and then builds this real estate empire. He gets married and stays with the same woman for like a century, not trading up for a shiny new model like every other rich jerk does in this town, and then as he gets older, just starts giving everything away. And I mean *everything*. Scholarships, charitable causes, trusts for needy kids, you get the picture?"

Chase did, and was now wondering aloud, "He sounds like a great guy; do you think he'd give me an interview?"

Jennifer took off her black Oliver Peoples glasses and placed them gently on the desk. "Well, that would be tough because he's dead, Chase," she said. "What we're looking for is . . ."

Chase cut her off. "An obituary. You want me to write an obituary for some rich guy I never met? Come on, Jen . . ."

Jennifer snapped back, "No. NO, absolutely not. We just want to know what made the guy tick. Why all the giving? Something must have motivated him."

Chase thought another moment while looking at Gavin and finally said, "So why do you need me? You must have someone who covers that world down here, the rich and famous types."

"Um, we do. Yes, we do," Jennifer replied, adding, "But we're having trouble getting any information from his point person on all things

Sebastian Winthrop. Her name is Charlotte Jackson. They call her Stonewall Jackson."

Chase shot a confused look at Gavin, who had stopped working on his computer and was intrigued by this conversation.

Chase then said, "I'm guessing they don't call her that because she fought in the Confederate Army?"

Jennifer laughed. "Um, no, that's her nickname because she's tough to get through, over or around in any way. A real . . ."

Chase finished her sentence: ". . . stone wall." There was silence on the phone line.

Chase then asked, "So why would she be any different with me?"

Jennifer stood up from her desk to stretch her legs and said, "People like talking to you, Chase, they always have. I tried with her, several times, but I'm more of a . . ."

Chase thought she was going to utter a word that rhymed with "itch," when Jennifer continued, ". . . acquired taste, a bit too abrasive. And you, you're like a soft little kitten. And such a brilliant writer."

Chase felt her laying it on thick and said, "Easy does it. Any more buttering me up and I'll have to get my cholesterol checked."

There was now silence on the phone, and Jennifer knew that meant her college friend was thinking.

Finally, Chase spoke, "Give me her info and I'll call right now. I can't promise anything, but I'll try to set something up with her. You want to meet in an hour so we can catch up and I'll tell you how I made out with the stone wall?"

Jennifer agreed, and a moment later a text message arrived on her smartphone, telling her the exact address of the Fur-Ever Java café.

Fifty-eight minutes after the two college friends hung up with each other, Chase's phone vibrated and the text read, *I'm here in the café, Jen.*

Chase changed into one of her favorite t-shirts. It was white with a Special Olympics logo on the front, and the back read, *I jumped in a frozen lake and all I got was this stupid t-shirt.* Back in high school she and her classmates had raised money for Special Olympics by taking pledges and doing a polar plunge in a lake near Seattle on New Year's Day. Twenty years later, it still fit and looked nice with her faded jeans and black Vince Camuto boots. She even tied a purple ribbon in her hair for maximum cuteness.

When Chase bounded into the café with Scooter at her side, Jennifer was seated in the center of the room where she couldn't be missed. To her left were a couple of construction workers on their twenty-minute break, and on her right was a familiar older woman, sitting with a dog on the chair right next to her. Chase waved hello to Jennifer, but her biggest smile was for the woman with the dog. It was Delores Wainright sipping a tea, while Penelope, the rescue Pug, was up on a chair close enough to put her paw in her lap. As she fed the pup treats from a fancy-looking bag, she gave Chase a welcoming smile.

"How are you, Jen?" Chase began, giving her best friend from college a warm hug.

"Give me one second, would you?" she said to Jennifer. Turning now to Delores, she said, "Excuse me, ma'am. A dog sitting at the table with all this food around; whatever would the health department say?"

Delores picked up on her sarcasm immediately and replied, "Well, since I sit on several boards with both the health commissioner and his wife, I doubt they'd say very much."

Chase smiled. "I'm just teasing. How are you today, Mrs. Wainwright?"

She smiled back while petting Penelope. "I'm well, Chase. Thank you."

Chase then turned her attention back to Jennifer and said, "First up, you look amazing. How are you?"

Jennifer smiled and said, "You always were a good liar. I look exactly five years older than the last time you saw me, but *you* actually do look great. What is that farmer Gavin feeding you? Oats? Is it oats and barley?"

Chase smiled again and said, "I think it's more the running three miles every day. That and sushi. I live on the stuff down here."

After a few more minutes of catching up, Chase finally said with a wry tone, "Anyway, thanks so much for giving me Stonewall Jackson to talk to. Geesh."

Jennifer had a pained look, "No good?"

Chase then changed her voice to sound very formal and snobby, "She said, and I quote, 'Everything we care to say about Mr. Winthrop is in the press release. Good day!'"

Jennifer nearly spit her coffee out. "She hung up on you!?"

Chase nodded, "Oh yeah, big time. Good day and then click. Dial tone."

Jennifer thought a moment, then said, "So you never even got to tell her who you were, the best-selling novel stuff?"

Chase reiterated for effect this time, "Oh I told her, and then, two words: DIAL TONE."

There was a pause when Chase said, "Listen, I'm sure Sebastian Winthrop is a fascinating guy with a great story to tell, but I can't tell it based on some bullet points in a press release. That document makes it sound like all he did was buy and sell things and give the money away. I'm afraid if there's a story there, we'll never know it."

"Samuel," a voice said from a few feet away. It was Delores speaking.

"You two are looking for information on Sebastian Winthrop? Then you want to talk to Samuel," she added.

Both women in unison said, "Who is Samuel?"

Delores, who could overhear their conversation, turned her chair to face them. "Samuel was his driver for, let me think, what had to be the last thirty years. He was also Sebastian's best friend, next to his wife, of course."

Chase quickly replied, "And you know this how? Were you friends with Sebastian? I mean this Mr. Winthrop?"

Delores gave another treat to Penelope, breaking it in half and saying to the dog, "Not too much, sweetie, and chew it slowly, we don't want you to choke."

Then, turning back to Chase and Jennifer, Delores continued, "I didn't know him well, but we did travel in some of the same circles, and I know for a fact he was close with Samuel. Very close."

Jennifer looked at Chase, knowing this was a promising lead, but before they could even ask, Delores offered up, "And now you want to know if I can put you in touch with him. Hmmm?"

Chase, looking a bit sheepish, answered, "If I said pretty please with sugar on top?"

Delores smiled and said, "My driver was friends with him. I think they played poker together or something. I can get you Samuel's number. After that you're on your own."

Chase and Jennifer both nodded and again in unison said, "Thank you."

Jennifer looked at the time on her phone and said she had to get back to the office. Chase gave her a hug goodbye and watched her friend from college push through the front door and disappear into a swirl of people outside. Chase was about to go back upstairs to Gavin when she looked at Delores and Penelope still sitting together, and something moved her to walk back over.

"Delores? Is it okay if I call you that?" Chase began.

The neatly dressed older woman smiled and said, "Of course."

Chase then shared a brief story.

"Delores, back where I lived before this place, I used to drive past a Christmas tree farm all the time. And the funny thing was, people would go to this big field full of trees, sometimes in the summer, and they'd pick one out for Christmas."

Delores was listening, not certain where this young lady was going with her story.

Chase continued, "They'd tie a ribbon around the tree that they wanted and write their name on it, so everyone knew it was theirs. And later, if they changed their minds, they could just take the ribbon off and the tree was free to go with another family."

Delores said, "I'm not following your meaning, dear. Why are you talking to me about trees?"

Chase looked down at Penelope and said, "I can't help but notice you've taken a liking to this sweet dog. You do know she's here to be adopted out?"

Delores put her wrinkled and shaky hand down on the pup's back and said, "I know. And I know I could walk in here one day and she'd be gone."

There was sad reality in the old woman's eyes now, realizing what she'd just said, as if saying it out loud somehow made it more real.

Chase replied softly, "She doesn't have to be. I don't know your living situation, but I'm guessing, a woman of your means, you could make room for a pup like Penelope."

Delores shook her head. "Me?" she said. "No, I don't think I could." She paused, and then looked at Chase. "She's a lovely dog, but seeing her here for an hour is different from taking her home. That's a real . . ."

Chase finished her sentence, "Commitment."

Chase then reached down to pet her dog, Scooter. "I know, believe me I know. But they do make great company. I'd be lost without my Scooter."

There was an awkward silence for a moment when Chase reached up into her hair and pulled out that purple ribbon that was helping to keep her ponytail in place. She turned her head toward the front counter of the café. "Deb, throw me a pen," she called out firmly.

Deb looked around her workspace and yelled back, "I only have a black Sharpie."

To which Chase replied, "That's perfect, actually."

Chase took the marker and wrote D E L O R E S in big block letters on the purple ribbon that had been in her hair a moment earlier.

"What are you doing?" Delores asked.

Chase then tied the ribbon around the collar that Penelope was wearing, with Delores's name facing out, for all to see the dog had been tagged. Chase touched the older woman's shoulder gently and said, "Just in case you change your mind."

As Chase made her way toward the door, Delores shouted after her, "Thank you, dear."

Chase could see the old woman's eyes were glistening, just barely holding back her tears. As old as she was, in that instant Delores's face reminded Chase of a four-year-old who had just been given the very present she was hoping for.

## CHAPTER 10

# Meet Me at the Bow

G avin needed to head back up to Vermont to help his dad with the farm.

"I promise, three days tops, and then I'm back down to be with you," he said before hugging Chase goodbye. Just as he put his hand on the doorknob to go, Chase's phone lit up and she said out loud, "What the heck?"

Gavin turned, "What's wrong?"

Chase sat down on a kitchen chair never taking her eyes off the phone's screen. She was staring, not speaking, her expression blank.

"Chase, you're scaring me, what's the matter?" Gavin asked, more insistently.

Chase broke her stare and looked up at her boyfriend and said, "So, Delores, the nice lady I told you about, she gives me the number for Samuel, the driver of the rich guy who died."

Gavin, still standing by the door, replied, "Okay, so?"

"So I call him and get his voicemail and I leave a detailed message. I name drop Delores and tell him I'm an accomplished writer and I'd really like to do a nice story on his former boss."

"Right, so what's the message on the phone?" asked Gavin again.

Chase held it up, but Gavin had to walk closer to see it clearly. He read aloud: "Checked you out and you seem like the real deal. Six o'clock tonight, meet me at the center of the bow. If you want the story, you'll figure this riddle out. If not, oh well—Samuel."

Chase looked from the phone back to Gavin, " 'Meet me at the center of the bow'—what is that supposed to mean?"

Gavin put his truck keys down on the kitchen table, knowing he might be staying a little while, and said, "No clue. This is Manhattan, though, and it's a big city. Is there a street or theater named bow? I mean, like the Bow Theater or something?"

Chase said, "No idea, but get your phone out, get on Google and start typing."

The two of them spent the next twenty minutes having no luck finding a place called *The Bow* in New York City.

Finally, Gavin snapped his fingers at her and said excitedly, "Wait, your driver, Matthew, he used to be a cop and drives all over the city. He might know." Gavin had barely finished the thought when Chase pulled his name up on her phone and hit send, putting the call on speaker.

Matthew was buying a hot dog from a vendor on Canal Street on the lower end of Manhattan when he saw Chase's name appear on his phone. He checked his watch and said into the receiver, "I lost track of time, is it 50th or 59th?"

Chase shook her head and said, "No, no, I'm not out for a run. Besides, I'm done staring at church windows. Listen, quick question."

Matthew took a healthy bite of the dog covered in spicy mustard and onions and said with his mouth full, "Shoop."

Chase looked at Gavin then back at the phone and said, "What?"

Matthew swallowed, cleared his throat and said, "Sorry. I said shoot, meaning go. What's your question?"

Chase grabbed Gavin's hand and pulled him closer, she felt like Nancy Drew in one of those mystery stories she read as a child. "Okay, listen. I have to meet a man, but he's being all cryptic. He said to me I'm to meet him at the center of the bow."

Matthew didn't quite catch it, "At the center of the boat, like a ferry?"

Chase, now yelling impatiently, replied, "NOT BOAT, BOW, B-O-W. BOW. Like a bow you'd put on a present."

There was silence for long time on the phone, and then Gavin spoke, "Matthew, it's Gavin. We checked out theaters, buildings, nothing in Manhattan is named bow. So, we're lost."

Matthew said, "Wait a minute. Read me the whole message exactly as you got it."

Chase swiped her finger across the phone bringing up the text message again and said, "The guy said and I'm quoting now, 'Checked you out and you seem like the real deal. Six o'clock tonight, meet me at the center of the bow.' Then he acknowledges that this is a riddle I have to solve if I want to meet him."

Matthew got back into his car, which was double parked with the flashers going, thought a moment, then said, "I think I know what he means. In Central Park, there's a bridge called the Bow. If you've watched a movie in the last twenty years you've seen it, trust me. They use it all the time in movies; it's pretty there. He must want you to meet him at six in the center of that bridge."

Chase, in an excited voice, said, "You just doubled your Christmas bonus."

Matthew snipped back, "I don't think you gave me one last year."

Chase giggled, "Well, then you just earned one. Thank you, Matthew."

Before she could hit "end" to finish the call, Matthew shouted, "WAIT UP. Who is this guy? You aren't going alone. GAVIN, don't let her go alone."

Gavin smiled because he liked this protective side of Chase's driver. "No way, Matthew, I'll be with her."

Matthew let out the breath he'd been holding, then said, "What's this about, anyway?"

Chase chimed back in, "Tell you when I see you, gotta go."

Matthew shouted again, "YOU'LL SEE ME IN TEN MINUTES 'cause I'm coming to get the two of you. I'm driving, unless either of you knows where it is in the park."

They both nodded in agreement and said, "See you in ten."

Once in the car, Chase explained to Matthew the reasons behind the clandestine meeting, and he parked as close as he could to their secret destination. Chase agreed to let Gavin walk her onto the bridge for the meeting, but she insisted he keep a respectable distance, once Samuel arrived, so the old man wouldn't feel ambushed or surprised.

Matthew was right when he told them the bridge was beautiful, nearly a hundred feet long, stretching out over the tranquil water below. The trees were deliberately cut back on both ends so the bridge stood out in the park. It was crowded today, lovers walking hand in hand, tourists taking photos, and Chase and Gavin both feeling like a bit like Jason Bourne meeting up with a spy. There was so much foot traffic on the bridge, and neither of them saw the man in his early seventies in a dark wool coat and knit driver's cap walk right up on them.

"You're prettier than the picture on your book," he said with a smile.

Chase and Gavin both turned, as she said, "Samuel?"

He took off his hat like a gentleman and extended his hand to shake hers, "Pleasure to meet you, miss. And I'm guessing this is Gavin."

Gavin was surprised he even knew his name and extended his hand. The older man continued, "I must confess, with such short notice, I could only scan your novel, but I could tell from what I read that you are the handsome boyfriend." He then turned his eyes toward Chase and added, "And you, my dear, have a good soul."

Samuel was short, five foot five at best, impeccably dressed, with shiny, tan slip-on loafers and a neatly trimmed gray beard. His green eyes twinkled like those of someone half his age.

They both felt comfortable with him instantly, as Gavin said, "I came along just in case, you understand."

Samuel looked him in the eye and nodded with respect the way knights might on a battlefield, and then said, "I do, sir. Most prudent. Very wise."

Gavin replied, "Why don't I go sit on the bench over there and let you two talk?"

Chase gave him a quick peck on the lips and said, "Would you do me a favor and text Matthew, so he knows we weren't kidnapped?"

She turned back toward Samuel. "My driver, Matthew, very protective of me."

Samuel smiled and said in a hushed voice, "It's nice to have friends."

After Gavin found a seat, Samuel and Chase both turned toward the railing of the beautiful cast iron bridge that crosses the lake in Central Park, leaned forward in a relaxed posture, and began their chat.

"I'm talking to you for three reasons. Would you like to know what they are?," Samuel began.

"Sure," Chase said with a smile.

"Delores says you're a nice person. I mostly know her by reputation, but she's a good woman. Second, I skimmed your book and read a couple of articles about you and saw that you helped the people in that little town in Vermont. Which means *you're* a good woman."

Chase felt warm inside, having this nice man speak so kindly of her. She asked, "And the third reason?"

Samuel took a deep breath. "Because when it comes to Sebastian, my best friend, they all got it wrong," he said.

"They?" Chase inquired.

"The newspapers and magazine and talking heads on TV. All they rambled on about was the money and giving, and trust me there was plenty of that, but the real story is a love story. That's why I had you meet me on this bridge."

Chase ran her hands back and forth on the railing and replied, "This bridge? Why?"

"Because this is where Sebastian asked his wife of fifty-three years to marry him. Vida. Vida Bushey, who then became Vida Winthrop."

Even though Samuel was in solid shape for his seventy-three years of age, he said, "Would you mind if we walked over near Gavin and grabbed a seat on one of those benches? My back sometimes . . ."

Chase instinctively took him by the hand and said, "Of course, walk with me."

As they made their way to the bench, Samuel looked down at her young hand with smooth skin holding his, and he felt a sense of nostalgia.

As they reached the bench and sat, he said, "Thank you, dear. That was kind of you. It gave me déjà vu of all the times I drove Sebastian here to the park, and he and Vida would walk hand in hand. Sometimes they'd come here for a concert or a play. Sometimes they just enjoyed splitting a hot pretzel from one of the carts and looking at the pretty chalk drawings on the sidewalks."

Chase thought she should be writing this down, but she couldn't risk ruining this moment of honesty.

"Go on," she said hopefully.

Samuel looked around at the park and said, "I can't possibly tell you the man's whole life in one conversation, but here's what you need to know. The newspapers said he turned one building into five and that into five hundred and built half of Manhattan and got rich. All true. But Vida, when she came into his life, his heart grew larger than this whole city. She changed him."

Chase asked, "Changed him how?"

Samuel went on, "Well, he never again stayed late at work to chase down some deal or another pile of money. His whole purpose in life seemed to be pleasing her. He was constantly buying her flowers or gifts and leaving them for her as a surprise. If she went to the salon to get her hair done, a dozen roses were already there waiting. As they sat in a Broadway theater, at intermission a man would walk in and hand her a box with diamond earrings inside."

Chase was smiling and said, "He adored her!"

Samuel shot back, "Yes, he did, Chase. And when he lost her, about five years ago, he realized the true riches in his life were not money or possessions, but Vida. So, he took the money and all the trappings of wealth and gave it all away to reset things."

Chase looked confused, and asked, "I'm not sure I know what you mean."

Samuel took her hand back in his again. "What I mean is he'd say to me, 'Samuel, I had next to nothing when she met me, and she loved me anyway. When I go to meet her in heaven, I want us to start the same way." So, he gave it all to charity."

"Everything?" Chase asked.

Samuel nodded, "Well, almost. There is still the house in Westchester County. Some fancy cars and artwork. A few million dollars' worth of stuff, I suspect. And in the end, that's all it was to him, *stuff.* They'll be auctioning it all off in a few weeks, with the money going to charity."

Chase was quiet a moment, thinking about everything she'd just heard, when Samuel concluded their conversation. "Do me this one favor. Whatever you write, understand Sebastian Winthrop cared about one thing, his Vida. Do you know why?"

Chase looked Samuel in the eyes and said, "Because she was his world."

Samuel looked off at some pigeons who were waiting patiently for someone to toss them a snack and said, "Yes, she was, and I'll tell you this. That man sat down with presidents, kings, celebrities, the pope even, but if you gave him his choice, he'd tell you every time, he'd rather be sitting here in Central Park with his Vida, watching happy people stroll by, or some street artist earning his keep, one dollar at a time."

Chase was looking down the cobblestone sidewalk at the row of vendors lined up, doing brisk business, as Samuel continued, "This park is where they met by chance a long time ago. One year later to the day they got engaged here. On the bridge over there, the Bow. In a world that always wanted something from them, this was their safe space where it was just them."

Chase sat silently, imagining this great American romance playing out right before her.

Samuel then turned back to her and said, "Do you know what the word Vida means?"

Chase shook her head no.

Samuel finished, "Vida is a Spanish word. It means *life.* Vida was his life. That's your story, Chase. A love story that still goes on to this day."

Chase thought a moment and asked, "You mean in heaven? Their love story."

Samuel smiled and said, "Yes, of course. Here and there."

Chase wasn't sure what that meant, about *here*, since they both had passed, but the older man looked tired, so she stood up and took both his hands, helping him to his feet, and asked, "So, I'm okay writing about Central Park and the bridge and all that ooey gooey stuff?"

Samuel motioned to Gavin that it was time for him to return to his lady, then answered, "Of course. That's the reason I'm here. You be as *ooey gooey* as you want."

With that the fragile, well-dressed man adjusted his cap, and with carefully measured steps slowly disappeared into the Central Park crowd. Chase took hold of Gavin's hand, glanced down at her fingers locked tightly around his, and said, "I need to get home to write a love story."

## CHAPTER 11

# The Lonely Hearts Club

Three weeks had passed since Chase met Samuel at the center of the Bow bridge and learned about the love between Sebastian and Vida Winthrop. Chase stayed up all night writing the story for the *New Yorker*, and Samuel was kind enough to send her an old photo of the couple to accompany it. The photograph was classic New York City, Sebastian and Vida dressed to the nines after a charity gala at the Waldorf Astoria; he in a tux and she in a shimmering silver gown. Vida never aged a moment in Sebastian's eyes; his love froze her in time.

As the two lovebirds climbed aboard a horse-drawn carriage, a photographer from the *Daily News* snapped a photo of them. When Sebastian saw it two days later in the *style* section of the newspaper, he purchased the print, had it professionally framed, and there it sat on an antique hutch in their country estate for the last twenty-two years.

After Sebastian died, Samuel went through his personal things and took the photo, knowing his friend would want him to have it. It was that picture he gave Chase to use for her article, and now Vida and Sebastian were glowing with joy from every news stand in the city.

When the *New Yorker* arrived, Chase's eyes flew open with astonishment, as she said, "They gave me the cover?"

Her friend Jennifer, handing her a stack of the magazines as keepsakes, responded with a smile, "You bet they did. I know it's not a best-selling novel, but not bad, eh?"

Chase gave her friend a hug, "Not bad indeed."

She paused a moment, thinking, then said, "We should celebrate with cappuccinos or something yummy. Want to go downstairs to the café? My treat."

It was early evening in Manhattan, and Gavin wasn't expected until morning, so Chase and Jennifer found their way to the coffee shop below.

As she came through the back door, her usual entrance, Oscar was taking the white dog named Ella outside on a leash for her evening walk and lesson in obedience.

"Hey Oscar, who it turns out is *not* a grouch," Chase yelled over to him with a wink in her eye.

Oscar grinned back and said, "Hey, Chase, would love to talk but gotta earn my daily bread."

Chase looked at him, confused, and said, "I thought they weren't paying you?"

Oscar nodded, "True, not cash, but I take my payment in muffins and hard rolls."

As he vanished out the back door with the puppy, Chase heard a commotion of voices in the café, unusual for this time of day. It was coming from a small gathering of unfamiliar faces. A half dozen or so women, all in their early forties, were sitting with three tables pushed together in the corner, giving them some measure of privacy. She spied Raylan across the café, but his attention was clearly on the group of women, bringing them a tray of treats and a pitcher of iced tea.

"Compliments of the house," Raylan said to the women, displaying his gentleman's charm.

An attractive woman, wearing a baggy blue sweater and large hoop earrings, looked up from the group and said, "Thanks, Freddy."

Chase was confused why the woman called him that, watching on as Raylan smiled and replied, "Anything for you, Adele."

As he turned to go back to the counter, Raylan started singing a sappy love song from the famous singer Adele very dramatically, teasing the woman who just called him by the wrong name.

The woman he called Adele made a face in response to his terrible singing voice, then called out, "Keep it up, smarty pants, keep it up."

Chase turned to Jennifer and said, "Would you excuse me for a minute?" as she darted across the café to Raylan.

"Hey, smarty pants," she began, clearly imitating the woman at the table. "Why did she call you Freddy?"

Raylan, busy stacking cups behind the counter now, never made eye contact with Chase when he replied, "It's just an inside joke."

Chase just stared, not understanding, prompting Raylan to explain further, "Freddy, as in Freddy Krueger, the Nightmare on Elm Street guy. You know, because of my face."

Chase was instantly fuming now, "She's making fun of your scar? I have a good mind to go over and smack her in the head. See what she calls you then."

"Whoa, whoa, down, girl," Raylan responded strongly, raising his hands up like someone surrendering to the police. "She's kidding. We joke like that all the time. Jeez, relax."

Chase looked back at the women sitting together pouring the iced tea, then back at Raylan, calming down a bit, and asked, "She's your friend?"

"Yes, well, sort of. Her name is Bonnie and she's part of the Lonely Hearts Club."

Chase looked over to her own friend, Jennifer from the magazine, and said, "Hey, Jen, this is going to be a minute, can you stay, or you need to run?"

Her friend looked at her watch and said, "I probably should go. Raincheck on the drink?"

Chase nodded yes and gave her a smile. "Definitely, hon. Bye."

Jennifer put the strap from her bag over her shoulder and started toward the café's front door, shouting back, "Congrats again on the cover."

As the door closed behind her, Raylan realized that Chase was holding the new issue of the *New Yorker* in her hand and said, "Hey, they gave you the cover for your story—that's great."

Chase looked down at the magazine and said, "Yes, thanks. Wait, go back. Bonnie? Didn't I just hear you call her Adele? And the lonely what's club?"

"Hearts," Raylan said.

He then extended his hand to a chair at the nearby table and said, "Take a seat."

After the two sat, Raylan explained, "The first Tuesday evening of each month a book club comes in here to discuss the latest thing they've read. Since they love to read cheesy romance novels and most of them have had like ZERO luck in the love department, they call themselves the *Lonely Hearts Club*."

Chase looked over and realized each of them did have an identical-looking book in their hands, then back to Raylan asking, "And Adele, or Bonnie, what's her deal?"

Raylan leaned in whispering now, "She's the ringleader and I love to tease her. I tell her she's like a walking Adele song, all misery, no happy ending."

Chase nodded, sort of understanding. "And she reciprocates by calling you . . ."

Raylan smiled now. ". . . Freddy. Yes, I know. Shocking, but it's all in fun, Chase."

Chase considered a moment and said, "Well, I'm not so sure I like it."

Raylan took her hand and gave it a friendly squeeze, saying, "That's because we're friends and you're being protective. And you don't see the scar like you used to because we're friends."

Chase thought a moment and said, "I guess you're right. If it's all in good fun."

With that, Bonnie walked over and said, "Don't mean to break up your conversation, but we need more iced tea, Raylan."

She then looked at Chase with kind eyes and said, "Hi, I'm Bonnie, or who smarty here calls Adele." She extended her hand to shake Chase's and it was clear now this woman wouldn't harm a fly.

"I'm Chase. Nice to meet you, Bonnie Adele."

The two giggled as Bonnie picked up the cloth Raylan used to wipe down tables and gave it a little snap at his backside. "Chop chop, male servant. Discussing literature is thirsty work."

There was something about the way Bonnie spoke to Raylan and the way he looked back that told Chase there might be something smoldering just beneath the surface between these two.

Being a writer, she would make note of things and then tuck them away in a *to be discussed later* file in her mind.

As Raylan got up to go, Chase said in a tender voice, "Hey Raylan, I have to tell you something."

There was silence now as Raylan waited for her to finish that thought. For some reason Chase was having trouble saying the words.

Finally, Chase just said it. "You know I'm not staying here forever, right? Upstairs in the apartment."

His hazel eyes went sad for a moment, as he replied, "Sure, I know that. You said a year and a deal's a deal, but I'm not kicking you out. If you want to leave this paradise . . ." He paused, now swallowing hard and looking down at his feet.

*Was he getting choked up?* Chase thought silently, looking away so he wouldn't feel embarrassed by her seeing it.

Raylan continued. "I was saying, if you want to leave, that's heavy lifting you'll have to do on your own. I'm not tossing you out. As far as I'm concerned you can stay as long as you like. And Gavin is welcome to visit anytime."

As Raylan went back to work, Chase couldn't deny the fondness she'd developed for this place and the people, especially Raylan.

She felt herself getting a little emotional at the thought of leaving this safe space, so she stepped outside to grab the cool evening air.

The Fur-Ever Java café was on York Avenue in Manhattan, positioned exactly in between 71st and 72nd street. As Chase stood out front, her eyes fell on the Sotheby's Auction House located directly across the street. Whenever anyone had something of real value to sell, this was the place they brought it. On more than a few occasions Chase had watched workers with armed guards unloading crates from expensive-looking trucks and carrying them in. Normally she paid it no mind, but now she was staring at the Sotheby's sign and remembering something she came across in her research on Sebastian Winthrop.

He'd given most of his money away, but his country estate, some expensive jewelry, and a few priceless paintings were all to be sold at auction at Sotheby's. Chase was looking at the building where the last remnants of a good man's life would be sold off like cattle to strangers— people who didn't know or care about this wonderful man and his bride, looking to cash in on his death. Chase understood that this is how some stories end, but there was something sullied about it just the same.

Chase was wearing only a t-shirt top, so with the cold evening air making her shiver, she returned to the warm café. Before she turned to go, she saw two men on ladders hanging a long yellow banner with bright blue lettering across the front of Sotheby's. It read, *Auction Winthrop Collection – Saturday at Noon.*

"Saturday, huh?" Chase thought out loud. She stared at the banner for the longest time, and the strongest impulse suddenly stirred inside her.

Chase had no earthly idea why, but deep in her bones she knew she needed to be at that auction. Perhaps to say goodbye to the man she had never met but now clearly admired. Or perhaps because something was about to happen at that auction that no one saw coming. Something that would get international headlines and change Chase's life forever.

## CHAPTER 12

# You Shouldn't Have Laughed

G avin arrived late Saturday morning with two homemade balsam fir wreaths bursting from his arms. There was no bow or other decoration on them, just the fresh pine tied together with wire, making them perfect in their simplicity. They smelled glorious too, having been cut and bundled not a dozen hours earlier on Gavin's farm in Vermont.

"Are you selling Christmas wreaths door to door now?" Raylan asked jokingly, as Gavin carried them into the café.

"Ha, ha. Nope. My dad makes these and sells them back home for ten bucks. Even though the holidays are still a ways off, he was practicing his technique, so I grabbed a couple and thought you could hang one on your door."

Raylan grabbed one of the wreaths, then asked, "Will you and Chase even be around for Christmas this year? I figured a big shiny ring might be making an appearance soon and you two would be outta here."

Gavin responded firmly, "I'm working on that. Trust me."

"Good man," Raylan said, as he held his fist out to give Gavin's a bump, showing respect for the answer.

In Raylan's mind there was nothing worse than a guy leading a woman on and burning years of her life with a promise never fulfilled. He could see that was not Gavin.

As Gavin turned to go upstairs, Matthew, Chase's driver, came through the front door in a hurry with his phone in hand and a concerned look on his face. "Is she okay, Gavin?"

Gavin just as quickly replied, "Yes, Why?"

Matthew replied, "She sent me a text saying she had someplace important to go today but she didn't need a ride. The last time she talked like this she was meeting a stranger on a bridge in the middle of the park."

Gavin took his own phone out and said, "You know, she sent me a weird text too. It said, 'Make sure you bring nice pants and a shirt with a collar.' " He held up a small black bag that was slung over his shoulder, indicating he had indeed brought both.

Raylan chimed in, "Sounds like you're going someplace fancy, or at least a spot where a Guns and Roses t-shirt won't do."

Matthew replied, "So, what's going on?"

Gavin said to Matthew, "Let's go up and ask her together."

In that instant, Chase appeared from the side door of the café, smiling and saying, "Ask me what?"

All three men turned their attention toward Chase, and not one of them could find the words. She looked stunning in a strapless red Halston cocktail dress that revealed her soft, smooth shoulders and was cut just above the knee. It was a dress that said *flirty but taken* to any wandering eye. Chase had found it in the Neiman Marcus store in a section of Manhattan they call Hudson Yards, her one big splurge with the money from her book sales.

"Babe, you look . . .," Gavin began, his eyes wide as dinner plates, staring at Chase as he did that first time he saw her years ago on a back country road in Vermont.

Seeing Gavin was now speechless, Raylan slapped him on the back and said, "*Great* is the word he's looking for."

Matthew looked at Chase like a daughter he was proud of, adding, "*Amazing* works too. You look amazing."

Chase blushed instantly and said, "Stop it, the three of you. I just wanted to make sure I looked appropriate."

"For what?" Gavin asked, as he set the wreath he was holding on a nearby table and made his way to take his lady's hand.

Chase realized in that moment she had never told any of them what was going on, so she blurted out, "An auction. *The* auction actually. For the Sebastian Winthrop estate."

Matthew nodded. "Yes, I read about that in the *Post*, lots of expensive stuff. That's the guy you wrote about in the magazine, right?"

Chase replied, "It is."

Gavin countered, "So that's why I needed pants with a crease and a nice shirt; I'm coming with you?"

Chase wrapped her arms around his broad shoulders, feeling his muscles through the t-shirt he was wearing, "I would never go without you," she replied.

Raylan then asked, "Are you planning to buy something?"

Chase laughed, "Oh, yeah." Then imitating a snooty, rich lady, Chase said, "My good fellow, I'd like to bid on that diamond necklace. How much is it, you say? A half million dollars. Sounds like a steal; I'll take two."

Raylan smiled and said, "Yeah, yeah, I see your point."

Matthew interrupted, "So if you're all dressed up, why don't you want a ride to this auction? You can't take the subway in that dress."

Chase took hold of Matthew's chin and turned his head, so he was now looking out the front window of the café, explaining, "'Cause it's right across the street, silly."

Matthew noticed the Sotheby's sign and replied, "Oh, duh. I keep forgetting that place is over there."

Matthew thought a moment, then added, "You sure you don't want to hop in the car, let me drive around the block and then drop you at their front door like some big shot?"

Gavin smiled, "Oh, that would be fun."

Chase interjected, "Nah, I'm fine walking over. I just want to go see what all that crazy expensive stuff goes for, and I figure if you're going to be a *lookie-loo* you better dress the part or they might toss you out."

Gavin asked, "A look-e-what?"

"Lou," Chased replied. "You know, someone who just wants to watch."

Raylan offered, "Not my business, but I'm sure if you told them you're the one who wrote the cover story for the magazine they'd treat you like someone important, whether you plan to bid or not."

Chase grabbed up her tiny Coach change purse and said, "I don't like trading on stuff like that or getting special treatment. I just want to watch from the back."

Gavin ran upstairs to change, and Matthew, now without a client to drive, made his way to the counter to order some egg whites. Deb, the always entertaining hypochondriac, pulled the collar down on the shirt she was wearing, exposing her neck and asking, "Does this look like a rash to you?"

Matthew raised his eyebrows in surprise and replied, "I flunked out of medical school. My specialty is driving, miss. I'll just wait down here on the end of the counter for my eggs."

Deb could see there was no audience for her antics today, so she got busy making Matthew his breakfast.

A very well-dressed Chase waited patiently for noon to arrive, noticing the curb across the street from the café was now filled with limousines, parking bumper to bumper outside of Sotheby's.

Gavin didn't disappoint, turning the corner in a teal-blue Polo dress shirt and neatly pressed light tan slacks, both fitting him like a glove. He was also wearing the beautiful cowboy boots Chase had gotten him as a gift their first Christmas together.

"Shall we?" he asked, holding his arm out formally for Chase to take hold. Together they walked the forty or so steps from the front door of the Fur-Ever Java café across to the entrance of Sotheby's.

The man working the front door knew many of the faces coming in, as these high-level auctions often attracted the same well-heeled crowd, so to his trained eyes Chase and Gavin were certainly new. There was no protocol on who to let in or keep out, but when he took one look at Chase's perfect make-up and form-fitting designer dress, he opened the door wide and said, "Welcome."

The room was less formal than Chase imagined an auction house might be. Large and square with cherrywood walls, it contained six rows of chairs, each with comfortable red velvet cushions. A small stage sat at the head of the room, raised a good two feet high, so items that were placed on pedestals or easels could be seen by the bidders.

The artwork was already arranged along the back of the stage, the single Monet the easiest to spot because of the unmistakable French

Impressionist style. The expensive jewelry, once worn by Sebastian's wife, Vida, was placed in glass cases under lock and key, with large, framed posters showing a close up of each piece next to them.

There was also a beautifully framed painting of the Winthrop estate in Westchester County, New York. It was an elegant English Tudor, with a large stone chimney and weathered red stones covered in thick green ivy. A single spire reached up toward the pale blue sky, the structure filled with peaks and valleys, mystery and romance. It was exactly the kind of place Chase could imagine Sebastian and Vida living in.

A man in a tuxedo appeared from a door behind the stage with a microphone already attached to his ear and cheek. It looked like something Brittney Spears might wear in one of her music videos. A small power pack clung to his belt on his left hip, and when he pushed down on the top with his thumb, the microphone came to life.

"I won't say testing one, two, three, I promise," the auctioneer began with a chuckle. It was clear he knew faces in the crowd as well as they knew his. At one point he covered the mic with his right hand and whispered to a woman sitting in the front row, "I already know which one you're taking home," giving her a wink.

Gavin and Chase didn't feel comfortable taking a seat, since they had no intention to bid. There was a table at which to register, and each bidder was given a paddle with a specific number on it. Chase had seen enough auctions on TV to know that when someone wanted to bid, they'd raise their paddle up high. She and Gavin made their way to the back of the room to stand quietly.

It was also obvious by the body language that some in attendance were not the actual bidders. The ones with the money were off in some far-away place, directing every move over the telephone that was glued to the ear of the person sitting at Sotheby's.

The auctioneer was everything Chase and Gavin assumed he'd be, fast and furious and speaking a language they could barely understand. An item would be held up by a lovely young woman in a black gown, the auctioneer would read a brief description, then paddles flew up and down like some very wealthy game of "Whack a Mole." In a matter of minutes each and every item was bidden on and sold. Unsurprisingly, the *Monet* fetched the most money thus far at 6.2 million dollars.

With everything purchased except the lavish country estate, a quiet hush fell over the room.

The auctioneer began, "I know many of you are here to bid on the mansion, but before we get to the Winthrop home, we had a last-minute piece of artwork come into our possession."

Many in the crowd were there only to buy the house, and they fidgeted impatiently in their seats, not happy they'd have to wait one second longer to bid on it.

With that the woman in the black gown reemerged from an unseen room with a small item covered in a beige cloth. People's necks were jutting left and right to get a better view. *Another Monet?* they silently hoped and wondered.

She pulled the covering back and placed the small ordinary frame on an easel, as the auctioneer said, "As you've seen today, Mr. Winthrop had a very impressive collection of art, which is going home with some of you, in fact. Congratulations."

The auctioneer could see the crowd staring with confusion at the ten-by-twelve frame that was now facing them, and the charcoal sketch it housed. It was a portrait of an older woman sketched on cheap construction paper of the kind one could find at any art supply store for five dollars. There was absolutely nothing remarkable about the sketch; it looked like the kind tourists bought from artists in Times Square a hundred times a day. No one in the room had a clue who the woman in the sketch was. Well, no one but Chase. She recognized the face immediately and smiled.

The auctioneer then pulled a small index card from the breast pocket of his suit and held it up high so all could see what he was holding, saying, "These are his words—of the late Mr. Winthrop—that I read to you now."

The auctioneer cleared his throat and said, "This drawing may look like nothing to you, but it meant the world to me. It was sketched 25 years ago in Central Park. The artist's name is unknown because he worked under the shade of a chestnut tree a short distance from The Bow bridge. He was, what you might call, a street artist. My loving wife, Vida, had a bit of a health scare that year, and we'd just gotten word from the doctor that she'd be fine, so I took her to the park for an ice cream cone to celebrate. The street artist, who sketched portraits, was lacking any customers, so Vida sat for him and he did this lovely sketch in just seven minutes. The man asked ten dollars for the sketch, but I was so taken by its beauty, I gave him twenty. Isn't it lovely?"

The auctioneer looked up for a reaction but was greeted by rows of confused and uninterested faces glaring back.

He continued reading Mr. Winthrop's words, "Because it was special to me, I wanted to make it part of the auction, after I was gone. I hope you bid high. I promise you won't regret it. Sincerely, Sebastian Winthrop."

The auctioneer put the card back in his pocket and said, "Before we get to the country estate, do we have any bids on this simple yet beautiful sketch?"

His eyes scanned the crowd and there was an unmistakable chill in the air. The looks on the faces of the bidders were icy, their eyes cold and dismissive as if they were shouting, *BE DONE WITH THIS NONSENSE, SELL US THE MANSION ALREADY.*

"It really did mean the world to him," the auctioneer encouraged again. "Do we have any bids? Anything at all?"

Chase's stomach tumbled, watching the room at this moment. There was audible giggling from the crowd, as if they couldn't be bothered with the sentimental wishes of some dead old man.

Gavin looked at her, knowing she was upset, and asked, "Are you okay?"

Chase didn't reply. She just stared at the room full of strangers with their condescending snickering. She couldn't stand it. She hated it when people thought they were better than others because of some perceived station in life. It reminded her of how she had felt as a little girl when she couldn't afford the right clothes or a designer bag the other girls had, and someone made fun of her.

She suddenly started fumbling with the change purse in her hands, the one she had bought at the Coach outlet in Lee, Massachusetts, years prior. Chase unzipped the small bag and began rummaging through to see if she had any cash. There was a lipstick in the way, a small packet of tissues and a plastic container with breath mints. Chase shook the bag trying to move things around, saying, "Come on, would ya," loud enough for others nearby to hear.

Her movements became so animated, heads in the room began to turn and focus on this beautiful young woman in the red dress standing in the back, now making a scene. Chase pulled out all the green bills she could find and handed Gavin the purse and other items to hold while she sorted this out.

She couldn't count without moving her lips. "Five, seven, twelve . . .," she said to herself.

Off to her right a woman who obviously had her plastic surgeon on speed dial, said to her husband, "Is she looking for bus fare?"

The snarky comment brought laughter from those around them, but then everyone's attention shifted back to the front of the room as the auctioneer, unaware of what Chase was doing, said even more loudly, "ANY bids at all? I really must insist we give this item the attention it deserves."

"HOLD UP," a female voice yelled from the back. It was Chase, still counting out the dirty, wrinkled bills.

People weren't hiding the fact that this was getting ridiculous. *Who is this woman?* they thought. *Get to the house, just sell us the house!*

The auctioneer then, "Sadly, it appears we have no interest in the . . ."

"I HAVE TWENTY-SEVEN DOLLARS!" It was Chase shouting from the back of the room, holding her clenched fist in the air with money sticking out, every which way, from between her knuckles.

While the crowd was laughing now, some covering their mouths to mask it, the auctioneer ignored them, his focus staying instead on the young woman in the back. He then stepped forward on the stage to better engage Chase's eyes, smiled, and said calmly into the microphone, "Is that a bid, young lady?"

She stood there, frozen, with her arm still in the air, looking like the Statue of Liberty, feeling every eye on her, absorbing their judgment and ridicule.

As the whole room went dead quiet, everyone watching and waiting, Gavin under his breath said, "Answer the man, sweetie."

But she didn't hear him. Chase, in that moment, was not in the room; she was back in the park talking to Samuel on the bridge, hearing about this wonderful love story and how in the end it was never about the money. She remembered how Sebastian asked Vida to marry him on that bridge and how important the park was to them. She was thinking that sketch must have meant the world to Sebastian, and here these strangers were mocking it. How dare they!

*How. Dare. They.*

The auctioneer a second time, "Miss, is that a bid on this priceless work of art?"

Chase looked at the crowd with fire in her eyes and shouted, "You're darn right it is. Twenty-seven dollars!"

The auctioneer surveyed the room briefly, but he knew this crowd all too well and was certain there would be no takers beyond this exquisite woman in the red dress.

With that he said, "No other offers? Once, twice, thrice, sold to the beauty in the back."

Chase gave Gavin a hug out of pure adrenaline and laughed so hard she started to cry. *What is wrong with me?* she thought in that instant. *Why so emotional? It's just a sketch.*

As she wiped the tears from her eyes and felt pride that she had honored Sebastian's memory by purchasing the portrait, a stern-looking woman with gray streaks in her hair appeared from the side of the stage and caught the auctioneer off guard. He clearly recognized the older woman, then covered his microphone with his hand as she whispered something into his ear. Whatever she said, he literally jumped back as if she hit him with a cattle prod.

"NO," he said out loud to her, raising his hand to his mouth and then starting to laugh. What could be so shocking and funny at the same time?

After composing himself, he leaned in closer to the woman and said out loud, "You are absolutely certain?"

The woman looked at the crowd, with disdain in her eyes, as if they were vultures picking over the bones of a good man who was gone.

Then back at the auctioneer, she said, "Yes. These are his wishes. Now, do it."

If a pin had dropped at Sotheby's in that moment, everyone would have heard it.

The auctioneer turned his attention back toward the packed auction house and said, "Of every possession put up for auction today, Mr. Winthrop placed the greatest value on the sketch that was just sold to the woman in the back. To him it *was* priceless. He felt the person who thought enough of his legacy to purchase that sketch of his wife, should also be the person who lives in their home at Briarcliff Manor in Westchester County."

The room went from silent to an eruption. "Wait, wait," a man in the third row yelled. "You're not selling the estate? You have to."

Others joined in the chorus of dissent, "The mansion, what about the mansion?" they were calling out in unison. This was not the type of crowd to storm a stage, but their anger was palpable, and it was clear the well-mannered auctioneer couldn't control them.

Just then, the stern woman with the gray hair ripped the microphone right off the head of the overwhelmed auctioneer.

"QUIET," she shouted into the mic. "QUIET RIGHT NOW."

The room fell silent again, as she lowered her voice, "My name is Charlotte Jackson, the executor who handled all of Mr. Winthrop's affairs. It was his last wish that the person who purchased the sketch gets the house. Those are his wishes, end of story."

The man in the third row again piped up, "But you didn't sell it! The house. You didn't sell it."

The woman smiled now, looking directly over the man's head to the back of the room and at a stunned Chase and Gavin, saying, "Sure we did."

She pointed at Chase now, adding, "We just sold it to her. For twenty-seven dollars."

As the entire room looked back at Chase and then at each other in astonishment, Ms. Jackson added one last thought, "I guess you shouldn't have laughed at her."

With that, the woman they called Stonewall Jackson, the very lady who had hung up on Chase only three weeks earlier, gave Chase a wink, and the auction was closed.

CHAPTER 13

## *The Letter*

In the late 1800s an Irishman named John David Ogilby purchased a
piece of land about 30 miles north of Manhattan. It was so beautiful,
he named it after his family estate back in Ireland, a place called Brier
Cliff. The large plot of land outside New York City changed hands
many times over the years, but the name, with a slightly different
spelling, stuck, and today a dashing young writer was about to call
it home.

Charlotte "Stonewall" Jackson proved true to her name, when word
of the wild auction leaked out. So, when reporters from the New York
tabloids contacted old Stonewall to know who this mystery woman in
the red dress was, the one who stole a mansion for twenty-seven bucks,
she told them, "None of your business." The auction was private, and
Charlotte kept it that way.

The drive from Chase's apartment in Manhattan to Briarcliff Manor
took a little less than an hour. Gavin drove his truck as Chase sat
motionless in the seat next to him, both hands clutching a brass key that
looked more suited to an ancient castle than a modern home. The key
was chunky but smooth, measured five inches long, and had just started
to tarnish. It had several large teeth that fed into a one-of-a-kind lock,
on a one-of-a-kind door, created specifically for this house.

When Ms. Jackson handed it to Chase and she and Gavin stared at
it with wonder, Stonewall said, "He treated that home like it was Vida's
castle, so he had the special door lock made that was straight out of the
Middle Ages. Regular keys don't work in it; that one does."

The drive was quiet until Gavin spoke. "I still can't believe you
bought this house for so little money, babe. This is insane," Gavin said,
looking over with a smile.

"Eyes on the road, cowboy," Chase shot back, adding, "I can't believe it either. I just couldn't let them laugh at that sketch of his wife. I had to . . ." Her voice drifted off.

Briarcliff is one of the wealthiest villages in the entire country, based on income, and as they drove the well-manicured streets their eyes were drinking in mansion after mansion on both sides of the road. Some homes had large shiny black gates with long driveways that led to houses you could not see, while others had huge front yards the size of a football field, making you wonder just how much they paid someone to cut all the grass.

Gavin's GPS, sitting on the dashboard, then spoke: "In one quarter mile, destination on the right."

"There's another good thing about you living here," Gavin observed.

"What's that?" she replied.

"My buddy's place where I sleep when I visit is two towns over, like ten minutes away."

Chase squeezed his hand and smiled, then her eyes flew open.

They both saw the gorgeous Tudor-style home at the same instant. Chase grabbed her own face and blurted out, "You've got to be kidding me."

If Chase could have dreamed up a house to live in, this was it. The dark red stones were covered in ivy, crawling up toward a half dozen windows, all different shapes and sizes without shutters or drapes that Chase could see. *So much light must come into this place*, she thought.

A large stone chimney jutted out on the left front of the home, and at the center was that antique-looking wooden door the strange key would work on. Just above that door, on the second floor, there was a single wood and gray stone spire that reached up for the clouds. Perfectly kept hedges dotted the house as well, not seeming to be in any sort of order. Tucked between the hedges were perennials planted by Vida and Sebastian over the many years they called this castle home. They were dormant now, but in the summer, the flowers would explode with color, perfectly timed so when one plant stopped blooming, the one next to it would start.

Gavin parked at the head of the circular driveway, not far from the front, and Scooter jumped down immediately after Chase opened her truck door. Her pup was good off-leash, so Chase trusted him to stay close, especially in this strange new place.

Chase tried to hand Gavin the large, bulky key, but he bowed his head in deference and said, "Oh, no. The lady of the house should be the first to try it."

As Chase pushed the key into the lock, she felt a bit like Cinderella, wondering if the shoe would fit. Either way, she smiled at Gavin, knowing she already had her prince charming.

"Here goes," she said with confidence. A hard turn to the right brought a loud CLICK, and with that Chase gave the door a gentle push, and open it most certainly did.

The Winthrop estate was a little over 5,000 square feet, with four bedrooms and a large bathroom upstairs, a kitchen, dining room, family room, bathroom, den, and library making up the lower level.

As they stepped inside, Gavin turned to Chase and said with a smile, "Did you ever play the game *Clue* as a kid? This house reminds me of that."

Chase shot playfully back, "So you're saying it was Mrs. Winthrop, in the billiard room with a candlestick?"

They were both laughing at the thought of it.

As they explored the halls and could hear Scooter's nails clicking and clacking along the hardwood floors, a *knock, knock, knock* could be heard from the backdoor off the kitchen, and Scooter's bark guided them to a man in his sixties, holding some kind of garden tool, standing just outside. The man was in brown Carhartt pants with a matching shirt, heavy steel-toed work boots that appeared to have about ten years of coffee stains on them, and wearing an odd-looking, faded red baseball cap with a decal of a mouse holding a hockey stick on the front.

"Can we help you?," Gavin asked firmly.

The man looked past Gavin directly at Chase and said, "You the lucky lady with the twenty-seven bucks and brass?"

Chase, a bit confused, replied, "I'm the one who bid on the sketch, but, um . . ." She looked at Gavin and then back at the man who was still on the other side of the screen door. "Brass? I don't know what that means."

The man replied, "Brass, guts, stones, ya know. There are other words for it, but you're a lady, so I won't say 'em."

The old timer grinned, now making himself less scary, adding, "What I mean, miss, is you're the one who stood up to those rich snots and took the house from them?"

Gavin chuckled now. "Oh, yes, sir, she's the one."

The man in soiled work clothes then broke into a broader smile revealing a missing tooth on the upper right side of his mouth, adding with a hint of admiration, "Good for you!"

He then opened the door himself, stepped inside, and said, "I'm Nick. Nick Hargrave. The caretaker of this place. I don't live here or nothing, but I come by a couple times a week to take care of the lawn, hedges, driveway, roof, chimney, and to patch up anything that might need patchin'."

Chase extended her hand to shake his. "Nice to meet you, Mr. Hargrave."

"Nick, please. Every time I hear 'Mister' in front of my name, I expect to turn around and see my dad standing behind me. So, call me Nick," he replied.

Gavin nodded. "You got it, Nick. Hey, anything we need to know about this house?"

Nick smiled again and said, "Nope, it's a great old place, you'll love it." He then paused a moment as if he were trying to remember something, and added, "There are some rules, though."

"Rules?" Chase asked, with curiosity in her voice.

"Yep, it's all in the letter." Nick responded.

Gavin and Chase both looked at each other, and before they could ask *What letter?* Nick added, "Oh, you probably haven't been in the library yet. It's down that-a-ways."

He was pointing his finger to better direct them down a hallway, and Gavin couldn't help noticing the poor man's digit was as crooked as a country road.

"How many times have you broken that thing?" Gavin asked, pointing at the man's hand.

He smiled with that errant tooth again. "Oh, two or three. Maybe ten." With that the old caretaker let out a cackle that caused both Gavin and Chase to laugh along with him.

Chase then caught herself and asked, "Wait, you mentioned a letter? What letter?"

Nick looked at Gavin now and said sarcastically, "She's not following along so good, is she?"

He then looked at Chase, deliberately speaking extra slow, "In the library, by the west window, is an antique hutch. On that hutch sits a letter with your name on it."

Chase nodded and said back to him, "Got it. Thank you, Mr., I mean, Nick."

As Nick opened the door to leave, Gavin said, "Whoa, hold up. You aren't going anywhere until you explain that hat. What's with the mouse playing hockey on the front of it?"

Nick took the hat off, held it closer so both Chase and Gavin could see it better, and said, "He's not a mouse, he's a rat. A river rat."

Both stood with their mouths open, not sure how to respond, when Nick explained, "Albany, ya know, upstate where they have cows, they used to have a hockey team called the Albany River Rats. The team stunk most of the time, but they had great merchandise. Isn't this hat cool?"

Chase smiled. "Oh yeah, can't say I've ever seen a rat playing hockey before."

Gavin then joked, "Soccer maybe—I hear rats like soccer."

Nick chuckled, "You two are funny. I'm gonna like working for ya."

With that, Nick put his hat back on and let the screen door slam behind him. As he walked off into the back yard, Nick called back, "Don't forget your letter, Chase. Gotta learn the rules."

Chase looked at Gavin, and without saying a word they both started racing through the kitchen and down the hall, and quickly they found the library.

It was a large room with built-in bookcases that stretched twelve feet into the air. Chase looked up at all those books, some appearing very old, and wondered how Sebastian and Vida even got them down, seeing they were so high.

There was an old fashioned rolltop desk on one side of the room, and a small, black leather sofa on the opposite end. A thick, expensive-looking, burgundy-colored rug lay beneath their feet, and a chandelier with what had to be a hundred tiny glass crystals hung from the ceiling in the center of the room, throwing light in all directions.

As her eyes drank in the warmth of it all. Gavin said, "Chase . . ."

He was standing by the hutch that Nick the caretaker had mentioned, and just as advertised, there sat a white business-sized envelope with the name C H A S E printed in bold black lettering across the front.

Gavin handed it to Chase, and she opened it immediately. As she fumbled with the flap her mind was thinking, *Rules . . . What does that even mean?* She'd know soon enough.

It was a short one-page typed letter that Chase read out loud:

*To whom it may concern: If you are reading this letter, thank you for buying the portrait of my wife. It is my favorite piece of art. Isn't Vida beautiful? At this moment your mind must be swimming with confusion, but let me assure you this is real; this is now your house. Congratulations, I'm sure you'll love it. I told my friend and groundskeeper Nick to tell you there are rules that go with living here, but that's not really true. They are more like "suggestions," and there are three of them. Ready?*

*Number one, when you walk out the front door, you'll notice a large maple tree to the left of the house. Please don't dig anywhere around that tree.*

*Number two, if you look up in the library you are standing in right now, you'll notice a set of three large windows, each with nine panes of glass and all of them facing the west. Please don't wash the center pane on the center window. Ever. Just leave it be.*

*And number three, each week a florist will deliver seven yellow roses to the house. Not a dozen, exactly seven. Directly behind the house, about a hundred or so feet back, you'll see a rock wall runs along the property line. Each night before you go to bed, please take one yellow rose and leave it on that rock wall. It's important to me, so please don't forget.*

*I know what you must be thinking: these are very odd things this dead man is asking me to do. I understand, and believe me I'd think the same thing were I you. All I can say is I have given you this beautiful home and asked nothing in return. Well, nothing but these three simple requests you just read. I hope you can honor an old man's wishes.*

*Thank you and God Bless, Sebastian Winthrop.*

*Oh, and P.S., you have to jiggle the handle on the bathroom toilet upstairs or it will run all night.*

Chase held the letter in her hand and looked at Gavin. Neither said a word, their minds too busy running with possibilities of what this was all about. They both looked at the window right in front of them and the pane of glass they were instructed to never wash. It looked exactly like the others around it. *Windows, trees, roses on rock walls; none of it made sense.* Chase placed the letter back in the envelope and left it on the hutch where she had found it. Gavin pulled her in close for a long, loving hug, and said, "New adventure, eh?"

Chase felt Gavin's arms loosen, but she wouldn't dare let him break their embrace, pulling Gavin's strong chest closer to her own, burying her beautiful face into his shoulder, and responding, "It seems so."

The happy couple was so taken with the house, library, and strange letter, neither one noticed that Scooter wasn't with them at that moment. He was on the opposite side of the mansion in a small room off the den, barking at a shelf filled with board games. It was a very insistent, distinctive bark that Chase had heard before, late at night in a church far away. Neither she nor Gavin knew it yet, but it appeared the magic and mystery of Manchester had followed her after all.

CHAPTER 14

*Charlie*

It never occurred to Chase to stop at a grocery store on the way to Briarcliff Manor, so she was pleasantly surprised when she woke her first morning in her new home to a refrigerator and cupboards filled with groceries. Gavin had just arrived, saw all the food, glanced at Chase, and wondered aloud, "Nick the handyman?"

Chase looked at what had to be two hundred dollars' worth of food and said, "That's pretty handy if you ask me."

After splitting a small cinnamon raisin bagel smothered in butter, the two of them took their hot coffees outside to see the rest of the property. Pear trees lined the long driveway that led to the house from the main road. On one side of the front yard was the large maple tree that Sebastian Winthrop mentioned in his letter, the one they were told not to dig around. One thick strong branch extended out, separate from the others, supporting two brown ropes that dropped down and attached to a simple wooden swing.

"Can we fit two on that thing?" Chase asked Gavin with a smile.

He just winked and said, "It would be fun to try."

Three oversized gray stone steps led up to that amazing front door. The windows to the sides and above were all different shapes and sizes, each seeming to tell a different story. On the opposite side of the yard, away from the maple tree, there was a pretty arrangement of boxwood hedges, each a foot tall. They formed a perfect circle, with a large stone bird bath standing at the center. Gavin had never seen a bird bath so large or heavy looking; an entire bird family could bathe together.

The two of them walked around the back of the home, and sure enough, there, off in the distance, was the rock wall on which they were instructed to place a yellow rose each night before turning in. The left side of the large back yard was lined with heavy woods, and to the right was a stately-looking, dark brown wooden fence that bordered the neighbor's land. It served more as a decoration than a deterrent, because anyone could duck under the slats if they wanted.

As the two of them turned, looking back at the house, wondering if this was all some kind of dream, a loud "Hello" echoed out from the neighbor's property. It was a woman about Chase's age with a rope in her hand, leading a beautiful snow-white horse along the fence line with a little girl sitting quietly in the saddle. She was a gorgeous child, with dark skin and dark eyes, her hair braided back perfectly in neat rows, and tiny pink bows in the back helping to keep it all in place.

Gavin and Chase turned immediately and started walking toward the woman and child on the horse as Chase replied, "Well, hello right back."

The woman, wearing a denim shirt to match her jeans and mud-covered boots, stopped the horse and reached up her hand to help the little girl jump down.

The child immediately cast her eyes away from Chase and Gavin as the woman said, "Welcome. I'm Mary, and this is Charlie."

Mary then turned to the little girl and began waving her right hand to get the child's attention. Once the girl looked up, engaging her eyes, Mary began moving her hands in sign language. Charlie watched carefully, clearly following along, then answered back by moving her own tiny hands. Mary then shook her head *no* and turned back to Chase and Gavin, "I'm sorry; she's being especially shy today."

Gavin smiled at Charlie, but she looked away again as if she were afraid. Chase then approached slowly and got down on one knee, resting her hands on the wooden fence, peeking through to say, "Hi Charlie, I'm Chase."

Mary translated for Charlie, pausing a moment, seeming uncertain of something. She looked back at the two of them and said, "There isn't really a sign for the name Chase so I can spell it or just do the sign for someone being chased. But that might confuse her." Mary then pointed at Chase and spelled the name with her fingers C H A S E. The child again gave no reaction to any of it.

Before Chase could speak again to her new neighbors, Charlie pulled at Mary's sleeve to get her attention and asked through sign language, "Can I go back to the barn?" Mary nodded yes and handed the brown leather reins to the silent little girl.

Before she could go, Chase waved her own hand to get Charlie's attention and said, "Wait, you can't leave until I know the name of your horse."

Charlie could read lips very well and looked up at Mary and signed, "You can tell her if you want."

Mary smiled then looked back at Chase and said, "Her horse's name is Hermione, like in Harry Potter."

Chase continued talking to Charlie, now saying, "Oh, I LOVED those books. Which one was your favorite?"

As kind as Chase was being, Charlie looked away and Mary signed to her, "It's okay, sweetie, you can go."

As the adorable child slowly led the horse back to the barn behind her home, Mary said to both Chase and Gavin, "Thank you for trying."

Chase gave Mary a concerned look and said, "Is she okay?"

Mary took on a serious tone and said, "Before we get to that, can I ask, are you the woman we heard bought Sebastian's home for thirty bucks?"

Gavin giggled as he replied, "It was actually twenty-seven."

Chase then spoke, "Yes, I'm sorry, I'm Chase Harrington. I did buy the sketch of Vida Winthrop at the auction and surprise, surprise, now I own a mansion. Crazy, right?"

Mary shook her head in approval and said, "Hey, why not. Good for you. I'm Mary Beal. I work for the Cartwrights. That's their daughter, Charlie."

Gavin interjected again, "And what do you do for them?"

Mary engaged Gavin's eyes, only now realizing how striking this man was in his white t-shirt and faded jeans. "I'm, um, well. I'm a tutor for Charlie and an interpreter. And if we're being honest, probably her only friend. I look after her, you might say."

Chase then said, "I'm sorry I asked if she was okay, that was presumptuous of me."

Mary appreciated Chase's manners and kindness, responding, "It's quite all right, Chase. And to answer your question honestly, no, not really. She's um . . ." Mary stopped herself there, uncertain if she should be sharing private matters with a stranger, nice as she may seem.

Chase gave Gavin a look he knew all too well. It was one that said, *Can you give me a minute alone, sweetie?* So he immediately looked at his watch and said, "I should go make that call. Nice to meet you, Mary."

As Gavin left, Mary said quietly to Chase, "Husband?"

Chase thought to herself, *Someday,* which made her blush a bit and smile, and then simply replied, "Boyfriend." Then after a pause she added, "Best friend."

Mary leaned her arms on the fence and said, "Those are the best kinds, the ones you keep."

Once Gavin was out of sight, Chase continued, "You were saying about Charlie . . ."

Mary looked away, a sadness falling over her face, then replied, "You can see she's deaf and painfully shy. Her parents had her in public school, but the class sizes were too large, and she got lost in the mix there."

Chase then, "Lost how?"

Mary, "Eating lunch alone. Sitting on the playground alone. Charlie is a wonderful little girl, but she needs help, you know, pulling her out of her shell."

Chase nodded, showing she understood, as Mary continued, "So they moved her to a small private school, but now she's not just the only deaf child but the only Black child in her grade. It's left her . . ."

Mary struggled to find the right word, then finished with, "Withdrawn. And a little lost right now."

Chase thought a moment then asked, "Does she have any friends, out here in the country, at Briarcliff?"

Mary shook her head, saying, "Not really. She loves her horse and rides her, but a horse is a horse you know. It's not the same. I feel like she needs a best friend to connect with."

Chase thought a moment, wishing she had a solution, but nothing immediately came to mind.

Mary then broke the silence saying, "I should be getting back to her. It was really nice meeting you and . . ."

Chase helped her then. "Gavin. His name is Gavin."

Mary again: "It was so nice meeting you and Gavin, and thank you for talking to me about Charlie. Her parents are very busy working in the city, and a lot of this falls on me. I worry about her."

Mary then looked toward the barn and saw Charlie in the distance sitting on the ground with her back against a bale of hay. She was fiddling with a pinecone she'd found on the ground, lost again in her own quiet world.

Without looking back at Chase, Mary just stared at the child and said, "What scares me, Chase, is . . . it's getting worse."

As Mary made her way back to the silent child, Chase went back to the mansion where Gavin was sitting on a stool in the kitchen, those deep blue eyes watching out the back window for her return. He could see the concern on Chase's face, so he immediately came outside on the stone patio and asked, "Everything all right, hon?"

Chase gave Gavin a hug and said, "Yeah, just that sweet little girl. The woman, Mary, said Charlie is a bit lost right now. She needs a friend."

Gavin pulled her away from the hug, looked in her eyes, and said, "Maybe you can be her friend."

Chase wasn't convinced, responding, "She wouldn't even talk to me."

Gavin looked over at the neighbor's barn off in the distance, and said, to comfort her, "First day. Give it time."

The two locked hands and started back into the house, uncertain what the first day of this new life might bring. One thing was certain, both were still ravenous. The tiny bagel they had split was not doing its job.

Gavin fished a packet of bacon and a carton of eggs out of the refrigerator, while Chase grabbed two more K-Cups to replenish their empty coffee mugs. Gavin then pulled up YouTube on his phone, and a few clicks later James Taylor started singing about how sweet it was to be loved by someone like Chase. Gavin changed the word *YOU* in the song to *CHASE* just to make her smile.

As she watched Gavin cooking, singing, and moving around the kitchen, mimicking dance steps he clearly didn't know, she realized again in that moment how much she loved this man. His uncomplicated life was on a farm in Vermont, yet his devotion to her was so strong, he had chased her all the way to the upper East Side of the big city. *Chasing Manhattan,* she thought, how poetic.

Now, without raising an objection, he had shifted his life again, helping her make sense of this new adventure in a new place. That woman Mary was right, he was indeed *a keeper!* If the moment came soon, where a shiny diamond was put before her eyes, Chase knew she couldn't say "YES" fast enough.

Whenever someone was cooking, especially bacon, Scooter was always at their feet hoping for a free sample. Chase realized her puppy wasn't with them, looked around the kitchen, and said to Gavin, "Hey, where's Scoot?"

Gavin was in full iron chef mode now, so without taking his eyes off the hot stove, he simply shrugged his shoulders, indicating he had no clue.

Had they ventured out of the kitchen, away from the soothing tones of James Taylor and the sound of sizzling bacon, they would have realized Scooter was back on the other side of the house in the room off the den, barking again at a dusty shelf filled with old board games. While Scooter seemed infatuated with Monopoly, Scrabble, Pictionary, and Battleship, Chase was deep in her own thoughts, worried now about a sweet little girl who spoke with her hands and protected her heart. Two words that the tutor, Mary, said more than once were tormenting Chase now: *She's lost.*

Chase knew she'd just met the child, so it made no sense to feel this connected already, as if she had to help her. Still, there was no denying it, this was the same strong feeling Chase had gotten in the pit of her stomach back in Manchester, when she had met the lovely people in that town and realized they needed help, and Chase had been the only one who could give it.

But what could she do? Chase didn't know sign language, nor did she have a child that Charlie could play and connect with. As Chase watched Gavin plate their delicious breakfast and glance over with those kind blue eyes, she could only hope in her heart that something would come to her.

What she didn't know was, just as in Manchester, it was Scooter who would unlock everything.

## CHAPTER 15

# Game Night

It took Chase less than a day to decide the library was her favorite room in this amazing house. Beautiful wooden bookcases blanketed the walls, housing many of literature's classic tales: *Moby Dick*, *Of Mice and Men*, *To Kill a Mockingbird*.

"You could be locked in here for ten years and not finish them all," Chase said to Gavin while holding a worn copy of *The Great Gatsby*.

Gavin put his hands in his pocket and smiled, looking like a little boy with a secret, when he said, "We may have to read them. I just checked and there's no cable TV hooked up right now. I called, and the guy on the phone said it got disconnected when the owner died. Could be a day or two till they can get somebody out here for you."

Chase gave him her best pouty face, then raised her eyebrows and said, "Then we'll just have to find something else to do with the time, hot stuff."

As the two of them smiled, there was a knock on the front door, loud enough to cause Scooter to bark and run in that direction.

"I got it," Gavin said, leaving Chase to continue looking at the literary works of art that adorned the room from floor to ceiling. Chase was busy thumbing through a copy of John Steinbeck's *The Pearl* when Gavin appeared in the doorway holding something green and yellow.

"Guess what just arrived?" he said.

Chase couldn't see from that distance, so she crossed the room slowly. Then her eyes went wide as she said, "The roses!"

"Yep," Gavin replied. "Seven of them, all yellow, just like the letter said."

They both turned and looked at the antique hutch by the window and realized the letter was still where Chase had left it.

Chase took the roses from Gavin's arms and said, "Who gave them to you? Who was at the door?"

Gavin went into his back pocket and pulled out a small business card and said, 'Flora's Florist.' The delivery guy said he comes once a week like clockwork. He left his card in case there was ever a problem, and said he'd bring more roses."

Chase smelled them, and they were divine, "Did you tip him, hon?"

Gavin shook his head, "He wouldn't take it. He said the previous owner set up a fund and he was well taken care of, whatever that means."

Chase looked around the well-appointed room and said, "Well, since Sebastian Winthrop used to own Monets, I'm guessing that means the flower guy is all set on the tip."

The thought made Gavin chuckle. "Nice to be rich, huh?"

Chase pulled a single rose from the bunch and said, "I guess so. Should I place it on the rock wall or you?"

Gavin rubbed his chin and said, "Well, since you wrote the nice article about him and you are the lady of the house, I think you should. But I'll keep watch from the patio in case a bear attacks you or something."

Chase threw Gavin a look and said, "Oh great, now I'll have that on my mind as I walk out there in the dark."

The two stepped outside, and luckily it was a clear night with a half-moon overhead. It was certainly not bright, but it made the yard look as though a flashlight low on batteries was shining down on it.

Chase was wearing her favorite high-top Converse sneakers with the star on the side, so navigating the mushy lawn was a piece of cake.

"You come running if I scream, now," she yelled back over her shoulder. Gavin called back, "In a heartbeat."

A moment later Chase found the wall and placed the yellow rose on top as instructed. She looked off into the woods behind the property, but nothing appeared to be looking back—just thick trees. Even though she was perfectly safe, there was something a bit spooky about doing this errand all by herself, so her steps back toward Gavin and the light from the kitchen quickened with each movement. As she got near, she saw

Gavin looking back into the house. There was no music playing or TV on, so sounds in the old home carried far and fast.

As Chase reached the patio she called out, "What's the matter?"

He looked back toward Chase and said, "Nothing—I hear Scooter going crazy. Barking."

Chase locked the back door behind them, and together, without saying a word, the two of them snaked their way through the house that Sebastian built, to the other side and the den. Once they were there, Scooter's barking seemed much louder, so they followed it through a door off the den into a small room that was used for storage. Boxes of blankets were on the floor, three or four old brooms were tucked neatly in a corner as if waiting for an owner to pick them up, and there was Scooter standing on all fours in an aggressive posture, barking at a shelf filled with board games.

Chase looked at Gavin and they both thought the same thing, then tried to push it out of their minds. This is what had happened at the old church in Manchester, Vermont. This is how the craziness had started, with Scooter seeing or knowing something they did not.

But there were no stained glass windows in the room to hide secrets. Just boring old walls that were painted white and as blank as a new sheet of typing paper. The only thing of any interest in the room were the games piled on top of each other on a shelf.

"Maybe a mouse is in there?" Gavin asked.

Chase thought, *we should be so lucky*, then said, "Maybe."

She then petted Scooter and said, "What's wrong, boy, something in there?"

With that he stepped forward, jumped up, and using his paw pulled down several of the board games, causing them to crash onto the wooden floor. Pieces of the Monopoly game sprawled in every direction.

"SCOOTER," Chase cried out. "Bad boy."

You'd expect the dog to look ashamed after such a scolding, but he wagged his tail as if he were pleased with himself. He acted as if he had done exactly what he intended to do.

Chase and Gavin got down on the floor and scooped up Park Place and Marvin Gardens, when Scooter stepped right between them and started clawing his right paw on a box that hadn't burst open from the fall. It was Scrabble.

Chase looked at Gavin and said, "If there IS a dead mouse in there, I'm gonna scream, you know that, right?"

Gavin finished putting the other games back in their boxes and then looked into Scooter's eyes. "What gives, buddy? You want me to open this box?"

With that, Gavin picked up the Scrabble game and gave it a quick shake. It felt full, as if everything was still inside. If a dog could smile, Scooter did in that instant, barking, whipping his tail quickly back and forth, and again striking the box with his paw, as it lay in Gavin's hands.

Gavin stood up, looked at Chase, and said, "I think he wants us to play Scrabble."

Chase loved her dog with all her heart but that didn't stop her from saying out loud, "Dogs can't want things like that, Gavin. Come on."

Gavin took her by the hand and led her into the den, saying as they walked, "Well, this one does."

There was a large couch to the side and two smaller chairs, but they needed something level, so Gavin grabbed two pillows off the furniture and tossed them down to the carpet.

"Cop a squat?" he suggested.

Chased looked confused so he added, "Don't tell me you never saw *Pretty Woman*. Remember they cop a squat under a tree? Julia Roberts and Richard Gere."

Chase thought a moment, then snapped her fingers when she remembered, saying, "She makes him take his shoes and socks off cause he's all too business."

Gavin smiled, "I'm not sure business-eeee is a word but okay, yes, now you have it."

The two sat down, and Gavin pried open the Scrabble box. All the pieces were neatly arranged, and it looked as if it hadn't been used more than once or twice.

They opened the board and placed it on the floor, took out the dozens of tiny brown wooden tiles, which were blank on one side and had letters on the other.

"How does this work again?" Gavin asked. "I mean, I know we spell words on the board and get points, but how many tiles do we get?"

Chase said, "Honestly, I don't remember. I haven't played this since I was fourteen at the Finns' house."

"The Finns?" Gavin asked curious.

"Bobby and Jimmy Finn, twin boys one year ahead of me in school. We hung out all the time as kids and they loved board games. They had them all."

Gavin glanced at a piece of paper with the rules printed on it and read out loud, "Place tiles into the Scrabble bag. Shake it up and have each player remove seven tiles and place them face up on their wooden rack. Use the tiles to form words on the board and score points. Abbreviations and names do not count."

He then tossed the paper down on the carpet and said, "It goes on from there, but that's the gist of it. You wanna play?"

Chase replied, "It says you need a hundred tiles to play. Make sure we have enough."

Gavin quickly counted them out and got 99.

"Let me count," Chase said, certain that Gavin had just missed one.

She then slowly counted the wooden tiles and a moment later concluded, "Looks like you were right: ninety-nine. We're missing one letter. No biggie, we can still play."

It was then they both realized Scooter was lying on the floor to Chase's left with a satisfied look on his face, watching every move.

Both took seven wooden tiles out of the bag and arranged them on their small rack. Gavin had an odd collection of letters: Z, T, V, O, R, R, L.

Chase on the other hand got L, O, Z, B, A, E, L.

They both tried to scramble their letters around to make something, anything, but Gavin was at a loss. "If I had another *L* I could make the word *ROLL*, but I got nothing. You?"

Chase looked at Gavin's letters and said, "Hold up, you have a couple. OR is a word. So is ROT."

Gavin looked again. "Oh, you're right. I guess I ROT at this game."

His awful joke brought a groan from Chase.

Gavin then asked, "How about you?"

Chase moved the pieces around and realized she could spell BALL or BELL. "Did you say we can't spell names?" she asked.

Gavin replied, "That's right, no names."

"Too bad," Chase said, as she placed the tiles on the game board. "I could have spelled BELLA."

Gavin saw she had some other words she could work with and told her to go with one of those.

They played to 100 points and the game went quickly, with Chase winning the first one easily.

"Rematch?" Gavin asked with a smile,

"Mix 'em up," Chase said as they placed the tiles back in the bag, adding, "Who needs cable TV?"

After taking the tiles back out for game number two Gavin said, "Oh, finally some good letters."

This time he was starting off with A, D, E, S, R, S, P. "Wow, I've got DRESS, PRESS, READ, tons of words this time. How'd you do?"

Chase turned her tiles over and had L, A, L, V, X, E, B. "Hmm, not so good. Look," she said, turning her rack around so Gavin could see.

Just then Scooter, who had been quiet for a half hour, let out a surprise bark that made them both jump. The dog looked at Chase and then over to her letters. As ridiculous as it seemed, it felt as if he were saying, "Look again, mommy. LOOK."

Chase patted his head and looked back, but her Scrabble letters still seemed like odds and ends. Then she relaxed her focus and saw it plain as day.

"Hey, I got Bella again," she said with surprise.

Gavin looked and said, "That's funny. What are the odds?"

Chase didn't say anything. Instead, she looked back at her dog, who was still staring as if waiting for something. Chase's mind started running away from logic and toward the impossible.

She stared silently at Scooter.

"Hello, we still playing?" Gavin asked.

Chase ignored his question, her mind now piecing together the evening's events.

His barking had led them to this room and he himself had pulled down this very game they were playing. It was all too familiar to her, since it was the same dog who, a couple years earlier, had been barking at windows in a church and at messages that only Chase could see in the stained glass windows. But this wasn't a church, was it? No, far from it. They were sitting on the floor of a million-dollar mansion, playing a stupid board game, so whatever this was, it couldn't be that. It had to be a silly coincidence. *What are the odds?* she wondered.

There was an awkward silence, and Chase's eyes appeared to be looking far away, causing Gavin to ask, "Are you okay?"

Chase finally returned to him, and said, "Let's find out."

"What?" Gavin answered.

Chase then, "You said, what are the odds of getting the same letters twice. Let's find out."

She took both of their wooden racks and tossed the tiles back into the bag, shaking it up extra hard this time.

"You go first, just you," she said to Gavin. He pulled out seven new letters: D, M, P, E, E, C, O.

Chase then grabbed a handful of tiles from the cloth sack and placed them down on her wooden rack: A, P, E, L, Y, B, L. If you took out the Y and P you had *BELLA*. Again.

More silence as Chase stared at the name, trying to convince herself this was just an incredible coincidence.

Finally she said, "It's a fluke. Just a fluke. That's all it is."

Gavin was the one who looked wonderstruck now, not saying a word.

With that she grabbed up the letters in her fist are threw them back into the bag aggressively.

"Are we done?" Gavin asked. Chase didn't answer. Instead, she began to shake up the tiles again, this time for a good twenty seconds. Her shaking of the small bag got even more aggressive, bordering on angry, as she shook and shook some more.

When it didn't look as if she'd ever stop, Gavin put his hand over hers and said, "I think you got it, hon." His voice sounded a bit concerned now.

Then she handed the bag back to Gavin, saying, "Shake it more."

Gavin was starting to think this was silly, saying, "I'm sure they're mixed up enough . . ."

"Shake it!" she said, more insistently.

Gavin did as instructed, then tentatively handed the bag back to Chase. She looked at Scooter, who was still watching silently, then met Gavin's gaze, as she, very slowly, pulled just five letters out this time. One by one, she placed the five she picked, face down on the floor so she could not see the letters. They both stared at the five blank tiles, wondering what might be hiding on the other side. There are exactly 100 tiles in a normal Scrabble game; they had 99. The odds of pulling out the precise five you want had to be a million to one, maybe more. She knew it and Gavin certainly knew it.

With that Chase smiled and said, "Oh, to heck with it. I have to know." She then turned over the five tiles and the letters were, in exact order, B E L L A.

Chase jumped back as if she were ten years old, playing with a Ouija board, and the game just said "Hello."

She wasn't sure if she should be scared or excited, only saying, "What the . . . Gavin."

Chase began pacing around the room in a circle, trying to make sense of what was happening. The church windows back in Manchester were something only she could see, but this, what in God's name was this?

Gavin didn't seem upset. He just sat on the floor and stared as if he were solving a puzzle. He took his right index finger and rubbed the letters one by one, spelling out the name. He then looked up at Chase and said, "We're asking the wrong question."

Chase shot back a look and raised her voice: "WHAT?"

Gavin then replied, "We're both asking what is going on. But that's not the right question."

Chase leaned in with a look that said, *So, what is the right question?* Then Gavin gave it to her: "Who is Bella?"

Chase sat back down on the floor, grabbing Scooter and pulling him close as if she needed a hug at the moment. "I, um, I . . ." She stared at the letters. "I have no clue."

Gavin stood up, now asking more questions quickly. "Think. Childhood friend? Someone from college? Someone you met in New York City?"

Chase thought as hard as she could. "I don't know anyone by that name."

Gavin then very methodically picked up the letters and place them back in the bag, put the bag and board back in the box, and led Chase by the hand, out of the room.

"Where are we going? she asked.

Gavin didn't answer, instead taking Chase into the kitchen, where he silently opened a bottle of Merlot that was resting on a small wrought iron rack on the granite countertop.

He poured two healthy glasses and began, "Let me say this first, because I know we're both thinking it. What happened in Vermont, might be happening here."

Chase took a sip of her wine and said, "But that was church windows; this is a silly game."

Gavin paced the kitchen now like a detective piecing a crime together. "True, but Manchester started with Scooter barking at windows. Here, he barks at those board games and then literally pulls down the one we just played."

Chase followed along said, "Right, but still . . ."

Gavin continued. "Then you get the same letters four times. All the same name. FOUR TIMES, Chase?"

Chase thought a moment, then said, "So let's say you're right, this, whatever it is, IS happening again. I don't know a Bella, so what am I supposed to do with this . . . information?"

Gavin took his seat again. "That I don't know. But I don't think you can ignore it."

Chase squeezed his strong hand, and they both sat quietly, sipping their wine.

That's when a thought came to Gavin. "Can I ask, what were you doing or thinking about right before Scooter started up with the barking?"

Chase thought a moment, trying to dial back her memory, then said, "I watched you dance, BADLY, I might add, around the kitchen while you made us dinner. We went to the library to look at books, the roses came, I placed one on the rock wall, and then he started barking."

Gavin paused, then asked, "Right, but were you thinking about anything in particular?"

Chase took another drink of her wine and said, "Not really. I mean, I was wondering why we're putting roses on rock walls, and about . . ." She paused then, her face changing as if something had just occurred to her.

"What?" Gavin asked.

Chase replied, "Charlie, that little girl we met. I've been thinking about her since we met her and wondering how I can help her."

Gavin saw her wine glass was nearly empty, so he poured her more, topping off his as well.

"Maybe that's it. Maybe that's what this is about." Gavin said in a supportive tone.

Chase looked at the wine in her glass and thought quietly a moment. Then she said, "So if I want to help Charlie, I keep my eye out for someone named Bella?"

Scooter walked into the kitchen now and sat between them. Gavin reached down to pet him and said, "I think so. Maybe. I don't know."

Gavin snapped his fingers then. "You said she had no friends at school. Maybe there's a girl named Bella who is going to be Charlie's friend and she just needs to meet her."

Chase nodded, but then observed, "But what does that have to do with me? Why tell me? I have nothing to do with her school."

Gavin shrugged his shoulders, realizing Chase had made a good point.

As the two of them sat, trying to sort this out in their minds, Chase's phone rang. It was a number she didn't recognize.

"Probably spam," Gavin said.

Chase was about to reject the call when she noticed it was a 212 area code, New York City.

She hit the green button to answer and put it on speaker.

"Hello, Chase, are you there?" It sounded like an older woman, her voice shaky and thin.

"This is Chase, can I help you?" she replied.

Then, "Chase, this is Delores Wainright. We met at the Fur-Ever Java, the café."

Chase lit up now. "Oh, yes, hello, Ms. Wainright."

There was a smile now, returning in the voice over the phone. "You can call me Delores. I'm calling, Chase, because, well, do you remember that purple ribbon you put around Penelope's neck, the rescue puppy?"

Chase looked at Gavin with joy in her eyes. "Yes, of course."

Delores replied, "Well, I'm taking the ribbon off and replacing it with a Chanel collar. Tomorrow."

Chase replied, "So what you're telling me is, you are . . .?"

Delores, "Yes, Chase. I'm adopting her. She's my Christmas tree."

Chase stood up, holding the phone. "Oh, that's wonderful. I'm so happy for both of you, Ms., I mean, Delores."

Delores replied, "The woman from the shelter is bringing me the paperwork right to the café tomorrow at noon. I'd love to see you."

Chase thought a moment and said, "I'm flattered, Delores, but I'm about an hour outside the city now, and I have my hands pretty full here."

Delores pleaded, "Chase? This puppy changed my life, and that only happened because of you. Please come."

Gavin shot Chase a look that said, *Babe, you gotta go!* to which Chase nodded yes and said, "I wouldn't miss it for the world, Delores. I'll see you at noon."

After a long hug ended their long day, Gavin made the short drive to his friend's home, promising to be back first thing in the morning.

A strong north wind shook the tree outside the bedroom where Chase turned in for the night, causing a lone branch to reach out and tap the glass on the tightly closed window. It was surprisingly loud and distracting. Still, all that scratching wasn't the reason Chase lay awake for hours. You could thank a board game and five letters for her sleepless night. As she stared at the ceiling of Briarcliff Manor, Chase could hear Scooter at the bottom of the bed snoring away. And why not? His work, at least for now, was done.

## CHAPTER 16

# The Missing "B"

S ound traveled far in Chase's new home. She learned this when she was awoken by a loud knocking on the front door downstairs.

"Coming," she shouted to this unseen alarm clock.

After bouncing down the stairs she put her hand on the doorknob and realized it wasn't wise to just open it blindly, so she called out, "Who is it?"

A woman's voice she didn't recognize said something back, but the door was so thick it muffled the sound, and Chase couldn't make it out.

She opened the door just a crack to find an older woman standing there holding a small metal carrier with two quarts of milk in glass bottles and a dozen eggs.

"Welcome to the neighborhood," the woman said with a smile.

She was wearing a simple blue house dress with a floral pattern and a white bow that tied in the front. Chase was still half asleep, but as she opened the door, she remembered well what had happened the night before while she was playing Scrabble and said without thinking, "If you tell me your name is Bella I may jump out of my shoes."

The woman had a kind face and appeared to be in her sixties. Looking down at Chase's feet, she said, "But you're not wearing shoes, dear."

Chase glanced down and realized she was barefoot.

Before she could respond, the woman handed her the milk and eggs and said, "I'm from Miller's Market, just around the bend. We work with a local farm and deliver items to homes in Briarcliff. The previous owner had us come by once a week, and I wasn't sure if you needed anything, but I thought, Helen, why not just bring something over and say hello. My treat."

Chase rubbed the sleep from her eyes and said, "I caught about half of that. But . . . your name is Helen, not Bella?"

Helen replied, "Nope. Helen. Who is Bella?"

Chase pointed at the delivery woman in the pretty dress and said, "That's the million-dollar question, Helen."

Chase then turned her head and said, "I wonder if Gavin is here yet? And where's Scooter?"

Helen replied, "If those names belong to a good-looking man and a cute dog, I think they're around back. I saw them when I came up the drive. This old bird still has twenty-twenty vision."

Chase was feeling more awake now, and said, "Thank you, Helen, for the four-one-one on my boyfriend, and the dairy."

Helen smiled and played along, replying, "Ten-four, good buddy."

Chase closed the door and was walking toward the back of the house when Gavin met her halfway with Scooter at his side. He looked adorable, wearing black sweatpants and a long sleeve white t-shirt.

"How long you been here, babe?" Chase asked, giving him a soft peck on the lips.

" 'Bout an hour or so. I was out back looking at nothing," he answered.

Chase scratched her scalp, trying to wake up, and asked, "Looking at nothing, what does that mean?"

Gavin turned and pointed toward the back of the mansion and said, "I mean nothing, as in the rock wall where you left that yellow rose last night is empty. The rose is gone."

Chase's eyes went wider. "You're kidding me?"

"Would I kid you? Well, maybe I would, but not about this. It's gone."

Chase believed Gavin, but still she walked into the kitchen and looked out the window toward the wall to see for herself. She turned back to him and said, "So, board games that talk to us and flowers that vanish. Fantastic. You know, when I told you at Spark's restaurant in Manhattan I was ready for a new adventure, I didn't mean this."

Gavin hugged her now. "I hear ya, but as you saw in Manchester, sometimes you don't get to choose the mischief this world brings you."

"Who was the lady at the front door?" Gavin wondered.

"Free milk and eggs," Chase replied. Seeing Gavin's confused look, she added, "Don't ask me, they're just friendly folks around here, I guess."

Chase then observed, "How did you let Scooter out?"

Gavin pointed, "Back door was unlocked. I didn't think you'd mind, and I didn't want to wake you."

Just then Chase's phone, which was charging on the marble island in the kitchen, buzzed, indicating it had a text. Chase picked it up and said one word, "Matthew."

Gavin replied, "Your driver? What's up with him?"

Chase said, "He's on his way. I've only been out of the city two days and he's feeling neglected, and so I told him he could drive us into Manhattan today."

Gavin thought a moment and then said, "Oh that's right, the nice lady is adopting that dog. You want me to come with you?"

Chase hugged him again and said, "I'd love the company. Maybe we can walk in Central Park afterward. Looks like a nice day."

Gavin then replied, a bit sarcastically, "Yeah, maybe we can call out the name *BELLA* and see if anyone answers."

The two of them ate, and Chase then showered and dressed, making sure to be ready by 11 a.m. for Matthew's pick-up. Chase wanted to show Matthew her new place, but she didn't want to miss Delores getting her puppy, so they hopped in the backseat of his shiny BMW and away they went.

They made it to the café in 53 minutes flat, perfect timing to grab another cup of coffee and watch the official adoption. As Gavin pushed open the café's front door, they both heard, "Shingles. I'm pretty sure it's shingles."

It was Deb, her short red hair spiked up in all directions, ignoring the customers standing at the counter and talking to her open laptop computer again.

Raylan came out of the kitchen with some clean cups on a tray and said, "I thought you got the shingles shot. And flu shot and pneumonia, and about a dozen others earlier this year."

Deb considered what he said and replied, "You know, I think you're right."

Chase noticed Bonnie, the woman from the book club, was sitting at a table by herself, pretending to read some novel. Chase knew she was pretending because she saw how often she looked up from the book to watch Raylan doing his chores. *Interesting,* Chase thought to herself.

Gavin, who loved to tease Deb, couldn't resist yelling across the café, "It could be skittles, not shingles, Deb."

She looked up, recognizing Chase's boyfriend, and said, "Don't you be messin' with me today, Gavin."

He held up three fingers and said, "Scout's honor, my uncle had them once. Look it up. It's a real thing."

Deb started typing into her computer, "Skittles, you called it?"

Gavin gave Chase a look, and she was ready to smack him for doing this again, as he continued, "Yeah, Skittles. There's more than one type. They come in different colors."

Deb kept clicking with the mouse and suddenly looked up with fire in her eyes. "Skittles are a candy, you idiot."

As a dozen or so customers in the café laughed out loud, Gavin responded, "Oh, wait. You might be right."

Deb closed the laptop hard and asked out loud, "When am I gonna stop falling for your nonsense?"

Gavin went over and did something he'd never done before, giving Deb a big hug and said, "I hope never."

Deb harbored a secret crush on Gavin, like half the women in Manhattan and Vermont, and started to blush.

Just then Oscar, the kind man who collected bottles for the poor and occasionally helped with the dogs, came in from the side door with Penelope on a leash, looking all groomed and perfect.

"I just gave her a bath, brushed her out, and clipped her nails. Our little girl is ready for her forever home," he announced.

He spotted Chase and said, "Oh, hey, Chase. How are you?"

Chase smiled and said, "Good, Oscar, I'm here for the lady of the hour. Where is she?"

As if on cue, the door clanged open and Delores Wainright came in, wearing a brand-new beige Burberry pantsuit she'd bought special for the day, saying with joy, "There's my girl."

Chase smiled and turned toward Delores, when Gavin said, "I think she's talking to the dog, hon."

She was, of course, crossing the room to give Penelope a hug.

"She's gorgeous. Oscar, let me give you a tip?" Delores said.

Oscar backed away, and replied, "No ma'am. No tips. I was happy to do it."

Delores, Chase, and Gavin all took a seat at the same table in the center of the café, waiting for the woman from the shelter to arrive and give the paperwork to Delores.

Raylan told Deb to take a short break, as Oscar crossed the room to take the café's other shelter dog, Ella, out for her walk. He realized she was curled up in a ball, leaning against the wall, sound asleep.

"I guess I'll let her finish her nap," Oscar said, as he picked up a magazine someone had left on one of the tables and started thumbing through it.

Just then a young woman with curly hair, big hoop earrings, and a pink dress bounced into the café with a small brown envelope in her hand, scanned the room and asked, "Is Delores here?"

Delores raised her hand and said, "Right here. You must be Crystal, from the shelter?"

The twenty-something woman said, "That's me. I just need you to sign two forms, mark that the adoption fee has been waived, and Penelope is all yours."

Delores scanned the two pages from the envelope, and as she signed her name she wondered aloud, "Waived. Why was the fee waived?"

Crystal said, "Oh, because the dogs technically have been living here at the café, they didn't cost us anything. So, no fee."

Delores looked over at Raylan behind the counter and remembered in that moment how rude she had been when she first met him, questioning why he'd have dogs in a place like this. She realized that his taking in those dogs had allowed her to meet Penelope, and his kindness even took care of the adoption fee. Raylan returned her stare, and as their eyes met, he smiled, knowing how happy this puppy made her feel. Delores mouthed the words *thank you* so only Raylan could see, and without missing a beat he quietly mouthed back, *you're welcome.*

As Crystal got ready to go, a young girl, of high school age, was off to the side looking over some of the pottery that Raylan sold. She attempted to take a large pitcher and bowl down from a shelf that was a few inches too high for her, when both slipped out of her hands.

"*CRASH!*" They both hit the hardwood floor, exploding into a dozen pieces. The sound was so loud and jarring, everyone in the café literally jumped in their seats. Gavin happened to be glancing in exactly that direction when the glass smashed and saw that the crash was only inches from the head of the sleeping dog Ella.

As the teenager apologized and looked on the verge of tears, Raylan ran over with a dustpan and broom in hand saying, "Nothing to be upset about, I put those up too high, that's MY fault, not yours, young lady."

That's when Gavin tilted his head to the side, the way a dog does when you say one of their favorite words like *ball* or *treat.*

He realized something that everyone else in the café apparently just missed, saying out loud, "She didn't move."

Chase looked over from where she was standing with Delores and asked, "Who didn't move?"

Gavin pointed at the still sleeping dog and said, "That dog. The dish crashed right next to her and she didn't move a muscle. Is she okay?"

Raylan, concerned now, reached down and touched the soft white fur on the dog's back, causing her to jerk awake, startled.

"She's fine," Raylan said, adding, "Ella must be a heavy sleeper."

Oscar, watching all of this from a nearby table, said, "You guys are kidding, right?"

Chase replied, "About what?"

Every face looking Oscar's way was blank, so he added, "She's deaf."

Raylan, Chase, Gavin, Delores, all of them were staring dumbfounded at Oscar now, none saying a word, when he added, "You guys didn't know that? How could you not know that?"

Raylan pointed down at the pup. "She's deaf. This dog right here?"

Oscar, "Yes, one hundred percent."

Chase thought a moment, and then remembered something. "Wait, that day I met you, I saw you training Ella with hand gestures. You weren't saying 'sit' and 'stay' out loud."

Oscar nodded in agreement. "That's right, because she can't hear. Did you think I trained all dogs like that, without speaking?" he added with a chuckle.

As Oscar went over to pet the small, thin puppy, and Raylan went back to cleaning up the broken glass, Crystal, the woman from the animal shelter, had a confused look on her face, now saying, "Can I ask you guys a question?"

All eyes turned in her direction, as she continued, "Why do you keep calling her Ella?

Raylan replied, " 'Cause that's her name."

Crystal, more insistent now, replied, "No it's not."

Raylan let out a loud sigh, frustrated, then pointed at the pup's neck. "LOOK. She has it sewn right into the collar you send with all the dogs when I take them in. Look right here, E L L A. *Ella.*"

Crystal looked away, confused, then snapped her fingers and said, "WAIT. I remember now. I was off the day she got dropped here at the café. The new girl who was filling in brought her here, remember?"

Deb, who was coming back from her break and caught the last part of this conversation, called out from behind the counter, "That's right. I was here when Ella got dropped. But, nobody told me she was deaf."

Crystal said, "I'm so sorry. This was a huge screw-up."

She looked over at Oscar now, saying, "Yes, she IS deaf. You were supposed to be told that. And her name . . ."

The young woman crossed the café, to get close to the dog, bent down and touched Ella's collar gently and said, "The lady who sews these collars for the shelter messed this one up. She missed the *B*, but because she sews the collars for free, I didn't want to send it back and make her redo it."

Crystal then looked at all their astonished faces and said with an embarrassed look, "And because the dog is deaf, I didn't think it really mattered. I mean deaf dogs can't answer to their name anyway, right?"

Raylan looked down at the scrawny puppy and said, "So all this time, her name wasn't Ella? It was . . ."

Chase beat him to the punch. "Bella. Her name is Bella."

She turned sharply and looked at Gavin. As their eyes met, he whispered, "Jesus, Mary, and Joseph."

## CHAPTER 17

# I'm Not Asking for You

The moment Delores and her new puppy left the café, Chase jumped to action, saying, "I need Gavin, Raylan, Oscar, and shelter lady. I'm sorry, I forgot your name . . ."

The woman replied, "Crystal, I'm Crystal."

Chase continued. "Yes, sorry, Crystal. I need the four of you in the kitchen right now, please."

Deb agreed to watch the register as the group disappeared into the back.

Chase, "I don't have time or the desire to explain why, but I think I know who is supposed to adopt Bella."

Chase then looked at Gavin and said to him, "Do you remember what I was worried about all day when Scooter started barking? *Who* I was worried about?"

Crystal smiled, "Who? Who is supposed to adopt her?"

Gavin, understanding where Chase was going with this, looked toward the shelter woman, explaining, "The place where Chase lives, there's a neighbor, a little girl . . ."

Gavin then directed his attention back to Chase, asking, "Why would you think this child would adopt a dog she's never met?"

Chase patted Bella on the head and said, "In a way she has met her. Every time she looks in the mirror."

Gavin then, "You lost me."

Raylan, "That makes two of us."

"Three," Oscar echoed.

Crystal raised her hand, "Fourzees."

Chase again, now more insistent, said to Gavin, "Think about it. Charlie, an only child, who is deaf and alone and nobody understands."

Crystal: "So this little girl, she's deaf like Bella?"

Gavin again: "Yes. But that's not the only reason we think they're a match."

Chase shot Gavin a look and said in a firm tone reserved just for him, "Yeah, best we not get into that, though, or we might *scrabble up* everyone's thinking, you know what I mean?"

She raised her eyebrows to drive home her point that she wanted him to *zip it* on their *other reasons.*

Gavin nodded. "Right, right."

Raylan asked, "What are you two talking about?"

Gavin turned to Raylan, "Another time. The important thing is Chase is right, this pup might be just what Charlie needs."

Oscar, who had been listening quietly, added, "The little deaf girl's name is Charlie? How sweet."

Chase turned toward Oscar, asking, "The sign language you do with the dog. Is that something you just made up or do you actually know sign language?"

Oscar looked at all of their faces that were waiting on his response, and said, "My best friend growing up was deaf. I learned sign language so I could communicate with him. Why?"

Chase bit her bottom lip and engaged Oscar's kind eyes. "I know it's a big ask, but can you disappear for a day and come with me to the country? I can't talk to Charlie, not the way you can. I think if you . . ."

Before Chase could finish that thought, Oscar took up Bella's leash and said, "We'll meet you out front."

Just then the kitchen door swung open, and Chase's friend and driver, Matthew, poked his head in. "Are we electing a new pope? What's going on?"

Gavin replied, "What's going on, my handsome Antonio Banderas-looking friend, is you are driving a bunch of us back to Briarcliff."

Chase interrupted. "Matthew, can you take us all back to the house in the country and stay for a few hours? Then when Oscar is done, bring him back wherever he needs to go?"

Matthew replied, "Of course, but who is Oscar?"

Oscar pushed passed him with the dog and said, "Me. Let's go, Antonio."

Matthew jokingly replied, "It's Matthew, actually—I'm better looking than him."

The drive from the city to Westchester County seemed to take twice as long as usual because of Chase's anticipation.

Her mind kept playing over and over again how she had reached into that Scrabble bag for the fourth time and pulled out that B E L L A in that exact order, and now a dog with the same name was sitting next to her in the back seat.

Gavin squeezed her hand, leaned in so only she could hear, and said, "Is this how it felt in Manchester for you, after the windows?"

Chase didn't need to answer. Her eyes told Gavin that feeling of nervousness and excitement in the pit of his stomach were familiar territory for her.

Luck was on their side. As Matthew pulled into the circular driveway in front of the house, she could see Mary the tutor and Charlie were already outside near the large red barn.

"Oscar, you and Bella come with me, everyone else hang back, okay?" Chase said, as they exited the vehicle. Mary waved hello as she saw her new neighbor and a harmless-looking man with a dog on a leash approaching.

Charlie saw them too, but looked away, pretending to be uninterested in this unexpected house call.

Chase began, "Hi, Mary, hi, Charlie. I wanted you both to meet a friend of mind. This is Oscar."

Mary translated what Chase said to Charlie using sign language, but there was no reaction.

Mary then asked, "I'm sorry, is Oscar the man or the dog?"

Chase giggled. "Oh, my fault. This is Oscar," she said, while patting him on the shoulder. Then Chase looked to Charlie and said, "And this is Bella," pointing down on the scared-looking pup.

Oscar noticed instantly that the little girl and the shelter dog were an almost mirror image of each other's movements. Both looked frightened and both avoided eye contact with anyone.

Chase took a beat, then said, "The place I used to live in Manhattan has a coffee shop below it that takes in dogs from the shelter, dogs that need homes. Bella here, is in need of a home."

Instead of relaying what Chase said, word for word, Mary turned to Charlie and signed, "Honey, give me a minute, I want to talk to Chase alone."

Mary then gently took Chase by the elbow, leading her twenty feet away so the conversation would be private. Charlie decided to sit down in the grass under an apple tree, so Oscar copied her exact movements, without saying a word. Bella the puppy was still on the leash at his side.

Mary, in a somewhat stern voice, said, "I know where you are going with this, and God bless you for thinking of her, but there's something you don't know."

Chase swallowed hard and just stayed quiet now, as Mary continued, "Charlie had a dog who died. They got the Golden Retriever before she was born, so when Charlie came along the dog was already seven years old. His name was Rex or something obvious like that."

Chase just listened said, "Okay."

Mary again, "So, Charlie was four when the dog died, and it just crushed her."

Mary looked back at Charlie to make sure she was all right with Oscar, then back at Chase. "If you ask me, her withdrawal really started not long after losing her dog. Her parents asked her about getting another one, but she refused. She said no dog could replace the one she lost. So, instead, they got her the horse, but you know from your own pup, a horse is not the same. They don't kiss your face or sleep at your feet."

Chase nodded in agreement. "No, they don't."

Mary finished. "So, as kind a gesture as this was you bringing— what's her name?"

"Bella," Chase said gently.

Mary continued, "As kind as this was bringing Bella, she's not going to want the dog."

As Chase listened, a short distance away, Oscar kept petting Bella and then did something that completely surprised Charlie.

When he saw her look over, Oscar used sign language to ask, "Have you ever thrown horse poop when it freezes?"

Charlie looked astonished for two reasons. First, this stranger she assumed was ignoring her knew sign language. And second, why was he talking about horse poop?

There was an awkward pause, so Oscar continued, "Horse poop. I see you have a barn, so you must have horses. In the winter, their poop freezes into small hard balls."

Charlie was fully engaged now, following his every unspoken word.

Oscar, laughing now, continued his slightly inappropriate tutorial. "You take those frozen poop balls and go down to the driveway where it's a smooth surface and you fling them like a snowball or a baseball."

Charlie's mouth opened wide, and she fought back a giggle.

Oscar continued, "Oh, you'd be amazed how far you can throw them."

For the first time since Oscar arrived, Charlie responded, signing back to him, "Don't your hands stink from touching the poop?"

Oscar replied, "Not really, because it's frozen solid. But you can wear gloves if you want. Works well either way."

Mary and Chase both turned when they heard the two of them laugh out loud together. Mary was about to return to see what was funny when Chase took her by the arm and said, "Hold up a sec."

The two women stood and watched. Only Mary was able to pick up parts of the private conversation, because she knew sign language.

Oscar looked down at Bella, who just lying still and being a good girl, and said, "Do you want to pet her? She doesn't bite."

Charlie stared at the quiet dog and seemed uncertain what to do. Just then Oscar waved his hand to get Bella's attention, touched his nose, and she jumped up in a perfect sitting position.

He then motioned for her to spin in a circle, which she did, causing Charlie to smile brightly. Then Oscar pointed to the spot next to Charlie, waved his finger, and Bella went over and laid down only inches from the little girl's knee.

Charlie wasn't stupid. She knew a set-up when she saw one, but before she could tell Oscar she didn't want the dog, no matter how cute she was, he surprised her again when he signed, "It's okay, I know. Don't worry about it. You aren't the only one who feels that way."

Charlie, confused, asked, "Feels what way?"

Oscar again, "That she's, sort of, well, I'll just say it . . . broken. Bella. She can't hear. Who wants a dog who can't hear? You can't call them. You have to teach them sign language, and I don't have to tell you, 'cause you know, that's a LOT of work."

Charlie reached out her hand cautiously toward Bella and she, just as carefully, returned the gesture, pushing her warm nose slowly toward the little girl's fingers, giving them a sniff.

Bella looked up at Charlie now with her light blue eyes, wagged her tail a bit, and took a chance by giving the tips of her fingers a kiss.

Charlie then said to Oscar, "She's not broken. Why would you say that?"

Oscar replied, "Isn't that how you feel sometimes? My best friend growing up did."

Charlie looked up. "What do you mean?"

Oscar replied, "I had a friend just like you. He was born deaf. It was hard sometimes. People don't understand what it's like."

Charlie put her tiny hands on the puppy's head, now feeling his soft fur, then signed, "No, they don't."

Charlie asked, "Is that who taught you sign language, your friend?"

Oscar smiled. "It sure is."

Oscar then looked over at Mary and Chase and then back at Charlie, saying, "My friend Chase thought you might like Bella, but it's okay if you don't want a dog right now. I'd take her myself, but they don't allow dogs where I live."

Charlie kept petting Bella, and now the pup inched closer, putting her tiny front paws on Charlie's bare arm, making them tickle a bit.

"What will happen to her then?" Charlie asked with a concerned look.

Oscar shrugged his shoulders. "I guess she'll go back to the café where she was living, and we'll hope a stranger comes in who likes deaf dogs and adopts her."

Oscar paused a moment and then touched Charlie's arm to get her full attention, signing, "Here's the thing, though, and I can only say this to you. Whoever takes her won't understand her the way someone like you would."

Charlie looked down at the puppy and emotion started to swell inside her. She remembered how it hurt losing her last dog, and now she wanted to open her heart to this poor, silent puppy.

Oscar continued. "These nice people think the dog is here to help you. That's not what I think."

Charlie signed back, "You don't?"

Oscar, "No, they got it backwards. I'm not asking for you. I just met you, but I care about Bella and I'm worried she won't find the kind of love she deserves."

Oscar paused a moment, then signed, "I took this long drive out here, to meet a little girl named Charlie, because I was hoping it was you who could help her."

Charlie and Bella just stared at each other a moment longer when Oscar added, "They say broken crayons still color just as bright. This little girl, this puppy, is a star, she just needs the right person to want her."

Oscar saw a single tear fall from Charlie's cheek as she reached down with both arms and scooped Bella up. She couldn't speak any longer through sign language because her hands and fingers were locked tight around the white fur in a hug, but her watery eyes told Oscar everything he needed to know.

Oscar gave Chase a nod and the two women returned.

Mary fought back tears, seeing Charlie so happy holding the dog, then whispered to Chase, "Thank you."

Chase then asked Oscar, "Is Bella staying? Did you want to head back with Matthew now?"

Oscar replied, "Um, yes to the first question and to the second, no, not yet. I have to show Charlie all my tricks I've taught Bella."

He then signed to Charlie, "Do you mind if I spend some time with you to teach you a few things?"

Mary smiled and said, signing at the same time, "Why don't I get the two of you lunch and we can call your mom and dad, Charlie, and let them know they might be getting a new family member."

Chase pulled Oscar to the side a moment and said, "You're a good man, Oscar."

He just smiled and replied, "I was happy to help. I owe?"

Chase was about to ask, *owe who,* when Charlie interrupted.

She took Oscar by the hand, then signed, "Let me show you my house and barn and my horse. Do you like Harry Potter?"

Oscar signed back, "I ADORE Harry Potter; just don't put me in Slytherin, okay?"

Before leaving, Oscar looked at his watch and called back to Chase, "Two hours? That should be enough time."

Chase nodded and said, "I'll tell Matthew to meet you out front in two. Thanks again, Oscar."

Just as Chase turned and started walking toward the back of her own home, two tiny arms suddenly wrapped around her legs, almost causing her to fall. It was Charlie, giving her the sweetest hug she'd ever received. Without saying a word, the silent girl released her embrace and took up Bella's leash to continue her short walk home with Oscar.

Gavin was out on the patio watching all of this, and waiting for Chase with a cup of hot tea with lemon. Scooter was there too, sitting tall at Gavin's side. Chase was probably imagining things, but she could swear her dog had a very satisfied look on his face, as if he had orchestrated the whole thing.

## CHAPTER 18
## *Losing Her Touch*

It was now early December, and the grounds, trees, and rock walls that dotted the estate at Briarcliff Manor were covered with a fresh coating of light snow. At first glance, it appeared as if Betty Crocker herself had slipped in while everyone slept and put a fresh layer of vanilla icing on everything.

While the snow was ever present, one thing was noticeably absent each morning when Chase awoke: the yellow rose they left on the stone wall behind the property. She had no idea what the significance of the rose was or who was taking it each night; Chase only knew she wanted to follow the instructions of the letter left for her by the previous owner. That meant the rose went on the wall, she was careful not to dig near the large maple tree out front, and one single pane of glass in the library must never be cleaned. She and Gavin looked at that specific patch of glass more than once, but it appeared exactly like the others around it.

No matter, keeping a promise meant keeping it, even if you didn't understand the reasons behind it. This was obviously a house that kept its secrets guarded. The worst-kept secret in the home, though, belonged to Gavin, who was working up the courage to ask the most important question a man can ask a woman he loves.

"I'm not saying we should get engaged right now, but if we did, I'm just curious what kind of ring you'd want," Gavin wondered aloud, while the two of them were side by side as Chase brushed her teeth.

Chase turned to look at Gavin, her mouth full of water and paste, with green oozing out like some swamp creature in a horror movie.

"Could you think of a more unromantic moment to ask such an important question?" Chase teased him.

She instantly felt bad when Gavin hung his head like a little boy who had just been scolded for eating the last cookie.

"Babe, I'm sorry, you just caught me off guard," she said with a warm hug, hoping to make things better.

Gavin smiled, and then said, "You're right. And I was definitely NOT asking you, just curious about the ring, that's all."

Chase squeezed Gavin's face with both hands, saying, "If the ring came from you, whatever you chose would be perfect."

The two walked hand in hand into the kitchen and shared a big bowl of steel-cut oatmeal and wheat toast for breakfast. Off in the distance, Chase could see her young neighbor Charlie in her warm barn, the large wide doors pulled open to let in the light, as the little girl played *fetch* with Bella.

The puppy that Chase had brought to Charlie three weeks earlier, after that strange game of Scrabble, had just the effect everyone hoped. Mary shared the news, not long after, that Charlie was indeed coming out of her shell and starting to make friends at school.

Chase couldn't take her eyes off of Charlie and the unbridled joy on her beautiful face.

"Wanna get out of here and visit your friends at the café?" Gavin asked Chase, as she broke her stare outside and turned to Gavin.

"Really?" She lit up with a smile. "I'd love that."

As she ran up the stairs to get changed, Chase said, "Do you want to drive, or should we get Matthew to come out and get us? With this bitter cold weather, I really don't feel like walking from the parking garage to the café, do you?"

Gavin, already dressed in black khaki pants and a gray sweater, looked up the stairs and said, "We're not walking. I knew you'd say you wanted to go to Manhattan, so I texted Matthew a half hour ago. He'll be here in a few minutes."

Chase stopped her ascent on a dime, turned, and came back down the stairs to give Gavin a kiss, saying, "Well, don't I just have the smartest boyfriend?"

He returned her affection with a wink and said, "You really do. I can't deny it any longer."

The drive into the city took twice as long due to the fresh snow blanketing the roads; most city drivers were terrified of even an inch of it under their tires. Matthew took the G.W. bridge and then the West Side Highway, giving Chase and Scooter a nice view of the Hudson river out the passenger side window. Chase made sure to bring her dog, figuring he'd want to catch up with some of his old friends as well.

As the dog sat between them in the back seat, Gavin was thinking of his father and the farm when he said, "I hope dad is okay. If this storm system dumped a couple inches of snow here, he may have gotten a foot that far north."

Chase replied, "Are you worried about him clearing the driveway or being able to get out?"

"God no," Gavin replied. "He has a snowmobile if he really needs to leave the farm. I'm more worried about snow piling up on the flat portion of the roof in the back of the house. After a storm, I climb up there and clear it off. I don't want him on a ladder."

"You should call him then," Chase said, with understanding in her voice.

"I did," Gavin said adding, "And he gave me a *yeah, yeah, yeah,* answer."

Chase's driver, Matthew, overheard their conversation and said, "You talking about snow on a roof? We get that in my building down in the meat packing district. They don't clear it off and I wish they did."

Chase, curious now, asked, "Why is that?"

Matthew continued, "When the snow melts it gets flooded up there and then drips into the building and my apartment sometimes."

Gavin caught Matthew's eyes in the rearview mirror and said, "That stinks. Sorry."

Matthew replied, "Thanks, Gavin. Hey, speaking of snow and buildings, do you two know what the weather looks like on Saturday? I ask because I have to move something heavy, and I don't want to freeze or get snowed on carrying it outside."

Gavin thought a moment and said, "I think the snow is over and we're about to warm up for the weekend."

Then, after a thoughtful pause, Gavin added, "You know, Matthew, if you need help moving anything let me know. I have the pick-up truck, remember."

Matthew nodded as he pulled in front of the café, and then said, "Thanks for the offer and the weather forecast. I'll let you know."

He put the car in park and added, "Okay, gang, we're here. Just text me when you need me."

Chase touched Matthew on the shoulder and said, "Probably an hour or so. And hey, thanks for coming out and getting us."

As Matthew gave Chase a wink, she and Gavin exited the car with Scooter in tow, heading toward the café's front door. Chase could tell, even before placing her hand on the doorknob, that the place was packed. Cold, snowy days made everyone crave hot coffee and muffins, it seemed.

Raylan's Fur-Ever Java café really was a melting pot of Gotham. One table was full of Wall Street types in two-thousand-dollar suits, and right next to them sat a group of teens who looked intent on bring back the *grunge* period of fashion. The owner of the coffee shop, Raylan, saw Chase and Gavin walk in, and immediately called Scooter over, giving him a bite of a blueberry muffin Deb had cut in half to split.

"Hey, is that my half?" she asked teasingly. Raylan flashed a smile and then gave the always hungry dog the rest of the muffin, even letting him lick the small white plate. Deb loved Scooter, so she didn't mind sharing her snack.

"Full house, eh?" Gavin said, looking around for a place to sit but realizing every table was occupied.

Raylan replied, "Hold up," disappearing into a closet where he stored extra chairs. He pulled two out and took a wobbly wooden table that was being used to hold stacks of *AM New York*, a free daily newspaper, turning it into a quick place to sit.

"Thanks, Ray Ray," Chase said.

Raylan pretended to frown and thought, only she could get away with calling him such a silly nickname.

As they took a seat, Deb brought over two fresh cups of coffee and Chase noticed a familiar middle-aged woman, wearing more make-up than usual, alone at a table but well positioned to see all the café's business, especially the front counter where Raylan was often perched.

"Bonnie again, huh?" she said to Raylan.

He glanced over, then back at Chase. "You mean Adele. Hadn't even noticed her."

Chase replied, sounding less convinced, "Ah ha."

Gavin wasn't following along and gave Chase a confused look, to which she said, "I'll tell ya later."

Once they had their coffee in hand, Gavin surprised Chase when he asked, completely out of the blue, "Why do you think Scooter hasn't done it again? With the board game. It has been a few weeks now."

Chase reached down to pet her dog, responding, "Honestly. I don't know."

She paused now, thinking carefully about a memory from back in Manchester, then added, "When it happened at the church in Vermont, there was no rhyme or reason to it."

Gavin stared at the pup and said, "Maybe that was it then, maybe it's done. We're done, I mean."

Chase sipped the coffee, then looked up toward the counter and yelled, "This coffee is perfect, Deb, thank you."

Deb waved back without looking up, and Chase continued Gavin's thought, saying, "Maybe it *was* a one-time thing."

Gavin stared off at the busy café when Chase added, "Of course that's what I thought before, until he started barking at the church windows again."

Gavin then shifted gears entirely, asking a series of rapid-fire questions. "Since we're in the puzzle-solving business today, who do you think takes the yellow roses off the wall? Why can't we dig by some tree in the yard? Why is that one window in the house special and can't be washed?"

Chase nearly spit out her coffee, he caught her so off guard.

After a quick pause, she replied, "Let's see. I'll answer them in the order you asked. I don't know, I don't know, and I don't know."

Gavin continued. "Do you think we should find out?"

Chase met his eyes. "Did we wake up today and confuse ourselves with Scooby-Doo and the gang from the mystery machine van?"

Gavin smiled and said, "NO. But if we were, let's both agree I'd be Fred, not Shaggy. And you are definitely more of a Daphne."

Chase fired back, "Hey, I like Velma, I'd just need the glasses."

The thought of it made them both smile.

Chase then got serious, saying, "I don't know, Gav. This whole thing, the article I wrote, the auction, the house, it's all a bit like a dream. And all the old man asked on his deathbed was for us to follow three simple rules. Do we really want to mess with that?"

Gavin thought a moment and said, "So respect his wishes?"

She touched his strong hand and said, "For now anyway."

Judging from his face, it was not the answer Gavin wanted, causing Chase to add, "In my experience the truth always comes out when it's ready, so let's leave it alone for now."

Gavin nodded in agreement, then got up to use the restroom. Chase noticed there was a new dog in the café. It looked like a Labrador mix, dark brown with big, sad eyes. She assumed it must be another one from the shelter, there to replace Penelope, who had recently been adopted out to Delores. Chase could see Scooter was eager to meet the new coffee house guest, so she dropped his leash, allowing him to go over and say hello. The two dogs gave each other a quick sniff, before wagging their tails and deciding they'd be fast friends.

She heard a giggle to her left and saw Raylan talking to Bonnie.

As he turned to go, Bonnie said, "You wish, Raylan."

Chase whispered to Raylan, "Hey, Romeo, yeah you, come here."

Raylan walked over, a dirty cup and saucer in his hand, "You need something?" he asked.

Chase looked at Bonnie then back at him and said, "Was that flirting I just saw going on?"

Raylan, incredulous, replied, "No, please. She's not even my type."

Chase continued. "Oh, we have a type, do we? Well, excuse me, then."

As he turned to go, appearing annoyed with her inquisition, she added, "I see she's calling you Raylan now, not the other thing."

Raylan shook his head and walked on, making it clear that if he did have a love life, he wasn't discussing it with Chase.

She then got up and walked over to Bonnie's table, taking a seat without being invited. "Hey, I've seen you here before and I wanted to introduce myself. I'm Chase."

Bonnie met her eyes, smiled, and said, "I know. I'm Bonnie, nice to finally meet you."

With the pleasantries out of the way, Chase dove right into the deep end of the pool, asking, "It's none of my business, but, I get a vibe coming off you two."

Bonnie looked away, her face turning a light shade of red, and she said, "You mean Raylan. Oh, no, we're just friends. Just friends."

Chase felt like pressing, but something told her to back off, so she said, "Okay. Fair enough. My mistake then. I really just came over to say hi. Enjoy your day."

Gavin returned and saw Chase returning to their tiny table and asked, "What was that about?"

Chase, sounding defeated, replied, "I thought I was playing matchmaker, but both parties shut me down. I guess I'm losing my touch."

Gavin took both of her hands, saying, "Well, I like your touch, and I don't think you've lost anything."

Chase looked deep in his eyes, and suddenly the café noise and crowd faded away.

"I've never lost you, have I?" Chase asked, thoughtfully.

Gavin gave her a light kiss and said, "Never."

Just then Chase's phone made a loud *DING,* revealing a text message from her driver, Matthew. It was two words all in caps: OUT FRONT.

A quick whistle from Gavin brought Scooter running back to join them, and the happy couple and pup made their way toward the door. The snow had stopped, and the sun was doing its best to break through the hazy December sky.

As they hit the sidewalk together, hand in hand, Chase asked, "You want to order a pizza and watch a movie tonight?"

Gavin squeezed her hand and said, "Sounds perfect."

Scooter looked up at the both of them, knowing something much more exciting was on the evening's agenda.

## CHAPTER 19

# *The Wrong Break*

By the time Matthew dropped them off at Briarcliff Manor the sun was already low in the western sky. For a quiet home in the country, it was busier than ants at a picnic, because Chase could see the flower delivery man was standing on the front steps talking with the groundskeeper, Nick. On the stone steps next to them was the woman from the market delivering another two quarts of fresh milk. Chase and Gavin rarely drank milk, except in their cereal and coffee, but Chase didn't have the heart to cancel the weekly order after the woman brought that first delivery in an act of pure kindness. Chase always believed unsolicited friendship was the rarest kind and deserved loyalty back. So, milk it was.

The woman waved goodbye to the group and made her way back to a small van with her store name stamped on the side. The florist had other deliveries to make and was next to go.

The driveway was clear of snow, and the sidewalks were shoveled and covered in a light dusting of rock salt, a clear indication Nick was indeed earning his keep.

As he walked toward his truck, Chase called out, "I forgot you worked winters too, Nick. Thank you."

He smiled, saying, "Of course. Lawn in the summer, driveway in the winter. I even sweep the chimney."

Gavin picked up the milk carrier, Chase the fresh bundle of roses, and the two went into the warm home.

"You wanna do rock, paper, scissors on who puts the flower out tonight?" Gavin asked playfully.

"Nah, I got it," Chase replied, placing six of the roses in a vase and marching out behind the house with the seventh rose in hand.

Nick made her jump when he suddenly appeared around the side of the house, saying, "I'm so sorry, ma'am. Didn't mean to startle you. I just wanted to see if you needed anything, before I left?'

Chase shook her head, then remembered, "Oh, wait, actually, yes. Question. Who has good pizza around here, a place that delivers?"

Nick scratched his balding head and said, "The fastest is Luigi's but they're not the best. The best, believe it or not, is Marty Burke's place, the South End Tavern. There on Mill Street, if you Google 'em."

Chase repeated his words out loud, so she wouldn't forget, "The South Side Tavern."

Nick quickly correcting her, "End, South End Tavern. Old Marty Burke's place. Ain't that funny. The best pizza in Briarcliff is made by an Irishman. Go figure."

Chase thanked him, continued her short walk, and placed the rose on the rock wall. She paused momentarily, looking into the woods beyond the property, wondering how the flower managed to vanish each night. Then she pushed the thought aside and headed back toward the house to open some wine and see if Gavin wanted to build a fire.

As she inched closer to the French doors that led to the kitchen, she could see through the door glass that Gavin was holding the bottle of Merlot in one hand and a corkscrew in the other, but his face instantly made her stomach turn.

She stopped, and through the window she mouthed the words *what's wrong?* Gavin just waved the hand holding the corkscrew, motioning for her to come in.

The moment she turned the latch and opened the glass doors she instantly understood why Gavin looked like he had seen a ghost. Faintly, but in a rhythm you could have set a clock to, Chase heard barking. It came every few seconds and always three times in a row, *bark, bark, bark*. A slight pause then, *bark, bark, bark*.

Gavin held up the unopened wine bottle and asked, "Should I even bother?"

Chase, with her own ashen face, now quipped sarcastically, "I'd wait. Something tells me we'll need a drink after."

After placing a pizza order by phone, the two of them walked through the house, neither one harboring any real hope that Scooter was barking at a squirrel or had his collar stuck in a door, anything *normal* to justify such a commotion. They knew what was happening before they even got there.

Sure enough, in the room off the den, they found Scooter standing upright, positioned like a watchdog who had cornered his prey, barking at the shelf full of board games again.

The moment Scooter saw them approach, he stopped barking and sat down as if his work here was done.

Chase patted his head and said, "Again, buddy? Really?

Gavin said, "Just to be certain, pick up a different game and see what he does."

Chase looked back and said, "You think? Okay, let's see."

She grabbed a box off the shelf and said loudly, as if to drive home the point, "SO, WHO WANTS TO PLAY BATTLESHIP?"

As she turned with the game in hand, Scooter gave her a low growl, his way of saying, *don't mess around, grab the right one.*

Chase put Battleship back and traded it for Scrabble. Once Scrabble was in her hand, Scooter lay down on the rug, put his ears back, and just stared at the two of them with contentment.

Gavin opened the box and said, "Stupid question, but, do we even bother playing or just see what happens when you pick letters?"

Chase sounded annoyed now: "You think I have a clue? Let's, um, let's both just pick letters."

They opened the game's board out of habit, laying it face up on the carpet, then took up the cloth bag that was filled with 99 Scrabble letters, all printed on wooden tiles.

"I'll go first," Gavin said, taking seven of them out in this order: V S T U E B O. He stared at them a quick second and observed, "I can make VEST, BUT, BOUT. I have a few words here. Now you."

Chase shook the bag briefly then retrieved E Z R A B K Y. Chase looked long and hard and said, "The words I see are KEY, YEAR, BEAR, BRAKE, the other spelling of BREAK, BAR, RAKE and BAKE."

They placed all the letters back into the sack, gave them a hearty shake and went again.

Gavin got M P X O D L R. He moved the letters around and said, "Okay, this time I can do MOP, ROD, POM, like something a cheerleader would have. None of my words repeated."

Chase reached back in and pulled seven new letters in one big bunch, getting K O E D R B A. They both looked them over carefully when Gavin said, "I see RED, BRA, BAKE, BAR again, ROB, DO, READ, RAKE again, and DARE. That's all I've got."

Chase agreed that she could only see the same nine words as Gavin. He was about to scoop them up and return them to the bag when Chase grabbed his arm to stop him.

"Wait. Gavin." She then moved the letters around, to spell once again the words BRAKE and BREAK.

They both were quiet a moment, thinking, then Gavin said, "So BAR, RAKE, BAKE and BRAKE with both spellings repeated. Skip me and just take out five letters, like we did with *Bella*, remember?"

Chase sat back and looked deep in thought, staring at the Scrabble pieces on the floor. Then she surprised him, saying, "What if we don't? What if we just leave it be, whatever this is."

Gavin rubbed her knee and said, "I'll do whatever you want but . . ."

Chase then, "But what?"

Gavin put the tiles back in the bag, stood up, and paced a moment as if he wanted to be certain how he said what needing saying next: "In Vermont and now here, what you saw helped people. There's no denying that. Look at Charlie and Bella. Chase . . . YOU help people."

He went silent now, and Chase stared at her dog who was also quiet and offering no opinion on the matter.

Finally, she relented, "You're right. But I'm getting sick of playing this game."

Chase grabbed the bag from Gavin's hand and instead of taking out five wooden tiles with letters on them, she moved off the carpet and shook the whole bag upside down violently, forcing them all to fall out.

"WHAT ARE YOU DOING? Gavin yelled, causing Scooter to get startled and jump.

Chase ignored him and kept shaking until all 99 tiles hit the hardwood floor and bounced in all directions. They scattered across the room in an area five feet wide.

Gavin was looking at Chase, worried this might be upsetting her, but she seemed calm as a cup of cocoa, gazing down at the floor.

She turned her head, and a slight grin crept up in the corners of her mouth, causing Gavin to ask, "What is it?"

Chase simply said, "Look."

Gavin glanced down and realized every single tile was face down on the floor except four of them. Chase knew if she dumped those tiles a thousand times, she couldn't get 95 of them to fall face down.

The only four tiles that were facing up were the letters- R A K E, in exactly that order.

Chase looked to Gavin and said, "Close. We got four out of five to land face up."

They both stood in silence when Chase added sarcastically, "Maybe I'm supposed to buy a rake."

Gavin replied, "Somehow I doubt that."

Then she paused and added, "It's possible this is just a weird coincidence."

Gavin answered, "Do you really believe that?"

Chase giggled, "No, but I'm trying not to lose my mind here, so let a girl dream, okay?"

Gavin again: "Maybe you're right, only four flipped over, so maybe this is all nonsense, Chase."

Chase, feeling a bit better about things, agreed, "Would you look at the two of us? We are making ourselves nuts over some random letters. It's just a stupid board game."

Just then Scooter barked, causing both of them to look. Once he secured their attention, the dog slowly walked over the shelf where the games were kept and scratched his paw at something on the floor. Sure enough, there was a single tile that bounced farther than all the others, a good ten feet away, and the letter was face up. They couldn't make it out from that distance, so Gavin walked over, picked it up and turned so Chase could see. It was a B.

Neither one felt like cleaning up the mess. Chase just looked at Gavin and said, "Wine?"

Gavin agreed, and as they started toward the kitchen, almost as if on cue, the door knocker banged loudly, and Scooter went running in that direction. It was the Irish pizza guy bringing them an Italian treat.

For the next hour they sat in the kitchen, chowing down on the best pizza either had ever had and finishing the bottle of wine.

Gavin, still holding the letter B in his hand, raised the tile up and said, "Break. Maybe someone is telling you to take a break."

Chase shook her head, "A break from what? I haven't written a word since that article for the *New Yorker*, and I barely worked before that."

Gavin was lost, responding, "I honestly don't know then."

Chase: "Besides, what if that's the wrong break."

Gavin: "What do you mean 'wrong break'?"

Chase, being a writer, explained, "B-R-E-A-K is the kind of break you're talking about. What if I'm supposed to be seeing B-R-A-K-E. Like a brake that stops something."

Gavin, now understanding, replied, "Oh, like when you pump the brakes in a car."

Chase again: "Yes, that kind of brake. But what does *brake* even mean?"

They sat silently, when Gavin observed, "Well, with the word Bella we didn't know what it meant until it whacked us over the head. Maybe this will be the same way."

Chase had a very uneasy feeling about this mystery word, although she couldn't put her finger on why.

As she placed the dirty dishes in the sink and the empty pizza box in the garbage she said, "Why don't we both sleep on it."

Chase faced another restless night. Something told her this message was different, and that the worry she felt deep down to her bones was not misplaced. By the time the sun rose on Manhattan, Chase knew what she needed to do.

## CHAPTER 20

## Check It Again

When Gavin arrived back at Briarcliff Manor the next morning, he could smell bacon and syrup wafting from the kitchen. Chase's hair was pulled back in a ponytail, no make-up in sight, and she was jumpy, having already finished three cups of coffee. Gavin had long ago stopped telling her how beautiful she was without a stitch of make-up, because she refused to believe him, but he thought it every time he saw her this way.

As he entered the kitchen, Chase pointed at the tall wooden chair with two slats on the back and said, "Sit."

Gavin, feeling a big like a Golden Retriever, did as he was told and saw his first cup of coffee was already waiting. He gave Chase a look that said, *Go ahead. I know you have a plan, so hit me with it.*

Chase took a large bite of toast and jumped right in, "Remember the snowmobile falling through the ice, back in Vermont? Of course, you do—you were there chasing after it. Anyway, I'm thinking this could be the same thing, sort of."

Gavin took a drink of his hot coffee and spoke for the first time this morning, saying, "Explain what *sort of* means?"

Chase continued. "I saw something in that church window back in Manchester that warned me the snowmobile and the rider were in danger, that they might fall through the ice. And it turned out to be true. I think it's happening again here. Not the same way, but kind of the same, me getting a warning, a premonition."

Gavin understood where she was going, so he replied, "Go on."

Chase then, "The words I kept getting last night in those Scrabble pieces were bar, rake, bake, break, and brake. And as we discussed over pizza, I don't go to bars, I don't bake, I don't need a rake or to take a *break,* so that leaves us with the spelling that means a BRAKE that stops something. And what has brakes?"

Gavin, following along, replied, "A car."

Chase, "Exactly, but that's not all. Trucks have them too. Like your pick-up truck."

Gavin reached over for a piece of slightly burnt bacon, placing it on his plate and said, "So you're worried my brakes are going to fail or something when I'm going down a hill?"

Chase then, "A hill or highway or wherever. Yes, I am worried about that, and not just you."

Gavin was curious, "Who else?"

Chase slid over a piece of paper that had a long list of names in black ink, "I was working on this while you slept. Obviously, we need you to get your brakes checked and Matthew, my driver. But I was also thinking of a few people back in Vermont, my mom in Seattle, of course, um, Raylan at the café, Deb, Oscar too, although I'm not sure he even has a car."

Gavin thought a moment and said, "And you plan to call them all and warn them something might happen?"

Chase corrected him, "Called, past tense, as in I already did it. At seven a.m."

Gavin shook his head, looking somewhat displeased. "*CHASE,* you must have woken people up and worried them with this."

Chase felt defensive at his comment, responding sharply, "Hey, these are the people I care about, and you were the one last night who said I can't ignore this stuff and, I might add, pointed out that all the messages in the past helped someone. So . . ."

Gavin could see she was getting annoyed, so he reached for her hand and said, "No, you're absolutely right. You can't mess around with this. Whatever it is, you did the right thing."

As Gavin took another bite of bacon, Chase said, "I called Nick Hargraves, the groundskeeper, and he told me he does his own brakes on his pick-up, you know, instead of a repair shop, and he said he knows his brakes are fine. As a favor, he's coming over this morning to check your truck."

Gavin smiled and said, "Man, that guy is a jack of all trades."

Chase continued: "And Matthew promised me he'd take his car directly to the BMW dealership that's like two blocks from his place in Manhattan, so he's covered."

Scooter scratched at the back door, letting them know he needed to go out and do his business. As Gavin opened the door, he glanced out toward the rock wall, and sure enough, the small yellow rose was gone as usual.

He turned to Chase and said, "You know I'm a patient man, but this rose thing is driving me crazy. At some point I'm going to have to sleep in the yard by that rock wall and see who takes that flower and why."

Chase joined him by the window, resting her hand on his shoulder, and said, "I'll be honest, it's driving me nuts too. Someday we'll figure this vanishing rose out and the rest of it."

Gavin replied, "Oh, you mean the window that can't be washed and the yard that can't be dug. Have we considered the possibility that the old man who left these rules was cuckoo and we are idiots for playing along and acting like the FTD florist every night?"

Chase looked away from the yard and back at Gavin saying, "Cuckoo enough to give me a mansion that's got to be worth, jeez, I don't even want to think about it."

Gavin seemed lost in thought, and then said, "Hey, something just occurred to me. The taxes on this have to be in the stratosphere. I wonder if you have to pay them."

Chase looked back out the window at the rock wall and said, "Maybe some money will suddenly appear on the wall where the rose was and pay them for me."

Gavin laughed and replied, "Wouldn't that be nice."

Just then a knock on the front door sent Scooter scrambling around the outside of the house.

It was Nick, the groundskeeper, saying, "I need the keys to the truck to check the brakes."

Gavin scooped them off a small table by a coat rack inside the front door and handed them over, prompting Nick to say, "I have no clue why you folks need your brakes checked this early in the day, but I'm here, so just give me a half hour or so."

Chase watched as the old man drove one side of Gavin's truck up on a metal riser that acted like a jack. Nick then proved he was doubly smart, taking a wooden block and jamming it against Gavin's back tire, making certain it couldn't move while he was underneath the two tons of steel. A moment later Nick got down on his back, facing the white December sky, and slid under the chassis.

Chase's grandmother Marge was fond of saying, "A watched pot never boils," so Chase stopped snooping through the front window and ran upstairs to take her morning shower. She figured by the time she got done, they'd have a verdict on Gavin's brakes.

Gavin was playing ball in the front yard with Scooter when, a short time later, Nick appeared to his left, his hands covered in dark grease.

He said confidently, "Your brakes are fine. Looking at the pads and rotors I'd say you have another eighteen thousand miles before you'll need to change 'em. That means you have more than a year before you'll need to worry about it."

Gavin saw Chase coming out of the house, wearing a pretty white sweater and a pair of Jordache jeans she found at a vintage shop in Boston, when he said, "We're all good, hon. No problems with the brakes. In fact, Nick says I've got at least another year before . . ."

Gavin couldn't finish that sentence before Chase cut him off, saying in a stern voice to Nick, "Check them again."

Nick, wiped his dirty hands on his pants, gave a loud sniff as if fighting an early winter cold, then said, "Miss, I just checked. He's fine."

Chase looked at the truck and said, "You checked all four tires? All four brakes? The brake lines, everything?"

Nick nodded, "Yes, ma'am. As you can see from the grease, I really got in there, and his brakes are fine. I promise you."

Gavin looked at Chase and shook his head in the affirmative, "I think we're okay, love."

Chase walked over and put her arm around Gavin, giving him a hug, turned her eyes back to Nick and said, "I appreciate you getting up and coming over here so early to do that dirty work."

Nick bowed his head and said, "It's no trouble, Miss Chase. I'll just grab my tools and be on my way."

Chase then, "One last thing, Mr. Hargraves."

He looked into her normally warm, beautiful eyes and saw they were hard and intense at this moment, as she said, "Check them again."

With that she turned and went back into the house, patting her leg, a sign to Scooter that she wanted his company for a while. The dutiful pup obliged, picking up the green tennis ball he'd been playing with and followed her into the house.

Gavin shot Nick a look, and said, "I'm sorry. I know this seems nuts. I swear I do, Nick. But please just do as she asks."

Nick could tell something was happening that he didn't understand, but he had lived long enough to know what it looked like when someone was scared, and there was no question, what he saw in Chase's eyes was fear. This young woman who had moved into his old friend's house was on edge about something this morning, so he let out a sigh, got down onto his back, and disappeared once again under Gavin's truck, as ordered.

By lunchtime not only had Chase heard from Nick, twice now, that Gavin's truck was safe, but also her phone had rung a half dozen times, and every person she alarmed with her early morning call was happy to report that the brakes on their vehicles were all fine as well. Matthew called, asking if Chase needed a ride into the city, but she told him that she and Gavin had plans to visit the nearby village of Sleepy Hollow and Gavin could drive his truck.

Chase devoured books as a child, and one of her favorite writers, Washington Irving, used to live a stone's throw from Sleepy Hollow, New York. His legend of the headless horseman was must-reading when Chase was a teen, and she wanted to visit the places Ichabod Crane would have frequented had he been real.

In Irving's world the characters and scares were all for fun, and Chase thought that right about now, something *make believe* sounded good for a woman who just lost another night's sleep worrying about Scrabble pieces and mysterious messages that even Einstein couldn't decipher.

*Brake, break, give me a break,* she thought. What Chase didn't know, what she couldn't know yet, was something frightening was coming, and it was anything but a work of fiction.

## CHAPTER 21

# So Glad You Came

Two days had passed since the odd incident with the board game. Everyone's brakes checked out fine, and nothing bad happened on their trip to Sleepy Hollow. The small town was anything but *sleepy* this time of year; it was all decked out for the upcoming holiday.

Gavin could see his sweetheart had been on edge for the last 48 hours, worried something bad would happen, so as they sat outside, enjoying a cup of hot chocolate with marshmallows on the front steps of the beautiful mansion, he said, "Looks like this time was a false alarm, eh?"

Chase looked over at the neighbor's property and saw Charlie riding her horse, Hermione, with her new puppy, Bella, walking right alongside and her tutor, Mary, close by, and replied unconvincingly, "I guess so."

After a slight pause she added, more positively now, "Which is fine with me. We've had enough excitement, don't you think?"

Gavin didn't answer, knowing that was a rhetorical question.

"So, what does my handsome boyfriend want to do today?" she asked with a smile.

Gavin stopped her there and said, "Don't you remember I promised to help your driver, Matthew, move something today, in the city?"

Chase bit down on her bottom lip and said, "Oh, rats, that's right. What time is that?"

Gavin pulled out his phone and scrolled through the text messages. "I'm meeting him at eleven a.m., but he told me it shouldn't take more than an hour. After that, I'm all yours."

Chase asked, "What are you moving, anyway?"

"Beats me," Gavin responded. "All I know is it's very heavy and he needs a truck to take it a few blocks away."

Chase reached over to touch Gavin's thick, long hair and said, "Want some company?"

Chase then batted her eyes for dramatic effect, adding, "I ask because my favorite nail salon in the whole wide world is down in Soho. We can go after you help Matthew."

Gavin replied, "And what exactly am I doing while you're getting your nails done?"

Chase blurted out, "You can get a pedicure!"

Gavin, right back at her, protested, "Ewwww, I am not letting a stranger touch my feet."

Chase again: "Fine, then, you can wait patiently outside to take me to lunch after. Tribeca Grill is only a few blocks from there."

Gavin frowned, as he said, "Why am I always the one sitting in the truck?"

Chase leaned in close now, "Oh, come on, babe, bring me along. I promise that later you'll look at me and say, 'I'm so glad you came.'"

Gavin smiled. "How could I say no to that face? Sure. Let's go."

Chase walked Scooter over to Charlie and asked Mary to sign a question: would she mind watching the pup for a couple of hours as Chase and Gavin went into the city? Bella, the deaf puppy, gave Chase her answer when she jumped up on Scooter's back and slobbered him with kisses.

Matthew lived in a section of Manhattan called *the meat packing district*. It got that moniker from days gone by when this section of the Big Apple housed a number of very busy meat packing plants. Today, there were a few of them left, but it was mostly filled with high-end restaurants, shops, and loft apartments tucked neatly in hundred-year-old brick buildings. Matthew's was ten stories high and was dwarfed, immediately to its south, by the skyscrapers that were home to Wall Street and the financial district.

As Gavin pulled in front of Matthew's place, their eyes drank in all the retail shops located just steps away: jewelry stores, banks, restaurants, a dry-cleaner's, and a dance studio. And right on the first floor of his building was an accountant you couldn't miss, *ROBERT RAKER CPA.*

The accountant had two signs, one made of wood, painted forest green with raised gold letters that advertised the accountant's name. It hung from a small pole that jutted out from the building, making it hard to miss for people walking up and down the sidewalk. The other was a large neon sign, with identical lettering, that hung in the front window facing the street. The neon letters were dark because the office was closed, but you could still read the accountant's name.

Gavin spied both signs and said jokingly to Chase, "If we need help with our taxes, I'll bet Matthew can hook us up."

Chased dismissed the humor, instead asking, "Why aren't you parking?"

The entire street in front of the shops and Matthew's building was marked "No Parking."

Gavin pointed at the bright red and white sign and said, "They don't mess around with No Parking zones down here. They'll tow me in a heartbeat."

He added, "I don't see anything close, and since we'll be carrying something really heavy, I think we'll have to leave the truck out front. Would you mind putting the flashing lights on and staying with the vehicle? If someone comes along and gives you a hard time, just drive around the block."

Chase replied, "Sounds like a plan. You go and I'll stay with the truck."

As Gavin got out and was heading toward the front door, Chase yelled after him, "Don't hurt yourself lifting anything. Remember, we have plans for later."

She winked, causing Gavin to wink back and flash that charming smile of his.

Chase put the radio on and looked around, noticing several of the businesses were not open yet.

She watched as the woman in the dry cleaner's unlocked her front door and flipped the *CLOSED* sign over to read *OPEN*. A steady line of people was going in and out of the Starbucks on the corner, and just to her left was an older gentleman, well dressed, sitting in a small chair in front of his jewelry store. This busy street reminded Chase a lot of her old neighborhood in Manhattan, Lenox Hill, offering so many options for spending your money.

Gavin went into the building and found a quaint lobby, with white marble floors and dark wood walls. A large grandfather clock stood watch in the corner, keeping the time. On the wall to Gavin's left was a row of brass mailboxes, each with tiny windows allowing a tenant to peek inside. It was typical of New York City, seeing a random building with such unexpected details hiding inside. It's what made these old buildings so great, he thought.

To Gavin's right were two elevators. One was the normal kind you'd find in any building in America, perfect for shuttling people up and down. Farther down the lobby wall was a freight elevator, a large metal contraption that looked more like a torture device than a mode of transportation. It had a steel door that housed a see-through cage. Inside this ancient contraption there were no buttons. Instead, it had a lever that you'd crank left or right, indicating which floor you need to travel too.

Gavin had never seen an elevator like this, outside of those old black and white movies his father was fond of watching on *Turner Classic*. Before heading up, he noticed something else too. Taped to the front of the freight elevator was a piece of cardboard with three large words printed in magic marker: DO NOT USE.

Gavin took the advice and rode the modern elevator up to the top floor, where Matthew was already waiting by his open front door.

"What's up, amigo?" Gavin offered, as a friendly hello.

Matthew shook his hand and replied, "Thanks for helping me out. I can't move this thing by myself."

The two walked into the spacious apartment, and there, in the center of one room, was the item that needed transport.

"What the heck is that?" Gavin inquired.

Matthew was used to the question, answering, "It's a late-nineteenth-century authentic butcher block."

What Gavin was looking at was a large square piece of wood that was two feet deep and four feet in length and width. It was solid as a rock.

Gavin was intrigued, saying, "So this is an original butcher block from more than a hundred years ago. Cool."

Matthew agreed, "Yes, cool and heavy. A normal butcher block is about 250 pounds. This one is double that weight. The steel rack that holds it is more than a hundred pounds just by itself."

Gavin squatted down, looking at the butcher block from below, then asked, "So where's it going?"

Matthew responded, "There's huge meat facility a few blocks from here. They sell choice cuts to most of the high-end restaurants in the city. I know the owner and asked if he wanted it, to display in his lobby."

Gavin nodded. "Makes sense. So, you need me to help you get it downstairs and into the truck."

"Exactly," Matthew replied. "It's tricky to move, but if we both put our legs into it, I think we can get it onto this dolly and wheel it into the elevator."

It took three attempts for the men to lift the heavy block of wood and rack, slamming it onto the dolly. It made such a loud thud that Gavin was certain it might buckle the wheels and render the device unable to roll. They then leaned hard into the handles to get the dolly moving, and slowly made their way to the outer hall.

Just as Gavin saw in the lobby, there were two elevators to choose from; the modern elevator that carried people and the freight elevator collecting cobwebs. Again, just as he saw downstairs, a white piece of paper was taped to the door with the words DO NOT USE.

Matthew had never used the freight elevator and couldn't recall the last time he even saw it moving, although he was certain the maintenance man did operate it from time to time. He pushed the button on the regular elevator and waited patiently with Gavin.

"You a Giants fan?" Matthew asked, trying to fill the silence.

"Um, no, Patriots. Being from Vermont we tend to follow the Boston teams," Gavin replied with a smile.

More silence, then Matthew said, "I can't thank you enough for doing this, Gavin."

"No problem, Matthew," Gavin responded, "Happy to help."

The elevator made a *ding*, and although the doors were closed, both men could hear laughter from within. When the doors opened there were a half-dozen college kids on board, and one of them, wearing a baseball cap backwards, looked at Gavin and Matthew and said, "This isn't the lobby."

Both men could see the butcher block wouldn't fit in the elevator with this crowd, so they stood motionless as the elevator doors slowly closed. The two gave each other a look that said *kids*, and both let out a sigh knowing it was going to take a while for that car to stop at each floor on the way back down and then find its way back up.

"I've waited ten minutes for an elevator in the past," Matthew explained, "It's the only thing that stinks about living on the tenth floor. I usually use the stairs."

Gavin tapped the butcher block with his hand, and said, "Yeah, I don't think that's an option."

Matthew laughed and replied, "Ha, no way."

Gavin pointed to the freight elevator and asked, "Does that work? I mean, I think this the kind of thing a freight elevator was meant for, right?"

Matthew couldn't argue with the logic and responded, "I think it does. I know there are signs all over telling tenants not to use it, but I think that's so the maintenance guy can get where he needs to go."

Gavin thought a moment and said, "There's an easy way to find out. If it's *out of service*, they'd cut power, right?"

Matthew walked over to the freight elevator and pushed the button on the wall just to see what would happen. Without hesitation, the air was filled with the sounds of the metal machine coming to life.

"See, it does work!" Gavin said happily.

Downstairs, still parked in front of a sign that said *NO PARKING,* Chase sat patiently with her lights flashing. She watched customers go in and out of various shops, as the late morning sun was just starting to creep over the building tops and warm the busy street. Up ahead she saw a policeman approaching on foot, and Chase said out loud, "Oh crap."

The fifty-something man in the NYPD blue uniform found his way to Chase's truck, looked at the plate, then smiled warmly and waved hello through the windshield.

Chase knew what was coming next, so she rolled down the window and offered her explanation: "My boyfriend is helping a man upstairs move something super-duper heavy. That's why I'm parked here. If you need me to move it . . ."

The cop shook his head and said, "No worries. If there was an emergency you're right there behind the wheel, so you're fine. You don't plan to be here all day, right?"

Chase replied, "God no. They should be out any second."

With that the officer moved on, giving her another friendly wave.

The streets were bone dry on 9th Avenue in lower Manhattan, something that was not the case a few days earlier when that minor snowstorm blew through. Chase remembered Matthew telling them about the snow on the roof melting and causing flooding in his building. What Chase, Gavin, and Matthew himself didn't know, was that for years water had been leaking into this old building and causing damage that no one could see.

Back upstairs the freight elevator finally arrived on the tenth floor, the steel door creaking open with a painful groan that reminded them of an old man trying to get out of a chair. Gavin and Matthew shifted their weight for better leverage and slowly pushed the butcher block into the center of the freight elevator. The exertion left both men wiping sweat from their brows and breathing heavily.

Before the elevator door shut, Matthew asked, "Hey, we still have a lot of lifting ahead of us. Do you want a bottle of water?"

Gavin nodded, "Yeah, that would be good."

The two men stepped out of the elevator car, Gavin standing in the hallway now, as Matthew ran back to his apartment to grab them both drinks.

Downstairs, Chase waited and watched and noticed an older gentleman in a nice suit making his way to the front door of Matthew's building. Just to the right of the main door was a separate door that led to the accountant's office, and the man was fiddling to get his key in the lock.

Chase looked up at his unlit sign and read it out loud: "Robert Raker CPA. You must be Robert. Can I call you Bob? Ya wanna check my deductions, Bob?"

With the windows of Gavin's truck rolled up, the man couldn't hear her joking, of course, but Chase had to do something to amuse herself.

She wasn't trying to be nosey, but through the CPA's large front window she could see the man toss his bag down on a desk and start turning on lights to begin his long day of crunching other people's numbers. *What a boring job,* she thought. Chase didn't know it, but her boredom was about to end.

Upstairs, Matthew returned with the bottle of Poland Spring water, handing it to Gavin, who then made a distressed face and said, "Don't kill me, but I think I have to use the bathroom really quick. Do you mind?"

Matthew had just locked up but tossed Gavin the keys and said, 'No problem. It's the first door on the left after the living room. Just do me a favor and lock it again when you leave."

Gavin went back into the apartment to take care of his business, while Matthew stepped just inside the open freight elevator, leaning on the large wooden block and drinking his water.

Downstairs, Chase was still watching the accountant set up shop for the day, and after finally getting situated in his seat, she saw him smack his forehead with an open palm. It was the kind of thing a person does when they realize they've forgotten something. The man then got up and walked toward the front window and reached for a small silver chain that was dangling there. He gave it a hard pull and the neon light advertising his business came to life.

Only it didn't, not even close. Chase saw, as is often the case with old neon signs, the bulbs in many letters had burned out and didn't light at all. So instead of ROBERT RAKER CPA, blinking on and off in bright red, Chase saw the O,E,R,T were missing in his first name, the R,A,R stayed dark in his last and the CPA had just the A lit up. His name was easy enough to read when the sign was off, but when it blinked on, the letters looked like gibberish.

A loud bang pulled Chase's attention to her left, where she saw a delivery man had slammed his truck's back door a bit too forcefully, startling Chase. *Why so jumpy? Everything is fine*, she thought.

Chase looked around some more and saw two men sitting on a front stoop laughing. Across the street, a young mother was pushing her newborn in a pearl-white baby carriage. There was more foot traffic in and out of Starbucks.

But as she occupied her mind with these random strangers, there was suddenly a sour feeling in her stomach, telling Chase something was wrong. She had an instant sense of dread, but no clue why. Everything was perfect on this beautiful December morning in lower Manhattan, except it wasn't.

*Look back, look back,* her mind nudged, *you saw it even though you don't realize it. Look back!*

"Look back at what?" Chase said out loud to herself, trying to tamp down this feeling of malice.

Then, she did as her mind instructed, and looked back at the front of Matthew's building. It was exactly the same. There was still no sign of her boyfriend or driver, and everything about the structure appeared precisely as it was twenty seconds ago.

Inside the accountant's office she saw the same man, now with his head down working on a computer. She relaxed her gaze and noticed the man's broken neon sign blinking on and off every few seconds. The missing letters were still missing, his name was mangled beyond repair, the O,E,R,T was gone in ROBERT, the R,A,R was not lit up in RAKER, and only the A was blinking on the very end.

Every four seconds when the sign came to life and blinked, this is what Chase saw: R B     K E     A

Chase just stared at it, still not seeing what her subconscious clearly could. Then she closed her eyes and imagined those letters in that exact order on a Scrabble board R B     K E     A.

Her mind started moving them around, the way you would playing the game, and that's when she finally caught it. Those exact letters, in different order, spelled the word BRAKE.

All week long she had been worried about everyone's cars and trucks. Now, here she was, outside of Matthew's building, and the word was staring her right in the face in bright red neon: BRAKE.

Her eyes traveled up the building and everything looked fine, so why did she know in her heart that it wasn't? *Gavin and Matthew* leapt to her mind.

Chase knew they were moving something heavy, and cars weren't the only things that had brakes. Chase grabbed her cell phone and dialed Gavin's number, but her heart sank when she heard his phone ringing on the passenger seat next to her. She punched in Matthew's name and hit "send" only to have it bounce directly to voice mail.

Chase kicked open the truck's door and jumped out. She started sprinting toward the building, with the vehicle still running, when the police officer she had spoken with a moment earlier bounded out of the barber shop and yelled, "HEY, YOU CAN'T LEAVE IT THERE LIKE THAT."

Chase didn't hear a word the cop said, ripping open the building's front door so hard it nearly shattered the glass. Her first instinct was to go to the elevator and hit the buttons to see where the car was at this instant. The numbers above lit up, revealing it was on the third floor and not moving. She quickly noticed the freight elevator to the left, and despite having a large DO NOT USE sign attached, the numbers above indicated the car was on the tenth, Matthew's floor. She placed her hand on the steel cage and felt it vibrating, meaning someone was using it.

*STAIRS*, her mind screamed, as she saw the door to the right. Chase was always impressed when, once a year, firefighters would raise money for the 9-11 charity by running up one hundred flights of stairs in full gear. Chase wasn't carrying a hose or an ax but a heavy heart that was about to break if she didn't make it in time.

On the tenth floor Gavin locked the apartment door and was slowly returning to the elevator to ride down with Matthew and his 500-pound antique.

Matthew was still inside the open elevator door, leaning back on the wooden table, when he saw Gavin meandering down the hall. He tapped his wristwatch impatiently and said, "Let's go, let's go. Times a-wastin', young man."

Gavin deliberately started walking in slow motion to tease Matthew and said, "Oh, did you mean don't walk like this?"

As the two let out a hearty laugh, the fire escape door crashed open and Chase fell to the floor in a heap. Covered in sweat, her hair down in her face, and completely out of breath, she screamed, "GET OFF THE ELEVATOR."

Matthew stood frozen and confused. All he could think to say was, "Chase?"

But he wasn't moving. *Why wasn't he moving?* Matthew just stood there inside the elevator, unaware of the danger.

Gavin was ten feet from the elevator when Chase crashed through the fire escape door, falling face down on the dirty carpet. After screaming at Matthew, her eyes met Gavin's and she looked frantic, wondering why Matthew just stood there, not moving.

She screamed at Gavin now, "BRAKE, BRAKE, BRAKE," pointing back to Matthew who was still standing inside the elevator car with the heavy butcher block table right behind him.

Gavin only needed a half-second to understand Chase's warning, lunging at Matthew and grabbing the front of his jacket with both hands, clenching his fists tightly around the material. He then yanked him backwards as hard as he could, causing both men to tumble on to the hard floor just outside the elevator car.

Chase and Gavin stared at the elevator door still open, the butcher block table idle inside. They watched and waited when . . . nothing happened. Nothing.

Matthew was rightly startled, and pushed Gavin's hands off of him, saying, "What is wrong with you?"

Gavin didn't know what to say, turning instead to Chase, his expression confused.

Chase was panting and tried to talk, still out of breath, "Downstairs, the accountant's sign, the one that lights up. Most of letters are off and only a few turn on. R-B-K-E-A."

Gavin wasn't following.

Chase continued, more insistent now, "BRAKE. Gavin, they spell brake."

Gavin nodded, finally getting it, as Matthew said, "A sign is broken, so you tackle me? So, you're both nuts then."

Chase and Gavin both looked at the elevator again and it seemed to be perfectly fine.

Just then the elevator doors closed on their own, the steel cage now shut tight, and the car began to rumble, announcing it was about to begin its painfully slow descent with the cargo.

"Oh great," Matthew said, annoyed, "Looks like the table is taking a ride down without us. Just great!"

It didn't move, though. The car just rumbled loudly as if waiting for someone to get on. It was as if the car were saying, *Come back in, Matthew, it's safe in here. Hop back in.*

Chase then gasped out, "Matthew, do you remember what I told you happened to me in Vermont, seeing things, *knowing things* ahead of time?"

Matthew, standing up now and dusting the dirt off his pants, responded, "Church windows, yeah, I remember. But we're not in church, Chase. Besides, what does that have to do with Gavin slamming me to the . . ."

Before the word *floor* left his mouth there was the piercing sound of steel cables snapping, and the freight car, with the heavy butcher block inside, dropped like a bag of soaking wet cement, disappearing out of sight.

Down in the lobby the police officer was waiting for Chase to return, to give her a piece of his mind, when he felt the building start shaking and heard a rumbling sound that was growing louder. It sounded like an angry animal charging toward them in the dark. The officer had no idea what it was, but he could tell it was coming from the elevator shaft and coming fast.

Instinctively, he screamed at a young couple standing in the lobby, "GET BACK."

Just as the two of them made it to the front door, the freight car, with all that weight and in a free fall, slammed into the ground floor like King Kong pounding his fist, causing pieces of the metal cage to shoot forward recklessly into the now-empty lobby. By some miracle, no one got hurt, but the force of impact managed to split the butcher block in two. If the fall did that to a solid 500-pound piece of wood, the officer couldn't imagine what would have happened had people been on board for the deadly ride down.

It turns out, the snow that melted on the roof, causing a leak inside Matthew's building a few days earlier, had repeated the same ritual hundreds of times over the past decade. Snow. Melt. Leak. Snow. Melt. Leak.

That dripping water didn't just leave a stain on the ceiling in Matthew's apartment, it also trickled down onto a mechanism called a *shiv* that sits above the freight elevator. That shiv holds in place the various cables that allow an elevator to go up and down, and after years of rust, it finally crumbled.

All that freight elevator needed was the right amount of weight to cause the mechanism to snap and send the car falling. The emergency brakes that all elevators have had long ago stopped working, which is why the city inspector had taken the freight elevator out of service years ago. DO NOT USE, on all the signs, did not mean it was frowned upon if tenants rode in that old clunky deathtrap. It meant, DO NOT USE, as in EVER.

Back upstairs, Gavin, still on his hands and knees from when he pulled Matthew out of the elevator, slowly crawled across the floor like a soldier ducking enemy fire. He reached the place where the freight elevator used to be and stuck his head into the dark shaft and looked down into the vast emptiness. Smoke and dust started billowing up from the ten-story drop, causing him to pull his head back out of the hole. Gavin looked up and found Chase's grateful eyes, saying the first thing that came to his mind: "You were right. I'm so glad you came."

CHAPTER 22

*Finding Time*

Acopy of the police report, via the insurance company at Matthew's building, blamed the elevator mishap on damage to the mechanism over time, and a building inspector who failed to do his job. Once the inspector had deemed that freight elevator unsafe, he should have cut the power so it couldn't move or tempt anyone to ever use it. The doors also should have been padlocked shut to keep people out.

The drive back to Briarcliff Manor was quiet as a church on Monday morning, Gavin and Chase both processing what had just happened and secretly worried about what might happen next. Back in Manchester, when Chase received messages through Tiffany glass windows, there were only four of them, so that strange adventure had a defined beginning, middle, and end. But this? The wooden tiles from an old board game had endless possibilities that neither of them wanted to entertain.

As Gavin's truck pulled in front of the mansion, he and Chase caught a glimpse of their young neighbor, Charlie, laughing and running between their two homes. Right on her heels were Chase's dog, Scooter, and Bella, the deaf pup that Charlie had adopted a couple of weeks prior. While elevators seemed to be dropping out of the sky in Manhattan, here in Briarcliff Manor, all was perfect in the world.

"Hey, Charlie," Chase yelled, as she waved.

Charlie and the dogs came over to the front of the house, as Mary the tutor came running from the barn with something in her hand.

"He forgot his present," she said to Charlie, holding a small white rawhide bone.

"Oh, I'm sorry, we probably should have asked first. Is Scooter allowed to have bones?" Mary asked Chase.

Chase looked at Gavin with a confused expression and replied, "I can't say if he's ever had one. I'm sure he'll like it, though."

With that, Mary gave it to Charlie, who turned toward Scooter, got him to sit, and then handed him his prize. The bone was bright white and about a half-foot long. At first, Scooter chomped on it, but then ran in a circle, not certain what to do with his unexpected gift. Suddenly, the dog looked around the yard and then darted over to the large maple tree out front.

"He must want to chew it in privacy," Gavin observed.

Chase turned to Charlie and said, "Thanks for watching him while we were gone."

Charlie, using sign language, replied, "We love Scooter; he can visit anytime."

As Mary, Charlie, and Bella turned to go, Gavin said, "Look at that. He buried it."

All of them looked toward the large maple tree, its bright red leaves long gone, replaced with a light coating of snow, and saw Scooter kicking dirt onto his buried treasure.

"He must be saving it for another day," Mary said.

Chase smiled and added, "Must be."

Mary and Charlie returned to their home, but as Chase and Gavin walked toward the front door of the house, they both noticed Scooter had something shiny in his mouth.

"Whatcha got there, boy?" Chase inquired.

The dog pranced over proudly and dropped it at their feet.

"Is that . . .?" Gavin asked, without finishing the question.

Chase bent down and scooped it up. "Holy moly. It's a Rolex."

It looked weathered, but the band was still gold, and the glass on the face was dirty but in excellent shape.

"Can I see that?" Gavin asked, taking it from Chase's hand.

He walked over to his truck, opened his glove compartment, and took out a packet of sanitized wipes. He pulled one out and started rubbing it on the watch, and in a matter of seconds the Rolex looked good enough to put in a display case at a jewelry store.

Chase was trying to make sense of this. She looked at Scooter and asked, "Where did you get this, buddy?"

The pup could only wag his tail, not understanding the question. At the same instant, Chase and Gavin both turned their heads toward the maple tree where Scooter had just been digging.

Chase said to Gavin, "Remember the letter that was left for us? The rules."

Gavin replied, "Don't dig under the maple tree in the front yard. Exact words."

After a long pause, Gavin added, "Why? Because you might find expensive jewelry. This house just keeps getting stranger and stranger."

Chase didn't respond, instead walking slowly toward the tree and the spot where Scooter had just buried his bone.

Gavin, anticipating what she might do next, said, "Chase, he was clear in the letter, don't dig!"

She turned with a sarcastic look, holding up the Rolex, and said, "It's a little late for that, Gav."

Together, they knelt, using their hands to pull away the loose soil that Scooter had just overturned. They quickly found his bone and handed it back to the pup, who promptly walked off looking for a better hiding place.

Below the spot where the bone was, Gavin saw something else shiny and another small item that was dark in color. He gently cleared the soil away to reveal a silver Timex watch and a black Bulova with a leather band.

He looked up at Chase in astonishment, and said, "I'm going to grab a shovel."

By the time he'd gone a foot or so down, Gavin retrieved eight watches total. All were of different brands, styles, and costs.

They took them to the kitchen, and, using soap and water, gently cleaned each timepiece. As Gavin would get one showroom ready, Chase was pulling up that exact model on her computer to reveal how much it cost. Some were worth as little as fifty dollars, but a Cartier they unearthed was valued at $11,000.

"This is insane, right?" Chase asked Gavin.

As he held three of the watches in his calloused hands, Gavin replied sarcastically, "In a house with vanishing flowers and talking board games? I'd say it's par for the course."

The two of them fixed a late lunch of tomato soup and grilled cheese, as the watches sat lined up on the kitchen counter.

Gavin was dipping his sandwich into the soup, when Chase suddenly grabbed her phone, scrolled through the contacts, and hit "send."

"Who you calling?" Gavin asked.

Chase just raised her eyebrows, an expression that told Gavin, *Oh, you'll see.*

An older woman answered, but Gavin didn't recognize the voice, causing him to move closer to see Chase's iPhone. Two words in all caps: STONEWALL JACKSON.

"Ah," Gavin said with a smile. "Brave."

Putting the phone on "speaker," Chase didn't beat around the bush. "Ms. Jackson, it's Chase Harrington, the one who bought the estate at Briarcliff. We found some watches buried in the front yard and I'm wondering if you could tell me why they are there?"

There was a loud sigh into the phone and then, "Didn't Nick the groundskeeper give you a letter with the rules?"

Chase confidently replied, "He did, and we are following them to the letter. We place the roses on the wall every night, we don't wash that one window and we never dig near that tree, I promise."

Ms. Jackson then, "And yet here you are calling me about the watches."

Gavin jumped in: "The dog did it, ma'am."

For some reason just saying those words out loud made Gavin laugh.

Stonewall heard the laughter and said, "And we think all this is amusing, do we?"

Gavin again, "No ma'am, sorry ma'am. I laughed 'cause it sounded like Chase was saying the dog ate my homework or something. Truth is, our dog was burying a bone and decided to dig in the exact spot where the watches were. None of this happened on purpose."

Another pause, then from the phone, "And I suppose telling you to go bury them again and forget you ever saw them won't quite do, correct?"

Chase then answered nervously, "We'll do as you ask, ma'am, but I'm curious if *you* know why they are there."

More silence followed, and then finally through the speakerphone came the words, "Fair enough, young lady. Go to the library in the house and find a novel called *Somewhere in Time* by Richard Matheson. You'll find what you're looking for in that book."

With that the phone went dead.

Gavin took a last bite of grilled cheese and tossed it to Scooter. He and Chase shared a quick glance, then both took off like school children in a foot race, down the hallway toward the library, giggling with every step. Chase had the lead before Gavin grabbed her by the belt loop on her jeans and pulled her back, allowing him to be first through the door.

"Cheater," Chase laughed, as she spilled into the room right behind him.

There had to be five hundred books spread out over two dozen shelves.

"You start on the right, me on the left, meet you in the middle," Gavin suggested, as if the two were on a treasure hunt.

Both began scanning the endless books and titles, which were arranged in absolutely no order at all. A biography, next to a book on engineering, next to something from Nicholas Sparks.

"GOT IT," Chase screamed, before snatching the book down.

She looked at the cover and then flipped it over, saying, "I knew it. I knew I'd heard of this."

Chase took a seat on the chair next to the desk, then explained what she meant.

"When I was a little girl my mom loved a romance movie with Christopher Reeve, you know, the guy who was the original Superman."

Gavin nodded, "Okay."

Chase continued, holding up the book now. "It's a story about a guy who was so in love with a woman's photo that he figured out a way to travel back in time to be with her. The movie had a terrible ending, but it was a beautiful love story. This must be the book it was based on."

Gavin replied, "Stonewall Jackson said the answer to your question about the buried watches was in this book. Are you supposed to read it?"

Chase cracked open the novel, and out fell a small white envelope that landed on the floor.

Gavin spoke: "Ah, when she said the answer was inside the book, she meant literally."

Chase opened the envelope, finding a short, handwritten note that read,

*Hello stranger,*

*If you are reading this note, one of two things has happened. You were going through my books and found it by accident, or someone told you to look in this specific book. If I was right on the first part, I strongly encourage you to put it back on the shelf and forget about it.*

*If someone sent you here, well then, that's a whole other kettle of fish. It means you found my watches. Let me end the mystery for you.*

*Many years ago, when I started to amass my fortune, I spent every waking hour at work wanting more. More money, more deals, more things to buy.*

*On my forty-second birthday, my wife Vida gave me a very expensive Cartier watch and had me try it on. I loved it. She then told me to take it off and she took it out into the front yard and buried it under the maple tree.*

*She told me my business had become more important than her or our marriage, so I wouldn't need a watch ever again. I could just stay at work and not worry about coming home. Can you imagine hearing those words from someone you love?*

*Seeing the hurt in her eyes broke my heart. That moment and every moment after, I told her I would put her first, and no matter what was happening at work, I was home for supper every night by six.*

*I probably missed out on some big financial deals, but I never regretted putting my sweetheart first.*

*In the years that followed, Vida would give me a new watch on my birthday, and we'd bury it together, with the promise to always put each other first.*

*I don't know how many watches you found, but if you dig around that old tree, I imagine you'd come up with quite a few. I can't tell you what to do with all those watches, but I'd leave them in the ground as a reminder of a man who lost his way and learned the true value of time.*

*I hope you're enjoying my home. It's a special place. Love grew here.*

*Sincerely,*

*Sebastian Winthrop*

Chase was moved by the letter and sat still a moment, thinking about the old man's words.

She let out a large breath, as if all the emotion were running out of her, causing Gavin to say, "You okay?"

Chase didn't answer, instead walking toward the front door, opening it, and letting the cool December air wash over her face.

Gavin joined her, looked out into the yard, then asked gently, "You want me to bury the watches again?"

Chase turned and gave him a deep kiss, pulled back from their embrace, and replied, "I do. And I need a favor."

Without hesitation, Gavin responded, "Anything."

Chase smiled and looked down at Gavin's left wrist and the old Casio timepiece that rested there.

She looked up and said with a wink, "Give me your watch."

As Gavin knelt under the maple tree returning the watches to the exact spot where Scooter had found them, Chase was fifty feet away, near a small pear tree, with Gavin's watch in one hand and a small garden tool in the other.

Gavin, realizing what she was about to do, called out, "Why?"

Chase turned, and as the late-day sun glimmered off her auburn hair, she shouted back, "Because love grows here."

## CHAPTER 23

## *Serendipity*

"Penny for your thoughts?" Gavin asked, as he pushed his foot, which was keeping warm in a red wool sock, against Chase's feet on the other side of the couch. Neither one could tell you why, but they loved sitting on the opposite sides of the furniture and pressing their feet together. It was one of those silly little things that made them a couple.

For ten minutes, Chase was staring off into nothing while Gavin was scanning the channels on the television with the remote, looking for a movie to watch.

"Just a penny? My thoughts should be at least worth a nickel," Chase teased.

As Gavin continued channel surfing, Chase added, "I guess I'm thinking about love."

Gavin looked over with a smile in his eyes as he said, "Ours? Yes, it is the classic American love story. Boy meets girl. Boy chases girl. Girl sees strange things in windows and game pieces and starts predicting the future and then moves into a big mansion, where they bury watches and play midnight florist."

Chase laughed out loud. "We are ridiculous, aren't we?"

Gavin reached over as far as he could to take her hand firmly. "I like our flavor of ridiculous."

Chase replied, "Me too. OH, WAIT, go back."

In Gavin's haste changing channels, he passed a movie Chase loved. "Cusack, John Cusack. You know the rules," she added firmly.

Gavin let out a sigh. "I know the rules: we always stop and watch a film if John Cusack is in it. What did you see?"

He clicked back three channels and she yelled, "THERE." It was a romantic comedy called *Serendipity*.

Gavin looked at the screen for a moment and said, "Ah, isn't this the one set in Manhattan where he loses her and in the end she shows up at an ice rink with a missing scarf?"

Chase nodded. "It's a glove, actually, but good memory. Keep it on."

As the familiar movie played out to a perfect happy ending, Chase said, without taking her eyes off the screen, "When I said I was thinking about love, I didn't mean just us. I was thinking about Raylan and Bonnie."

Gavin hit the mute button and shifted his body to face Chase. "I thought they both told you to butt out."

Chase shrugged her shoulders. "Yeah, technically they did, but I have a nose for this stuff, and I can tell they both like each other. A LOT. So . . ."

Gavin interrupted. "So you're *not* going to listen and stick your nose into it anyway."

Chase moaned, then replied, "Geez, when you say it that way . . ."

Gavin knew Chase well enough to know he couldn't stop her, so he asked, "So what's the plan, cupid?"

Chase replied, "If we're being honest, I think the problem is Raylan's scar on his face. He won't pursue anyone because he thinks all they can see is the scar. And I think if Bonnie could look past that imperfection, if she could see him how he used to be and really still is . . ."

Chase stopped talking and disappeared in her head again.

Gavin interjected, "Chase? You were saying."

Chase jumped up and snapped her finger. "Where's my phone? I have an idea."

She darted across the room to grab her phone off the charger, punched in a name, and said to Gavin, "You'll think I'm crazy but just don't say a—Matthew, hi, it's me."

She had her driver on the phone. The two hadn't talked much since the elevator dropped. She thought it wise to let that day's drama process a bit with Matthew.

Chase continued. "Matthew, you're a retired NYPD detective. I have an odd question. Do you still have access to DMV records?"

Gavin stood up now, confused over where this was going.

Matthew, on the other end of the phone, replied, "I have friends who do. Why? Did someone hit your truck or something? You need to run a plate number?"

Chase hesitated, then said, "No, nothing like that. What I'm wondering is, can you access an old driver's license photo of someone from years ago. Not the one they use now, I mean one when they were younger?"

Matthew thought a moment and replied, "I'm sure old photos still live somewhere in the system. But Chase, I have to ask why."

Chase walked out of the room so Gavin wouldn't hear, raising her hand like a stop sign, so he wouldn't follow.

A minute later she came back into the room and found Gavin sitting upright on a chair with his arms folded, and asking, "What are you up to?"

Chase replied, "Rather than me tell you, let me do my match-making, and if all goes well you can come along for the big moment. Okay?"

Gavin let out a deep breath and said, "Whatever you say, my love, I just hope you know what you're doing."

Chase looked down at her phone and said, "Me too. But it's worth a shot. I have three calls to make. One to Raylan, one to Bonnie, and one to Serendipity."

Gavin looked confused, "The movie we just watched?"

Chase replied, "No, goofball, the place. Serendipity is an actual restaurant only a few blocks from Raylan's café in Manhattan. Home of the famous *frozen hot chocolate*. Anyway, I want to book a table for two for tomorrow night."

Gavin was more confused than ever, but with Chase he knew sometimes he just needed to trust her.

Because Bonnie was the head of the *Lonely Hearts Book Club*, Deb at the café had her number tacked up behind the counter. She gave it to Chase without hesitation and then put Raylan on the phone, as instructed.

Chase's conversation with Raylan was simple and direct, "I've never asked you for a favor, but I need you to do something for me, please."

He just nodded and agreed. Chase's call to Bonnie went exactly the same way.

The next evening at seven o'clock sharp, Raylan arrived at Serendipity on East 60th Street and was led to a table where Bonnie was already seated. He approached with a surprised look, and after an exchange of "hello's," it was clear both had no clue why they were there.

"Are you here to meet me?" Raylan asked cautiously.

Bonnie looked down at her hands resting on the table and said shyly, "I don't know. Chase, who used to live above the café, asked me to come here and said it was important."

Raylan, uncertain whether to even take a seat at the small table, looked to his right and saw a photo of actors John Cusack and Kate Beckinsale, neatly framed and on the wall next to Bonnie's chair.

Then a voice said, "This is where they sat, John and Kate, when they shot the movie here."

It was Chase, standing with Gavin near a door that led to the kitchen. "I phoned the owner and explained what I wanted to do, and she told me she'd reserve this table for the two of you. Raylan, please sit and I'll explain."

Raylan looked uncomfortable as he slid into the chair, and his eyes met Bonnie's, saying, "So you had no idea?"

She shook her head no. Both then looked up at Chase with expressions that said *Well? Explain yourself!*

Chase looked at Gavin, regretting this whole escapade already, then pressed on. "You're both wondering why you're here. Well, I think you two like each other and neither one will admit it, so I wanted to put you together on a date."

Both squirmed in their chairs uncomfortably as Raylan said, "I asked you nicely, Chase, to stay out of it."

As Bonnie looked away with embarrassment, Chase produced a small white envelope from the back pocket of her jeans and decided to finish what she started.

"I'm just gonna say it. I think Raylan's scar, which he got saving a life and defending this country, by the way, is the only thing that's keeping you two apart."

She then handed the envelope to Bonnie adding, "I wanted you to see Raylan as he was, before the injury, so maybe you could see him, more clearly, as he is."

Raylan looked at Chase, confused, wondering how she could have gotten a photo of him from before the war. Bonnie opened the envelope slowly, slid out the 3 x 5 image, and it was Raylan, a good ten years younger, with his perfect, unscarred face. He reminded her of Mel Gibson when he was young. Everyone held their breath a moment, watching Bonnie's eyes. Even customers at other tables nearby had stopped their conversations and were looking over to see what would happen next.

Bonnie gently placed the photo back in the envelope, slid it across the table to Raylan, and said, "This is not what I want."

Bonnie got up, pulled the strap of her red Brighton bag off the back of her chair, slid it over her shoulder and said, "I'm sorry. If you'll all excuse me."

No one spoke as Bonnie quietly left Serendipity, her eyes on the floor filling up with tears with each step. Raylan took the photo out of the envelope and was looking at the man he used to be.

Without looking up, and in a surprisingly timid voice, he said to Chase, "I asked you to stay out of it. Maybe now . . ." He didn't finish that thought. He didn't need to.

Gavin stood there, dumbstruck, uncertain what to do or say, so he gently put his arm around Chase and said, "Let's go."

Chase turned to leave and whispered, "I'm so sorry. I should have listened."

As the two of them left and Raylan tucked the old photograph into his jacket pocket, everyone in the restaurant thought for certain the man with the scar on his face had just been rejected. They couldn't have been more wrong.

## CHAPTER 24

# Mirror, Mirror

Nick Hargraves, the groundskeeper at Briarcliff Manor, found Chase sitting on the rock wall behind the house, looking as if her best friend had died. She had the yellow rose in her hand, the one she'd place on the wall each night, only to find it gone with the sunrise.

"You okay, young lady?" he asked softly, sensing, by the look of her, any loud noise might make Chase crack into pieces.

"Yeah, I'm just the fart at church today," Chase replied.

The expression made the old man laugh out loud, as he replied, "Excuse me?"

Chase continued. "You know the expression, something went over like a fart in church?"

Nick scratched his favorite red baseball cap. "Can't say I know that one. It doesn't sound good, though." He sat down on the rock wall next to her.

Chase put the rose down beside her and said, "I was trying to play matchmaker for a friend last night, and it blew up in my face."

Nick paused a moment, thinking, then asked, "Not a good match then?"

Chase: "Nope. And I think both people are pretty mad at me now."

Nick asked, "So they told you they don't like each other and wondered why you tried to put them together?"

Chase thought a moment and responded, "No, not exactly. He, the guy, said he didn't want me helping his love life, and the woman said it was not what she wanted."

Nick continued, "So, she did say she didn't want the man, whatever his name is?"

Chase corrected him, "No. She never actually said that. She said she didn't want *this*, while holding a photo of what the man used to look like. Raylan, his name is Raylan."

Nick then asked, still a bit confused, "And he doesn't look the photo anymore, this Raylan? Did he get old or fat or something?"

"Hmm," Chase replied. "More *or something*. He got hurt in the war, so he looks different now. Different but the same, it's hard to explain. All I know is I meant well, and I screwed it up."

Nick smiled. "Like a fart in church?"

As Chase stood up to go, Nick added, "Did I never tell you about my eyes?"

Chase shrugged her shoulders, "Nope. I think I'd remember that."

Nick patted the stone and motioned for her to sit, so Chase rested back on the rock wall again.

Nick began, "About five years ago I was having trouble seeing, so I went into the city to get Lasik eye surgery to fix it. It was going to be expensive, about five thousand bucks."

Chase was curious where this story was going, so she added, "Okay, and?"

"And so, the doctor does all these tests, and I can tell, by his reaction, something is really wrong. He says, 'Mr. Hargraves, you have a tear on your retina and cataracts in both eyes. That's why you can't see right.' "

Chase replied, "Oh my, I'm so sorry. How awful."

"That's what I thought, Chase," Nick continued. "Until I saw a specialist and he said he could do a surgery on both eyes and fix me good as new."

Chase nodded, "And did he?"

Nick, "He did, but here's the kicker. Lasik surgery was considered optional, almost cosmetic, so my insurance wouldn't pay a dime. But, because my eyes were so messed up, it was a required medical procedure, and it was covered by my insurance. So, it cost me nothing."

"Oh, so you saved that five grand you would have spent?" Chase asked.

"That's exactly right. My point is, sometimes what you think is bad news is good news."

Chase just paused, and both were silent a moment, when Nick added, "You said your lady friend looked at an old photo of this Raylan guy, who was hurt and looks different now, and she said it wasn't what she wanted. Maybe she wants him the way he is now."

Chase considered the old man's words and replied, "You're saying she loves the broken version of the man? Scars and all?"

Nick stood up and retrieved a shovel that was leaning against the rock wall, adding. "Nothing wrong with scars, young lady. Show's you've done some livin."

As Nick walked away to go back to his work, Chase called after him, "Can I tell you something, Nick? You're pretty smart for a groundskeeper."

He turned with that half-crooked smile and shouted back, "And you're not so bad for a fart in church."

Chase left the rose on the wall and returned to the patio where Gavin was waiting outside with Scooter. She could see he was talking to Mary, the neighbor, and young Charlie.

As she grew closer to the group, Gavin said to Chase, "You wanna play dress up?"

Chase could see Charlie smiling, her brown eyes waiting for Chase's response.

Mary said, "I was just telling Gavin that Charlie's birthday is next week. Christmas isn't that far off, so we're having a big party right next door at Charlie's house in three days."

Chase smiled. "Parties are fun, but what did you say about dressing up?"

Charlie started signing, as Mary interpreted. "Charlie is saying that on Halloween she had a cold, and it was raining so her parents wouldn't let her trick or treat. When they asked if she wanted a big birthday party, Charlie asked if people could dress up, kind of like Halloween, just for fun."

Chase looked at Gavin, who shrugged his shoulders in a *hey, why not* kind of way, then she looked at Charlie and said, "We'd love to come to your party. Can I invite some friends?"

Charlie nodded as Chase turned to Gavin and said, "We wanted to have a holiday party anyway, to see everyone. This is perfect."

Gavin smiled and agreed, and Charlie started running back toward her house to plan.

Once she was out of earshot, Mary said, "She's made so many friends now at school, since getting Bella. Her parents thought this might be a nice way to get them all together. I'm sorry about the costumes. I know that's weird for a party in December."

Chase interrupted, "Are you kidding? We'll have fun."

Gavin wondered, "So with this cold December air, they're doing it all inside, I assume, in Charlie's house?"

Mary replied, "Oh God, no, her parents have more money than the Rockefellers. They're bringing in huge, heated tents, a heated bounce castle, a hall of mirrors, and another tent just for food and games. This is a big deal."

"Sounds like the party of the season," Gavin replied.

Mary looked at her watch and said, "I gotta go. Hey, listen, invite whomever you want. The more the merrier. Costumes are optional but encouraged."

With that, Mary scooted back over to the neighboring property, as Chase pulled out her phone and said, "I have some calls to make. Maybe I can get Matthew to rent a big SUV and drive the gang out."

Gavin wondered, "The gang?"

Chase continued, "Nick told me sometimes when things look bad, they're actually good. And this party idea is good. I think maybe I was looking for Lasik when all along something else was needed."

"Lasik? Huh?" Gavin said confused.

Chase took his face in her hands and gave him a hard smack on the lips. "You'll see."

Three days passed quickly, and Chase, Gavin, and the others she invited from the café all scrambled to find costumes to wear to Charlie's party.

When Chase dressed as Dorothy from the Wizard of Oz, Gavin jumped at the chance to go as the Scarecrow. Deb went as the cowardly lion and Raylan completed the ensemble looking exactly like the tin man.

Raylan's costume was silver from the tips of his toes to the top of his head, with a thin metal mask covering his entire face. Raylan liked costume parties because he could easily hide his scar.

Oscar, the kind man who helped with the dogs, came dressed as a medieval knight. All of them piled into a large Lincoln Navigator that Chase arranged for Matthew to drive, taking the group of friends out to the country.

When they arrived, they weren't halfway down Chase's driveway when they heard music booming from the large tents behind Charlie's house. There had to be more than a hundred people in attendance on that chilly December day, with adults hanging around the food tent and the children attracted to the rides and games. More than a dozen of Charlie's classmates came with their parents, all dressed up and having a blast.

It was the first opportunity Chase had to see Raylan since the debacle at Serendipity, so she walked over holding Gavin's hand and said sheepishly, "Hey, you look great. I know you're not supposed to have a heart in there, being the tin man, but if you do, I hope you can find it in your heart to forgive me for the other day."

Raylan raised the mask, revealing his real face, and said, "Nothing to forgive. I know you meant well. It's done. Let's not worry about it."

Chase nodded in agreement, and just like that, the awkwardness between them was gone. She cared for Raylan and was happy her misstep hadn't caused real damage to the friendship.

"I'm going to check out the rest of the party," Raylan said, as he peeled off and walked toward the tents filled with games of chance.

A moment or two later, a female voice from behind called out to Gavin, "Excuse me. Mr. Scarecrow, can you tell me which way to the wizard?"

It was Bonnie, dressed like a flight attendant.

Gavin smiled and said, "Hey, yourself. I love the outfit, spot on."

Bonnie looked down at her uniform and said, "It should be—it's real."

Chase replied, "You're a flight attendant, for real?'"

Bonnie replied, with a smile, "Fifteen years with Southwest."

Chase smiled back. "I had no idea. Good for you."

Chase then added, "Thank you for coming to the party."

There was an awkward pause when Chase said, "I'm sorry about the other day. I didn't mean to . . ." With that, her voice drifted off.

Bonnie leaned in closer, whispering now, "Yeah, you did. You were trying to get us together. I wasn't mad at you, Chase."

Gavin, sensing the two needed privacy, said, "I'm gonna go grab some lemonade and chat with Oscar. Be right back."

Once Gavin walked away, Bonnie continued, "Your instincts are right. I do like him, a lot. And I think he likes me. But I'm not so sure he likes himself."

Chase reached for her arm and said, "He does, he does, he just, you know . . . the war."

Bonnie met Chase's kind eyes and said, "I understand, but I can't chase after him. That's not how this works. Not for me."

Chase for the first time really understood why the two of them weren't together, and said, "I get it and I agree. I do. I guess you'll have to wait and see when he's ready."

Bonnie then said, "In the meantime, do you want to go grab something to eat and find your boyfriend?"

As the two ladies started walking toward the food tent, some children came scampering from the left side of the property, running away from the rides and games. The kids looked upset.

A parent Chase didn't know asked a little girl, "What's wrong, sweetie?"

The child turned and pointed toward the house of mirrors and said, "There's a strange man in there, staring at himself."

Another parent heard her and said, "Is it like a haunted house? Maybe it's part of a show or something, dear."

The child replied, "No. We called out to him and asked if he was okay. I'm not sure he could even hear us."

Chase then asked, "What does he look like, hon?"

The child said, "He's tall with all silver on and he has a big scar on his face."

Chase said under her breath, but loud enough for Bonnie to hear, "Raylan."

Chase's first instinct was to run into the house of mirrors, but as she started to move, Bonnie took her arm firmly and said, "Let me go."

Bonnie walked the forty paces to a small structure not much bigger than a mobile home. One side was marked *Entrance,* the other *Exit.* A larger sign on the house of mirrors announced *Prepare To Be Amazed.*

Bonnie slowly entered the house and was immediately greeted by a glass maze. Some of the mirrors made her look tall and thin, the others short and stout, or they squished her face into an odd shape. *Kids love this kind of stuff,* she thought.

She carefully made her way through the hall of mirrors until she reached a large circular room at the center. There she found Raylan, just as the children described, standing still, his silver tin man mask dangling in his right hand, his eyes transfixed on the mirrors in front of him.

At first, Bonnie couldn't tell what Raylan was staring at, but as she inched closer, she saw it. The menagerie of mirrors directly in front of Raylan took the left side of his face and flipped it to the opposite side. So, as Raylan looked directly into the glass, his own image was staring back, but the scars were completely gone. Because his left side was on both sides, his face looked normal again, the skin smooth, his features as handsome as they were the day he dove into a burning vehicle to save a stranger long ago.

Raylan rarely looked at old photos of himself before the accident, before he was burned, because they revealed what he *used to* be. Now this image staring back showed Raylan what he would look like today if he had not traded half his face for another man's life. It was odd seeing himself this old and yet whole again. He knew it was an illusion, yet still he couldn't look away.

That's when a familiar and loving voice broke the spell: "I told you that's not what I want."

Raylan turned away from the mirror and saw Bonnie with tears in her eyes. For the first time in a long time, he really looked at her. Bonnie was in her late thirties, carrying the few extra pounds everyone tries to lose at that age. The wrinkles were just starting to creep around her eyes, her short dark hair hinting at the gray that would inevitably come. She never had the face of a runway model, but she was pretty, and Raylan wondered more than a few times what it would be like to caress that face and hold her in his arms.

Raylan took a deep breath and replied, "What do you want, then?"

Bonnie crossed the twelve steps between them and gently placed her hands on Raylan's face, her fingertips lightly touching his scar. "I want this, you idiot. I've always wanted this."

Chase and Gavin stumbled around the corner, bringing themselves to the center of the house of mirrors, just as Raylan put his own hands on Bonnie's face and drew her in close for a soft kiss.

The tin man mask fell to the floor as Chase put both of her hands over her own mouth, trying to stifle the gasp that revealed her joy. Gavin grabbed hold of her hips and silently pulled her away, giving the two lovebirds privacy.

As they left the small house of mirrors, Gavin realized that while Chase was most certainly a fine writer, her real gift was in helping people. She was the rarest find a man could hope for, because seeing others happy brought her more joy than anything she could want for herself.

As they walked hand in hand back toward the crowded party, Gavin paused, then looked up at the clear starry night and realized something else too. He was going to ask Chase to marry him, very soon. But there was something he wanted to show her first. A place she'd love, where Chase would not only shame the angels, but where the heavens above look down with wonder.

CHAPTER 25

## *Money over Memories*

The morning after the party, Chase assumed, would be a quiet one. Gavin had already gone back to Vermont to help his dad on the farm for a couple of days, so it was just Chase and Scooter wandering around the big old house. She noticed the rose was gone again from the back wall, while her pup was busy sitting just outside the room where they kept the board games and those strange messages had appeared.

She walked past Scooter, pulled Scrabble off the top of the pile, and said, "What da'ya say, champ? You want to play? You've been quiet since the elevator scare."

The dog, looking unamused, got up and walked down the hallway in silence, causing Chase to say, "Alrighty then."

As Chase tossed the box back on the shelf, she heard the doorknocker bang.

*Nick the handyman?* She wondered as she marched back toward the front of the house. Once she pulled the heavy wooden door open, she was greeted by an unfamiliar face. The man was in his early forties, dressed in a jet-black three-piece suit with shoes so shiny you could comb your hair in the reflection. She also spotted a brand-new Bentley automobile idling in her circular driveway, a man with a chauffeur's outfit and matching cap, still as a statue, behind the wheel.

"Excuse me for the unannounced visit. I'm Clayton Philmont, and I'm looking for Chase Harrington," is how the man in the suit began.

Chase, wearing an oversized flannel shirt and faded jeans, replied, "You found her."

Clayton continued, "I'd invite myself in at your request, but it's such a pleasant morning—might we converse on the steps of your portico?"

Chase replied, "My what?"

The stranger gestured with his hand like a game show host showing a contestant the car they may win, repeating, "Your portico, this area right outside the door."

Chase possessed a strong vocabulary, but even that one threw her, responding, "Sure. Why not. How can I help you?"

Clayton then, "You're a writer, correct?"

Chase replied, "I am."

Clayton, "Well let me employ a catchphrase of your occupation and say I don't want to bury the lead."

Chase understood him this time adding, "That's a newspaper term, meaning you want to get right to the point. So?"

Clayton produced a single sheet of paper, folded in three, from his inside breast pocket saying, "I'm here to buy your house. I've taken the liberty of having three independent assessors estimate the value of the home and land, and all are within a few thousand of each other. I'm prepared to pay the highest one and add five percent as a sweetener so we can hurry this along."

Chase took the document from Clayton and could immediately see all three appraisals were in the millions, and each started with the number four.

All she could do was stare at all those zeros, then ask, "Who are you again?"

He replied, "Clayton Philmont. I was planning to buy this house at auction, and then that incredible turn of events happened with you buying the sketch, and well, here we are. It's your lucky day, though. I'm here to make you rich. Looking at your outfit, it appears you could use the money."

Chase ignored the insult, instead looking over at the driver in the gas-guzzling car that was still running.

Chase turned to Clayton, saying, "You know about climate change and all, right? Could he possibly shut off the engine while we talk?"

Without hesitation the man in the natty suit called out, "Franklin. Kill the engine."

Just like that the car went silent.

"Thank you," Chase said, and then asked, "Can I ask you how you got my name? Everything with the auction was kept private."

Clayton shrugged his shoulders and said, "I could lie to you, but what's the point? I bribed a guy I know at Sotheby's to give me your name."

Chase nodded, a bit impressed with his ingenuity, and asked, "So how much is my name going for these days?"

Clayton leaned in, "Two premium tickets to the Met Gala next spring. That's worth about four thousand bucks."

Chase raised her eyebrows, "Wow, that's a lot of money for prime rib."

Clayton again, "Well, Celine Dion is performing, so there's that."

Chase nodded, adding, "Gotcha."

Chase then rubbed her hands together to stave off the cold and added bluntly, "I'm sorry you spent all that money and drove all the way out here, Clayton, but the house isn't for sale."

The obviously wealthy man walked away from her now, looking up at the roofline and windows, talking as he walked, "Oh, come, come now, everything is for sale at the right price."

Chase raised an eyebrow and followed after him. "Everything?"

Clayton then, "You know what I mean."

He then stopped snooping around the yard and turned back to her, "I looked into you. You're a writer who went to an auction and meant to buy an old sketch, nothing more. The rest was dumb luck. You're not from here, you have no family in Manhattan or Briarcliff, none that I could find, and so you have no attachment to the place."

Chase folded her arms a bit defiantly. "And you do? Have an attachment to this home?"

Clayton responded, "Oh yes, I've had my eye on this property for a decade, and when the old coot finally went, I mean when Sebastian Winthrop passed on to a better place, I planned to buy it."

Chase ignored his snarky insult to the previous owner and observed, "It's funny, I don't remember seeing you at the auction."

"I don't go to those things," he replied in a cocky tone. "I send someone to place my bid. If you saw someone with a cell phone pressed to their ear, that was me on the other end."

Chase looked back at the property and was thinking about all the things that had already happened in such a short time, and her new friends Mary and Charlie next door.

As she was lost in those nice memories, Clayton said, "I apologize if I come off a bit pushy. I just want what I want and I'm willing to pay you handsomely for it. Imagine what a young writer could do with all that money."

Chase turned to him, engaging his eyes, then asked sincerely, "And what about memories? The ones I already have here, the million more that I might make?"

Clayton took out his phone from his breast pocket, checking messages and sighing, indicating that this was already taking too long.

He then said smugly, "I'm offering money over memories. You'd be wise to take it."

Just then a familiar old truck, with rust holding the bumper together, pulled into the driveway. The groundskeeper, Nick, opened the door with a loud squeak, then slammed it shut. He peered across the lawn and was troubled by something he saw in Chase's body language.

Nick reached into the flatbed of the truck and retrieved a sharp spade used for stabbing weeds, and marched over with purpose, shouting, "Everything all right, Chase?"

Chase put her hand up, motioning him to stop his approach. "All good, Mr. Hargraves. All good. The gentleman is just going."

Clayton gave the old man with the garden tool a hard look and realized, despite his age, the groundskeeper looked like he could snap someone's leg like a rotted-out tree branch.

Sensing his welcome was well worn out, he retrieved a business card from the vest pocket and said, "Keep the appraisals, add five percent, and think about my offer. Here's my card."

She looked down and said, "I promise I'll think about it Mr. . . . Philmont?" Suddenly a memory nudged Chase. *Why do I know that name?*

She took on a blank look and her eyes were unfocused as she stared off in the distance.

"Are you okay, Miss Harrington?" the confused millionaire asked.

That's when it hit her: the story Raylan told her about the man he saved in the war, the one he dragged from the fire, his name was Philmont too. Paul? No. Patrick? That wasn't it. *PETER! It was Peter.*

Chase then asked, "Hey, you aren't from the Philmont family that owns the oil wells and stuff, are ya?

Clayton's eyes revealed the answer before he said it, "We are. Don't think about fluffing up the price on the house. A five percent markup is very generous."

"No, no," Chase replied, "That's not why I ask. Do you know a Peter Philmont?"

Clayton nodded and said, "There are two of them, a cousin and my brother."

Chase, not sure which was which, quickly said, "This one would have been in the war and almost got killed."

Clayton then smiled in a way that reminded her of a jackal. "Ah yes, that would be my good-hearted idiot brother."

Chase then, "Why do you call him that?"

Clayton responded, "An idiot for joining up to fight in a war he had no business being in and good-hearted because he wants nothing to do with the family business. He'd rather give his money away. Why do you ask? Do you know him?"

Chase's mind was racing with questions. Should she seize this unexpected opportunity and ask further about Peter Philmont or just stay out of it? The last time she stuck her nose in Raylan's business it didn't go so well.

*Oh, to heck with it,* she thought.

"No, I don't know him, but I'd like to meet him, and I'll make you a promise," Chase replied.

Clayton was intrigued, "Go on."

Chase, "If you introduce me to your brother Peter, I'll seriously consider your offer to buy my house."

Clayton glanced back at his phone and replied, "I'm running late, so walk me to my car."

As the two approached the expensive vehicle, Clayton said, "I can't promise you a meeting, but here's what I can do. I'll call him and tell him to expect you. I'll give you his address on Park Avenue, and if you can get by his doorman, you're in. Fair enough?"

Chase pondered the offer, then said, "So the doorman is tough, huh? Yeah, I'll take my chances. It's a deal."

Clayton took back the business card he'd just given Chase and wrote the address on the back of it. "I'll call him now and tell him to expect you. Good luck. You'll need it."

The Bentley, and the abrasive man with all that money, weren't fifty yards down the road when Chase texted Matthew in Manhattan and wrote, "Need you ASAP."

She wasn't sure if she'd sell the house or live there forever, but this was a chance to help her friend Raylan close that one final chapter that had been haunting him. Besides, Park Avenue was less than an hour away.

CHAPTER 26

## *Let It Be*

If the road to hell was paved with good intentions, the boulevard known as Park Avenue was lined with twenty-story stone buildings, with watchful gargoyles above and beautiful awnings below. Most were hunter green with large white numbers printed on the front, helping drivers find their destinations without delay.

"Are you watching for it?" Matthew asked Chase, as he slowly maneuvered down the opulent street.

"I am," she replied, her head craning out the window, the cold December air making her pay for not wearing a hat or scarf. "801, 807, there it is on the right, 813. Huh, that's funny," Chase added.

"What's funny?" Matthew asked.

Chase pointed at the awning. "My birthday is August thirteenth, eight-one-three."

Matthew ignored the coincidence as he pulled up front, saying, "They won't let me just sit, but I'll circle the block a few times until you need me."

"Roger dodger," Chase said, as she bounced out of her seat and shut the car door firmly behind.

Her eyes immediately saw the words *The Philmont* in raised lettering on the front of the building. It was clear this family had money to spare. Two impressive urns filled with evergreen branches stood like soldiers to the right and left of the large front door, as Chase reached for the brass handle and gave it a tug.

The lobby was small but well-appointed, with artwork on the walls and a checkered marble floor that shined as if someone waxed it every night while the millionaires slept soundly above.

To her left was a large desk that looked like a police command center. A walkie-talkie sat on top of the wooden counter, next to an old-fashioned phone, the kind your grandfather might have had back in the 1930s. A well-dressed man in a dark blue sport coat and white collared shirt buttoned to the top, sat directly behind the desk, his eyes on Chase the moment she entered his building. Behind him was a row of six television monitors switching automatically between a series of cameras that were strategically placed both inside and outside of the building.

"Help you, miss?" the man asked politely. Chase noticed he had a nametag on his right breast pocket that said Mel.

"Yes, thank you, um, Mel," she began, feeling nervous all of the sudden. Chase pressed on, "I'm here to see a Peter Philmont. His brother Clayton sent me and told me he'd call in advance."

Mel looked Chase up and down and thought she appeared harmless, but said, "Yes, well, he may have called but I can't send you up without announcing you and getting approval. You understand."

Chase nodded in agreement, "Of course, please announce away."

Mel grinned at Chase's good humor, then reached for the antique-looking phone and began pushing buttons, causing Chase to observe, "That thing still works?"

As the number rang, Mel glanced back at Chase and said, "It's new, actually. One of those re-creations, looks antique but it's no older than your socks."

He gave Chase a wink, causing her to giggle a bit, then spoke into the phone, "Yes, it's Mel downstairs. There's a . . ." he then looked over, waiting for a name to be offered.

"Oh, I'm sorry. Chase, Chase Harrington. Clayton sent me." Chased said encouragingly.

Mel repeated it louder into the phone, "A CHASE HARRINGTON to see you. Your brother said he called about this."

She could hear the muffled sounds of someone responding, but wasn't close enough to make out the words. Mel just kept nodding and saying, "I see. I see. Got it."

He then said to Chase, "Look up behind me above the monitors. Do you see that small camera? Look toward that for a moment."

Chase did as instructed. Clearly, they had a closed-circuit TV system so the tenants could see who was at the front desk before allowing them up.

Mel kept the phone pressed to his ear and said, "Understood." He then handed the phone to Chase saying, "He wants to talk to you."

"Hello," Chase said into the phone, making certain to keep looking at the camera so it felt like she was talking to someone.

A man's voice came over the phone softly, "Why is it you wish to see me, Miss Harrington?" His voice was so low, it was difficult to hear.

Chase swallowed hard and tried to say it exactly as she had rehearsed it in her head, "Well sir, I'm friends with a man named Raylan and he . . . I mean . . . he . . ."

Chase hesitated. *How do you just blurt something like that out?* She froze, not saying a thing.

"Hello, are you still there, Miss Harrington?" the voice inquired, a bit louder this time.

"Yes, I'm sorry, Mr. Philmont. Apologies, it's just a strange thing to say, so I guess I'll just say it. My friend Raylan, I believe, is the man who pulled you out of a burning vehicle in the war. Do you know what I'm talking about?"

There was a long silence, a good thirty seconds worth, and Chase called out more than once, "Hello? Sir, are you still there?"

She finally turned to the doorman and handed him back the phone, saying, "I think he hung up."

Mel put the phone up to his own ear, and after a brief pause the voice said, "Put her back on."

He handed Chase the phone a second time. She raised it up and said, "Yes?"

The voice again, still soft and faint: "What is it you want?"

Chase, feeling a bit more confident, replied, "I guess I wanted to see if you were the Peter Philmont my friend saved and if you were, I wanted to meet you. My friend Raylan lives not ten blocks from here, and despite getting hurt that day, he's doing well."

Peter Philmont's voice took on a more friendly tone now, "I am the young man he pulled from the burning truck. I'm forever sorry that he was injured saving me. I'm glad he's doing well. Can I ask *you* a question?"

Chase, looking back to the camera, "Yes, of course."

"Did he send you here to find me? Does he need my help in some way?" Peter inquired.

Chase shook her head, saying, "No, he doesn't need anything. I guess I just thought since you're both in Manhattan . . . Oh, I don't know."

Chase sighed then, wondering if this was a good idea after all.

Peter again, "Miss Harrington, does this Raymond even know you're here?"

Chase looked away now, like a child caught in a lie, responding, "It's Raylan, his name, Raylan, and no sir, he does not. In fact, he told me once he tracked you down, but he decided not to meet you in person, he just wanted to make sure you were okay."

Another pause and then, "As you can see, I am, okay as you put it, and it sounds like he's doing fine also. Perhaps, Chase—can I call you Chase?" Peter continued.

"Yes, of course," she replied.

Peter then, "Perhaps, Chase, you should respect your friend's wishes and just let it be."

Chase was the one being quiet now, wondering if she was trying to force something that neither man wanted.

"Chase, are you all right?" he asked, his voice fading again on the phone line.

Finally Chase responded, "I am, Mr. Philmont. You know, the last time I pushed something against Raylan's wishes it blew up in my face, so this time I'm going to listen and just, in your words, let it be."

Peter again, "I think that's best. And Chase?"

"Yes, Mr. Philmont," she replied,

"Sometimes things work out all on their own. You just have to trust the universe to sort things the way they are supposed to be sorted; do you understand?"

Chase smiled and looked back at the camera, unconvinced. "I'm not sure I do, sir, but I do know I'll have that Beatles song stuck in my head for the rest of the day."

Mel could hear laughter coming from the phone now as Peter concluded, "Yes, *Let it Be* is one of my favorites of theirs. You take care now."

With that the phone went dead and Chase handed it back to Mel. She looked at his name tag again and said, "You like Paul McCartney, Mel?"

The doorman looked around as if he were about to tell a secret, then said, "The early stuff, not so much later."

Chase nodded her head, "Me too, Mel. I hope they tip you well at Christmas."

The doorman smiled and said, "They do, miss, especially Mr. Peter."

With that Chase marched toward the front door and gave it a hard push; the last thing Mel heard was Chase singing to herself. Something about *whispering words of wisdom* as her lovely frame vanished from sight.

CHAPTER 27

*Charlie's Game*

It was mid-December in Manhattan, which meant the store windows on Fifth Avenue were decorated beautifully for the holidays. However, as Chase rode by, her mind was not on nutcrackers and gingerbread houses, but instead on her brief conversation with Peter Philmont. She asked Matthew his opinion, and he agreed that some things are better left alone. It was rare for Chase to let something go this easily, but this time she would listen to everyone's sage advice and drop it.

When her mansion pulled into sight, Chase noticed a small wreath with a red bow hanging from the black lamppost out front, and the simplicity of it made her smile. Chase wasn't one for gaudy decorations; she preferred modest and classy.

After kicking off her boots and hopping onto the warm couch in front of the fireplace, Chase's mind was on to other things, mainly Gavin and how he was acting lately. His glances were longer, his kisses were sweeter, and more than once if a commercial came on TV for a jewelry store, he'd casually ask again what kind of diamond she liked.

Chase told him the size or cut of the stone didn't matter, as long as it was Gavin slipping it on her finger. She still remembered the first time she ever laid eyes on him, opening a huge barn door in East Arlington, a tiny village just outside of Manchester, Vermont, that thick hair a girl could only dream of running her hands through pushing out from beneath a cowboy hat. It wasn't fair how good he looked that day, and just the memory of it made her tummy twirl the way it did that sunny afternoon long ago.

Chase was so lost in the memory, she didn't hear the light tapping on the front door. Scooter did, and it was his bark that shook her back to reality and sent her scurrying to see who it was.

"Hey, neighbor," Mary, the woman from next door, called out.

Chase smiled. 'Oh, hi, Mare, how are you? And hi, Charlie!" The beautiful child was tucked behind Mary just out of view. Charlie smiled, then used her delicate hands to sign *Hello* right back.

"What's up?" Chase inquired.

Mary bit her lip and made a face like someone needing a favor. "Can I ask you to do me a solid?" she began. "Charlie's parents are in Boston for a couple of days, and I need to run some errands that are not really fun for a little girl to tag along. I was wondering if you aren't too busy, can Charlie visit here for like ninety minutes or so?"

Chase flung open the large wooden door, "Of course, I'd love to hang with Charlie. She can keep me and Scooter company."

"You're a lifesaver, Chase, thank you," Mary responded, before making a dash for her car, the Burberry purse on her shoulder swinging back and forth as she jogged across the lawn.

Even though she lived right next door, Charlie had never actually been in Sebastian Winthrop's estate, so her eyes went wide as she walked in and saw all the beautiful stone, artwork, and furnishings. It was just then that it hit Chase: she didn't know sign language.

She knew Charlie could read lips, so she touched her on the sleeve and said, "Do you want something to drink?"

Chase motioned with her hand as if holding a glass, causing Charlie to smile and give her a thumbs up. *Maybe this won't be so hard after all,* Chase thought.

After pouring Charlie a large glass of ice-cold milk and placing a few Oreo cookies on a plate in the kitchen, Chase tapped Charlie's arm again and asked, "Do you want to do something fun?"

Charlie took a quick sip of the milk, nodded her head, and Chase led her to the room with the board games. Despite all the drama in the past, Chase figured it was safe to play one of the kids' games. Scooter tagged along, just to watch.

"How about this one?" Chase asked, holding up a game called *Chutes and Ladders*.

Charlie shook her head *NO.*

Chase pointed at Monopoly, followed by UNO and a game called Sorry, then Battleship, but again Charlie scrunched her face, looking like she'd just bit into a lemon.

It was clear the little girl didn't feel like playing *any* board games. As she took Charlie's hand to go back to the kitchen for her snack, Scooter walked by both of them, hopped up to the shelf and scratched his paw on the Scrabble box.

"Seriously, Scooter?" Chase asked her pup.

If dogs could smile, that's exactly what Scooter did, wagging his tail, then marching straight over to Charlie, giving her a bump with his body, as if to say, *Play this one, Charlie. It's FULL of surprises!*

Charlie patted the dog's head, then pointed at Scrabble, and nodded her head.

Chase reluctantly grabbed the game box, and the two of them sat down on the carpet, as a nervousness instantly filled the room. *What if something weird happens?* Chase thought.

The last thing she wanted was for any kind of strangeness to frighten this innocent child. Charlie pulled out the pieces and lined things up, making it obvious she had played Scrabble before. She took up the bag of tiles and gave them a shake, then urged Chase to pick first.

Chase's first seven letters were D B Z I Q V R.

After Charlie picked her own letters, she encouraged Chase to go first. Chase stared at the random letters a moment, then spelled the word B I R D.

Charlie went next and spelled the word C A R, and the game was off and running. To Chase's delight and surprise, nothing odd happened as they played. And with some carefully disguised maneuvers, Chase let Charlie win, without the child being any the wiser.

Happy with her victory, Charlie quickly grabbed a few tiles off the carpet and spelled two words: PLAY AGAIN. Her deep brown eyes looked up to Chase's, making it impossible to say no.

Chase smiled and gave her a high five, before they put all the tiles back in the cloth bag to give them another shake.

Charlie picked first and got several vowels, making it easy to spell a few words. Then Chase chose and her letters were E A D Y R I B.

Chase turned her tiles toward Charlie to show her and said, "I think you're in trouble this game, because I can spell lots of words."

Charlie looked at the tiles and asked, mouthing the words as she signed, "How many?"

Chase scratched her chin and said, "Let's see, I have BEAD. I have DEAR. I have BAD. What else? DAY, READ, BED, RED, READY, RIB, BID. Oh my, I have a lot, don't I?"

Charlie nodded with approval at Chase's good fortune, and then Chase looked for another moment, finally saying, "Hmm . . . I think that's all I can spell."

As Charlie was about to place her own letters on the board, she looked back at Chase's wooden tiles and then at Chase, holding up a single finger and then pointing it toward Chase's letters.

Chase said, "One more? Are you saying I have another word I didn't see?" Chase stared at the random letters and said, "I don't see it."

Charlie reached over and moved the tiles around, spelling B I R D. It was the same word Chase got on the first game.

"You're right, I didn't see that," Chase said, looking down at the word.

Chase didn't let on, but her first thought was, *Is this happening again?*

As Charlie began to play the game and place letters on the board, Chase interrupted, "Hey, can I do something really quick?"

Charlie shrugged her shoulders indicating, *sure.*

Chase then said to Charlie, "I'm not trying to cheat, I just want to see something."

Chase, remembering how certain words had repeated themselves in the past, pushed her chosen letters aside, picked up the bag of tiles again, and took out seven new ones: Q R D E I V B.

She just looked at them, not saying a word, and watched as Charlie's small hand reached over, slid the tiles around, and spelled out the word B I R D. Again!

Then the child put her right hand up to her mouth and nose, making the sign of an L, and suddenly closed the thumb and pointer finger together. She snapped them open and shut several times. It looked like the mouth of a baby bird opening and closing.

Chase smiled and asked, "Is that the sign for BIRD?"

Charlie took Chase's hand and showed her how to do it, nodding her head and silently mouthing, *YES, BIRD.* Charlie and Chase were both doing the silly sign in front of their noses, causing both to laugh.

Chase tossed the extra letters back into the bag, asking, "Do you want to finish this game or take a break and go get a snack in the kitchen?"

Charlie rubbed her hand on her tummy, indicating she was hungry. As they folded the game board and placed it back into the box, Charlie did the sign for BIRD one last time, causing Chase to say, "Yes, bird."

Charlie then spelled something with her hands that Chase didn't understand and started slapping the back of her own neck. Charlie could see Chase was confused, so she did it again, spelling something with her hands and touching the back of her neck.

Chase threw her hands in the air and said, "I'm sorry, I'm not following, sweetie."

Charlie shook the letters back out of the Scrabble bag and quickly spelled a name: OSCAR.

Chase looked down and said, "Oscar. You mean Oscar, my friend, the man who brought you Bella, that Oscar?"

Charlie nodded and then made the sign for a bird again and slapped the back of her neck.

Chase sat silently, trying to piece this together.

After Charlie did it a third time Chase said, "Wait. Are you saying Oscar had a bird land on the back of his neck?"

Charlie looked frustrated and shook her head *no* once again. There was a pencil in the Scrabble box for keeping score, so Charlie grabbed it. She then pretended to write on Chase's arm and made a buzzing sound. Charlie then pointed at Oscar's name in the Scrabble letters, did the sign for *bird*, and slapped the back of her neck. She did it twice and waited for Chase to solve this impossible puzzle.

Finally, Chase's eyes flew open as she asked, "Wait, are you trying to show me a tattoo? Is that what you're doing with the pencil? A tattoo?"

Charlie, reading her lips, shook her head yes and then did the sign for a bird again, pointed to Oscar's name in letters, and slapped the back of her neck.

Chase then, "Got it. Got it. You're saying Oscar has a tattoo of a bird on his neck."

Charlie smiled and gave her a thumbs-up sign.

Chase thought a moment then asked, "How do you know that? I've never seen it."

Charlie pointed to Scooter on the floor next to them and then she threw herself on the floor and rolled over like a dog. This caused Scooter to climb onto Charlie's back to play. After rolling on the floor for a brief moment, she popped back up and pointed at Oscar's name again in the wooden letters, then at the dog.

Chase asked, "Are you saying you saw it when Oscar was on the ground playing with my dog?"

Charlie pointed to her own chest.

"Your dog! When he was playing with your dog, Bella?" Chase added.

Charlie nodded her head again, *YES.*

Chase was nearly exhausted playing this game of charades, so she smiled and said, "Gotcha. Hey, let's clean this up and get that snack."

They finished putting away the game, and as Chase was about to leave the room and get Charlie those Oreos, a memory jolted her like a slap in the face.

"WAIT. WAIT. A bird? Charlie, what kind of bird is on Oscar's neck?"

Charlie thought a moment and then put two fingers together, almost crossed, right in front of her nose, making it look like she had a hooked nose.

Chase just stared, trying to understand, finally saying, "I'm sorry, Charlie, I don't know sign language. Is that thing you're doing with your hand a sign for a type of bird?"

Charlie, looking frustrated, took the letters back out of the Scrabble box and searched through them frantically for five specific letters. When she had them, she spelled it out for Chase to see: EAGLE.

Chase was staring off into a wall now, trying to unpack a memory from months ago, when Raylan told her the story about the day he was injured at war and the man he saved from the burning truck. There was one very identifiable thing that Raylan saw and would never forget, a tattoo on the back of the man's neck. A *screaming eagle*, he called it.

But this made no sense. Whatever Charlie saw, even if it was a tattoo of an eagle, it had to be some strange coincidence. Right? Chase was lost in thought when Charlie tugged at her sleeve, then rubbed her tummy again, reminding Chase of her promise.

"I'm sorry, sweetie, let's get you those cookies and milk." Chase said.

As the two started toward the kitchen, Chase turned back to Scooter who was still sitting on the carpet not three feet from the stack of board games, and said, "Troublemaker."

Once they were in the kitchen and Charlie was dunking her Oreos into the cold milk, Chase took her cell phone out and texted her friend and driver, Matthew, in all caps: TURN AROUND. I NEED YOU ASAP.

She hated making Matthew take her back to Manhattan on such short notice, but she needed to know if she was losing her mind. As Charlie sat at the kitchen island making cookies disappear, Chase knew in her heart that sometimes things were connected in ways we can't always see. She was 99.9 percent certain this wasn't what she thought it was, but she couldn't rest until she knew for sure.

## CHAPTER 28

# How's Your Brother?

Charlie's tutor, Mary, came to collect her an hour later, and Chase was a busy little bee as they waited. She called Deb at the Fur-Ever Java café in Manhattan and asked if she had a way to reach Oscar, the kind man who had brought Bella into Charlie's life. She did, telling Chase that when they had something special to donate to the homeless shelter, they'd call Oscar to come get it. Chase asked Deb to contact Oscar and get him to the café by 7 p.m., telling her only that it was for something important.

As she awaited her driver, Matthew, to come take her to the meeting, Chase called Gavin, who was back on the farm in Vermont, sharing her suspicion about Oscar and his hidden tattoo.

"Chase, I don't like telling you what to do, but the last time you made an assumption that involved Raylan it backfired and it could have cost you the friendship," Gavin said firmly over the phone.

Then he added, "If you do it again and you're wrong again . . ." He let that last part remain unsaid.

Chase nodded. "I know, hon, I know. But I have a way of doing this that doesn't show all my cards until I'm sure."

Gavin could only wish her luck as Chase hung up and opened Google on her smartphone. Chase had a hunch about the Philmont family and the voice on the telephone in that Park Avenue lobby who told her to let things be. She *would* let things drop, if that made sense, but right now, she needed to know more about this wealthy family and the son who was saved by Raylan. One good photograph of Peter Philmont would solve this one way or the other.

She searched the Philmonts and their story of oil and riches, scanning several articles for the better part of a half hour. There was a lot written about the parents and the grandfather, but very little about their three sons: Clayton, Peter, and Paul. It was clear from every article that Clayton, the oldest, ran the show, and that Peter had little to do with the company. The youngest, Paul, was also like a ghost, never mentioned unless there was a family photo at some event, and you saw his name in the caption beneath. Oddly, Peter was missing from almost every photograph.

The Philmont family was quite philanthropic, donating money to causes around the city. Chase saw an article about them giving $25,000 to start a community garden in the Bronx. Another had them building a new playground in Harlem. There was a nice photo of the family at a ribbon cutting at the Lexington School for the Deaf in East Elmhurst, New York, part of Queens. Clayton looked about twenty years old in the photo, standing next to his parents and a younger boy identified as Paul. The boy on the end was Peter, but he was no older than twelve, and the image not very clear, making it of little help to Chase.

A car horn beeped, and Chase jumped up and grabbed her purse, knowing she and Matthew still had an hour's drive before they'd reach the city. That gave her an hour to decide if she had the courage to follow through with what she was thinking of doing.

The ride to Manhattan was stone-cold silent, and Matthew, being a retired police detective, was skilled in reading people. He could tell Chase's mind was far outside the black BMW she was sitting in. He didn't say a word, only asking once if she was okay. To which he received a terse, "Sure."

When they arrived at the café on the upper East Side, Matthew decided not to stay in the car but to follow Chase in. He knew she wasn't in danger, but something told him to tag along just in case she needed his help. That's what made Matthew so much more than a paid driver to Chase. He was a friend who had her back even when she didn't ask for it.

The coffee shop was half-empty as the two entered. Chase saw Deb behind the counter, and Oscar was off in the corner playing fetch with the latest puppy visiting from the animal shelter. In between throwing the ball, Oscar saw Chase and gave her a wave, then went back to his fun.

"Coffee or water, Chase?" Deb asked kindly from behind the register.

"No, no thank you, Deb, I'm not here for that. I'm here for you," she added pointing over at Oscar. "You got a minute to talk?"

Oscar began a game of tug-of-war with the dog, calling back to Chase, "Sure, what's up?"

Chase realized the music in the café was louder than usual and might get in the way of her questioning, so she turned back to Deb, "Hey, would you mind lowering the volume on Josh Groban for a minute?"

Deb quickly obliged, realizing in that moment that no one had ever asked her to turn down the music in the whole five years she worked there. Something about Chase's voice when she asked made Deb turn it off completely.

"Thank you, dear," Chase said. Now she had the silence and the floor. *Are you SURE you want to do this?* was the last thought in her head before she began.

"Oscar, do you remember the day we met?"

Still playing with the dog, he said, "Sure, I was out back, and you brought me some treats to take to the homeless shelter."

Chase then, "That's right, and you were training a dog, who turned out to be Bella. The one we thought was named Ella."

Oscar thought a moment, then replied, "Right. That's right."

Chase continued. "And that day I asked you about your name. I said, so your name is Oscar? And you replied, 'That's what they call me.' Do you remember that part?"

Oscar, still not looking at Chase and playing with the pup, said, "Yep, that's right."

Chase, a bit sharper and louder now, "Only that's not really an answer, is it? *That's what they call me.* I didn't ask what they called you. I asked if that was your name."

The café fell dead quiet, and Matthew got uneasy standing by the door, enough so that he intervened. "Chase? What's going on?"

Deb repeated his words like a parrot. "What *is* going on?

Raylan was in the back office sitting at a small desk going over the monthly bills when he realized two things: the soft music that always filled his café was turned off, and he could hear someone, a woman, raising her voice. He got up immediately and went to the door, pushing through unnoticed by Chase and the others.

Oscar stopped playing with the dog, stood up, and asked in a tone matching Chase's, "Why do you care?"

Chase, a bit calmer now, replied, "Don't worry about my reasons. I'm just asking you what your real name is."

Oscar, feeling a bit on trial, responded, "Mark Retzlaff."

"Spell it," Chase asked.

Oscar now with a terse tone, "R E T Z L A F F. Do you need me to spell Mark?"

Chase again, "What do you do for a living, Mark, besides train dogs and collect empty bottles for nickels?"

Raylan hadn't said a word yet; he just stood, silently watching this inquisition.

Oscar replied, "I was a stockbroker."

Chase then, "Really. Can you tell me where the Dow or NASDAQ closed today?"

Oscar, without missing a beat, replied, "No, I can't."

Chase, "You trade stocks but you don't know where the Dow closed?"

Oscar again, "I said I *was* a stockbroker. I don't do it anymore."

Chase paused a moment, thinking of a new way to test his story, then continued: "If you were a broker, tell me the stock trading symbol for Proctor and Gamble?"

Oscar instantly, "PG."

Chase: "And Verizon?"

Oscar: "VZ."

Chase thought harder for something less obvious, "What's the trading symbol for Pfizer, the drug company?"

Oscar, "PFE. Are we going to play this all day? Please tell me if there's a prize at the end."

Raylan finally spoke. "What's going on out here?"

Chase ignored him. "Do you have any tattoos?"

Deb intervened: "That's kind of personal, Chase."

Oscar held his hand up as if waving her away, "No, it's all right, Deb." Then in a slightly sarcastic tone, he said, "Why yes, I do, Chase. I have two. Do you want the stock symbols for those as well?"

Raylan jumped in: "Chase, what the heck is going on?"

She continued to ignore all the others in the room, focusing only on Oscar. "No, I was just curious what they are."

Oscar replied, "There's a date tattoo on my left arm, up here, of a significant day in my life. And I have a small bird on the top of my back."

Raylan wasn't sure where any of this was going, but he continued to listen, along with everyone else in the café.

Chase asked, "What kind of bird is it? The one on the back of your neck?"

Oscar smiled. "It's an eagle. Any more personal questions? Or are we done for the day?"

Chase continued. "Why an eagle?"

Oscar right back at her, "My high school football team. The Cambridge Eagles. A bunch of us got them senior year without our parents' permission. I was grounded for two weeks."

Then in an angry voice, Oscar added, "Are we finished with the inquisition, Chase? Because this stopped being fun for me about five questions ago."

Chase looked at the faces in the café that were looking back at her, and every one of them was a mixture of confusion and dismay. Oscar was a fixture of this place and a good person. Why was Chase acting in such an aggressive, what some might call rude, way?

Chase read the room and decided enough was enough. "I'm sorry, Oscar, or Mark. I just was curious. I thought I knew something, but obviously I was wrong."

A wounded Oscar replied, "OBVIOUSLY."

Raylan finally spoke, "I don't know what this was about, you two, but let's have it be done. Chase, can I talk to you privately a minute? Now, please."

Chase looked at Raylan and could see he wasn't happy with her behavior, and said, "Sure."

Before she could move her feet, though, Chase remembered that every time some strange message had come to her in the past, it always had meaning and always came true. She stared at the floor, remembering what happened with Bella and then the elevator in Matthew's building and now this word BIRD, over and over again. It was Charlie, in fact, who raised this suspicion about Oscar. Yet he did have an answer for everything, so she must be wrong. Despite all evidence to the contrary, and the anger she felt in the room, something pushed Chase to ask one final question.

"Before we chat, Raylan, would Oscar mind if I ask one more thing?" Chase said sheepishly.

She then looked at Oscar, adding, "I promise, answer me honestly and I'll never ask you another personal question again. Ever."

Oscar let out a sigh and said, "Shoot."

Chase locked eyes with his and said, "I just wanted to ask you how is your little . . ."

Just then, Chase made her thumb and pointer finger on her right hand into an L, closing the remaining three fingers into a fist. Chase placed the thumb against her forehead and then brought the L down onto her left hand like a hammer. It was the sign for the word BROTHER.

She was asking Oscar, *How is your little brother?*

Oscar stood frozen now, not certain what to say.

Chase continued, "His name is Paul, right? And he's . . ."

With that she put her thumb in her ear with an open palm, the sign for DEAF.

Oscar didn't say a word. he just took two steps back and almost collapsed into a small wooden chair that sat next to an empty table. His face went blank.

Chase moved toward Oscar gently now, as if walking on eggshells and in the softest tone, "You told my neighbor Charlie that you learned sign language because your best friend growing up was deaf."

Chase's eyes were filling with tears now. "I think that's true. But he wasn't just a best friend, was he? He was your little brother, Paul, who you love dearly."

Oscar continued to stare, not saying a word.

Chase then, "I saw lots of photos of your family, but there was only one with both you and Paul in it. Your family was donating money to a school for the deaf in Queens. I'm guessing Paul went there and because you loved him, you wanted to be there for him that day."

Chase got down on one knee in front of Oscar, taking his hand in hers, "It's no wonder you worked so hard to help Bella and did so much for Charlie."

Oscar's eyes looked away, a sense of shame on his face.

Chase assured him then, "Please understand, I'm not here to hurt you; I just want you to stop pretending you're someone you're not."

He gave Chase a half-smile, then let out a large sigh as if the weight of the world had been taken off his shoulders, saying, "I'd like that too."

Everyone in the café continued to stare in silence, unclear on what was happening. Chase stood up, looked over at Raylan, who was watching quietly, and said, "Raylan, I'd like you to meet Peter Philmont."

Raylan turned his head toward the man he'd known for years as "Oscar," his face an expression of absolute bewilderment. He just stared, then finally asked, "Peter Philmont, from the war?"

Peter, the charade now over, stood up and faced Raylan and said, "Yes. It's me. And before you speak or get upset, please allow me to explain."

As a Marine, Raylan had trained himself how to control emotion and not overreact, so he summoned that ability as he slowly crossed the café floor and took a seat at the table near Peter, saying calmly, "I'm listening."

Chase stepped away, allowing the two men to have a conversation that took a decade to finally happen.

Peter started, "I'm not sure where to even begin. I guess the best place is the day we met."

Raylan interrupted, "Do you remember anything from that day, what happened?"

Peter continued, "Yes, parts of it. We were on forward patrol and there was an explosion. I was dizzy and confused and realized I was upside down in the truck. I also felt warmth on my leg, which I learned later was blood from a wound on my thigh. I knew I was in trouble but I couldn't get my hands to work, I was shaking so bad. That's when I felt someone grab hold me and pull me out. I was face down in the dirt so I couldn't see who had me, only that I was being dragged to safety."

Raylan nodded, "That's right. Anything else?"

Peter continued, "After I was patched up, I asked my commander to find out who saved me, and all I got was a name, Raylan. It's a unique name, not one you forget."

Raylan nodded silently then, "Go on."

Peter again, "They told me this Raylan was from another unit, a Marine, and he got burned pretty badly in the fire pulling me and my friend out."

Raylan touched the scar on his right cheek and just nodded in obvious agreement.

Peter continued, "I tried to find you at the camp medical tent, but they had already shipped you out to a real hospital. So, I tried to put it out of my mind, finish my tour, go home and return to my life. My family owns an oil company."

Raylan replied, "Yes, I know."

"But I couldn't go back to it," Peter continued. "My life before, I mean. After nearly dying that way, I had no interest in running an oil business. We were already rich—what was the point?"

No one interrupted, so Peter continued, "I'm not a religious man, Raylan, but I do believe in God and I figured he wanted me saved from that truck and fire for some reason, and it wasn't to sit in a board room and count stacks of money."

Chase finally spoke, "So what did you do?"

Peter spoke in a much friendlier tone to Chase now. "I started a charitable foundation at the company, and we awarded grants all over the city to needy causes, giving money to places like the school where my brother went. You were right about that, by the way; he spent six years there."

Everyone was silently listening, so Peter continued, "I helped the homeless shelter around the corner from here. I didn't want them knowing I had money or treating me different, so I went there dressed down, like this, my Oscar outfit, you could call it. When I saw the good work they did, I decided I wanted to become a volunteer and help even more."

Deb, listening to all of this, interjected, "So that's why you collect cans and bottles?"

Peter replied, "Yes, Deb, that's why."

She shot back, "But you're rich! Why not just write a check to them?"

Peter smiled again, "You sound like my family now. I could write a check, but I'd have no skin in the game. It's easy for a rich person to use money to wash away sins. It's another thing to roll up your sleeves and actually help."

Chase asked, "What sins?"

Peter looked back at Raylan and his scar. "My life cost him that. And for that I owe."

Matthew, Chase's driver, who had been listening to everything from the start, then asked, "I have a question, Peter. Can I call you Peter?"

Peter nodded, "Of course. Although people do call me Oscar."

The whole room laughed now as Matthew asked, "I'm wondering, Peter, there's a million coffee shops in New York City. How did you end up in this exact one? Did you know Raylan owned it and was the man who saved you?"

Peter looked back at Raylan. "No, not at first. I started collecting cans and bottles in the neighborhood, and eventually I came in here, and after a few visits I met the owner. I saw the scar, but lots of people have scars. Then one day he shook my hand and said, 'Oh, by the way, my name is Raylan.' Well, that was just too much of a coincidence, but still, I couldn't be sure."

Raylan, half smiling now, said, "So why didn't you just ask me?"

Peter let out a breath with a huff and said, "Well, I did in a roundabout way. I asked someone else who worked here how you got the scar. When they told me it happened to you during the war, I knew it had to be you."

Chase fixated on every word, and then asked, "But that's not the only reason you didn't say anything, is it?"

Peter replied in a hushed tone, "No it's not. I could see Raylan was a strong, proud man, and the last thing he'd want from me is pity."

Peter looked at Raylan again more intensely and continued. "And at first, I did have pity for you, for the price you paid saving me. But then, after knowing you about a year, I didn't feel that way anymore. You are not some broken thing, you're a proud veteran with a thriving business and lots of friends."

Raylan seemed touched by his words, as Peter continued. "But by the time I realized who you were, I couldn't tell you who I was. You all knew me as Oscar, so I just left it alone."

Something just occurred to Chase: "So yesterday, on Park Avenue, in that building's lobby?"

Peter smiled again, "Yeah, that was me on the phone. Now you know why I couldn't invite you up."

Chase smiled back. "And why you told me to *let it be*. I've been singing that stupid song in my head ever since, ya know," Chase added with a giggle.

Peter bent down to pet the shelter dog that was waiting by his feet, and then added, "Yeah, sorry about that."

Raylan then asked, "Earlier, Chase did something in sign language —what was that?"

Peter's face and features became soft as a pillow, answering, "She was asking about my little brother, Paul, who was born deaf. Everyone in my family learned sign language so we could communicate with him. That's how I was able to teach Bella, the deaf dog that Charlie adopted. Hey, how are they doing by the way, Charlie and Bella?"

Chase smiled warmly, "Great. That puppy changed her life."

Peter then extended his hand across the table to Raylan and said, "This is long overdue. I never got to thank you for saving my life. Thank you, Raylan."

Raylan had lied to everyone when he told them what happened to him in battle was buried deep in the past. Every time he caught a glimpse of his reflection in the mirror, that horrible day was looking back. He was proud and strong and was doing well, as Peter had observed, and now he had a wonderful woman in his life who cared for him. Still, it was a wound that had never quite closed, a scar that had never healed—until this moment, when he heard those two simple words from the man he saved: *Thank you.*

Raylan gripped his hand tight and shook it up and down twice, looked Peter in the eyes, and said, "You're welcome, Peter, and it's nice to finally meet you."

Both men were hardened by life and not prone to emotion, yet both sets of eyes welled up with tears. The room spontaneously broke into applause in that instant. Suddenly, strangers who just happened to pick that afternoon to go out for a cappuccino found themselves clearing their throats and pretending not to feel something stirring deep inside.

Chase knew the two men had lots of catching up to do, so she said, "Listen, I have to get back to Briarcliff. It's nice to finally meet you, Peter."

He crossed the room and gave Chase a hug, whispering in her ear, "You have a good heart."

Deb interrupted the moment with a question, "Excuse me but . . . what did the tattoo he has have to do with any of this?"

Peter pulled down the back of his shirt collar, revealing the screaming eagle that represented his army unit in the war, the same one Charlie spotted when Peter was playing. Raylan looked at it and smiled, adding, "That's the one."

Deb then asked, "If your real name is Peter, not Oscar, who is that guy you mentioned when you were fibbing. Mark something?"

Peter chuckled, "Oh, Mark Retzlaff. He was my college roommate. He sells real estate upstate. Doesn't even look like me."

Chase then, "And the Cambridge Eagles?"

Peter again, "Mark went to Cambridge High School, in Washington County, New York, but they were the Indians, not the eagles."

The whole room was quietly looking on with wonder, as Peter added, "Hey, you have to give me an A for creativity. Now, before you go, Chase, I have a question for you: How did you know the signs for 'brother' and 'deaf'? Chase smiled and answered, 'I asked Charlie's tutor, Mary, before I came down to meet you today.'"

As Chase turned toward the door to go, Matthew, her driver, opened it partially, then stopped himself and asked, "Wait. One more question. The tattoo you mentioned you have on your left arm that bears some significant date. Is that real?"

Peter looked around the room and realized every single person was watching and waiting for his answer. Finally, he said, "Yes, it is, Matthew. Very real. It's the most important date of my life. Who can guess when that was?"

As everyone paused and pondered, Raylan said, "The day we met."

Peter looked out the front window at the busy sidewalk, a fresh tear falling from his right eye. He couldn't speak, but there was no need for words. Everyone knew Raylan was right.

## CHAPTER 29

# What Would JC Do?

For the first time in the four years she had known Gavin, Chase was sick to her stomach with worry. It was the morning after she had revealed Oscar's true identity, and Chase and her pup, Scooter, sat on the chilly back patio staring at the stone wall. The yellow rose she placed on the rocks was gone, and she was left with an empty wall and an equally empty feeling in her heart.

She and Gavin spoke on the phone the entire ride home from Manhattan the night before, as she shared the amazing news about the man they called Oscar. Gavin was stunned, as anyone would be, then told her he loved her and said goodbye from his father's farm in Vermont. Only, that's not where he was.

After Chase woke, she called Gavin to wish him a good morning, but it went directly to voicemail. That meant either Gavin was on the phone or the phone was shut off. When Gavin didn't call back, she tried him twice more with no luck. Now worried, she called Gavin's father at the farm and felt ill when he told her Gavin wasn't there and he hadn't seen him in two weeks. It left her with only one possibility: Gavin had lied to her.

Chase paced for the next few hours, her half dozen more calls and text messages going painfully unanswered. Like a pot on the back burner of the stove, Chase was slowly reaching a boiling point, a mixture of worry and anger spilling over the sides.

Finally, at suppertime, her phone lit up with a loud "ding." It was Gavin with a cryptic message: *Matthew will pick you up at seven p.m. and bring you to meet me. Everything is fine, I'm sorry for the subterfuge. All will be explained soon. Love you so much, Gavin.*

Chase's first thought was, *Thank God he's alive. Now I'm going to kill him.*

Her driver arrived and assured Chase that he had no idea what was going on. Matthew only knew he was to take her to a specific address which she would recognize when she got there. Forty-seven minutes later the black sedan pulled up in front of Grand Central Station in Manhattan.

"The train station? Am I going somewhere?" she asked Matthew.

He could only shrug his shoulders, not knowing either.

Chase walked into the busy station and dodged commuters who were darting in all directions. She ventured toward the center of the station, and that's where she found Gavin waiting with a bouquet of flowers.

"Thank you for coming, and I'm sorry if any of this upset you," he began, giving Chase a hug.

Normally, she'd hug him back as if she'd never let go, but Chase was too upset.

Rather than beat around the bush she cut right to it. "You lied to me. I want to know why?"

Gavin flashed that warm country boy smile that was always so disarming, and for the first time it had zero effect.

When he saw the hurt in Chase's eyes, he said, "I did, but it's nothing bad. I promise. Before we get to that, though . . ."

Gavin then looked to his left toward the wall of the train station and waved his hand back and forth to get someone's attention.

"You see those two guys, the ones waving back at me?" he asked Chase.

She looked and saw two men, one of college age and the other in his sixties with gray hair and a pot belly that extended over his belt.

"Yes, I see them. Who are they?" she replied.

Gavin said, "That's Ronnie, and I think the older one called himself Jinx."

Chase, then completely confused, replied, "Jinx?"

Gavin, "Yeah, must be a nickname. They work at the furniture emporium on West 58th, and if you look behind them, you'll see two recliners. I paid them two hundred dollars each to do this."

Gavin gave them a thumbs up, prompting the men to drag two recliners from the side of Grand Central over to the center where Chase and Gavin were standing.

When they got there, Jinx said to Gavin, "Remember, ten minutes, no more."

Gavin nodded and said, "Absolutely. Deal's a deal."

Chase, still confused, looked at Gavin as he said, "Now, look over to that side of the station and you'll see a man in a suit with a bald head and glasses. Do you see him?"

Chase craned her neck and, looking through the sea of people, replied, "I think so, wait, yes, I see him. Who is he?"

Gavin, looking proud of himself now, said, "That is Stu Winkle, the night manager of this train station, and for a hundred bucks he's going to do something for me."

Chase was starting to lose patience and said, "Gavin, why did you lie and say you were in Vermont when you weren't? Where were you?"

Gavin turned to her and took up both of her soft hands in his. "I promise we'll get to that, but first I have a speech I practiced on the plane."

"Plane? You were on a plane? From where?" Chase inquired firmly.

Gavin cleared his throat dramatically, then began, "When I thought of how I wanted to do this, I asked myself what would JC do?"

Chase looked at him and said, "What would Jesus do?"

Gavin laughed nervously. "Oh, God no, I mean, yes, of course we should do what that JC would do, but in *this* case I'm talking about the other JC. The one you love watching."

Chase was completely lost now, asking, confused, "The one I, what?"

Gavin explained: "John Cusack. JC. Your favorite actor. You love all his schmaltzy romantic movies—*Serendipity* that we watched recently, and the one where he holds the boom box over his head, or the one where he runs a record store. Sorry, I don't know all the names."

Chase thought a moment, then said, "*Say Anything* and *High Fidelity*."

Gavin again, "Right, right. So, I asked myself, what would JC do if he were me in this moment, and here we are."

Chase looked at the recliners sitting empty next to them, then asked, "Okay, so explain where you've been and why we're standing in the middle of a train station?"

There was a loud whistle just then, and Gavin looked over to see the bald man holding up his wrist and pointing to his watch, as if it was time for something to happen.

Gavin smiled and said to Chase, "Right. Quick, sit down in the recliner. Stu Winkle says it's time."

Chase sat in one of the cloth chairs and said, "That can't possibly be his real name, Stu Winkle?"

Gavin ignored her comment, taking the chair next to her, then said, "Now, lean back."

When Chase did, she found herself looking up at the ceiling of Grand Central station, which, she hadn't noticed until now, was painted to look like the sky at night, with all the stars and constellations. Suddenly, they heard another whistle from Stu, and the lights in the train station went dim, causing the stars above to brighten.

Gavin began, "Do you remember our very first date back in Vermont? We had a picnic by a stream and then I did something special for you in a field."

Chase's heart warmed to the memory, responding, "You took me to a field at dusk and made all the lightning bugs put on a show just for me."

Gavin took her hand. "That's right. They don't have lightning bugs in Manhattan in December, but they do have this."

Both of them looked up at the stars above, as Gavin continued, "This ceiling was first made in the early nineteen hundreds, and they spent a lot of time and money on it. It's a replica of the sky above the earth."

Chase looked up at the twinkling lights and was taking it all in.

"After it was up for a while people started to notice that it's actually backwards," Gavin added.

"Backwards? Backwards how?" Chase asked.

Gavin pointed. "East and west are backwards, so you're not seeing things the way they're supposed to be."

Chase asked, "How could that happen?"

Gavin stared up. "Well, the theory is when they projected the image up on the ceiling to paint, it flipped everything left to right, and nobody noticed until it was all done."

Chase smiled now. "That's crazy. And they never fixed it?"

Gavin replied, "No. In fact, years later when the ceiling got damaged and it had to be fixed, they decided to just do the new ceiling the same way as the original."

Chase asked, "Backwards again?"

Smiling, Gavin replied, "Yep."

Chase didn't know what to make of it.

Then Gavin did something that reminded her why she loved him.

"I did a little digging, and there's a story no one talks about," he began.

"They say after years of everyone calling the stars backwards, a little girl no older than six came through the station with her grandmother and looked up. She pointed out that it's only backwards if you are looking up from the earth, but it looks PERFECT if you are looking down from heaven. So, this is how the angels see it."

Chase squeezed his hand and looked at Gavin, saying, "I like that explanation."

Gavin smiled. "Me too. Raise your chair up now so I can tell you the rest."

Chase and Gavin both sat upright at the center of the train station, and as people walked around them, he explained, "I lied to you because I didn't want you to know I was going to Seattle."

Chase was from Seattle, and her eyes went wide with wonder, as he continued, "I know your dad was never part of the picture and your mom raised you alone. I wanted to talk to your mom, to ask her a very important question."

Chase leaned in closer to Gavin now, "What question?"

Gavin fiddled with his hands nervously, then, "I wanted her blessing when I ask you to marry me."

Gavin looked in Chase's soft eyes, and suddenly hers darted down toward Gavin's hands looking for a ring box.

This caused Gavin to blurt out, "NO, NO, not now. I didn't mean this moment. I mean this is pretty neat with the romantic ceiling and all but, I'm not asking you tonight."

Chase let out a sigh of relief, saying, "Good. Not that I wouldn't say YES but I'm in jeans and a sweatshirt with no makeup on, Gavin. A girl wants to look pretty for that, ya know, moment."

Gavin replied with a smile, "The lady wants to look nice. Got it. I'll make a note of it."

Gavin paused a second, then said, "Well, that about covers it."

Chase replied in a most serious tone, "I love you and I understand why you kept this secret until now, but please don't ever lie to me again. I don't like the way it made me feel inside."

Gavin understood completely saying, "I promise. Never again."

Gavin looked up and realized Ronnie and Jinx were standing over them both. "Oh, sorry, guys, you did say ten minutes. We're all set."

They both got up, surrendering their recliners.

As the workers dragged away the recliners, Gavin waved over to Stu and the lights in the train station became bright again, causing Gavin to say, "Let there be light."

Chase teasing him, said, "Oh, do we fashion ourselves to be God now?"

Gavin gave her a hug and looked in her eyes. "No, just a man in love who wanted to give you the stars."

With that they both looked up at the ceiling again.

They stared a moment, then Gavin said, "That question *is* coming and coming soon, you know that, right? The big one. I just need to get a few ducks in a row."

Chase looked from the stars above to the light gleaming in Gavin's eyes, then said, "Well, good luck with those ducks then."

As the two walked hand in hand to exit Grand Central, Chase said, "Bravo, by the way. All this. It is what JC would do."

Gavin didn't say a word. When things go perfectly you shut your mouth and hold your girl's hand like you mean it.

CHAPTER 30

*Tag, You're It*

A week had passed since Gavin gave Chase the stars, but today it would be the groundskeeper, Nick, showing everyone some fun. His knock, bright and early, brought Chase to the front door, wearing a pair of oversized flannel pajamas.

Nick took off his wool cap, out of respect, saying, "Morning, ma'am. I wanted to stop by and talk to you about taggin' a tree."

Gavin walked up to join the conversation with his coffee in one hand and a piping hot cup for Chase in the other. On cold days like this, Chase enjoyed holding the mug between her chilly fingers almost as much as drinking it.

"Do you mean Christmas trees?" Chase asked. "We used to do that in Vermont."

Nick replied, "Yes, ma'am. I figured we'd head over to Faddegon's nursery in Hawthorne."

Chase replied, "Hawthorne? Like the famous writer?"

Nick played along. "No. Hawthorne like the not-so-famous hamlet, a couple of towns over."

Gavin then asked, "What's the difference between a town and a hamlet?"

Nick replied, "A town has more than one stop sign."

Chase then asked Gavin, "Did we want to get a tree? We hadn't really talked about it."

Nick, sensing they might say no, quickly added, "I should tell you Bob, the owner, has a big horse-drawn wagon with room for a dozen people. We ride out, everyone picks a tree, and by the time you come back, Bob's wife, Ginny, has a fire going, and there's cider donuts and hot cocoa."

Gavin rubbed Chase's back, and said, "Hot cocoa on a chilly day sounds fun."

Chase smiled and looked at Nick's kind, wrinkled face, realizing, in his own way, he was a handsome man for his age.

She then asked, "Did you say the wagon can hold a dozen people?"

Nick replied, "Oh, yes, ma'am. The more the merrier."

Chase looked at Gavin and started counting on her fingers, "You and me, Charlie and Mary from next door, maybe her parents, that's six."

Gavin interjected, "Raylan and Bonnie makes eight. Matthew, your driver, is nine. Oscar, I mean Peter, is ten."

They were both thinking about those last two spots open when Chase said, "We shouldn't leave out Deb from the cafe. I don't think she's seeing anyone, though."

Gavin, smirking, replied, "Do you blame them?"

Chase whacked his arm, lightly joking, "Hey, none of that, she's sweet once you get past the hypochondria. So, she'd make it eleven."

Chase looked back at Nick and realized he wasn't that much older than Deb, asking, "What about you, Nick? Would you come with us?"

He thought a moment and said, "Sure, if you wanted me to, why not."

Gavin smiled and said, "Nick, my man, how do you feel about a pretty woman with crazy red hair who spends all day on the internet searching for something to be wrong with her?"

Nick smiled with that tooth still missing, then said, "Sounds like my kinda gal."

The three of them laughed as Chase took a quick sip of her coffee and said, "We have some calls to make, then. How about we all meet here at the house at four?"

Nick nodded and said, "Sounds like a plan."

Gavin took Chase by the hand and led her back inside to start dialing their friends.

Everyone arrived on schedule, and the drive over to Hawthorne took less than ten minutes. Bob, the owner of the nursery, was waiting—an older gentleman wearing a leather cowboy hat atop his thinning gray hair. He also had a red and white Santa jacket on with a thick black belt that was too small to clip over his belly.

Bob removed the hat like a circus ringmaster, saying, "Good evening, one and all, welcome to my farm. You'll find the perfect Christmas tree a short wagon ride away. There's a nip in the air, making this officially *hug your honey* weather, so sit tight together on that wagon, and don't be shy with your affection."

Bonnie looked beautiful in a pink jacket, her hair and make-up done up more than Chase had ever seen her. It was her hand that drew Chase's attention, however, wrapped tightly around Raylan's as they walked over to the wagon and he helped her up to a seat.

Charlie and Mary were signing something back and forth, and while Chase didn't understand, it must have been something funny, because both were grinning as they talked. Peter, the man everyone knew as Oscar until just recently, was there too, and more than once he'd sign something to Charlie and she'd give him thumbs up in reply.

Peter saw others watching his silent conversation and said to the group, "I was asking about her dog, Bella. She's doing great."

Charlie's parents were not in attendance, as a prior engagement kept them away, but that was okay because it gave everyone more room to spread out. Matthew, Chase's driver, was wearing a faded Wrangler denim jacket and matching jeans, prompting Gavin to observe, "Matthew, I don't think I've ever seen you *not* in a suit. You look good, amigo!"

"Ah, this," Matthew said, running his fingers down the front of the jacket, "seemed more appropriate for a wagon ride."

Deb was there as well in a bright orange jogging suit, that on anyone else would have looked out of place, but she somehow pulled it off.

"You must be the beautiful Deborah I've heard so much about," Nick, the groundskeeper, said with a smile.

Blushing instantly, Deb giggled and replied, "Stop it now, I mean it."

Nick took her hand to help her up into the wagon and said, "Impossible. I could never stop complimenting a beauty like you."

That last line made everyone smile. In that moment, Deb felt as young as a teenager; the aches and pains that were the bane of her daily existence were suddenly gone.

Bob did a quick head count and said, "So ten is what we have, and ten is what we'll return with. Let's go find everyone a tree."

With that he snapped a whip in the air, and the pair of large horses sprang to life, tossing the wagon backward as they marched toward the woods and the mysteries of the forest.

It took less than twenty minutes for each couple to find and tag a tree. No one would cut it down today; Bob told them to return the following weekend to take their prizes home. The ride back to the nursery was quick, and everyone smelled the warm fire that had been lit in their absence.

"Oh my gosh, are those cider donuts?" Deb exclaimed.

All eyes turned toward a long table filled with hot mulled cider, cocoa, and those donuts they'd heard so much about. Everyone was looking at the sweet treats, with the exception of Nick, his dreamy gaze fixed instead on Deb.

As the group gathered with their drinks by the crackling fire, Matthew surprised everyone when he asked, "So, Chase, we've never really talked about what's been happening at the house."

Chase almost choked on her cider, taken so off guard by the question.

The looks on at least some of their faces told Chase they knew something strange was afoot at Briarcliff Manor: Bella, the elevator, her knowing Oscar was really Peter. They waited in silence for her explanation.

"Yes, happening." Chase began. "Well, when I came here, to Manhattan, I thought for certain what happened before in Vermont..." Chase stopped herself there, then asked, "Are you sure you want me getting into all this here?"

Nick, Deb, Charlie, and Mary had no idea what Chase was talking about, but they were eager to hear it just the same.

She glanced at Gavin as if looking for advice, and he said, "It's up to you."

Chase continued. "What happened in Vermont didn't happen here, you know, me knowing stuff, until I purchased the house in Briarcliff."

Raylan had read Chase's novel cover to cover, so he asked, "Is it like before, with the church windows?"

Matthew interrupted then. "No, not at church. I took her to Saint Pat's a million times. Nothing happened there."

Chase looked at Matthew. "That's right, he's right, not at church."

She paused now, knowing how ridiculous what she was about to say sounded.

Finally, she just spilled it. "You'll think this sounds nuts, but after I lived a little while in the new house at Briarcliff Manor, my dog, Scooter, became obsessed with the board game Scrabble."

Deb, without thinking, blurted out, "Your dog knows how to play Scrabble? Now that's impressive!"

Several of them burst out laughing, but Chase ignored their reaction, instead reaching over to touch Deb's hand, showing she was not mocking her, saying, "No, Deb. He doesn't play. He just kept barking at the game, so Gavin and I played it, and when we did, I kept getting the same words over and over again."

She could tell no one was following, so she explained further, "First it was the name Bella. Every time I mixed up the little wooden tiles in the Scrabble game, I got the name *Bella*. Every. Single. Time. Bella, Bella, Bella. Which led us to bring Bella to meet Charlie."

Gavin then, trying to help her, added, "You see, Chase had been worried all day about Charlie, and then we play Scrabble, and she gets the name Bella. We had no idea what it meant, but the next day we were in the café, and that's the day everyone learned the dog we all called Ella . . ."

Raylan finished his sentence: ". . . was really named Bella. So, you put two and two together?"

Chase replied, "That's right."

Nick was curious. "You said you got the same *words,* plural. What other words did you get?"

Chase turned to Nick. "The first time we played it was Bella. A couple weeks later when we played it was *brake.*"

Matthew spoke then. "That's why Chase had us all check the brakes on our cars—remember that day?"

Several of them shook their heads in the affirmative.

Matthew continued. "Everyone's car brakes were fine. Then, a few days later, Chase was parked outside my building and saw the word again, BRAKE, literally lighting up on a sign. She ran upstairs to warn us."

Bonnie, who had been silent as a monk up to this point, finally spoke. "This is crazy. You really think letters from a board game were talking to you?"

Chase turned to her, "I'm not sure what to make of it, Bonnie, I'm just telling you what happened."

Peter interrupted then, asking, "Was this how you knew about me?"

Chase replied. "Yes, I was playing the game with Charlie when the word *bird* kept coming up, and she told me about the tattoo on your neck, the screaming eagle."

Matthew asked, "And is that it?"

Gavin jumped in again. "Yes, that's it, and that's all there's going to be."

Chase looked at him, surprised, and saw Gavin glance toward Nick, the groundskeeper, with a guilty expression.

"What? What don't I know?" Chase asked the two of them.

Nick spoke first: "Earlier today, when you were upstairs in the shower, Gavin asked me to take those board games and put them in storage down in the basement. They're locked away in an old chest."

Chase then looked at Gavin, searching for an explanation, so he offered one. "You just seemed so stressed over it, and I know you probably don't realize it, Chase, but you walk by that room where the games were kept a dozen times a day and look in as if one of them is going to start talking to you. I'm sorry, but I just thought it would be best to give you a break."

Chase paused a moment, and her flash of anger was replaced by understanding, realizing both men were only trying to help.

Finally, Chase said, "Well, nothing has happened for a while anyway, so, I'm fine with it. It will be Christmas soon, and we need some peace and quiet anyway, don't you think?"

Bob, the owner of the nursery, raised his glass and said, "I don't know what the heck any of you people are talking about, and frankly you all sound nuttier than my aunt Lu Lu's fruit cake, but *here here,* let's toast to a peaceful holiday."

As everyone joined in, Chase noticed Bonnie looking down at her left-hand ring finger and fidgeting with something shiny, asking, "Hey girl, whatcha got there?"

Bonnie touched the stone and said, "Raylan gave me a promise ring. I'm not sure what we're promising each other but it means the world to me."

Chase looked down at her own hand bearing the promise ring Gavin had given her years earlier, and replied, "I know exactly what you mean, Bonnie."

Nick reached over on impulse and took Deb's hand. Without hesitation, she squeezed his right back.

Charlie then made two fists with her tiny hands, bumped them together, and pointed toward the sky.

Deb saw Charlie make that sign and asked, "What did she just say?"

Peter responded, "Charlie says there's a lot of romance in the air."

As the group of ten boarded their vehicles for the short drive back to the house, Scooter, Chase's loyal dog, was sitting in the library back home in Briarcliff Manor, staring at the windows. He was looking specifically at one pane of glass in the center, the one Chase was told to never, ever, clean or touch.

Scooter started barking as if he saw something that clearly was not there. The Scrabble game was indeed locked away, but that did not mean the mansion at Briarcliff, so full of history, shadows, and mischief, had finished revealing its secrets. And a big one was about to show itself the moment Chase got home.

CHAPTER 31

## *Hidden Heart*

Despite the colder weather, Gavin had left a window open in the front of the mansion at Briarcliff. So, before Chase reached for the doorknob to go in, they both heard Scooter barking loudly from deep inside the house. Any pet owner can tell you that dogs have different barks: one when they're excited, one when they feel threatened, and one when they want your attention. That was the bark Chase heard four times at the church back in Manchester, Vermont, years earlier, and the same one she was hearing right now.

Scooter's unrelenting call led them to the library. Before even entering the room, both Gavin and Chase knew something was about to happen that would likely alter their evening plans.

Scooter heard them approach, but he didn't look back to acknowledge them. He kept staring at the wall of windows, specifically the one in the center, a tiny pane of glass that was identical to the rest. The pup was lying down on the thick rug, his tail straight as a string, eyes fixed and unwavering. Chase looked at Gavin, and they both looked at the windows and saw nothing.

"Maybe a squirrel or something spooked him outside?" Gavin asked.

Chase looked at the height of the windows and said, "Even if that were true, how could a squirrel get high enough on the window to do that. I've never seen a squirrel with a ladder, have you?"

It was a rhetorical question meant to make Gavin smile, which he did before not answering. Just silence, as they both looked at the clear glass panes facing due west. It was late in the day, so the sun had almost set, and since the sky was clear, the big ball of red burned bright on the horizon. Chase called Scooter over, but he refused to move from his spot or even turn his head to her command. He did stop barking, though, while continuing to look at the windows in front of him.

Chase then moved closer to her dog and slid down onto the rug to sit right by his side on the floor. She put her arm around his neck, rubbed his scalp, and leaned her face against his. Her soft skin was flush against his warm fur, cheek to cheek, giving Chase the dog's exact vantage point.

"What are you looking at, boy? What's the matter?" she asked in a loving tone.

"Do you see anything down there?" Gavin asked, still standing a few feet away near a row of busy bookcases.

"No, just glass and the yard and the sunset," Chase replied. She put her lips down on Scooter's head to give him a kiss and shifted her eyes back toward the windows, seeing them now from Scooter's exact angle. That's when she said, "What the . . ."

Gavin looked at the glass, then back to Chase, "What? What do you see?"

Chase shifted her head left a few inches, then to the right, and then back where it was on top of Scooter's head.

"It goes away unless you are looking exactly right," she said, out loud.

"What goes away?" Gavin asked more insistently, moving now to join Chase on the floor.

Chase took Gavin by the chin and pushed his head down onto the dog's, and said, "Look straight at that center pane of glass, the one we aren't allowed to wash."

Gavin did, not seeing anything at first and then exclaiming, "WOW, I see it! Is that a . . ."

Chase interrupted him. "It's a heart, with what looks like little wings coming out of the sides."

Gavin squinted his eyes and then confirmed it. "Yes, you're right. It's a heart with wings. Angel wings, I think."

With that Scooter got up and walked to the other side of the room, spinning in a circle twice, before lying down, his body curled up like a warm crescent roll. He closed his eyes as if he were exhausted. Chase could only wonder how long he'd been in this room barking, waiting for them to get home.

Gavin stood up first and then lifted Chase by both hands. They were nose to nose now, and he was thinking of giving her a kiss when Chase turned toward the window and said, "Two questions. How did that get there, and why didn't we see it until now?"

Gavin walked toward the window and rubbed his hair back and forth, a habit that told Chase he was thinking hard for a solution.

"How's this?" he began. "When I was a kid, my dad had an old junk car he kept in a back barn. It was covered in dust, and one day I wrote my name in the dust on the windshield."

Chase was listening, not certain where this was going, only saying, "Okay, so?"

"So," he continued, "years later, after the dust was brushed away, you could still see the outline of the letters in my name if the sunlight hit it just right. It left a kind of invisible imprint on the glass."

Chase got down on the floor again and tried to duplicate the exact angle to see the heart again. The sun was a tiny bit lower in the sky, and only part of the heart was visible now.

"It's already going," she said to Gavin. "You must only be able to see it at a certain time of the day or year when the sun hits it exactly right."

She got back up and said, "So, dust can do that, you say?"

Gavin replied, "It did for me. As for how a heart got there on this window—you said Sebastian Winthrop was madly in love with his wife, right?"

Chase nodded, "Yes, very much so."

Gavin continued, "Maybe he drew that heart for her, or better yet, could it be she drew it for him, and when they saw it stayed, they never wanted to wash it away."

Chase pondered Gavin's theory, then added, "Makes sense."

She paced the floor of the library now, not saying a word, prompting Gavin to ask, "But that's a guess, and you need to know, don't you?"

Chase made a face as if she were wincing and replied, "I kinda do. I'm sorry, Gav, but you know me. I have to know for sure."

Gavin walked over to Chase's brown Louis Vuitton bag that was sitting on the desk and fished out her cell phone.

As he handed it to her, he said, "The last time we stumbled on a mystery at this house you got the answer from that Stonewall Jackson woman. Call her."

Chase paused a moment, staring at the phone, and then said, "You think she'll be mad?"

Gavin replied, "It's not like we went looking for this. Blame it on Scooter—he's the troublemaker around here."

Chase pulled up her number and put it on speaker so Gavin could hear. It didn't finish half a ring when . . .

"Yes, Miss Harrington?" she answered without saying hello, reminding Chase how direct this woman could be.

"I'm sorry to bother you, Ms. Jackson, but I was staring at the sunset in the library of the house in Briarcliff and noticed what looks like a heart with wings, drawn on one of the panes. I know the letter Sebastian left said not to wash that window, and we haven't. We've respected his wishes. But we saw the heart by accident, so I'm hoping you can shed some light on it, no pun intended."

There was silence for a good ten seconds, before the stern voice responded, "And I suppose if I tell you to drop it, you'll just end up tearing every book off the shelf looking for an answer?"

Chase looked at Gavin, then back at the phone, and replied, "You know me well, ma'am. I probably would."

More silence, and then, "There's nothing in the books to help you this time, but there is something."

Another pause, then she asked, "Are you in the library right now?"

Chase responded eagerly, "We are."

"Look toward the east wall, opposite the windows and the rows of books," she instructed.

Chase turned and did as she was told. "Okay, I'm looking that way."

Ms. Jackson again, "On the lower right side you'll see a white wooden cabinet with a silver latch—do you see it?"

They both crossed the room as Chase yelled back, "Yes, should I open it?"

"Yes," the voice continued. "In that cabinet are music CDs and some movies on DVD. You'll find one that looks different from the others. It's marked *TELETHON,* in big letters. Let me know when you have it."

Gavin scooped out a dozen discs and shuffled through them, and suddenly Chase said, "There! We have it, Ms. Jackson."

After another beat of silence, and the voice said, "The reason for the hidden heart is on that video. That's all the help I can give. Good day."

With that the phone went dead, causing Chase to look at Gavin and say, "Why is everything so dramatic with her?"

Gavin shrugged his shoulders and said, "I saw a DVD player in the living room next to the TV," causing both to dash out of the room and down the hall.

After popping the disc in the machine, Gavin joined Chase on the couch and pushed "play," causing the screen to suddenly come to life. As advertised, it was a telethon of some sorts, being hosted by a local news station in New York City.

A handsome man in a tux began, "Hello everyone, I'm Dave Rush. Welcome to our annual telethon to benefit the children's hospital at St. Mary's in the Bronx."

The woman, in a beautiful gown, followed, "And I'm Katie Ranno. As we come on the air, we want to send it out to our reporter who is at the hospital with a special presentation."

Chase and Gavin watched as a reporter in the field talked about the children's hospital and then turned to interview someone they both recognized.

Reporter: "Joining me now is philanthropist Sebastian Winthrop and his wife, Vida, here to cut the ribbon on a very special place."

The camera turned to Sebastian, looking a good dozen years younger than Chase imagined him, as he said, "Thank you. Today we are opening the *Heart Center*. Over the years we've given money to the hospital for equipment and treatment, but it took a frank conversation with a child to make this place happen."

The reporter then asked, "What do you mean, sir?"

Sebastian stepped aside so the camera could better see the room behind them, then explained, "A special little girl told Vida and myself that what this place needed was a playroom just for kids, no adults allowed. And if you look around, that's precisely what the *Heart Room* is. Video games, coloring books, every Disney movie a child could want."

The reporter just nodded along, so Sebastian continued. "There's just one rule in this room: have fun. No shots, no medical machines making you scared. Just play for these children who have already been through so much."

The reporter started to wrap things up, saying, "Well, it's fabulous. Thank you for allowing us to take a look inside today."

Sebastian interrupted, saying, "WAIT. Let me show you one last thing. That back wall has pictures of several of the children we met who inspired us to create the *Heart Room*. Can you get a shot of them, please?"

The camera zoomed in, revealing a small stone wall with photographs of five children. From left to right was a little boy with glasses, smiling brightly. Next to him, a teenaged girl in a wheelchair. In the middle, a beautiful little girl in a bright yellow dress with blonde, curly hair. To her right another boy in some kid of a special walker. And the last photo was a boy about ten, dressed like Superman.

"These children are the reason we are here today," Sebastian said, adding, "They are forever in our hearts." Gavin suddenly shouted, "LOOK! THERE!"

He was pointing at the TV, to a small red wooden heart with white wings, etched into the wall above the children's photographs. It was identical to the heart Gavin and Chase had just seen on the window in the library. It was the *Heart Room*'s emblem.

The reporter tossed it back to the studio for the rest of the telethon, but the video turned to static, revealing there was nothing left to see.

Chase thought a moment, and then said to Gavin, "So, let's talk this out."

Gavin took her hand in his and said, "Go."

Chase replied, "We knew Sebastian and his wife helped lots of charities. They help this hospital and meet some kids and decide to do this special room we just saw."

Gavin interrupted, "The *Heart Room*."

Chase continued, "Exactly, the *Heart Room*. The two of them sit in the library one day talking about what they want to build and one of them draws the heart in the glass, like you said earlier about your dad's truck, and they decide it's so pretty they don't want to erase it. They end up using it for the logo at the hospital."

Gavin was the one pausing now, and then said, "Makes sense. I mean Stonewall Jackson told you on the phone that the answer to the heart in the window was on the DVD, and that's what it showed us. So that has to be it."

Both were quiet now, mulling over Chase's theory, and neither could find fault with it.

Still, Chase said, "Don't be mad at me, but I have to know for sure."

"How can you do that?" Gavin wondered.

Chase picked up the phone and hit redial. After two rings a harsh voice answered, "I thought we were done, Miss Harrington."

Chase, in a less than apologetic tone, said, "I know, I know, I'm annoying, but how about this, Ms. Jackson. I watched the telethon video and I have a theory. So, here's my plan. I tell you what I think is up with that window in the library, and if I'm right you don't even need to speak. You just hang up."

Another pause, and then the voice from the phone's speaker replied, "I'd love nothing more than to hang up on you. All right, hurry up."

Chase started: "Sebastian and his wife meet some great kids at this hospital, and a little girl tells them they need a playroom. They build it and decide to name it after the *heart* that one of them drew on the window here at the house. Because those kids are special to them, they never erase the heart or wash the glass. It's a silent, beautiful reminder of the good they did. Knowing they can't live forever, they leave a letter for the next owner, telling them not to touch that window, so the heart stays. How's that?"

Silence over the phone and then, "Very good, Chase. And now we're done."

With that the phone went dead again, and Chase looked at Gavin with a satisfied smile. "I should write mysteries—I'm really good at this stuff."

Gavin glanced at his watch and said, "It's late. You wanna split a bowl of ice cream before I head out? You know, to celebrate your brilliance."

"Only if it's chocolate chip cookie dough," Chase replied, before giving Gavin a hug.

A few moments later both were sitting at the kitchen island, with Scooter watching every spoonful of ice cream leaving the dish, hoping the next one would come in his direction.

"I promise to save you the last bite," Gavin said, prompting the dog to wag his tail.

Chase was sitting only inches from Gavin, but he could sense she was miles away. "Where are you?" he asked.

"I was just thinking about the letter we were given when we moved in here," she replied.

"What about it?" Gavin asked.

"Well, there were three mysteries in there. Don't dig under the tree, don't wash the window, and place the rose on the rock wall behind the house every night."

Gavin, following along, agreed. "Right, what about them?"

Chase took on a mischievous look, which told Gavin she was about to propose something adventurous.

"What now?" Gavin asked, as he gave the last scoop of ice cream to Scooter, as promised.

"Well, we've solved two of the three mysteries, but the biggest one, these roses on the wall that vanish, that one . . ." She stopped talking, keeping whatever was next in her head.

Gavin loved and knew Chase better than anyone on the planet, so after a moment of silence he finished her thought. "So, you want to solve that one as well. You want to know who is taking the roses, where they are going, and why?"

Chase smiled and said, "Is that so bad?"

Gavin replied, "No, I wouldn't say it's bad, but you are deliberately going against the old man's wishes, the one who gave you the house. We solved the first two by accident. This would be different."

Chase thought a moment, giving serious consideration to what Gavin just said.

Finally, she responded, "You're right. We'd be breaking his wishes. Forget I even mentioned it."

Gavin, sorry to see her disappointed, added, "You know, if we think about it, we can probably guess what's happening with the roses anyway."

Chase turned to Gavin now and said enthusiastically, "You've thought about it too? Tell me your theory and let's see if it's the same as mine."

Gavin placed the empty dish on the floor for Scooter and started. "Sebastian adored his wife and probably gave her roses every day. When she died, he likely took roses to her grave and did it for years. When he was starting to get sick, and knew he wouldn't be around forever, he decided to have roses delivered to the house and ask the new owner to place one on the rock wall each night. Then someone he paid in advance comes along and takes them to make sure his Vida still has her rose. That's my theory. You?"

Chase's eyes went as wide as they could go, and she giggled and covered her mouth. "That's EXACTLY what I think is happening. Has to be right? Right? I mean, what else makes sense?"

Gavin put the empty ice cream dish in the sink, gave Chase a hug goodnight and started toward the door.

Just as he was about to leave, Chase added, "Unless we're wrong."

Gavin silently spun around, returned to the sink, and turned on the cold water.

"What are you doing?" Chase asked.

"Making fresh coffee," Gavin replied. "If we're staying up all night to follow the rose, we'll both need caffeine. Lots of it."

Chase met his eyes and said, "I'm sorry. Do you hate me? I have to know where that rose goes, I have to."

Gavin took her firmly in his strong arms and said, "I love you, and I wouldn't have you any other way."

Before the sun would rise again in the tiny village of Briarcliff Manor, New York, Chase Harrington would solve this last mystery of her mansion. She'd also learn, much to her surprise, that their theory on the vanishing roses was completely wrong.

CHAPTER 32

*Follow the Rose*

In the few months that Chase had lived in the mansion, Gavin had walked the property dozens of times with Scooter on his leash. He noticed in the back, beyond the stone wall where they left the yellow rose each night, was twenty feet of grass, then a row of tightly grown arborvitae trees. From left to right they stretched a hundred yards and acted like a fence, giving the property privacy.

On one such walk, he took Scooter beyond the wall of trees and found a single-lane gravel road that ran behind several of the nearby properties, including Chase's. Gavin assumed it was a maintenance road for workers to make deliveries and have less conspicuous access.

He told Chase, "Whoever is taking the roses at night must be using that road to drive in, then cutting through the trees on foot to retrieve them."

Chase thought about this and agreed, so after pouring coffee into a pair of large travel mugs, the two of them hopped into Gavin's truck and drove around the block to access the gravel road. It was pitch dark, making it no easy task, but with Chase aiming a flashlight out of the truck's window, they found it. Chase left three candles burning on the patio behind her house, so when they drove up the gravel road, they could peek through and make sure they were in the right spot.

Gavin parked the truck off the road, in a spot where they wouldn't be seen. The cold December night was black as a witch's hat, but with the help of a flashlight, he could just make out the shape of the rock wall and the yellow rose on top.

Now they'd wait to see who or what came for the flower. *Who or what?* Did Chase think a mysterious creature from the woods was taking the rose? It was that kind of silliness that crept into your head when you were playing Nancy Drew with your best friend in the dark.

"You okay?" Gavin asked. "I can tell your mind is off someplace again."

Chase squeezed his hand and said, "I'm here, babe, don't worry. Thank you for doing this with me."

Gavin held her hand tight, telling her, without words, that they were indeed a team.

As Chase looked out the window at the moonless night, she mumbled quietly to herself, "The watch, the window, the rose. Sounds like a Disney movie."

Gavin didn't catch what she said, asking, "What, hon?"

She smiled and replied, "Nothing, babe."

The two took turns choosing the music on the truck's radio, Gavin going for country and classic rock, Chase opting for pop and hip-hop.

By 3 a.m., when no one appeared to gather the flower, both were fading fast, so they decided to take shifts the way cops do on stakeouts. Gavin would keep watch from 3 to 4 a.m. while she slept. Chase would then take 4 to 5 a.m. while Gavin napped, and so on.

It was during the third hour of watch, just before 6 a.m., when Gavin saw headlights approaching in the distance. He quickly killed the engine on his own truck, making it silent as well as invisible. A dark colored SUV drove right by, not noticing Gavin's truck hiding in the shadows.

The sun was almost up over the horizon, casting a faint light that farmers call *false dawn*. The light was just bright enough to see a man of small stature exit the SUV, careful not to slam the door shut, and make his way to the row of trees that bordered Chase's property. He vanished into them, prompting Gavin to nudge his sleepy girlfriend, "Hey, wake up, it's show time."

Chase rubbed her eyes and took a moment to remember where she was, and then those tired eyes grew wide as she asked, "Someone's here?"

Gavin pointed and said, "Watch the row of trees and, bam, there he is," just as the mystery man reappeared and returned with something in his left hand. Dark as it was, there was just enough light to tell he was holding something small and yellow.

"That's our flower thief," Gavin said with a smile.

The man went to his vehicle, closed the door gently, did a quick U-turn, and drove back in the direction from which he had first come.

"Wait, not yet," Chase said, worried Gavin might give their position away too soon. Gavin waited another beat before firing up the truck and cranking on the heater to warm their legs and feet.

"Here we go, Sherlock Holmes," Chase said with a smile.

Gavin waited until they hit the main road to turn his headlights on and begin his pursuit. Whoever was driving the SUV was not in a hurry, so Gavin stayed back, never taking his eyes off the man's taillights.

They weren't more than a mile or two down the road when he saw a right directional blinking, and Gavin mirrored the man's every move. After turning right, he soon saw a left directional engage, and the vehicle with the mystery driver slowly turned into Mt. Moriah Cemetery.

"I KNEW IT," Chase exclaimed. "We called it."

Gavin remembered what they had discussed the night before about Vida Winthrop loving yellow roses and her husband Sebastian keeping a promise to always bring her one, even after death. Gavin couldn't help thinking there was something terribly romantic and sad about it at the same time.

Chase's mind was on the article she wrote in the *New Yorker*, telling the world that this wealthy man wasn't really about money, it was a love story from start to finish. In this case, even beyond the finish of life.

Gavin didn't want to spook the man delivering the rose to Vida's grave, so he killed the truck's lights and took a parallel road in the cemetery, parking a short distance away.

"So now what?" he asked Chase. "Have we gone far enough, or do you need to actually see him putting the rose on her grave?"

Maybe Gavin was overtired, but there was a hint of sarcasm in his tone, so Chase shot him a look and said, "In for a penny, in for a dime, I say."

With that she popped her passenger side door and stepped down from the truck. Gavin got out right after her, and the two of them slowly made their way through the rows of gravestones, each telling short stories of people who were once here and now gone.

The sun was peeking over the horizon now, making the light noticeably better, as the pair watched the man walk with the rose toward a small fenced-in area of the cemetery. A black gate was surrounded by a wrought iron fence that housed a half-dozen headstones, separate from all the others in the graveyard. It was like a private cemetery in the middle of the cemetery.

The man's walk and steps were slow and shaky at times, indicating he must be quite old. No doubt, too old to be playing florist in the dark of night on uneven ground. From this distance, they couldn't make out his face, so Chase and Gavin hid quietly, watching him open the latch and enter the private burial plot.

There was a large statue of Jesus laying his hands on someone who was kneeling, perhaps healing the sick. Even in this bad light it looked majestic, exactly the kind of extravagant marker you'd expect to find at the grave of a wealthy man. It was mounted on a large white marble pedestal with the names Sebastian and Vida Winthrop etched in large letters below.

The man, in a long dark overcoat and a gray felt fedora hat, took the lone rose and approached the large stone. Chase elbowed Gavin as if to say *SEE, TOLD YA*. Gavin silently nodded his head, impressed with Chase's ability to solve any puzzle.

Yet the true puzzle was about to reveal itself, when the elderly man walked by the large stone and disappeared behind it. There was something back there, but neither Chase nor Gavin could see it.

Suddenly, the man appeared again, the rose missing from his hand, taking a seat on a cast iron bench just to the right of the grave. He rested his hat on the empty seat next to him, took a deep breath, and then said out loud, "Are you two going to stay in the shadows all morning or come talk to me?"

Gavin and Chase were secluded behind a large gravestone twenty feet away, but there was no mistaking that the man on the bench was talking to them.

"Um, hello?" Chase said, as she took Gavin's hand and yanked him out of their hiding spot.

Slowly they approached and carefully opened the gate to the private plot, as Gavin said, "We're so sorry to bother you, sir, we just, uh, we just were curious who was taking the rose every night."

The man didn't turn to look at them. Instead, he slowly took off his black leather gloves and said, "I told him when he wrote that letter nobody was going to follow his silly rules."

Chase thought the voice sounded familiar, so she inched closer trying to make out the face in the shadows, finally saying, "Hello, sir, my name is . . ."

"Chase," he replied, "You're Chase Harrington, the nice young lady who wrote that lovely article about my friend."

Chase's jaw dropped as she called out, "SAMUEL? Is that Samuel from the bridge in Central Park?"

The older man stood up, hat in hand now, and took a half bow, "One and the same."

Gavin smiled now. "So you're the person taking the roses?"

Samuel turned his eyes toward Gavin and responded in a most serious way, "A promise to your best friend is a promise to your best friend. And when that friend says bring my girl a rose every morning, you do it! Without question. Do you disagree?"

Gavin, being a gentleman who honored friendship, nodded, "No sir. I totally understand."

Samuel smiled, pointed at Gavin and replied, "You only think you do."

Gavin had no idea what that meant. Just then, Chase looked around Vida and Sebastian's stone and saw the rose was nowhere to be found, prompting her ask, "If you're bringing the rose to Vida, where is it?"

Samuel looked at Chase now, replying, "I never said I brought the flower to Vida."

Chase, clearly confused said, "But who then . . ."

With that, Samuel waved his hand, gesturing for the two of them to enter further and see what they could not see from just inside the gate. Hiding behind the large gravestone was a much smaller white stone with an angel, smiling and holding a heart in his hands. On the sides of the heart there were wings.

The perfectly shaped heart looked exactly like the drawing Chase and Gavin had seen in the window at the house, the same emblem they had seen at the children's hospital.

Chase tentatively moved closer to the tiny grave and saw one word carved in large letters: ROSE. Beneath that, in a slightly smaller font, it read, *Forever Our Angel.*

Chase had done extensive research when writing the article about Sebastian and Vida Winthrop, prompting her to say to Samuel, "But they didn't have children. So . . . who is Rose?"

Samuel sat back down and tapped the seat next to him on the bench, encouraging Chase to join him. Gavin approached the child's grave and saw beneath the beautiful angel and heart was the yellow rose that he had placed on the rock wall behind the house only hours earlier.

Samuel explained. "Years ago, when Sebastian and Vida started helping the children's hospital, they met a lot of great kids. But one in particular was special; her name was . . ."

Gavin, still staring at the stone, called out, "Rose."

"That's right, young man," Samuel said. "Rose was born with a tumor where the spinal cord attaches to the brain. Her parents were told she'd never live beyond the age of two and would need constant expensive care, which they could not afford."

Samuel stopped to make certain both Gavin and Chase were listening to the next part, then added, "So they left her, at birth, right there in a crib at St. Mary's hospital."

Gavin came to stand by Chase's side now, and she took his hand.

Samuel continued, "Sebastian and Vida met her when she was almost three, and she didn't even have a full name. Everyone just called her Rose, because she was beautiful like the flower."

Samuel glanced at the angel statue, now adding, "At first they'd visit her at the hospital, in the residential wing where the children who are very sick live full time. But when it got toward the end, when she was getting *very* sick, they decided to take her home so she wouldn't face what was coming, alone."

Chase was filling up with tears at the thought of it, her voice cracking as she asked, "My home, where I live now?"

Samuel replied, "Yes, dear. They brought nurses in round the clock, and she received the best care and was made comfortable for several months. On her good days, you'd find Rose running around that big house. I even played board games with her sometimes. We kept them in a room off the den."

Chase covered her mouth, trying to push back the tears. "Yes, we know. I mean, we saw those games."

Gavin, then looking at Chase, said, "That's why there was Candyland and Chutes and Ladders with the adult games. They had a little girl with them."

Up until that moment, neither Chase nor Gavin had ever wondered why a home without children would have children's games. Now it made perfect sense.

Chase then asked, "Did she, by any chance, like to play Scrabble?"

Samuel smiled and, in a surprised voice, replied, "Now, how did you know that?"

Chase started to cry, and Gavin gave her shoulder a squeeze to comfort her.

Samuel corrected himself. "Actually, when I say *play* Scrabble it wasn't like you or I would play. Rose liked to shake the letters up, dump them out and spell words that she knew. Cat. Dog. Bug. You know, most children under five can't spell a single word, but Rose was sharp."

Chase and Gavin were smiling now at the thought of it. They could picture a beautiful child sitting on that thick rug in the den laying out the little wooden tiles.

Samuel continued. "Her favorite letter was R, for Rose of course. Most days you'd find Rose walking around the house with the 'R' from the Scrabble game in her tiny hand. Watching TV, playing with her dolls, sitting in the kitchen eating frosted flakes; that little wooden R was right there with her."

Samuel looked off, as if trying to retrieve a memory, then added, "In fact, she lost that letter not long before she died. We looked everywhere but couldn't find it."

Gavin turned to Chase, who was a mess now with tears, whispering, "That's the missing letter. Remember the first time we played Scrabble and counted the tiles, one was missing."

Chase nodded and said, "There were only ninety-nine. I remember we counted twice."

Gavin replied, "Rose had it."

Samuel's own eyes were filling with tears, as he said, "The things that little girl could have been, if she were only able to grow up. They said she'd never see the age of two, but Rose lived four years, seven months, three days."

Chase collected herself, as Gavin walked back over to the child's grave, pointed, and then asked, "This heart the angel is holding. We saw it in the window back in the library. We wondered, which one drew it on the glass, Vida or Sebastian?"

Samuel got up, joined Gavin near the stone, touched the heart, and said, "Neither."

He looked up from the heart and added, "Rose drew it."

Chase's head spun around to look at Samuel, "Rose?"

Samuel answered, "Yes, ma'am. They had an early frost one October, and the heat wasn't turned up in the library yet, so those panes of glass all glazed over with ice. Rose went out in the yard, got up on a chair to reach the center window, and with her tiny finger drew a heart with angel wings. She said, um . . ."

Samuel stopped now, biting his bottom lip, which was quivering. It was clear he was getting too emotional to speak, the memory too strong.

Gavin asked, "Are you all right, sir?"

Samuel clinched his hand in a fist as if to catch the sadness sweeping through his body and squeeze it away.

He then finished his thought. "She said she knew she was sick and going to heaven soon, and then Rose said, 'I'm giving my heart wings because I'll be getting my angel wings soon.'"

After a long pause he added, "God bless that child."

No one knew what to say. Gavin broke the silence: "Samuel, did you know they use her heart with wings at the hospital? We saw it on the telethon video."

Samuel perked up at that thought, responding, "Oh yes, I know. I was there when they built that place. Did you see her picture? They have photos of, um, I think it's five kids who all passed away, on the wall in the children's playroom."

Gavin and Chase both searched their minds for the images they saw in the telethon video when Chase snapped her fingers and said, "The girl in the center photograph in the bright yellow dress with the curly hair!"

Samuel gave Chase a smile, "That's right. That's our Rose. Yellow was her favorite color."

Gavin put his arm around Chase now, and said, "So all this time, placing yellow roses on the rock wall. Rose was never just a flower."

Chase looked at the grave. "She was an angel."

Samuel picked up his hat and added, "Indeed she was, and now you know why you put them out each night. It's for her."

Chase and Gavin sensed it was time to go, when Samuel added, "Do you remember when I met you, Chase, I told you everyone got it wrong. How Sebastian's story was really a love story?"

Chase wiped a tear away and said, "I do, Samuel. And now I see it was more of a love story than even I knew. He had love for two special girls."

Samuel started toward the gate and touched the statue with Vida and Sebastian's names, answering, "Yes, he did. And he adored them both."

After closing the gate behind him, Samuel slowly made his way toward his car, calling out, "I do hope you'll keep those roses coming. One on the rock wall. Every night. Thank you."

As the taillights of his car vanished over the hill, the sunrise was in full splendor now, making even a cemetery look breathtaking.

In the shadow of Rose's angel statue, Gavin took Chase in his arms and said, "Manchester and now here . . ."

There was a long pause as Gavin took a deep breath, finally saying, "I don't know if you are drawn to these amazing things by forces we can't see, or if the opposite is true and your mere presence conjures up this magic."

Chase looked back into his loving eyes, not sure what to say, as Gavin added, "Just know, it doesn't matter. What I do know for absolute certain is you are special, Chase, and I love you."

The short ride home was quiet. Chase busy thinking about an important decision she needed to make regarding the future, while Gavin focused on finding someone from the past. If it all went as planned, the lady of Briarcliff Manor was about to see how all things connect, and sometimes dreams really do come true.

## CHAPTER 33

## *Not Again*

The next week went by uneventfully as Chase and Gavin both kept busy with their own secret projects. Chase received several calls from Clayton Philmont, the wealthy brother of Peter, formerly known as Oscar, pressuring her to sell him the mansion. When he had arrived in his fancy car weeks earlier, Clayton had offered full value for the property, plus an additional five percent. In the days since, he bumped his offer up another ten, fifteen, then twenty percent, making it $4.8 million. He told Chase, in his last message, that he'd go to an even five, if they could get it done quickly.

For someone who had grown up poor, the thought of someone handing you that much money was mind-boggling to Chase, yet something didn't feel right about it. After all, she had come to possess the property by accident after buying a cheap sketch. Emotion and blind loyalty to a man she never met caused Chase to raise her hand that day in the auction house, not greed. If she sold, it had to be for the right reasons.

It was December 17th, one week before Christmas Eve, and Chase asked Gavin to connect the printer to the laptop computer.

"What do you need printed?" he asked.

"Documents," she replied. "But if you don't mind, I don't want you reading them until the right moment."

Gavin asked sincerely, "And how will I know when that is?"

Chase hugged him, saying, "Oh, trust me, you'll know."

As the printer came to life and started spitting out papers filled with words, Gavin joked, "If this is a prenup, I have to tell you I'm fine giving you my truck and half of my interest in Dad's farm. I believe he has four goats now, two of which are mine, so there's definitely a goat in this for you if we get married and things go south."

The thought made Chase laugh, as she said, "No, sweetheart, it's not a prenup and I'm not worried about your fortune or mine. As long as we love each other, that's good enough for me."

"Ditto," Gavin replied, as he lifted the half dozen pages off the printer, making sure not to read them.

Outside, a loud beep echoed into the mansion, sending Scooter scurrying, his nails clicking and clacking on the hardwood floor as he darted for the front door.

"Good. Our guests have arrived, just in time," Chase said, taking the documents from Gavin's hands.

Parked outside was the same expensive car Chase had seen before, and out stepped Clayton Philmont with his younger brother Peter.

Gavin saw them standing together and said, "I keep forgetting they're brothers, they're so different from each other."

His observation was a bit too loud, causing Clayton to reply, "Indeed we are, Gilbert."

"Um," Gavin responded with a half smirk. "It's Gavin. GAVIN."

Clayton ignored the correction as Peter circled the car and clapped his hands, urging Scooter to come see him. "Who's a good boy?" he asked, as the pup jumped in his arms.

"Ms. Harrington," Clayton began, "If I'm here to buy the house, why did you want my brother to tag along?"

Chase looked from one Philmont brother to the other and said, "He's here because I asked him to be, and who knows, maybe he wants to buy the house."

Peter looked up from the dog, who was now lying on his back having his tummy rubbed, and said, "ME? I don't have enough money to buy this place."

Chase gave him a mischievous wink and said, "Ya never know, Oscar."

Clayton spoke: "Oscar?"

Gavin, still annoyed that this rich snob got his name wrong, replied, "It's a long story, Clem."

Clayton shot a snarky look at Gavin, "It's Clayton."

Gavin then, "You sure? You kind of look like a Clem to me."

Chase could see none of this banter amused Clayton, so she asked, "Did you both bring the things I asked of you?"

Clayton tapped his breast pocket, and said, "Yes, I have my checkbook right here, and I wore my most expensive watch from my collection."

With that Clayton held up his right wrist, revealing a shiny gold time piece.

"And you, OSS . . . I mean, Peter?" Chase said in a silly tone.

This caused him to giggle a bit, then answer, "Yes, ma'am, I have an envelope right here in my back pocket, and I'm sorry to say my most expensive watch is this Fossil brand that I picked up at JCPenney for eighty-one bucks."

Gavin looked at Chase and asked, "What's going on?"

Chase smiled wryly and said, "You're about to find out."

With that, a man walked around from the side yard holding a shovel in his hand and gave Chase a wave. It was Nick, the groundskeeper.

"Hole is all set," he said, giving Chase a thumbs up.

"Thank you, Nick, we're coming now," she replied.

Chase walked them around the large house, and there, already waiting, was a freshly dug hole in the ground. It was two feet square and revealed a three-foot drop to the bottom. With the ground hard from the recent frost, it had taken Nick twenty minutes to dig it.

Chase turned her attention to Clayton Philmont and said, "Sir, you said you want to buy my house. I brought you here today to say, I *will* sell it to you."

Before Chase could finish that thought, the well-dressed man clapped his hands in celebration and said under his breath, "I knew you had your price. I knew five million would turn you around."

Chase gave him a hard look, then said, "Nothing turned me around, sir, and I'd have you hold your tongue and checkbook until you hear the terms."

"Terms?" Peter asked, curious what Chase had up her sleeve, and loving the fact that someone was finally putting his pompous brother in his place.

"Yes, terms. I'll sell you the house, Clayton, on two conditions. We'll call them . . . parts. Part one and part two."

Clayton could see the documents in Chase's hands, and reached toward her, saying, "Let me read them."

This gesture caused Chase to recoil back and say, "Slow down, tiger. I'll tell you the terms, and they don't involve you touching that, at least not yet."

Clayton, feeling thoroughly scolded, looked down toward his feet and said, "Apologies. Continue."

Chase pressed on. "As I was saying, the terms come in two parts, parts one and two. You can't get to part two until you do part one."

Nick, having no clue what any of this was about, chimed in. "Sounds logical to me."

This caused Chase to look at him lovingly and say, "Why, thank you, Nick, and nice job on the hole, by the way."

Nick grinned proudly, heard a buzz, then looked down at his phone and said, "She won't stop texting me. Deb."

Gavin was smiling now, because he could tell Nick loved it.

Chase's eyes went back to Clayton. "Let's get to part one. I asked you to wear the most expensive watch you own. So, what is that on your wrist?"

Clayton held his hand up high and said, "This is a Patek Philippe eighteen-carat brushed gold watch with a sterling silver dial and alligator band. It's accurate to one ten-thousandth of a second and worth one hundred and forty-eight thousand dollars."

That price caused Gavin to whistle loudly.

Chase replied, "Wow, sounds impressive. What time is it exactly?"

Clayton looked at the face of the watch and said, "Four minutes past noon."

Chase then turned to Nick, still holding the shovel, and said, "Nick, I see you have a Timex on. What time do you have?"

The groundskeeper glanced down at his old watch that was smeared with mud, and said, "Same. 12:04."

Gavin looked away, trying to stifle a laugh, as Chase turned to Clayton and said, "Imagine that, they both keep the same time, and he paid a hundred grand less than you."

Clayton didn't appreciate the joke, saying, "Did you bring me here to mock me, young lady?"

Chase gave him a serious look and said, "No sir, I did not. Just teasing."

Peter chimed in. "My brother doesn't like being teased."

Clayton gave Peter a look that said, *Butt out.*

Chase then surprised everyone when she said, "Part one of my offer to sell the house involves you taking that Patek whatcha-ma-call-it off your wrist and tossing it in the hole."

Clayton looked at the dark hole in the ground and said, "Why?"

Chase then, "Because you can't bury it if it's not in the hole."

Clayton, "And why in God's name would I bury a hundred-thousand-dollar watch?"

All eyes were on Chase now as she smiled and said, "Because that's part one of my deal."

Clayton raised his voice then, sounding a bit upset: "DESTROYING a priceless watch, that's your idea of a deal?"

Chase didn't say a word, she just stood silent, everyone watching Clayton think.

Finally, he said, "So this is a test. If I bury the watch you sell me the house?"

Chase shrugged her shoulders and said, "No, I sell you the house if you agree to step two, which only happens if you complete step one."

Clayton then replied in a dismissive tone, "Are you playing games with me, girl?"

Gavin stepped back from the group, throwing his hands in the air, thinking, *You did NOT just call her GIRL.*

But Chase, cool as the ground beneath their feet, smiled like a Cheshire Cat, saying firmly, "I'm not a girl, I'm a woman, and I assure you, sir, you *can* buy the house. You just need to complete my two steps."

Clayton paced in a circle around the hole and then said in an accusatory tone, "So I destroy my watch and then you tell me you'll only sell me the house for twenty million bucks or something ridiculous, and what then, I don't get the mansion and I'm out a watch? I don't think so."

Chase again, "I can promise you, sir, I'm not looking to trick you or get any more money than you've already offered. In fact, how's this? You can forget the five million dollars you were willing to pay. I'm asking way less. The number in this document will more than offset the cost of that expensive watch. You have my word."

Clayton thought some more, then asked, "But what are the conditions? What is step two?"

Gavin, having no clue what Chase was up to, intervened now. "Isn't it clear she's not telling you that until you demonstrate that you'll bury the watch? So, if you want the house, bury it."

With that last word, Gavin grabbed the shovel from Nick's hands and tossed it on the ground at Clayton's feet.

Another pause, and then Clayton said, "Do I have to throw it in, or can I place the watch in gently?"

Chase just smiled. "Hey, it's your watch."

Clayton took the very expensive timepiece off his wrist, got down on his belly on the cold ground, reached in as far as he could, and gently dropped the watch into the hole. He stood up, took the shovel, and scooped up a large pile of fresh dirt.

Nick smiled, thinking, *Oh, man, he's really gonna do it.*

Clayton lifted the shovel of dirt high, ready to dump it in, and then his eyes shifted from everyone watching, down to his prize watch now in its eternal grave. As everyone held their breath, the next sound they heard was not dirt hitting the hole but the shovel falling to the ground, followed by Clayton quickly diving down to retrieve his watch.

As he rose from the ground, dirt now covering his chest, he said, "I can't do it. I'm not ruining this expensive watch so you can make some point that nobody here understands. Forget it."

Chase walked over and touched Clayton kindly on the shoulder and said, "I understand completely, and I'm sorry I put you through that."

Clayton kept touching the watch, making sure he didn't damage it, replying, "You should be sorry. So, what now? You don't sell, after all this nonsense, you don't sell?"

Chase smiled again and said, "Hmm, let's find out. Peter, did you wonder why I asked you to come along with your brother today?"

Peter scratched his head and said, "Kinda."

Chase smiled warmly and said, "I planned on selling my home to a Philmont today, but I had my doubts that your brother would pass my two steps. Would you like to try?"

Clayton folded his arms and glared at his brother, saying rudely, "Yeah, like he has four million bucks lying around, the guy who collects empty bottles for nickels."

Peter gave him a sarcastic smirk back, then turned to Chase and said, "My arrogant brother is right. I have some trust fund dough put aside, but nowhere near that amount, Chase. I appreciate you asking, though."

With that Chase said, "But you haven't heard my price."

Peter looked confused, as Chase continued, "And you won't, because that's part of step two. As you just saw, I won't do step two until we dispense with step one. So, would you please toss your watch in the hole and bury it? Call it an act of faith."

Without hesitation Peter took off the Fossil watch and thew it in the hole. He picked up the shovel and put his shoulder into the task at hand, quickly filling the gap and making the watch disappear. When he had finished, he leaned on the shovel, and said, "How's that?"

Chase said, "I know what you just did looks insane, but there is a point to it that I'm happy to explain later, something I learned from the previous owner about what matters in life."

Peter nodded in agreement and said, "I look forward to that conversation. So, what's step two?"

Chase replied, "I asked Clayton to bring his checkbook, but when it came to you, I asked you to bring something *very* specific in an envelope. Do you have that with you?"

Peter pulled a sealed white envelope out of the back pocket of his jeans and held it up. "It's right here."

Gavin, Nick, and Clayton all stood silently looking on, with no clue what was about to happen.

Chase handed Peter the contract she had Gavin print earlier, "Step two is you agree to two things in this document, the price for the house and the way in which it's to be used."

Peter started reading the first page of the contract, when Chase said, "Rather than have you read it, why don't I tell you what it says."

Peter looked up and replied, "Okay."

Chase then addressed the group of them, "Have you ever heard of a Ronald McDonald house?"

Peter thought a moment and said, "Yes, it's a place for families to stay if their child is sick in the hospital."

Chase smiled, "That's exactly right. Free food and a roof over their head for a day, a week, whatever they need. There are more than 300 of them all over the country."

Peter nodded in agreement as Chase continued. "Before he died, Sebastian Winthrop, the man who owned this place before me, let a sick little girl stay with him here. He made her final days happy."

Chase then looked up at the stately mansion and said, "This house is so full of love. First Vida and Sebastian and then Rose, the girl they brought here."

She looked back at Peter, now adding, "I think it should stay that way."

Peter replied, "I'm sorry, how exactly do we do that?"

Chase again, "Here's how. If you agree to buy my home, all I ask is, if a family with a sick child at St. Mary's Hospital needs a place to crash for a night or two, you'll let them stay in one of those empty bedrooms upstairs. There's a trust fund already set up by the Winthrops—his executor, Charlotte Jackson, took care of that—and it will cover all your costs. All you need do is open the front door to these families."

Before Peter could even answer she said, "You volunteer at the homeless shelter because you want to help the less fortunate, correct?"

Peter replied, "Yes, I do."

Chase then, "Well, you can do that right here for moms and dads who are out of their minds with worry and need a quiet place to stay. Would you be willing to do that, Peter, if I sell you the house?"

Peter loved Chase's heart and what she was proposing, but reality set in as he said, "I would, Chase, I mean, it all sounds great, what you want to do here. But I told you, I can't pay you what this place is worth."

Chase turned to Clayton now and said, "Feel like loaning your little brother four million, just for old time's sake?"

Clayton shot her an incredulous look and said, "I DO NOT."

Chase smiled at Clayton and replied, "Yeah, I didn't think you would. That's why I priced it to sell."

She looked back at Peter again and said, "Turn to page three of the contract and look at the bottom for the price."

Peter quickly turned the pages in the document, then exclaimed, "WHAT?"

He looked at Chase and the others, stunned.

Gavin asked, "What does it say, Peter?"

Peter laughed out loud and held the document up so they could all read the two numbers in bold black ink.

"She wants *twenty-seven dollars*."

Everyone's jaws dropped as Chase explained. "It didn't feel right, making money on this property, and after all, twenty-seven bucks is what I paid for it, so, it only seems fair."

Everyone stood speechless, when Chase asked, "Peter, you don't happen to have that amount of money on you by chance, do you?"

Peter opened the white envelope he'd been carrying and took out a twenty-dollar bill, a five, and two ones. It was exactly the amount he was told to bring, and precisely what he'd need to buy the four-million-dollar estate.

Clayton grabbed the contract out of his brother's hand and said, "Not again. Is this a joke?"

Then, after scanning the legal document and their satisfied faces, he screamed, "NOT AGAIN!"

Nick leaned in and broke the tension when he said, "At least you still have your fancy watch. It keeps lovely time."

Everyone laughed at that comment except for Clayton, who shook his finger at Chase and said, "You're insane. You know that? You were insane to buy that sketch at the auction, and you're insane now. I could have made you rich."

Chase took Gavin's hand in hers, locking fingers, and said, "I'm already rich, Mr. Philmont."

With that, Clayton started walking back toward his car and his driver, barking at his brother, Peter, "Find your own ride back to the city."

Nick gave Peter a playful shove and said, "Don't worry, buddy, I got ya. Long as you don't mind riding shotgun in a pickup with no heat."

The thought made Peter laugh out loud with delight.

As Clayton's expensive ride disappeared down the driveway, Chase said to Peter, "Oh, there is one request I have. It's not in the contract, just a favor for me."

Peter turned to meet her eyes, his own eyes swelling with tears over such an emotional morning, saying, "Name it."

She smiled at Gavin, still holding his hand, then said, "I'd like you to call this house *Rose Garden,* after a special little girl. Can you do that for me?"

Peter looked at the huge mansion, his head still spinning from what had just happened, and said, "You bet. Rose Garden. I promise to honor your wishes."

Gavin joined in: "Oh, Peter, speaking of honoring wishes, there's a letter that was left for us by the former owner you'll want to read. It's nothing major, just a few chores that go with living here."

Peter climbed into Nick's pickup and said, "Anything you need."

As Gavin waved goodbye, Chase pulled his sleeve and said softly, "Hey, you okay with me giving the place away? I mean, Clayton was right, it *is* a lot of money."

Gavin gave her a soft kiss, looked deep in her eyes, and replied, "As you said, we're already rich in all the ways that matter, babe. Besides, I have plans of my own for us."

Chase pulled back from his embrace for a better look at his handsome face, then asked, "Such as?"

Gavin took the ring finger on her left hand, giving the promise ring she wore a gentle kiss, and said, "Such as, keep your schedule clear for Christmas Eve. I have a surprise for you."

Chase looked back at the home she had just sold for a song and, as a cold December wind swept across the frost-covered pines, she swore she could hear an old man whisper from heaven, "Well done, young lady, well done."

## CHAPTER 34

# Finding Grace

Chase was sound asleep on Christmas Eve morning when Scooter licked her face, as if to say, *Get up, already!* Her unfocused eyes saw movement outside the window, and it took her a moment to realize there was fluffy light snow drifting by the glass. She thought Manchester, Vermont, was the prettiest place on earth at Christmastime, but the mansion at Briarcliff Manor held a close second. A half-dozen pine trees dotted the property, the tops of each coated in white, while the grounds looked as if an invisible chef had shaken powdered sugar atop everything.

Once in her slippers and robe, Chase crept downstairs to the smell of something delicious. Her nose led her to the kitchen, where a single pan with a copper bottom was sitting on the back burner of the stove, the heat set at the lowest level. Chase lifted the lid and found a vegetable omelet shaped perfectly like a heart.

"What in God's name?" Chase said out loud, before dashing to the front window to see Gavin's truck was not there.

"Did he stop by, make me breakfast and leave?" she asked to the empty room.

As she turned to go back to the kitchen and make a cup of coffee, Scooter stood in front of her and barked.

"It's too early for that, buddy. Let mommy wake up," she replied.

But as she went to walk by, her pup stepped directly into her path and barked again, deliberately blocking her advance. Chase glanced down and realized there was something red tied around his neck. She looked closer and saw it was a ribbon that had not been there the night before. Curious, she slid it off Scooter's neck, and on the ribbon she found a message written in black Sharpie: *Eat your breakfast, brush your hair, dress for warmth and a special dare.*

"Poetry? I'm starting my day with poetry?" Chase mumbled.

She could tell it was Gavin's handwriting, but she had no clue what he was up to. Chase knew he was close to popping the question and had told her a week earlier to keep Christmas Eve free for a surprise. Apparently, whatever adventure awaited, it involved following her future fiancé's riddles.

"Okay, sweetie, I'll play along," she said with glee.

After eating the delicious omelet and taking a quick shower, Chase went to her closet to dress for the day. A gray knit sweater and a pair of jeans should get it done, she thought, and then she remembered Gavin's instructions to *dress for warmth.*

On the right side of Chase's large walk-in closet, she kept an array of scarves and hats. After she pulled on a thin chain that hung down from the light fixture, the 75-watt bulb came alive, and the dark closet was now fully visible. Chase smiled when she saw another red ribbon tied around the hook that held her favorite white wool scarf.

She slid the ribbon off the hook and turned it over to read the next clue: *One need not live near water to find a river. They run through the strangest places. - N.M.*

Chase realized Scooter was standing in the doorway of the closet watching all this unfold, and she smiled and said, "We've got another clue, buddy, but this one has mommy stumped."

Chase took the ribbon in her hand and walked over to the large, fluffy bed she had been sleeping in only a half hour earlier. She sat down and patted the blanket, prompting Scooter to jump up next to her.

She then read the riddle once again out loud: " 'One need not live near water to find a river. They run through the strangest places.' Then the initials N and M."

Chase stared at the phrase for the longest time and said to her dog, "There are no rivers around the property, not even a pond. And I have no clue who N.M. is."

She got up and stared out the bedroom window, searching for water, but there was none to be found, not even a puddle. Then she looked back at the ribbon and said, "They run through the strangest places. Run through . . ."

Chase snapped her fingers and yelled to Scooter, "I THINK I'VE GOT IT. Follow me."

With that she darted out of the bedroom, down the stairs, and into the library. Chase started scanning the bookshelves for one title in particular.

It took a moment before Chase called out, "There you are!"

Her eyes fell upon a book by a writer named Norman Maclean, initials N.M. The story was a modern classic that Chase had read more than once after seeing the movie that was based on it. Scooter walked into the library and looked at Chase, as she held up the book and said, "*A River Runs Through It.* Our clue is a book. That's the *river* that's running through a strange place. This library."

There was no need to open the book, because she saw another red ribbon tucked in the center of the pages like a bookmark. The note on the ribbon read, *Today is the day where our love will grow, so at the stroke of noon meet me at the Bow.*

Chase squeezed the soft ribbon in her hand and then raised it to her face, covering her mouth to contain the excitement. She knew what this had to mean. Back when she wrote the great love story of Sebastian and Vida Winthrop for the *New Yorker* magazine, Samuel told her to meet him at *The Bow.* It was that special, romantic bridge in Central Park in New York City.

It was the exact spot where Sebastian popped the question to his sweetheart. If Gavin were going to take a knee and ask for her hand, it most certainly would be there. One thing puzzled Chase, though. Gavin said the big moment would be a surprise, so why was he tipping his hand this way?

"I'll know soon enough," she said to herself.

Chase reached for her phone to call Matthew and arrange a ride to the city when she heard a car horn beep out front. "Gavin?" she yelled, as she ran for the door.

No, it was Matthew already sitting in the circular driveway, waiting to take Cinderella to Prince Charming. But it was only 9:30. Surely, Chase didn't need two hours to get to the city. Why so early?

Matthew's window slowly rolled down and his hand reached out with a bright white envelope in his grasp.

"For me?" she asked with a smile.

Matthew smiled back and said, "Big day for you, sweetheart."

Chase opened the envelope, and it was a gift certificate for a posh spa in Manhattan. The note on the front told Chase she had an appointment to get her nails, makeup, and hair done this morning, all of it pre-arranged by Gavin.

"I should change," Chase said to her driver. "I mean, if he's going to, you know, I can't be wearing old jeans and a lumpy sweater."

With that Matthew cleared his throat dramatically and pointed to the back seat and a large silver box with a silky red bow. Chase opened the car's back door, slid in, and opened the box. It was a gorgeous black cashmere Veronica Beard dress cut just below the knee. Perfect for a chilly day in the park. Without saying another word, Matthew put the car in drive, and with each mile, Chase was moving closer to her destiny.

"Wait," she said, "Who's gonna feed Scooter and let him out?"

Matthew found her face in the rearview mirror and said, "Just like your breakfast. All taken care of."

Chase's mind was now swimming with so many things: *the day they met, their first kiss, the moment she realized Gavin was her happy ever after.* She wished it was already noon, so she could race to that bridge and leap in his arms.

The spa was exquisite, complete with a soft robe, slippers, and a perfectly chilled mimosa. With her nails and makeup done and auburn hair fluffed to perfection, Chase returned to the backseat of Matthew's car, and he headed for Central Park. Being a retired NYPD detective, Matthew had a special badge that gave him access to places others could not go. When a street cop in blue tried to wave him off, Matthew just flashed the badge, and Chase was allowed straight through.

He drove as close as he could to the Bow bridge in Central Park, shut off the engine, and said, "Before you get out, I have two things to say."

Chase put her chin on the top of the backseat, moving closer to her friend.

"First," he began, "thank you for saving my life. I won't pretend to understand exactly how you do what you do, but I'm so grateful to have you as my friend. That's who saved me that day, not some talented writer I drive around for money—my friend."

Chase felt emotion well up in her, whispering back, "You're welcome."

Matthew continued, "The second thing is, I'm pretty sure your life is about to change in two minutes. Just know, no matter what, Chase, no matter where you go, day or night, I'm always a phone call away."

Chase reached over the seat to grasp Matthew's hand and squeezed it lovingly. "Thank you so much, for everything."

He could see her eyes glistening over and said, "Don't cry or you'll wreck your makeup."

Chase smiled and said, "You're one to talk."

Matthew's eyes were moist with tears, something Chase had never seen in all the time she had known him. He cleared his throat, hit the unlock button on the car doors, and said, "Go get your man."

Chase let go of his hand and sprang from the car in her brand-new dress. Even though it looked a bit out of place, she kept the white scarf she'd taken from the closet tied around her neck, to keep warm. The chill in the air gave her white cheeks a red glow, and her heart started beating a mile a minute as she made her way to the bridge.

The Bow is the longest of all the bridges in Central Park, standing at 87 feet. While most bridges in the park were built to be inconspicuous, almost hidden, the Bow was the opposite. It spanned a stretch of water, and the trees were cut back on both sides, making it stand out. The light snow that had greeted Chase in Briarcliff Manor found its way to Manhattan as well, making the park look magical.

Normally the bridge would be busy with foot traffic, but Chase saw a well-dressed man standing on each end, stopping people from crossing. They were retired NYPD officers that Gavin asked Matthew to hire for just this moment. Whatever was about to happen, it would just be the two of them alone on the bridge. Or so Chase thought. Gavin promised a surprise, and indeed, one was coming.

Chase carefully walked on the cobblestones to one end of the bridge. She could see Gavin waiting by himself directly in the center of the Bow, wearing a beautiful black peacoat. It was buttoned up to the top and fit Gavin perfectly, hugging his strong frame. Chase was so in love with Gavin's heart, she sometimes forgot how drop-dead gorgeous he could be when he made the tiniest effort. Today his look was spot on, complete with a new haircut and shave he'd gotten just an hour before.

As Chase was about to step onto the bridge, she noticed something strange on the other side. Just up from the water, sat a beautiful horse-drawn carriage. It wasn't like the open carriages that carried tourists in the park; it was enclosed with a small door, hiding whoever was inside. The driver on top was dressed to the nines, holding the leather reins that led down to a pair of stunning white horses. The image reminded Chase of something from a fairy tale.

Gavin was why she was here, though, not the carriage, so she smiled at the officer who was guarding her side of the bridge as he motioned for her to enter. The center of the bridge was forty paces, and Chase covered them as quickly as she could. Gavin turned as she reached him, and just as he had done on their first date back in Manchester, he paused before kissing her, making certain their eyes met, long before their lips.

After the gentlest of kisses, Gavin said, "I see you followed my clues."

Chase smiled and said, "It took me a minute to figure out the second one, about the book, *A River Runs Through It.*"

Gavin nodded and said, "I knew you loved that story. Remind me, what did Norman Maclean say are the three things you should never be late for?"

Chase, without missing a beat, responded, "Church, work, and fishing."

Gavin pointed toward the water and said, "I don't plan on catching any fish today, so why don't we change it to, you should never be late for church, work, or your fiancé."

Chase knew the moment was coming for months now, but hearing him say that word out loud, *fiancé*, still caused her knees to wobble. She could see in Gavin's face it had the same effect on him too.

Gavin stood there then, not saying a word, just drinking in Chase's beauty. The silence made her eyes look down at Gavin's hands and pockets. Surely, if this was about to happen, he'd be producing a ring any second.

But there was no ring, just Gavin looking lovingly at her in that moment.

Finally, he said, "Did you notice the beautiful Cinderella carriage over there?"

Chase looked at it again, and replied, "Sure, who could miss it?"

Gavin continued, "Once, a long time ago, you told me a story about the first time you ever left home. It was a trip here to New York City. A high school graduation present, if I recall."

Chase confirmed, "Yes, that's right."

Gavin went on: "You saw a Broadway show, ran all over Manhattan, even shopped on Fifth Avenue."

Chase nodded. "We did."

Gavin continued. "And Matthew tells me that sometimes when you walk down Fifth Avenue, you stop in front of Tiffany's and stare in the window, but you never go in."

Chase wasn't sure what any of this had to do with getting engaged. All she could muster was a confused, "Okay?"

"You told me, on that first trip here, when you were just a kid, that you wanted to buy something that came in the pretty Tiffany's blue box, but you didn't have enough money."

Chase paused and looked away from the Gavin, down at the water beneath the bridge reflecting the nearby trees, and said, "That's right."

Gavin went on, "And if I remember correctly, you told me a very nice saleslady, an older woman, pulled you aside and was kind to you. She didn't embarrass you; she actually gave you an empty Tiffany's box to take home as a keepsake."

The memory pulled at Chase's heart now, as she looked back to Gavin's eyes. "She did. She wanted me to have it, even if I couldn't afford to put anything inside. It was such a nice thing to do."

Gavin again, "And yet, now that you live here, you never go back in to buy anything, even though you have the money. Did you ever ask yourself why?"

Chase thought a moment then said, "No. I guess . . . Oh, I don't know, Gavin. I guess part of me never felt good enough."

Gavin took her by both hands and said, "Well, that, my dear, ends today. Right here and right now."

Chase's eyes were welling with tears.

"When I was in Seattle on my secret mission, I asked your mom about that Tiffany's box that the nice lady gave you all those years ago, and she told me it was still in your old bedroom just sitting there on a shelf."

Chase's eyes went wide with surprise, "I didn't realize it was even still there."

"It is, or at least it was," Gavin continued, "until I took it. I figured if I was going to get you the engagement ring that *you* deserved it should be from Tiffany's and it should be in *that* very box."

Chase was astonished now at Gavin's thoughtfulness, then was so excited she started to stammer, "So you, um, got me? Ya know . . . from?"

Gavin took Chase by both shoulders and said firmly, "I DID!!"

Chase again looked at Gavin's hands, then his pockets, but there was no sign of the box. "So?" she asked hopefully.

"Well," Gavin replied, "Once there was a girl who went into Tiffany's and couldn't afford a thing. A nice lady gave her an empty box and a promise that someday it would be filled with something special. It only makes sense to me that if you are to be handed that box . . ."

Gavin looked toward the horse-drawn carriage and waved his hand over his head to get the driver's attention, then said to Chase, "Don't you think it would be amazing if the very woman who was kind to you that day, was here to give us the ring?"

Chase's eyes traveled over to the carriage just as the tiny door opened, and a much older woman slowly stepped out. The carriage driver took her hand and carefully led her to the edge of the bridge. The woman, with snow-white hair, was dressed beautifully and had a small blue bag clutched in her hands. She eased her way across the Bow to the waiting couple, but even before she reached them, Chase recognized the face. Older now, but in many ways exactly the same.

Gavin spoke: "This, Chase, is Grace O'Reilly. And, Mrs. O'Reilly, this is my sweetheart, Chase."

The elderly woman took one hand off the blue Tiffany's bag she was holding and reached out to shake Chase's hand. "So lovely to see you again, dear."

Chase smiled and said, "You as well, ma'am, but, with all due respect, there's no way you could remember me."

Grace gave her a stern look and said, "I beg your pardon. This old mind is as sharp as a tack, and I do remember meeting you. Not so much the face, but I remember what you said to me that day."

Chase looked puzzled. "I only remember not being able to afford a keychain, and you gave me the Tiffany's box anyway. Which was so sweet. I don't recall saying anything else."

Grace replied, "After I gave you the tiny box, I asked what your plans were, and you told me you were going off to college and hoping to be a writer someday."

Chase was astonished the woman remembered that part when Chase did not.

Grace continued, "I always wondered what happened to that young lady who wanted to write. And you know what, Chase?"

Chase responded, "What, Mrs. O'Reilly?"

"Grace, please call me Grace," she replied.

Then she continued, "I didn't realize it, but I've read some of your stories and never knew it was you. When Gavin contacted me through my old store manager and told me why he wanted me to be here today, he told me about your most recent article on Sebastian Winthrop. And I told him, *I read that and loved it.* So, you see, dear, I was a fan of your writing and didn't even know it."

Chase smiled warmly. "That's amazing, Mrs., I mean Grace."

The old woman replied, "But look at me, blathering on when there is work to be done by this young man."

With that, Gavin reached into the bag and produced the same Tiffany blue box that Grace had given to Chase nearly twenty years earlier. He dropped to one knee, and there at the center of the Bow Bridge, just as Sebastian had done for Vida fifty years ago, opened a ring box to reveal a perfect stone. It was a little over two carats, in a traditional round cut. The light bouncing off the diamond was nearly blinding, making it clear this was an exquisite ring.

Chase nearly burst into tears at the sight of her man down at her feet, looking up with those blue eyes which were now filling with water.

"Chase," he began, "from the moment I met you on the side of a country road, until this one, I've been in love with you. Only a fool could believe someone so beautiful on the outside could be equally beautiful inside, but you are. Your whole life is about helping others."

Chase could swear her feet were lifting off the ground as Gavin continued.

"You are the only woman I know who is comfortable dressing up and standing shoulder to shoulder with millionaires at an auction and then grabbing a flashlight and work boots and searching for a missing dog in the woods at midnight. Pretty as they are, I don't need lightning bugs or the stars at Grand Central Station. You, Chase, are my light. I know I'm just a plainspoken man, so I'll put it to you like this. I don't want you to be my girlfriend anymore."

With that Gavin stood up and took the ring out of the box, adding, "I want you to be my wife."

He took her left ring finger and touched the promise ring he had placed there three years earlier and said, "This ring made you a promise. Today we keep that promise and replace it with a ring that means forever."

Gavin slid the ring with Chase's birthstone off and onto another finger on her hand, and then put the incredible Tiffany diamond in its place.

Most women would have been transfixed by the diamond, but Chase couldn't stop looking into Gavin's eyes. She just stared as tears streamed down her cheeks.

Finally, Grace leaned in and said, "He's waiting for an answer, dear."

Chase kissed Gavin passionately and then said in the softest, most loving voice, "Yes."

Strangers, who were waiting patiently to cross the Bow Bridge, broke into spontaneous applause, and one let out a loud whistle, causing everyone else in the park to turn and see what all the celebrating was about.

Chase looked down at her stunning ring and then gave Grace a hug, thanking her for making this moment so perfect.

She then turned to Gavin and said, "This WAS a surprise. Well done."

Gavin gave her a mischievous look and didn't answer right away, causing Chase to ask, "The ring, the box, you finding Grace, was my big surprise, yes?"

Gavin took her by the hand and said, "Most of it. But there's still one part left."

Gavin led her by the hand off the bridge and said, "We have one last stop."

Chase pointed toward the carriage and said, "Are we riding in that?"

Gavin smiled, "As much as you remind me of Cinderella, no, we have almost two miles to cover, and I think we'd freeze in this December air. I believe we can manage something a bit more comfortable than that."

Chase now noticed a short distance away a shiny black limousine was waiting by the curb. Gavin escorted his brand-new fiancée and Grace into the back of the limo, where chilled Dom Perignon was waiting in a silver ice bucket.

"WOW, top shelf," Chase exclaimed, picking up the bottle to pour the three of them a glass.

"Look at the date," Gavin replied, smiling.

Chase found it on the bottle and bit down on her lip, causing Grace to say, "What is it?"

Chase then said to Grace, "It was bottled the year Gavin and I met."

The limo driver, another friend of Matthew's who was pressed into service, took less than ten minutes to reach their destination in Central Park. They could have been driving to the moon and Chase wouldn't have noticed, having never taken her eyes off the ring.

When the vehicle came to a stop, Chase asked, "Where are we?"

Gavin replied, "Do you remember the end of that movie you loved, *Serendipity*?"

Chase smiled and said, "NO! Are we at the ice rink?"

It was the Wollman Rink, another famous landmark in the park, filled with Christmas Eve skaters holding hands, falling down, some falling in love on this perfect December day.

Chase turned to Grace and explained, "In one of my favorite movies the boy and girl find each other, lose each other, and eventually find each other again right here at this ice rink."

Grace smiled and then surprised Chase when she said, "I love a good John Cusack movie, young lady—I know it well."

The limo driver opened the back door to help Chase out, and she was immediately greeted with a loud cry of, "CONGRATULATIONS!!!"

Chase almost burst into tears again when she saw who was waiting for them: Raylan and Bonnie from the café, Peter, Mary, Charlie, Matthew her driver, Deb and Nick holding hands, no less, her college roommate Jennifer, and a half dozen other faces from the neighborhood whom Chase used to wave hello to every day.

"I thought such a special occasion should be shared by friends. I hope you don't mind," Gavin said, as he wrapped his arm around Chase's shoulders.

A children's choir was in the park that day, singing a festive Christmas song about hope and love. Directly to their left, Chase saw an array of street vendors selling hats, scarves, bags, and artwork, roasting chestnuts and heating pretzels, the very essence of Christmas in Manhattan.

As Chase looked from her friends to Gavin and then down to her ring, she couldn't believe how perfect this all was. Then . . .

"How's the house?" a voice asked from the crowd. It was Charlotte *Stonewall* Jackson, dressed in a pretty pink sweater, her hair all done up, making her seem soft and approachable.

Chase just stared, her mouth slightly open, shocked by how good she looked.

"What? A lady can't dress up now and again? This *is* a special occasion," Charlotte said, smiling now at Chase.

Chase smiled back, "You look amazing."

Charlotte moved closer and said out loud, "I heard you sold Briarcliff for twenty-seven bucks. Not a very smart businesswoman, are you?"

Chase and everyone looked on, not sure what to say, then Charlotte winked and added playfully, "You could have gotten at least twenty-eight."

Everyone chuckled at her good humor.

Then Chase met Charlotte's eyes and said, "I sold it to Peter over there, so it could become a home to help the families of sick children. The way the Winthrops did with Rose. You okay with that?"

The big mean woman the world knew as Stonewall stepped forward, gave Chase a hug, then said, "I couldn't be prouder of you. Sebastian and Vida would have loved the idea."

Charlie and Mary approached Chase and Gavin to offer congratulations, when Charlie reached into her coat pocket, taking something out and then holding her closed fist in front of Chase.

"What's this?" Chase asked, with curiosity.

"I guess she has a gift for you," Mary said,

Charlie shook her fist up and down, urging Chase to open her own hand so she could give it to her.

Chase did as instructed, and then Charlie released her grasp, dropping a small square piece of wood into Chase's palm.

Gavin let out a gasp and said, "Is that the . . .?"

Chase turned it over and revealed the missing R from the Scrabble game back at Briarcliff. It was the very tile that Rose carried around and lost shortly before her death.

"Where did you get this, honey?" Chase asked, almost breathless.

Charlie then signed, "I was chasing my dog, Bella, from my yard into yours when she stopped to rest by the rock wall behind your house. It was just sitting there near the place where I see you leave yellow roses. I think it goes with your game."

Gavin gave Chase a look and she read his mind, bending down now so she could whisper to Charlie, "This belonged to a very special little girl like you. I think she'd want you to have it."

Charlie picked the R up with her tiny fingers and smiled, then gave Chase a loving hug.

Raylan interrupted the moment and said to Chase, "Hold up, hold up! We see, Chase, that you now have the ring—gorgeous, by the way—but Bonnie and the rest of us want to know the big question: when and where's the wedding?"

Chase looked at Gavin, then back at all their waiting faces, and replied, "We haven't gotten that far yet. I mean, Vermont? Seattle? Here in the city?"

Peter joined in: "Maybe Briarcliff Manor?"

Chase nodded in agreement, thinking that was certainly a romantic option.

There were endless possibilities, but before anyone could offer up another suggestion, Gavin tapped his champagne glass to get everyone's attention and dramatically cleared his throat saying, "Ahem, I have one last announcement to make."

With that, Gavin shouted, "*SAMUEL!!*"

Suddenly, from behind a row of strangers, Sebastian's old driver, Samuel, appeared, pushing through the crowd with Chase's dog, Scooter, on a leash. He said, "Go to your mom, boy."

Scooter pranced over and sat directly in front of Chase, looking up adoringly, with a thin white envelope attached to a red ribbon that was tied around his neck.

"Take it," Gavin said to his now fiancée.

Chase unclipped the envelope from the ribbon, and as she started to open it, Gavin said, "It's a surprise."

Chase looked over and said, "From you?"

Gavin just responded, "Not me."

As Chase opened the envelope and the card inside, with everyone watching in silence, Gavin added, "The day I got on the plane to come home from my visit to Seattle, your mom met me at the airport and handed me that. She said she's been saving a long time and she wanted it to be her wedding gift."

Chase just looked at it silently, her expression one of pure astonishment.

"What is it, Chase?" Bonnie asked.

Raylan then joked, "A subscription to *Sports Illustrated*?"

Gavin replied, "Oh, it's a bit more than that."

Little Charlie then signed, "Tell us, Chase, tell us."

Chase then blurted out, "It's an all-expenses paid trip, first-class air and four-star hotels, private tours, meals, the best of the best . . ."

A long pause, then . . . "to Italy."

There was an audible gasp from everyone.

Charlotte Jackson asked, "A honeymoon, perhaps?"

Gavin then took Chase's left hand and held her ring up high, for all to see, and said, "How about a wedding!"

Chase looked up from her perfect ring and then at her fiancé, then over to her friends' loving faces, and said, "Ya think?"

Gavin put his strong arms around her like he'd never let her go and said, "You spent the last year Chasing Manhattan. You wanna go *Chasing Rome*?"

With that, Scooter let out a loud bark of approval, and everyone smiled, their hearts bursting with joy for their favorite couple.

Charlie then stepped forward directly in front of Chase and Gavin, bringing both arms across her chest in the form of an X and squeezed.

"What does that sign mean?" Gavin asked.

Chase nodded her head at the child, then looked into Gavin's eyes, and said, "It means LOVE."

# ACKNOWLEDGMENTS

Writing and publishing a book is a bit like taking a canoe down the rapids; nobody paddles alone if they want to avoid hitting the jagged rocks. I wish to thank the wonderful staff of talented people at Paraclete Press for their help and dedication in bringing you Chase's latest adventure. Specifically, I wish to thank Jon Sweeney, Robert Edmonson, Michelle Rich, Sister Estelle Cole, Jennifer Lynch, and Rachel McKendree.

I owe a debt of gratitude to not one, but two *New York Times* best-selling authors for taking the time to look at my humble work and showing the kindness to share their encouragement.

The first of these is Dana Perino, who is not only a talented journalist and writer but a huge animal lover, devoted to her husband, Peter, and her fabulous furry friend, Jasper. Dana is not just a role model for young women, but she is also a champion for the underdogs of this world and a big fan of my blind and deaf pup Keller.

A tip of the hat as well to Richard Paul Evans, author of one of my favorite books, *The Christmas Box,* for his continued support of my prose. No Christmas is complete without a Richard Paul Evans novel nearby, and his new novel *The Walk* is a treasure as well.

A huge thank you for the beautiful artwork on the cover from my immensely talented friend Shanna Brickell.

I want to thank the wonderful and eclectic people of New York City for inspiring the characters in this novel. Taking a seat in any coffee shop in Manhattan gives you a window to the world, in all its beauty.

I also want to thank my mother and my sister, Mary Ellen, for dragging me to Manhattan every December when I was but a teenager. Those long, bumpy bus rides that dumped me in Rockefeller Center opened my eyes to a big and different world, one that at first was scary, but eventually it became a place I loved to go to. Many of my personal experiences, including the reference to Tiffany's in this story, are drawn from my own life.

I wish to thank my wife, Courtney, for her unwavering support of my writing and patience with me when the words stumble and my work keeps us apart longer than I promised.

Last but certainly not least, I thank God for the blessings and gifts he has given me. The older I get and the more I write, the more I realize I am not the rapids, but the canoe meant to carry his message to those with an open and willing heart.

—*John*

# ABOUT PARACLETE PRESS

## *Who We Are*

As the publishing arm of the Community of Jesus, Paraclete Press presents a full expression of Christian belief and practice—from Catholic to Evangelical, from Protestant to Orthodox, reflecting the ecumenical charism of the Community and its dedication to sacred music, the fine arts, and the written word. We publish books, recordings, sheet music, and video/DVDs that nourish the vibrant life of the church and its people.

## *What We Are Doing*

BOOKS | PARACLETE PRESS BOOKS show the richness and depth of what it means to be Christian. While Benedictine spirituality is at the heart of who we are and all that we do, our books reflect the Christian experience across many cultures, time periods, and houses of worship.

We have many series, including *Paraclete Essentials*; *Raven* (fiction); *Iron Pen* (poetry); *Paraclete Giants*; for children and adults, *All God's Creatures*, books about animals and faith; and *San Damiano Books*, focusing on Franciscan spirituality. Others include *Voices from the Monastery* (men and women monastics writing about living a spiritual life today), *Active Prayer*, and new for young readers: *The Pope's Cat*. We also specialize in gift books for children on the occasions of Baptism and First Communion, as well as other important times in a child's life, and books that bring creativity and liveliness to any adult spiritual life.

The MOUNT TABOR BOOKS series focuses on the arts and literature as well as liturgical worship and spirituality; it was created in conjunction with the Mount Tabor Ecumenical Centre for Art and Spirituality in Barga, Italy.

MUSIC | PARACLETE PRESS DISTRIBUTES RECORDINGS of the internationally acclaimed choir *Gloriæ Dei Cantores*, the *Gloriæ Dei Cantores Schola*, and the other instrumental artists of the *Arts Empowering Life Foundation*.

PARACLETE PRESS IS THE EXCLUSIVE NORTH AMERICAN DISTRIBUTOR for the Gregorian chant recordings from St. Peter's Abbey in Solesmes, France. Paraclete also carries all of the Solesmes chant publications for Mass and the Divine Office, as well as their academic research publications.

In addition, PARACLETE PRESS SHEET MUSIC publishes the work of today's finest composers of sacred choral music, annually reviewing over 1,000 works and releasing between 40 and 60 works for both choir and organ.

VIDEO | Our video/DVDs offer spiritual help, healing, and biblical guidance for a broad range of life issues including grief and loss, marriage, forgiveness, facing death, understanding suicide, bullying, addictions, Alzheimer's, and Christian formation.

Learn more about us at our website
www.paracletepress.com
or phone us toll-free at 1.800.451.5006

SCAN
TO READ
MORE